#1* New York Times *bestselling author Sylvia Day returns to the decadence of the multimillion-selling Crossfire® Saga with* Ireland*, a searing new tale of temptation, deception, and ice-cold vengeance.

Ireland Vidal is the third generation to control Vidal Records, and she's on track to lead the recording company to greater heights. She's the youngest of an affluent, prominent family headed by her eldest brother, Gideon Cross — one of the richest men in the world. Despite her siblings' outsized shadows, Ireland has carved her own identity. But the clever, stunning beauty with fierce tenacity and a heart of gold has yet to find a man with whom to share her life — someone who doesn't need her connections to be successful.

Then a chance meeting with Ronan Boudreaux sparks an irresistible attraction. He has it all: wealth, charm, a wickedly provocative talent for seduction, and he can hold his own against her powerful family. He offers Ireland everything she's ever wanted, but at what price?

Waiting in the wings, someone from the distant past bides his time until he can unleash his vendetta against the Vidals. He's got old scores to settle and when he sets his plans in motion, everything and everyone Ireland loves is in his crosshairs.

From the soaring penthouses of high-stakes Manhattan to the opulent mansions and mysterious bayous of Louisiana, *Ireland* draws readers back into the illustrious lives of the beloved Vidal / Cross family, where the only thing more dangerous than desire is falling in love.

"You know you're in for a good book when other authors—and I mean LOTS of other authors—recommend it."
—*USA Today*

"A page-turner!"
—*Access Hollywood Live*

"Glamorous people, swanky settings, steamy sex, and passionate married love make this a heartwarming, gratifying conclusion to the series."
—*Publishers Weekly*

"[A] highly charged story that flows and hits the mark."
—*Kirkus Reviews*

"Will have you furiously flipping pages."
—*Glamour*

"Sophisticated, engaging, clever and sweet."
—*Irish Independent*

"Superb writing... I can't wait to see what Day does next!"
—*RT Book Reviews*

"When it comes to brewing up scorchingly hot sexual chemistry, Day has few literary rivals."
—*Booklist*

"Day writes indulgent fantasy at its most enjoyable, in a story populated by high-society beauties and rakes, all of them hiding dark passions and darker secrets behind their glittering facades."
—*Shelf Awareness*

"This bold, erotic tale of passion and revenge features a cast of colorful characters and a complex and intriguing plot."
—*Library Journal*

Contemporary Romance

THE CROSSFIRE® SAGA

Bared to You

Reflected in You

Entwined with You

Captivated by You

One with You

THE CROSSROADS SERIES

Illusive

Mystery/Thriller

THE BLACKLIST DUOLOGY

So Close

Too Far

Historical Romance

Pride and Pleasure

Seven Years to Sin

The Stranger I Married

THE GEORGIAN SERIES

Ask for It

Passion for the Game

A Passion for Him

Don't Tempt Me

Paranormal Romance

THE RENEGADE ANGELS

A Dark Kiss of Rapture

A Touch of Crimson

A Caress of Wings

A Hunger So Wild

Urban Fantasy

MARKED CITY

Eve of Darkness

Eve of Destruction

Eve of Chaos

Marked

Fantasy Romance

In the Flesh

THE DREAM GUARDIANS

Pleasures of the Night

Heat of the Night

Omnibus

Afterburn | Aftershock

Blacklist

Carnal Thirst

Love Affairs

Scandalous Liaisons

Spellbound

Novellas

All Revved Up

Butterfly in Frost

Wish List

"Hard to Breathe" in *Premiere*

"Mischief and the Marquess" in *The Arrangement*

"On Carnegie Lane" in Fourteen Days

THE SHADOW STALKERS MINISERIES

Razor's Edge

Taking the Heat

Blood and Roses

On Fire

#1 *New York Times* Bestselling Author of *Bared to You*

SYLVIA DAY

Ireland

A CROSSROADS NOVEL

This book is a work of fiction. All names, characters, locations, and incidents are products of the author's imagination, or have been used fictitiously. Any resemblance to actual persons living or dead, locales, or events is entirely coincidental.

www.sylviaday.com

Library of Congress Control Number: 2025907455

ISBN 978-1-62650-011-2 (e-book)
ISBN 978-1-62650-012-9 (trade paperback)
ISBN 978-1-62650-013-6 (hardcover)
ISBN 978-1-62650-982-5 (large print)

Edited by Hilary Sares
Character Illustration by Penny Mae Harris
Cover concept and design by Croco Designs
Woman © Svetlana Sokolova, Manhattan Skyline © Delphostock, Swamp © nat693, Man's Eyes © PKpix, all Adobe Stock.

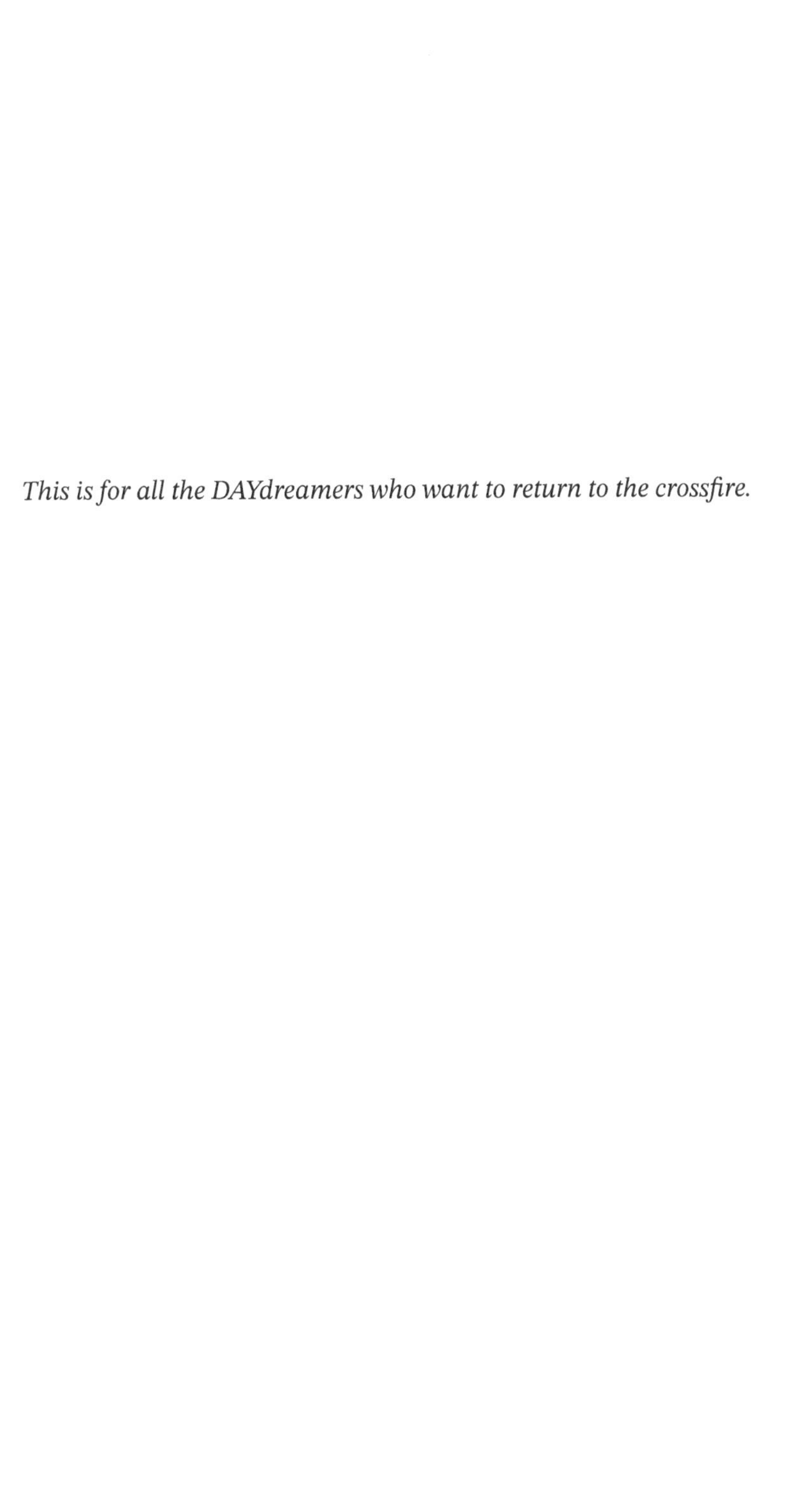

This is for all the DAYdreamers who want to return to the crossfire.

Dear DAYdreamer,

Thank you so much for choosing to read *Ireland*.

It's important to tell you that this story, the first installment of the ongoing Crossroads series, is a direct spinoff of another series of mine, the Crossfire® Saga. That means this book is a major spoiler for that series.

While it's possible to enjoy *Ireland* without first reading the five Crossfire® novels and the companion novella, "*Butterfly in Frost,*" doing so will enrich the reading experience of Ireland's story. So if you're just stepping into the crossfire for the first time, I recommend starting with *Bared to You.*

Every writer has a theme that flows through their works; mine is survivorship. That means it's possible something my characters have suffered or are suffering may trigger you. You can find a list of trigger warnings for this book on my website: SylviaDay.com

Stay fierce and happy reading!
Sylvia

Ireland
A CROSSROADS NOVEL

one

"I HOPE YOU'RE READY TO CELEBRATE!" IRELAND VIDAL tapped her pen against her desktop and grinned at the woman on her left monitor. On the right, the music video she'd just watched was frozen on the last frame. She resisted the urge to replay it for a third time. "You've outdone yourself *again!*"

Alina Rurik beamed with pleasure. She was a striking woman. Her hair draped her slim shoulders in soft brown waves, framing a face boasting luminous, makeup-free skin. "I'm glad you love it, too," she said. "I'm especially proud of this one."

"As you should be!"

A true bohemian soul, Alina's easygoing and drama-free nature appealed to Ireland when they'd met as students at Columbia. They'd been best friends ever since and were now a powerhouse production team. There were some things Ireland loved about her job; working with Alina was one of them.

"Thanks, Ireland."

A text message appeared above Alina's head, and Ireland immediately glanced at it. Only family messages appeared on her work monitors because they were always her priority.

> We need to talk. Leaving the Crossfire now.

Gideon never wasted words or time, and she straightened at the sight of his name and photo. As usual, she'd kicked off her spiked, towering Rockstud heels because she worked better barefoot, but she slid her feet into them again. Gideon Cross might be her eldest brother, but that didn't negate his standing as one of the wealthiest and most influential men in the world.

"What's wrong?" Alina frowned. "Did I miss something?"

"You never miss anything," Ireland reassured her. "It's just that my brother's driving over to see me." Being chauffeured over, rather.

You can get a lot of work done in Manhattan traffic.

Alina's dark eyes lit with excitement. "Well, since Christopher's office shares a wall with yours, you must be talking about the sinfully delectable Mr. Cross." She gave an exaggerated sigh.

Ireland shook her head. She'd spent too many of her twenty-nine years hearing about how good-looking her brother was. She got it. She saw it. Didn't mean she wasn't over it.

"Since Gideon happens to *live* next door to me," she pointed out, "it's weird for him to stop by my office. Especially" —she glanced at the time— "at three in the afternoon. And considering how rigidly he maintains his ridiculously packed schedule, taking the time instead of calling or waiting until I get home probably isn't good."

Even when Gideon had managed her and their mother's shares in Vidal Records, he seldom came by the Music Row headquarters. He'd worked on Vidal matters from the top of the Crossfire Building, where he oversaw his global conglomerate, Cross Industries. In a few weeks, he'd be turning the Big 4-0, and media outlets far and wide would laud what he'd accomplished in that relatively short time.

"Well, it can't be bad." Alina gave a dismissive wave of her hand. "He coddles you."

"Coddles? That's a weird word. Anyway, let me know when you're settled at home on Monday, and I'll come by with champagne."

"Of course. Can't wait to see you." Alina blew a kiss and ended the call.

Standing, Ireland walked to her coatrack. Gideon saw her nearly every day because she lived in his penthouse's adjacent guest apartment, but he rarely saw her at work, in her element, and she strove to make him proud. Not that he ever wasn't. But was his pride rooted in his love for her or because she'd earned it? The metalized records framed on the walls of her office proved she had. Still, she struggled with doubts.

She grabbed the buttery black leather blazer that matched her shorts and pulled it on over her blue silk bandeau. Having an ownership stake in a recording company was a headache more than anything, but there were a few benefits. She listened to the hottest and freshest music, worked with extraordinarily talented creatives, and could take her sartorial choices to the edge and beyond.

Before she sat again, she did a quick check in the ornate oversized mirror leaning against the wall. She was the one member of her family who looked like a music exec. Her father, Christopher Vidal, Sr., preferred cardigans over blazers and quirky brass glasses. Gideon's wife, Eva, once said he looked more like a college professor, and Ireland could see that, even though none of her professors at Columbia had dressed like her dad. Her brother, Christopher Vidal, Jr., fell somewhere in the middle. And while Gideon no longer held a stake in the company, he practically invented quiet luxury. Everything he wore was bespoke.

When he arrived, Gideon filled her office's open doorway in an expertly tailored pinstriped three-piece suit, his Berluti oxfords polished to a high shine, and subtle cufflinks at his wrists. As usual, he commanded the expansive space the moment he walked into it, a tall and dominating presence with unmistakable authority who always struck awe and a little fear into her.

But she played it off, rocking back in her seat and grinning. "Hey, bro. How many people have you managed to scare the shit out of today?"

His brow arched. "Not enough, but there's still time."

He moved to one of the two gray velvet visitors' chairs in front of her desk. In a choreography of deft and practiced moves, he tugged up his slacks and unbuttoned his jacket while sinking gracefully into the seat.

She'd actually seen TikTok tutorials of women dissecting how he sat so other men could learn how to up their game.

In many ways, looking at him was like looking at a masculine version of herself. They both had their mother's aqua eyes and inky hair, although Gideon cut his glossy locks off at the collarbone while she wore hers to the hip. She marveled that he didn't have a single strand of silver in his hair yet, although she had seen more than a few in his morning stubble the few times she'd caught him before he shaved. They had the same aquiline nose and full mouth, the same cheekbones and sculpted jaws.

It was strange how genetics worked. Gideon's father was their mother's first husband. Christopher shared both of Ireland's parents, but they looked nothing alike.

"To what do I owe the immense pleasure?" She leaned forward and linked her hands on her smoked glass desktop so she didn't fidget. "Did you piss off Eva again?" she teased, appreciating that his petite wife's fiery temper was the one thing on earth that could make him change course. “Is Mom acting up? Want me to shoot another campaign for ECRA+?”

“None of the above. I’m here about Graham Teller,” he said with deceptive mildness while studying her with that unnervingly focused gaze.

She stiffened, shocked at hearing her brother say a name she’d never expected to hear again and certainly never from anyone in her family. “Graham? What about him?”

“How do you know him?”

“How do *you* know him?” she countered.

Leaning back, he crossed one ankle atop the opposite knee. “He dropped by the Crossfire on Wednesday, and when he couldn’t get past security, he left a proposed legal filing behind.”

Her entire body absorbed the blow. “*What?*”

“How do you know him, Ireland?” he repeated patiently.

She squirmed inwardly, hating having to discuss any of her failures with him. “He was a fling that didn’t end up amounting to anything important.”

“He’s a musician.” It wasn’t a question, and there was no censure in his tone, but she felt it anyway.

“He sings and plays guitar. Gideon, wherever this is going, can you get there quicker? What legal filing?”

“He’s alleging you and he had a verbal agreement to produce an album, and he turned down other work because of it, which has had a negative career and financial impact for him.”

What the ever-loving fuck?!

“What career?” she scoffed. “He was playing in random bars. And I never promised him *anything*. I told him before we hooked up that my work and personal life are totally separate. I was very clear. I always am.”

She’d also made it clear that there would be no introductions to her brothers, but she didn’t include that caveat now because it was obvious by her actions. There hadn't been anyone yet whom she'd taken to meet the family.

Closing his eyes, Gideon pinched the bridge of his nose. "Do not ever mention hooking up in my presence again."

Her breath came swift and fast as the icy knot in her gut tightened painfully. Adrenaline pumped through her veins. It wasn't because a man she'd once been intimate with betrayed her trust so callously because they all did.

They all wanted something but never her.

What was truly horrific was the targeting of her eldest brother. She did everything within her power to cause him no difficulties, ever. "I'm so sorry, Gideon. This isn't your problem. I'll fix it. You won't hear about this again."

Gideon's voice softened from its usual clipped command. "Don't apologize, and don't worry. I've got it handled."

"No!" Words rushed out of her mouth in near panic. "Please don't give this another thought. I understand why he would try to serve *you* the paperwork but forget about this. I can deal with him. He won't be an issue."

"I wasn't served—he hasn't filed anything yet. He wants a settlement, not a lawsuit."

Her nostrils flared. "I'm not caving to extortion. He's not getting a fucking cent."

Turning her head, she winced at how curt her tone was. It was a side of herself she never wanted Gideon to see.

"His lawyer heard exactly that from Arash yesterday," he informed her.

Gideon's attorney was also one of his closest friends, one of Ireland's favorites. Arash Madani was fun and funny, not to mention extremely attractive, but when he did his job, he went straight for the jugular. If anyone could nip this in the bud, it was

Arash. Hearing that the lawyer was involved wasn't what upset her further.

Standing, Ireland turned to face the window and crossed her arms. Vidal Records was one of the last few holdouts on historic Music Row in the heart of Midtown. Situated on 48th between Sixth and Seventh Avenues, Music Row had once been a vibrant community of music shops selling a wide variety of instruments. Most were gone now, torn down to build ever higher, more modern buildings. New York City never stopped evolving, too often to the point of destroying its storied history.

"You've known about this for two days," she noted faintly, "and I'm only just hearing about it."

"I would never bring you a problem without a solution."

She blinked hard against the sudden sting of tears. "Does everyone else know?"

"Your father and Christopher do. Vidal Records was named as a co-defendant."

"You've all known since Wednesday? Am I the last to know? Did you tell Eva before me?"

"I tell Eva everything," he said simply. "I wasn't about to upset you unduly. Now, I can tell you it's been settled, and you won't hear from Teller again. That's what I want you to know and all you need to know."

He was so unbothered by the whole thing. Mildly annoyed and nothing more. It wasn't the threat to him that it was to her.

She took a deep, bracing breath and then faced him with a sunny smile—even while feeling like she was vibrating violently on the inside. "Well, that's a relief. How was it resolved, if you don't mind my asking?"

Her tone was light. Studiously unconcerned. Which took colossal effort. Her dismay began to shift into icy rage toward the man who'd brought his bullshit to her family and laid it at their feet.

Gideon waved it all off in the most casual of gestures. "Your father will distribute Teller's demo to three people he requested specifically. What happens from there isn't our business, and we've got that in writing."

She hid her fisted hands in the crooks of her elbows, her entire being rebelling against the thought of Graham Teller benefitting in any way from putting her in this position.

You've got a broken picker, Alina often said. *You should stick to guys you're* not *attracted to.*

"You're being more generous than he deserves," she told him, careful to keep any resentment from her voice.

Her brother shrugged. "He's not getting a check, and he's not slandering you in the press. It's a win all around."

Ireland would've preferred tearing Graham's lies to shreds, getting the threatened suit dismissed, and watching him leave the courthouse humiliated and empty-handed, but her opinion hadn't been factored in, so she didn't offer it now. Doing so wasn't worth antagonizing her family.

"Thanks for coming over and telling me personally."

Standing, Gideon rounded the desk and lifted his hands to rest on her shoulders. She could see the fondness in his gaze—they were nearly eye-level when she wore heels. She basked in that warmth, even though it didn't touch the chilling fury building within her.

His eyes give him away, Eva once told her. *I always know where he's at if I look into his eyes.*

Gideon had been estranged from the family the entirety of Ireland's childhood. It wasn't until Eva came into their lives that they formed a relationship. Ireland cherished his involvement in her life now.

She would do whatever she must to protect it.

Gideon stopped in the doorway to his wife's office, taking a minute to absorb the sight of her lost in concentration. Eva stood at her mirrored desk, intently studying whatever was atop it. Her blond hair was shorter than his own, grazing her jaw in soft waves. It obscured her breathtaking face from his view, but since it was always front of his mind regardless, that freed him to take in the rest of her. Petite and voluptuously curved, she was more than a handful in every way possible, and he wouldn't change a single thing about her.

"You coming in?" she queried without glancing up. "Or are you just going to stand there and stare?"

"Both. In good time." With its profusion of pastel colors and mirrored accents, her office was decidedly feminine. But she alone was what made any room sparkle.

Behind him, the main floor and its sea of cubicles was thrumming with activity. His office was on the other side, with the same dividing wall of glass so he could look across at his wife whenever the mood struck him.

Turning her head, Eva hit him with the full force of her attention. Her gaze raked him from head to toe, heating as it slid over him in a near-tangible caress. Time hadn't lessened the attraction between them. It was primal and deeply rooted, two halves of a whole drawn inexorably together.

"So, which of us was right?" she asked, returning her attention to her work. She'd sworn Ireland would lose her mind if not told about Teller sooner rather than later, while he'd known his sister would take the news in stride.

"You'll note that I'm in one piece."

She flipped a page over to read the one beneath it. "And Ireland? How would you say she is?"

"She was surprised at first, then brushed it off. You know how easygoing she is."

"I know you think that," she retorted.

"I don't understand why you're upset it went well."

Straightening, Eva faced him with her stormy gray eyes narrowed. "However well it went, you did what you always do: you went ahead and fixed the problem without consulting her."

"My understanding is that's what older brothers are for."

She shook her head. "I've been telling you the same thing for years, ace, and you still don't get it."

"This was going to be the resolution, period." He leaned casually against the jamb and slid his hands into his trouser pockets. "Why waste time convincing her that taking this to court wouldn't be worth the win? I, too, would prefer to legally annihilate this douchebag, but not at the cost of Ireland's private life becoming fodder for Page Six and TMZ."

"It's not about whether you're right," Eva argued, half-sitting on the edge of her desk. "It's about respecting Ireland enough to value her opinion."

"If I didn't respect her, I wouldn't have pressed her to start taking the reins at Vidal," he reminded. And his sister had paid him full market value to repurchase her shares from him, insisting he'd earned it because he'd brought Vidal Records back from the brink and turned it around. Unfortunately, while her father had the heart and soul for music, Chris didn't have the head for business.

Eva glared at him. "That's work stuff. And I know you've categorized this situation as solely that, but it has to be very personal for your sister."

"Because of that moron Teller?" he scoffed. "No way."

"In part. But mostly because you're you."

His mouth curved. "The love of your life? The man of your dreams?"

"You're baiting me on purpose!" she complained.

Releasing a deep breath, Gideon said evenly, "She still has a lot to learn about playing the game."

"Then take the opportunity to teach her. She's not a child! She's the same age you were when we got married."

"But she's still dating losers. She needs to stop wasting her time on idiots." He'd been saying so for years. If there was a guy on the planet worthy of dating his sister, he'd yet to meet him, and he met a lot of people all the time.

Eva sighed. "You have no idea how hard it is to find a decent guy."

Standing, his wife approached him on towering stilettos with needle-thin heels. He had no idea how she walked in shoes like that, but he certainly loved how her full hips rocked back and forth with every step. She'd elected to wear a dress in soft gray that matched her eyes. It was a garment that would be modest on most women. Long sleeves, a neckline that reached her collarbone, and a hemline that brushed the tops of her knees. But it clung to her lush body like a second skin, taunting him with reminders of how good she felt in his arms.

She reached up and began to fuss over the knot of his tie and the point of the handkerchief in his breast pocket. It was something she did often, not because he wasn't pristine, but because it gave her a socially acceptable reason to run her hands over him. "Ireland has a right to participate in decisions concerning her."

"No one is saying she doesn't." He caught her wrist and gave a gentle squeeze. "I'll argue, however, that since Teller approached *me* with the matter, it's my problem to solve."

"My god, you're infuriating!"

Eva watched her husband straighten away from the jamb in an elegant unfolding of powerful muscle and steely-eyed determination. Butting heads with him was an exercise in patience—and arousal. He was a man who knew what he wanted and how to achieve it, and that level of supreme confidence turned her on as much as his devastating handsomeness.

It also exasperated the hell out of her sometimes.

As Gideon's hands slid around to cup her buttocks and pull her close, Eva's head tilted back to look up at him. A dozen blissful years together, yet the impact of his strikingly gorgeous face hadn't lessened even a little. There were lines now. Faintly in his forehead and around the wickedly sensual mouth she'd felt over every inch of her body. They were also around his eyes. She loved them all but especially the crow's-feet because they were laugh lines. Permanent echoes of joy. She'd helped to put them there, and it was what she was most proud of.

A pervasive and all-too-familiar frustration agitated her. There was so much she wanted to give him, so much more they deserved to have. But he never complained or even mentioned it.

Tension entered the space between them. Had he followed the direction of her thoughts as he so often did?

"I'll concede that I could've handled things differently," he murmured, studying her intently with those magnificently blue eyes.

"But not that you should have," she countered, her voice husky. "I know both Chris and Christopher were on board with the way you handled it, but still..."

"I went to her office based solely on your input. So, I did at least take a step in the right direction."

His body was so hard and warm, Eva couldn't help but feel protected and safe. It was intrinsically crucial to her husband to provide a shield for those he loved because he hadn't been protected or kept safe as a child. If he believed that delaying a response would give a bad actor an opening, Gideon wouldn't wait. He simply couldn't.

She pressed her lips sweetly to his. "You see a problem and handle it, and I love you for that. I really do. I'm just saying that sometimes you overlook the human component."

"That's not true. I factor it in, I just don't give it the same weight you would." He bent and nuzzled her cheek.

"She's your sister. You've got to weigh her feelings with a different scale."

"Angel, you're way more upset about this than she is, I promise you. It's fine. She's fine. So fine, in fact, that I have a free hour because I carved out more time to meet with her than was needed."

Reaching up, Eva ran her fingers through his luxuriously sexy hair. He lifted her feet from the floor and walked toward the pink velvet sofa in the seating area.

"Lauren," he called out, using the wake word for the office's latent artificial intelligence. "Privacy."

The glass wall that divided her office from the main floor instantly turned opaque, and the door swung shut and locked.

She laughed softly. "I don't have an hour, Mr. Cross. Maybe fifteen minutes."

"Well, I do love a challenge, Mrs. Cross."

Ireland strode through the revolving lobby door of the Vidal Hotel in Midtown, her heels clicking across the brightly hued crushed glass floor. Her fury was ice cold. That Graham had dared to come here was another level of insult she couldn't and wouldn't stand for.

The immense space, with its mirrored walls and massive chandeliers, was packed with people. Guests and tourists alike. When she'd first envisioned a Vidal Records-themed hotel, Ireland had pictured something much smaller than the tower she was presently cutting through. Gideon had expanded her idea into majestic proportions.

Suites at the Midtown flagship sold out months before opening, and now, a half dozen Vidal Hotels were scattered across the country. All were part of Cross Industries' hospitality portfolio, with a licensing fee paid to Vidal for the brand and access to memorabilia.

There were numerous musically themed bars and restaurants on the property, but the one Graham had posted a selfie from an hour ago would've been her last choice for him. He must have chosen the opulent jazz club because it was one of her favorites. *And* he'd been posting from there every day since Wednesday just to needle her and rub salt in her wounds.

Graham didn't know her well enough to understand that the more wounded she was, the more dangerous she became.

Her steps didn't slow until she reached the hostess stand at Jazzie's, then she stopped walking altogether. Friday nights were always busy, but the place seemed more packed than usual. The band was in full swing with a rendition of "Blue Train," and all eyes were on the stage.

With a nod to the hostess, Ireland walked past the throng of guests waiting for tables and went to the bar, where three bartenders were moving nonstop to fill orders. One of them, an older gentleman with a voluminous white pompadour and precisely trimmed salt and pepper goatee, gave her a nod of acknowledgment. She went to the service bar and settled in to wait, her gaze scanning the crowded space for the man she was hunting down.

It didn't take long to find him. Graham stuck out in a jarring way with his spiked leather accessories and faded Megadeth T-shirt. He had a pretty blonde with him, her hair tousled and eyes thickly lined. They both looked bored as they scrolled through their phones.

The music faded into silence, and applause swelled. Ireland stared daggers at Graham until the trumpeter broke through with a series of plaintive notes that almost immediately lowered the volume of voices in the room. Her gaze cut to the stage.

She froze in place. Her breath left her in a rush.

A broad-shouldered man half-sat on a barstool with a trumpet to his lips. His hair was thick, a deep dark gold, and worn longer than Gideon's in a luxuriant lion's mane. If he'd sported a tie earlier, he had removed it and opened his collar, revealing a tanned throat that worked reflexively as he played. His powerful thighs and biceps strained against his gray slacks and white dress shirt in a spectacular display of potent virility.

Something stirred low and deep inside her, unfurling with luxuriant heat.

The bartender's voice pulled her attention, if not her gaze. "What can I get you?"

"Who's the new guy, Sam?" Ireland asked, unable to take her eyes off the stage.

"He's a guest of the hotel."

"No." The man was accomplished, his performance masterful.

"I wouldn't lie to you, boss. He's been here a week. Came down a few days ago with his trumpet and talked to the band for a bit. They invited him to jam, and now it's a thing. Every night, he comes down for an hour or so. Plays and sings sometimes, too. The ladies love him."

"I bet." Ireland studied the man more closely. His clothes

were clearly tailored expressly for his tall, strong frame. His rolled-up cuffs revealed a full-sleeve tribal tattoo, and the sharp, talon-like tips crept beneath the cognac leather band of the expensive watch on his wrist. He was savagely alluring masculinity wrapped in wealth; assured in his posture, and skilled with his instrument. The dichotomy of his vitally aggressive attractiveness and the melancholic way he played the jazz standard "Nature Boy" shocked the senses.

Abruptly, he looked up and caught her gaze, held it without blinking for a heartbeat, then another. A frisson of awareness arced between them like an electric current.

She was aware of him in the most elemental sense. Drawn to him so powerfully, she fought taking a step toward him. It was a visceral attraction. And she didn't like it at all.

"I'll take my usual," she said, forcing herself to turn away. "Send the trumpeter a drink when he's done. Tell him it's on the house. And call security, would you, please?"

Sam didn't question the nature of her requests. "You got it."

Pushing away from the bar, Ireland weaved through the crowd, skirting club chairs and candlelit tables to reach Graham, who sat near the stage. She'd entered the club in a high rage but unexpectedly found herself in a different mood entirely. The trumpet's slow, drawn-out notes felt like a requiem, which aligned with Ireland's realization that Graham was dead to her, and she didn't care to waste her rage on him. There was no point after all. The man had dug his own grave.

Graham happened to glance up then and see her. She watched him flinch and schooled her expression into something more pleasant. It worked because he recovered and flashed her a cocky grin. It was that mischievous smile that first attracted her to him. He had the rockstar aesthetic down to a science and a face so handsome it bordered on pretty.

Musically inclined bad boys were her downfall. She really needed to find a new type.

"Well, hello," she greeted with a bright smile, coming to a halt at his table. "Fancy seeing you here."

Graham smirked. "You're following me."

"It's more like you're following me since this is my place." The song ended with a moment of stunned silence. Then the applause started again, the truest sign that the performance had resonated with its audience.

"I meant on social," he qualified.

"God no," she dismissed with a wave of her hand.

"Right." He sneered. "Gail and I are just celebrating."

"Of course you are. Hi, Gail." She shot a sympathetic look at the other woman. "Listen, I don't mean to keep you. I just wanted to say thanks so much for signing that settlement agreement today. I had my fingers crossed."

His smile lost a little of its shine. "Why?"

She ignored the question. "You know… most people will do just about anything to avoid pissing off my brother, but then you *are* dumber than most."

Gail's brows lifted while his smile fled altogether, his denim blue eyes taking on a hard, mean edge. Why hadn't she seen that nastiness in him before?

"I'm not afraid of him."

"As I said…" She grinned. "In any case, I'm the one you should be worried about. I hold grudges, and my memory is long. Then again, you're going to rot in obscurity somewhere, and that might satisfy. Maybe."

Graham scowled. "You'll eat those words when you hear my songs everywhere you go."

Tossing her head back, Ireland laughed uproariously. "Stand-up might be an option if you ever stop being delusional.

Although, you don't have the presence to hold an audience hostage like the guy onstage right now."

"Okay, bitch," Gail said, shifting to stand.

He thrust his arm out to stop her. "Fuck you, Ireland."

"No, thank you." She made a face. Then she stopped playing with him. "The truth is you're passable enough for cruise ship entertainment and local bars, but you don't have star quality. Yeah, you'll get your demo seen by the eyes you want, but they'll know my father is humoring someone by sending it. Maybe you're his housekeeper's kid, they'll think. Or a nephew. No one important or with any true talent."

"What do you know, nepo baby?" Graham jeered. "You've got your job because you were born into it, not because you know what you're doing."

He looked past her, and his jaw clenched.

Ireland glanced at the two burly security guards who walked up on either side of her. "Show him out, please, gentlemen, after he's closed their tab. She's welcome to stay, but put his name on the DNR list. We're an upscale establishment. We don't cater to losers."

"You're going to regret fucking with me," he snapped.

"Okay. Bye now." She walked away, glancing at her favorite table tucked in the corner by stage left. A *Reserved* sign was already on it, and she silently thanked the staff for doing that for her despite not calling ahead as usual.

Piped music blended with the din of the crowd while the band took a break. She dropped into the club chair facing the wall and heaved a weary sigh. The ways her job fucked with her emotional wellbeing seemed endless.

Long, strong legs draped in expensive gray material rounded her chair, drawing both her attention and her gaze down to a pair of lustrous black crocodile dress boots. From there, she *had* to look upward... over lean hips and waist, muscled torso, and powerful shoulders. She stared at the full, firm lips—a sinner's mouth that softened his intensely focused stare.

Goddamn.

In an instant, the crowded club seemed to fade away. Her heart skipped a beat, then her pulse began to race. The trumpet had obscured the lower half of his magnificent face. Now, she saw the chiseled bone structure. The sculpted cheekbones and the perfect symmetry of his features. And that impossibly tempting mouth which promised the most decadent pleasures.

He looked to be about Gideon's age—an irresistibly gorgeous, highly sensual man in his prime. She'd met so many celebrities and musical superstars in her life, people whose livelihoods depended on their extraordinary good looks, and none held a candle to the enthralling and overtly sexual male in front of her. She'd never even imagined a man could be so heart-stoppingly beautiful.

It was an effort to dismiss him by returning her gaze to the photo of Louis Armstrong on the wall. "I don't want company," she said brusquely, acutely aware of his proximity—and unwavering stare.

He stood there, unmoving, for another endless minute. Then he spoke.

"Fine by me," he replied, his voice like smoked whiskey. There was a subtle drawl in it, smooth as molasses. It was a lover's voice, intimate and unhurried, and like evocative lyrics, it made her think of those voluptuary's lips moving in a caress against bare skin. The hairs on her nape raised, causing the tiniest, most delicious shiver.

He moved to the loveseat across from her, directly in her line of sight so that she couldn't help but watch as he folded into the cushions like a lounging jungle cat, all sinuous muscle and dangerous grace.

And there was no doubt that he was a danger. As relaxed and leisurely as he appeared at first glance, his heady charisma was a potent lure—a silent provocation to play on the wild side. For all his urbanity, the man inside the custom-made clothing was not to be taken lightly.

When he merely watched her, she narrowed her eyes. "Which part of what I said did you not understand?"

"It's my table." His gaze shifted to where a previously unnoticed jacket matching his slacks draped a trumpet case.

She stood in a rush, her face hot with embarrassment. He stood with her, and she saw he was an inch or two taller than Gideon's 6'2" height, putting her at eye level with that wickedly alluring mouth. She turned to move somewhere else.

"Behind," Sam warned, skirting her to set two beautifully presented Old Fashioneds on cork coasters. "One for the lady and one she bought for you."

Ireland scowled at the bartender. He waggled his brows in response.

"If you want him to enjoy that," he told her, "you should sit back down and keep his fan club at bay."

Sam headed back to the bar.

Her unwanted companion collected his drink but remained standing. "Thank you."

Ireland's attention went to his forearm. Golden skin coursed with veins over flexing muscle. It shouldn't be sexy. It was just an arm for chrissakes.

"The place is packed," he pointed out casually. "You're leaving the only open seat, and you've got a drink it'll take a while to enjoy. You're welcome to stay, but let me be clear: while I very much enjoy an exchange of harmless flirting with a beautiful woman—and you are, without question, the most beautiful woman I've ever seen—I'm not looking for a hookup."

It wasn't remotely fair that a man who looked like a golden god had that voice, too. The combo was a one-two punch to her common sense.

She stood there, staring at him for a long moment, refusing to be disappointed or flattered by what he said.

But she was more than a little curious. And too reckless for her own good.

Ireland sat.

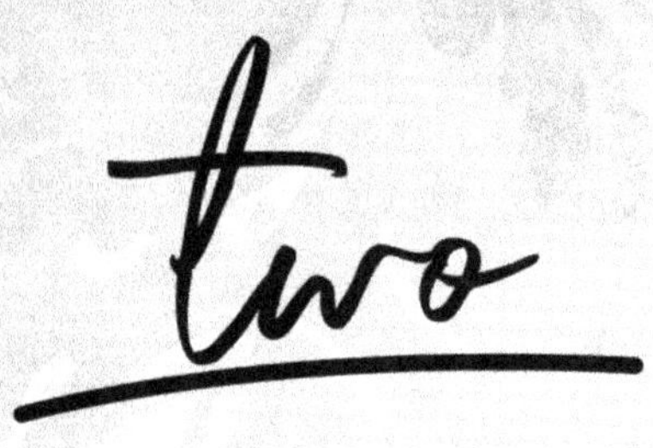

"YOU WEREN'T SUPPOSED TO KNOW THAT DRINK CAME from me," Ireland said wryly as he settled back into the loveseat. Picking up her tumbler, she tipped it slightly in a silent toast. "It's meant as a thank-you for sharing your talent. I'm not looking for a hookup, either."

One corner of his delectable mouth lifted with amusement. "Ah, well, I appreciate the compliment. And I'll enjoy the drink far more with your company, so thank you for staying."

A gentleman. And unbelievably sexier for it.

He brushed a wayward lock of his thick hair back from his face. The color was a sumptuous blend of sable, toffee, and honey. Women paid a small fortune to get hair like that, but she would bet Mother Nature was his colorist. Her fingers itched to run through it, to learn its texture and feel the warmth transferred from his body.

Ireland took a larger-than-usual swallow, rolling the liquor around her tongue with a near-silent hum of pleasure. His smokey eyes watched her with a focus so intense it gave her butterflies.

"Where did you learn to play like that?" she asked, hoping his answer was long so she could listen to his voice again.

"On street corners, mostly."

Ireland blinked, processing that. "You've had no formal training?"

"I didn't have the means, so I was fortunate to find exceptional and generous mentors."

She leaned back in her seat, taking in the implications of what he'd said. "Wow."

"Lady Luck does find me on occasion, however rarely." His smile was as faint as his drawl but carried the same high impact. "Possibly, she was waiting for just this moment when I'd have the only empty seat available for the most stunning woman alive. If so, I have no complaints whatsoever."

"Well, aren't you a charmer?" she managed to say with some semblance of elan. That sense of profound awareness continued to ripple through her, lapping like waves against the shore, and Ireland knew she was in over her head.

She'd only ever encountered his level of self-possession in Gideon and his closest friends, who knew better than to flirt with her or risk her brothers' wrath. It was a revelation to experience such dynamic confidence in someone she found herself powerfully attracted to.

Until now, and too often, the men she dated had unrealized dreams and unappeased ambition. They hadn't "made it" yet and worried they never would. This man knew exactly who he was and what he wanted.

"What brings you to New York?" she asked.

"The culmination of years of meticulous planning." He flashed a devastating smile. "Although, most would simply call it 'work.'"

Ireland's interest sharpened to a fine point. The first half of his answer was the truth; the smile was meant to defuse the importance of it. She knew the tactic well because she employed it often when dealing with her family. But this guy didn't need to use it with her. He could say anything, a polite white lie about a wedding or a reunion. Whatever.

"Won't you ask me what it is I do?" His languid voice and relaxed pose were deceptive.

Anyone looking at him would think he hadn't a care in the world, but she suspected very little escaped his notice. His focus on her was unwavering and incisive despite his heavy-lidded gaze.

She couldn't say why it felt like they were playing a chess match, and he'd already strategized every move to the finish. "If you wanted me to know, you'd volunteer the information."

The smile he gave her was brilliant, as if he'd intuited her cool reply in advance. "I confess to being curious about what it is you do."

She blinked. Did he really not know who she was?

Of course, it was possible for her to go unrecognized. If not for the advertisements she did for Eva's makeup and skincare line—which the golden god wouldn't be likely to see—and occasional guest appearances on musical competition TV shows, most people outside her family's circle of interests probably didn't know her by sight.

Opportunistic guys like Graham were making her cynical. She didn't have to overthink a random encounter with a man who looked too good to be real.

"I read somewhere that discussing occupations is a very American thing to do," she prevaricated because being anonymous with a magnetically appealing man was a situation she wanted to enjoy as long as she could. "Maybe we put too much importance on work."

"And maybe you won't tell me." The perceptiveness in his gaze belied his nonchalance.

She relaxed deeper into her chair. “Why don’t you take a guess, and I’ll tell you if you’re warm.”

“The obvious would be to say supermodel because you certainly look like one.”

Ireland laughed at his flirtatious tone. “And I could guess that you’re a musician, but that’s too easy.”

“The trumpet’s a hobby. It doesn’t pay the bills.”

And his bills were not inconsiderable if she based them on his attire alone. His boots were easily double the cost of Gideon’s oxfords, and those sold for thousands. The Patek Philippe watch would have lowered his bank balance by the mid-six figures. And like Gideon, there were no belt loops on his dress slacks because they’d been made for his body and required no accessories to keep them in place.

“I’ve done some modeling,” she conceded, “if you can call it that, as a favor for a family member’s business. It’s definitely not something I’d do full-time because I don’t like being the center of attention.”

He’d set his glass on the flat, wide armrest and was spinning it slowly with leisurely turns of his fingers. “Tell me what you do like.”

She had noticed his fingers earlier when he’d been playing. He wore no rings, which didn’t signify anything but was intriguing, nonetheless. “Music—I can’t live without it. Whiskey, scotch, bourbon. Coffee. Late nights, later mornings. Rain. Thunderstorms. Fall. Cats *and* dogs. Sunlight on my face and a midnight breeze in my hair.”

His chest lifted and fell on a slow, deep breath. “That’s quite a list, *cher*.”

Ireland gave a careless shrug, but his endearment was revealing. Pronounced *sha* instead of *share*, it was unmistakably Cajun. Suddenly, so much about him was explained. No wonder he'd learned the trumpet; the instrument was the heart and soul of Louisiana.

She wished she could tell him about how she'd once found the most amazing zydeco band in Baton Rouge and signed them to a distribution deal the next day, but that would reveal everything she'd rather keep hidden—including how some decisions she made were based on passion rather than good fiscal sense.

Taking another sip, Ireland discreetly considered him. He had an unfair advantage with her. From that sexy mane of hair down to the sleek crocodile boots and all the musical talent in between, he was like an AI-generated dream man based on her wish list of traits.

"There are companies that have something I want," he told her as if her openness warranted the same in return. "I follow them, sometimes for years, then leverage their weak points and take them over."

"Why not merge or collaborate?"

"Then their weaknesses become mine," he said matter-of-factly.

"Who are you after now?"

"There's never just one, but I'm focused on a clothing factory in Queens this week. Their location and building are ideal for warehousing."

"You couldn't buy one or the other?"

"It's a family-run business on its fourth generation. They're more sentimental than smart."

She knew that scenario all too well. Vidal Records had once been a music shop like so many others on Music Row, established by her grandfather. It was her father who'd shifted from selling music and instruments to selling the talent itself. As the third generation to run the company, Ireland sometimes felt trapped by the legacy, but Christopher intended to raise his children to take over. Perhaps that would be the saving grace of Vidal Records, a new generation with their father's ruthlessness rather than their grandfather's recklessness.

Ireland sighed. "That's heartbreaking."

"That's business," he countered. "If it's not me, it'll be someone else."

"I get that it's not personal—"

"It can be." He looked away from her for the first time, down into his tumbler. His sudden contemplative mood was yet another facet to him, one of many in a kaleidoscope—a dazzling but fractured picture.

Complicated. That's what he was. And if she could tell that over a drink in a bar, the still waters must run deep. Call her crazy, but she'd love to have someone in her life who challenged her. It struck her that she'd been looking for the wrong things with guys like Graham.

The band returned to the stage. All four members looked at her companion questioningly. He bowed out with a hand over his heart, and the gesture moved her.

"Tell me what *you* like," Ireland said, setting her drink aside and leaning forward. "But first, tell me your name."

Lifting his glass to his lips, he eyed her over the rim as he swallowed, his attention fully returned to her as she'd intended.

The sax kicked off "Ain't Nobody Here but Us Chickens" with gusto. But his silence stretched.

Her brow furrowed. Why wasn't he answering?

"Don't frown at me, *cher*. You need to give a man time to gather his thoughts after you waylay his best intentions." He set his drink down, leaned forward, and extended his hand over the table. "Ronan Boudreaux."

"Ronan," she repeated softly as she leaned forward and slid her hand into his.

His strong fingers enfolded hers, conveying his charisma and sensuality in tangible form. The moment their skin came into contact, heat raced up her arm and spread throughout her body in a surge of fiery attraction. Her breath quickened along with her heartbeat.

"I have to ask," she began, "are you married? Engaged? Otherwise committed? Or just not interested."

"None of the above." He sat back, his fingertips sliding intimately over her palm as he pulled away. He gifted her with a sinful smile.

Ireland was stupidly thrilled by his answer. A lavishly attractive alpha male like him, at his age, was either taken or incapable of being so. Either way, it wasn't good news for her. He was a bad decision wrapped in a good time. Nothing but ruin for a woman who trusted men she shouldn't.

"And you?" he asked, seeming more relaxed than he'd been previously as if in giving his name, he'd opened a door.

She elected to give him the truth instead. "I've sworn off men."

Ronan laughed, and the full-throated sound felt like a caress. He made her feel like she was slightly out of tilt. She was nearly breathless, her pulse fluttering. Her eyes were probably dilated as her system tried to absorb the intense temptation he presented, the sense of being pulled into something dangerously exhilarating.

His eyes sparkled with amusement. "For how long?"

They were really beautiful eyes. She'd love to see them in daylight. In the moody, intimate lighting of the club, the shadows nestled in the hollows of his chiseled features. If the moment hadn't been so temporary and if he hadn't been passing through, she'd be very afraid she would end up regretting him. "As long as it takes for me to make better choices."

Ronan kept that piercing gaze on her as he lifted his drink to his mouth. When he slid his tongue along his lower lip, she felt it between her legs. "And who will be the judge of that? If you're making ill-advised choices, who's to say the choice to make better ones isn't also ill-advised?"

She recrossed her legs. "Well, when you put it like that..."

"Be bad. It's much more fun than being safe." His gaze lifted and focused past her, breaking the moment.

"I'm going to say he won't be changing his mind."

The intruding voice was drenched in the same accent that Ronan's had only a hint of. She shifted in her chair to look behind her and saw a couple approaching. They both glanced at her. The woman's head tilted faintly as if she couldn't quite place who she was looking at. Dressed in a simple black dress that let her curves steal the show, she wore her dark hair in a voluminous blowout that feathered around her pretty face. The man wore black slacks and dress shirt, and looked ready to find all the best kinds of trouble. They were obviously related.

A few more steps, and they arrived at the table. The man grinned. "Not that I blame you, *beau-frère*, when you have such a tantalizing new option."

He extended his hand to her, and Ireland took it, arching an eyebrow when he pressed his lips to her knuckles with exaggerated gallantry. "Although, admit it. I'm more your type than my brother is."

At another time, she'd say he was right. He was closer to her age and smug with his handsomeness—the Jack Daniels to his brother's Macallan Rare Cask.

Ronan introduced them. "My brother, Jules, and my sister, Claudette. This is..." He gave Ireland a look of silent inquiry.

"Elizabeth." Ireland gave her middle name before she really examined why. "Or Liz. Lizzie. Beth. I'm not picky."

Jules rocked back on his heels. "Lizzie it is then."

Neither of Ronan's siblings looked like him. Their hair was darker, their skin paler, and their eyes were a soft brown.

Ireland looked at him with a wistful smile. "As much as I'd like to keep chatting with you, Ronan, don't let me throw off your plans."

"Too late for that, *cher*." He narrowed his gaze with warning when Jules laughed.

"Leave him behind," Jules told her. "Come make mischief with Claudy and me instead."

If not for her fascination with Ronan, she might have taken his younger brother up on his offer. She loved to explore the city with people who came from elsewhere. They saw New York in ways she never had because she'd been born here and took it for granted.

"Ah..." Ireland hesitated and glanced at Ronan.

He gave a curt shake of his head. "Pass a good time, you two, but do *not* get into trouble."

"I brought bail money," Claudette said deadpan, but there was laughter in her eyes.

"Behave yourselves," Ronan reiterated.

"I'll be disappointed if *you* behave," Jules retorted. "Let's go, Claudy. I'm starving. *À bientôt*, Lizzie."

She watched the two weave their way back through the crowded space. "I hope you and your brother let Claudette have fun. Going out with my brothers is like being escorted by the Secret Service—no one gets close."

"Two brothers?"

Ireland turned back to him. "Yes, both older. I love them to death, but I'm pretty sure one wants me to become a nun, and the other wants me to wait until I'm geriatric to settle down."

"I understand why they're protective." His mouth curved.

"You're very sure of yourself. You considered going when Jules asked."

"If you left with them and wanted me to go, yes. I would have." She settled back into her seat. "Did you want to spend more time with me alone, or did you just not want to go out?"

"I want you."

"Well..." Ireland ran the tip of her tongue over her suddenly dry lips. "You weren't kidding. You're an exceptional flirt."

"You know we've moved past flirting." He leaned forward and set his elbows on his knees. All the indolence he'd displayed before was tossed aside like a discarded mask. "The question now is, how far do you want this to go?"

Ronan sat in front of her, framed by the sapphire blue velvet of the loveseat—legs spread, hands linked—and looked like a king in a sultry underworld.

She wanted to be sophisticated enough to play his game but knew when she was outmatched. "I don't know," she said with brutal honesty. "I know if I leave now, I'll regret it, but if I stay, I might regret that, too."

He held out his hand to her.

Reaching for him felt like making a deal with the devil, but when she did, she was inundated with a red-hot, sizzling sexual attraction. It was heady and overwhelming. She'd never experienced anything like it. It was lust on another level, heightened by her intense interest. Yes, she wanted him. But just sitting with him, talking to him, was satisfying, too.

"Do you remember the first thing I told you?" he asked, holding her fingers lightly. "That hasn't changed."

Ireland frowned, confused. *I'm not looking for a hookup.*

"And you said," he went on, "that you make bad choices. So, get to know me. See who I am. And let me see you."

Her fingers tightened reflexively on his. She felt like she was careening out of control, but holding on to him made the sensation seem less scary, and she didn't know why. It made no sense when he was the reason she was spinning. "This is really intense, Ronan."

"Do I frighten you?"

"You should. I don't know why you're not."

"You're scaring the hell out of me," he said bluntly.

She laughed, and the tension inside her loosened enough to be bearable… until she returned his gaze. Her leather blazer suddenly became too warm.

No man had ever looked at her with such absolute interest and desire. It seemed impossible for a man with his assets—and he had so many of them—to feel what she felt. And his directness was as unique and appealing as the rest of him.

"Have dinner with me." Ronan's thumb stroked the backs of her fingers. "I have friends who've recently opened a restaurant in Harlem, and I promised to check it out while I'm here."

Ireland wavered between relief that he wanted to leave the hotel, where most of the servers knew her by name, and concern about going out, where an eager tourist could recognize her. But she'd cross that bridge if they came to it. "That sounds lovely."

His brilliant smile and the way his delight glowed in his gaze was gratifying enough, but then he bent his tawny head to press an electrifying kiss to the palm of her hand. "You're a tigress."

"I have to grab a few things beforehand," she advised because she'd marched over from the Vidal offices without her purse after realizing where Graham was. "Give me the address, and I'll meet you there."

Ronan reached for his jacket, and they both pulled their phones out of their pockets simultaneously. He typed deftly with both thumbs. She watched him, seeing shades of her eldest brother in his easy command. *Beau-frère* Jules had called him—

half-brother. Like Gideon, Ronan had younger half-siblings he looked out for. Did she feel such a strong connection to him because of that? She swiftly dismissed the thought.

She woke her screen with a quick tap and paused when she saw that she'd missed a text notification from her mother. She opened the hour-old group message.

It was a photo with no caption, but the image of a massive emerald-cut diamond on the fourth finger of her mother's left hand told her everything she needed to know. Elizabeth Duffy Cross Vidal would soon be known as Mrs. Elizabeth Pearson, wife of Daniel Pearson.

Congratulations!

It was all she could manage in reply. She was the last to chime in since her brothers apparently paid more attention to their messages. It wasn't that she didn't like Daniel because she did—a lot. But the thought of her mother remarrying was a bit too much to process now.

"Is there a problem?" Ronan asked, his handsome face sobering with concern.

"No." She pushed her mother's news from her mind. "I'm ready for the address."

He read it off to her. "Take my number, too."

Such a simple thing to get a man's number but having his gave her a little thrill. "Got it."

Their server stopped by their table with a tray of empty glasses. Dressed in the tight black shorts and white halter waistcoat with bow tie that was the club's uniform, the pretty blonde gave Ronan a very warm and appreciative smile. "How are you two doing over here? Want another round, mack?"

Then she glanced at Ireland and sobered instantly. "Hey, boss."

"We're good, Tracy," Ronan declined. "Thanks."

As the server sashayed away, he shot Ireland an arch look. "She calls you 'boss,' but I'm just 'mack.'"

Ireland laughed, grateful that he didn't question the erroneous title the bar servers used with her. Even though the hotel bore her last name, Gideon was their ultimate boss.

She checked the time and stood. "Eight o'clock, okay?"

He stood with her. "Perfect."

They didn't move for a moment, separated by the squat brass-topped table. She hesitated to leave him. It was too exciting being in his presence.

Ireland grinned, feigning nonchalance. "*À très bientôt.*"

"Hey, Jimmy," Ireland greeted the evening security guard as he unlocked and opened the front door of the Vidal Records offices for her. The newly renovated, cutting-edge recording studios on the second floor were available at all hours for their artists; they had only to reserve the time. There were no office hours for creativity.

"You're in late," he noted as he relocked the door.

"I forgot my bag," she explained. "I'll be out of your hair in a minute."

"That'd be a neat trick," he said, then lifted his uniform cap to show off his bald head.

Laughing, she took the stairs because she was bursting with energy. She couldn't wait to grab her purse and freshen up. She hadn't bothered pulling herself together for Graham. What little makeup she wore was twelve hours old.

Rage had driven her to march the three blocks to Times Square, where the dirty sidewalks were clogged with pedestrians spilling over into the street in an eclectic blend of loitering tourists in T-shirts and shorts, and rushed theatergoers in finery. They swarmed around the taxis and town cars inching their way through the chaos while gawking at bikini-clad street performers and helmeted police officers mounted on massive horses.

There were so many beautiful, magical places in New York City, yet some people traveled from around the world to see only the most garish, claustrophobic part of it. She would never understand that.

Exiting on the third floor, Ireland hummed and felt a mad impatience. Straight ahead was the reception desk, backed by a dividing privacy wall featuring the Vidal Records logo. Visitors could pass it on either side to access the offices lining the wide hallway, with the assistants' desks in a row down the middle. To her left was the large conference room, with glass walls on two sides and windows on the third. To her right was a smaller, more intimate meeting room that looked like a living room. Both were visible to visitors immediately upon exiting the elevator or stairwell, and you never knew which recording artist or band you might catch a glimpse of.

The overall style was decidedly midcentury because the Vidal company had been in the building since its inception in the 1970s, and they'd elected to keep many of the original fixtures. It had been modernized with updated paint, wallpaper, and furnishings, but the vibe remained retro-hip in the best way. It was a happy, comfortable place to work in an industry that too often felt like a pressure cooker.

The janitorial team was already busy cleaning the vacant offices, and she waved at the man vacuuming as she passed him. She noticed the cleaning cart positioned in front of the main bathrooms, and her nose scrunched. Hopefully, no one was in her father's office since he had a private bathroom she could use instead.

She withdrew her purse from the locked filing cabinet drawer where she stored it. A quick scan confirmed everything was orderly enough for the crew to clean. She left the overhead lights on and headed across the hallway with long, impatient strides.

Ireland stutter-stepped to a halt on the threshold of Christopher Vidal, Sr.'s office, startled to see him behind his desk. He sat with his glasses removed, eyes closed, and headphones on. There were tears on his face.

Her excitement dissipated instantly.

She crossed the room to him and leaned across the desk to set her hand over his.

"What?!" His eyes popped open as his body jolted. He straightened in a rush, throwing the headphones onto the loose papers on his desktop and wiping his cheeks with impatient hands.

"Are you okay, Dad?"

"Jesus," he muttered. "You scared the hell of me, Ireland!"

The auburn waves of his hair, so like her brother Christopher's, were now liberally shot with silver strands. In the years since the divorce, the lines around his mouth and across his forehead had deepened. But he remained an attractive man with a winning smile and an easy-going disposition that made people want to be in his orbit.

"Why are you still here?" she queried gently.

Sliding his glasses onto his face, he glanced at his computer. "I didn't realize how late it was."

"What's going on?" she asked, even though she knew. She settled into one of his visitors' chairs.

"New song," he said. "It's not finished, but wow."

Ireland could hear the lie in his voice, so she didn't ask to listen to the music. "That's great. We love wow."

"We do, yes." He began straightening the papers on his desktop and kept his gaze averted. "What are you still doing here? I thought you'd left."

"I just ran out for a bit. I had to come back for my things."

Opening his middle desk drawer, he swiped the paperwork into it. "I didn't even hear the janitors working."

"They have to. You don't." She forced optimism into her voice. "No working late on Fridays, Dad. Weekends are for fun."

He huffed out a weary laugh. "I think I was just avoiding going home and staring into an empty fridge. I need to shop."

"Order groceries for delivery instead. Tomorrow, though. Tonight, call Sandy and take her out to dinner. Or invite her over for takeout and a movie."

It broke her heart thinking about her father floundering in bachelorhood. He'd expected to live out his days with her mother, madly in love. While he was now seeing Sandy and Ireland liked her, she knew their relationship wasn't anything like what her parents had before. But the cause of the divorce was yet another thing no one in the family wanted to enlighten her about.

"What about you, honey? Do you have plans?"

"I accepted an invite to dinner. I'm happy to cancel, though," she offered, "if you want to hang out with me. I'm here for you, Dad. Always."

If Ronan Boudreaux was the right guy—even if only a right-now right guy—he'd understand and hopefully be in town long enough to reschedule. She crossed her fingers for good measure. If not, she wasn't opposed to traveling his way. Alina was always up for an adventure, which was one of innumerable reasons why they were the best of friends.

But her father waved the offer away. “You go have fun; you’ve earned it. And you’re right—I’ll call Sandy. She mentioned streaming a new movie the other day.”

“You’ll have to tell me how it is.”

“Why don’t you tell me how *you* are,” he countered, his slate green eyes studying her keenly. “You’ve had a lot thrown at you today.”

“I’m good, Dad.” When he just kept looking at her with that knowing gaze, she reiterated. “Really. Nothing that’s come my way has knocked me off my stride.”

His mouth curved affectionately. “Very little does. You’re a wonder to me, you know that? What would you have chosen to do if Vidal Records didn’t exist?”

Ireland stared at him, surprised and alarmed. Her father was in the throes of rethinking his life choices now that he faced the finality of his ex-wife remarrying. In turn, he worried needlessly about his daughter’s choices.

“I’ve never considered it.” There was no point in wishing for things to be different. “Vidal does exist and is partly mine, so that’s my focus.”

And it was his great love. His attachment to their familial legacy ran bone deep. She would nurture and protect it for him as long as was needed.

“Are you happy?” he asked softly.

“I’m not unhappy. Lonely sometimes, but that has nothing to do with work.”

Smiling ruefully, her father stood and stretched, his back popping audibly. “And here I am keeping you from your dinner out.”

“And *your* dinner.” Pushing past her worry and mixed feelings, she focused on what she had to look forward to. She would've canceled on Ronan but was glad she didn't have to. "Walk out with me."

Her tone brooked no argument. She wanted to see him leave so that she knew for a fact he had. She could touch up her minimal makeup on the way to Harlem. And she'd text Christopher and let him know she was concerned about their father.

Unlike the rest of her family, she had no trouble being a team player.

Ireland took the time on the long ride uptown to type a more thorough reply to her mother, letting her know how excited she was for her and how she looked forward to supporting her through the chaotic joy of wedding arrangements. She briefly thought of how amusing it was that she would help plan her mother's wedding before her own, but she was happy to do it. She wanted nothing more than to have everyone in her family settled, safe, and happy.

After she added a promise to talk later, maybe in the morning, she put her phone away and looked out the window, contrasting the city with her memories of Southern Louisiana. She spotted Ronan waiting for her on the sidewalk outside Valentin's restaurant and felt a rush of giddy excitement. Even from a distance, he drew her gaze like a magnet. He carried that tall and powerfully built body with a fluid gracefulness that made her think of sex on tangled sheets beneath a lazily turning fan. Did he fuck like he talked—slow and smooth? Or was the heated demand she sensed in him unleashed with his passion?

Ronan Boudreaux had the kind of magnetism commonly referred to as stage presence, and like the artists she worked with, she found it surreal that someone so extraordinary could walk among mortals like he was one of them. Was he oblivious to how women's heads turned when they walked by? Their furtive glances and outright covetous stares.

No, he couldn't be. He'd been so quick to set boundaries when they first spoke.

What changed his mind? It wasn't her looks; he'd admired them from the first. It wasn't her occupation or family ties because he didn't know of them. For all of the exquisite packaging he came with, it was the idea of being wanted for something invisible and innate that most enthralled her.

Although to be honest, ripping into that packaging with careful teeth and greedy hands was something she'd very much like to do.

Ronan stood beside the entrance awning, conversing with a neatly dressed woman with a cascade of salt and pepper hair. He caught Ireland's gaze as her taxi pulled up to the curb, and his lips curved into a heated smile that made her so very glad that she was able to come.

He'd pulled on his suit jacket and wore a burgundy tie that she noticed had a subtle fleur-de-lis texture when he leaned in to help her get out. The impact of his gorgeous face, so much closer now that they stood a mere few inches from each other, scattered her thoughts to the wind. God, he was stunning. And so totally *male*. He exuded sex and sin. And he smelled like the darkest of temptations blended with whiskey and spice.

"I'm sorry I'm late," she said breathlessly.

"Moments that felt like hours," he teased. "I worried I'd have to track you down in this huge city."

She grinned. "Would you have gone to the trouble?"

"Without question." He led her to the waiting woman. "This is Genevieve, Valentin's wife and a dear friend."

"Hello." Ireland extended her hand. "Elizabeth. It's a pleasure to meet you."

Genevieve pulled her in for air kisses to each cheek. "The pleasure is mine, *petite*. Come in, come in."

The restaurant was situated on a corner, with windows on two sides. All the tables with a view were occupied, but it was much less crowded deeper in where they were seated. The interior was decorated to resemble the French Quarter of New Orleans, with wrought iron railings separating the dining area from the servers' stations, faux shutters on a massive mural that looked like a street, and baskets of flowers hanging from hooks between the wide windows. It was charming, and the savory smells emanating from the open kitchen made her stomach growl in anticipation.

Menus were already waiting on the table, as were two bottles of wine in cooling sleeves and four place settings. Louis Armstrong sang "*La vie en rose*" from hidden speakers.

"White or red?" Genevieve asked, and Ireland glanced briefly at the menu, searching for and finding the dish she ordered whenever she came across it.

"White, please. Thank you."

"I'll have the same," Ronan said, his gaze on her as their glasses were filled.

"I'll give you a minute with the menu," Genevieve told them before walking away.

Ireland couldn't take her eyes off Ronan, either. Against the backdrop of the brightly lit restaurant, his innate vitality was even more apparent. Strands of gold and dark copper shone in his hair, luring her to touch it and learn its texture. The gray of his irises reminded her of a storm rolling in from the Atlantic, swirling with mystery.

"I'm glad I could make it," she told him.

"Me, too. I worried you might be having second thoughts." His confident smile belied his words.

"I don't entertain those as a rule," she admitted. "I just ran into my dad unexpectedly and thought he might need me." Her eyes widened. "Oh. Sorry. You might not have realized I'm from here. New York, I mean. I'm not visiting. I go to Jazzie's sometimes because I like it."

"It's a great place. Everything turned out to be okay with your father, I take it?"

"He'll be fine. Eventually. My mom just told us she's getting remarried, and I think he's going through some grief over it. They've been divorced over a decade now, so it's not fresh, but it's still going to be a shift in our family." She sighed. "I don't really know, honestly. I'm the last one in my family to find out when something's wrong."

"Are you estranged?" Reaching over, Ronan took her hand in his. An intimate undertone warmed his voice, and the way he held both her gaze and hand was comforting. That a man with his relentlessly powerful physicality could demonstrate such tenderness was irresistible.

"No, we're very tight. I see all of them practically every day. Well, except my mother. I don't see her every day, but we talk every day. I don't know why they avoid telling me things. *Important* things. They tell me stupid, trivial stuff all the time, but if there's a problem, they don't want me to know about it until it's resolved and tied up with a bow."

His fingers squeezed hers gently before releasing her. "You're too fierce for them. They fear what you'll do."

That made her smile. "They don't know how fierce I am. I try to tell them, but I don't think they believe me."

"You must hide it then, although I don't know how. The minute you walked into the bar, I saw it."

"Yeah, well…" She laughed, delighted he'd noticed her before she'd inadvertently sat at his table. "I was a little angry when I got there."

"A little? You verbally castrated a guy in front of his woman. And you relished every minute of it."

Her mouth agape, it took her a moment to reply in disbelief. "There's no way you heard that! No way. You were playing… the band was behind you…"

"I can read lips."

"No."

"I'm a man of many talents." He gave her a roguish wink.

Ireland laughed. "Well… Now I know. And now *you* know—don't piss me off."

"I admire your ferocity. I'm sure I'll enjoy it even when directed at me."

The simple statement touched her. It was a side of her even those closest to her had seldom seen.

"Genevieve is headed this way," he told her. "Do you know what you want?"

You.

She almost said it. Instead, she confessed, "If I see shrimp and grits on a menu, that's what I'm getting. You add andouille to it, as they do here, and it's ultra guaranteed that's what I'm ordering."

"No one does it better than Valentin, except maybe his sister, Marcelle, but don't tell him I said that."

Ronan ordered for both of them, choosing the pork chop and Southern braised greens for himself. Genevieve inputted the order on a tablet, then smiled affectionately at him and gave a quick tug on the ends of his hair. Ireland had never felt such envy. Not that Genevieve was so transparently fond of him, but that the woman knew what his hair felt like and was free to touch it.

"You've forgotten to cut your hair," she teased him.

Shrugging, he said, "Too busy."

"I like it," Ireland interjected. "Your hair."

The curve of his lips deepened, and his eyes mirrored that heated smile. "Do you?"

"You've got the sexiest hair I've ever seen. If it doesn't drive you crazy, you could leave it just as it is."

"Done."

She melted a little. Genevieve noticed and gave a nod of approval before moving to another table.

Ireland changed the subject, hoping she didn't have little hearts as pupils. "How do you know them?"

"Through Marcelle." He sat back. "She lived down the road from my childhood home and caught me stealing tomatoes from her garden."

"Ah, so thievery isn't one of your talents."

"I'd be much better at it now. I was thirteen then, tortured by a growth spurt and starving. My mother's work in New Orleans allowed her one day a week at home, and Jules' and Claudette's father left the three of us to our own devices. So, I found what I could for us to eat and took it. Success outweighed stealth."

Ireland paused with her wineglass half-lifted to her mouth. He told his story in the most casual of tones, just as he'd told her how he learned to play the trumpet so consummately, but her ear caught turbulent undercurrents in his silky-smooth cadence.

"Marcelle had learned to hunt in the bayou," he went on. "She can be as silent as a shadow. I didn't fight when she caught me by the ear." His smile was wry, but affection softened his gaze. "Even then, she was smaller than me."

The picture forming in her mind was unexpected. And

Ronan's revelations were startlingly intimate. She wasn't prepared for that, either.

See who I am, he'd said. And he was showing her.

"I prefer when you look at me with desire," he said gently, "not sympathy."

"I'm sorry." She set her glass down on the table.

"Don't be. I've managed just fine. That's just the story of how —and why—we found each other. I wasn't ever hungry after that, and neither was Jules or Claudette. Marcelle was widowed in her early twenties and never remarried or had children. We became family, including Valentin and Genevieve." He sipped his wine. "Our food's here."

Turning her head, she saw the chef in his white coat approaching with a plate in his hands. Genevieve was beside him with Ronan's meal. They set the food on the table simultaneously.

Ronan pushed away from the table with effortless grace and embraced the shorter man in a back-slapping hug. Ireland stood, too, and returned Valentin's brief kisses to each of her cheeks.

Valentin pulled back but kept both of his hands on her shoulders. He was short, shorter even than his diminutive wife. His thick white hair was contained in a net, and his face was tanned and deeply lined. Dark brown eyes studied her for a long minute, then he gave her a broad smile. "Finally, a woman to bring this boy to his knees. He could use the humility. Give him no quarter."

Ireland laughed, not just at what he said but at using the term "boy" for Ronan, who was so utterly a *man* in every sense. "I'm doing my best."

"Give me a chance to woo her first, Val," Ronan said with that smooth, mellow whiskey drawl. "Before she decides to break my heart."

The older couple joined them, with Valentin sitting by Ronan. Genevieve poured red wine for herself and her husband.

The chef waited while Ireland took the first bite and watched as she grew still with pleasured surprise, her eyes widening. She chewed slowly, relishing every burst of flavor.

Ronan watched her, too, with a hint of a smile and warm, gleaming eyes.

"I now know what heaven tastes like," she said finally. "This is amazing, Valentin."

He blushed. "It's nothing special, *ma belle.* And please, call me Val."

Reaching into his jacket pocket, Ronan pulled out his phone. He looked at Ireland as he slid his chair back. "Excuse me a moment. It's Jules."

"There's an empty room for private parties down the hallway," Genevieve directed. "Send him our love."

Ireland followed him with her gaze. When she caught herself, she looked away and noted that she wasn't the only woman in the restaurant who couldn't take her eyes off Ronan.

She smiled sheepishly at her hosts. "Your restaurant is lovely. I can't wait to tell my friends and family about it."

"*Merci, petite,*" Genevieve said as she grabbed the white wine bottle and refilled their glasses. "We hope to make a success of it. Ronan put so much faith in us by buying this building so we could have this space and the condo above it. Without him, we wouldn't have been able to move closer to our grandchildren."

Swallowing, she said, "Oh, I didn't know that."

"We miss home, of course." Valentin's smile was wistful. "My sister, most of all. But we know she's in good hands with Ronan. You'll meet her, I'm sure."

Ireland didn't know what to say to that. It was a lovely idea, a tremulous and exciting possibility. "He told me how he met Marcelle."

"To come so far," Val murmured, his gaze distant as he revisited the memory. "I couldn't be prouder."

"Tell me you're not embarrassing me," Ronan admonished as he returned to the table.

"Is everything all right?" she asked.

"As much as it can be with Jules. They're heading up to Mohegan Sun."

A server stopped by the table and spoke discreetly to Valentin, who then stood. "I'll be right back."

Genevieve stood, too. "Excuse me while I make the rounds. We close at ten. Then we'll be free to relax."

When Ireland set her fork down again, it was because she'd eaten every bite, and only a pile of tails remained.

"A woman of lusty appetites," Ronan observed, having finished first. "You captivate me."

Ireland drank her wine and studied the fascinating man across from her. "I was just thinking the same about you. You knew they'd sing your praises when you brought me here."

His smile was devilish as his strong, talented fingers stroked the stem of his glass. He sat partially reclined, his long legs stretched out and crossed at the ankles, his left arm draped across his chairback and his right on the table. Lucifer himself had to envy Ronan's effortless flair.

"In my defense," he murmured, "I'd planned for dinner with them weeks ago, but yes, I thought their endorsement might shore up your goodwill toward me, so I moved the dates around. Now, I just have to convince you to see me again tomorrow."

Leaning forward, she spoke in a conspiratorial whisper. "Not that I'm complaining, but… You had me with the trumpet."

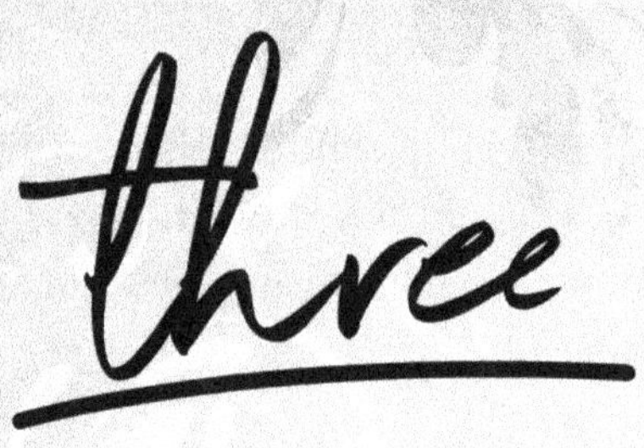

EVA RANG THE DOORBELL OF IRELAND'S APARTMENT AND smiled when she heard her sister-in-law humming loudly as she approached the door. It swung open, and the statuesque brunette stood barefoot, her toned arms and legs bared by a tank top and shorts.

Pulling a spoon out of her mouth, Ireland grinned at her. "Good morning!"

She appeared to be in such good spirits that Eva laughed, relieved. "Good morning to you, too."

Ireland stepped back and held the door open with her foot, extending her arm in invitation. She had a bowl of cereal in one hand and a television remote tucked under her arm. Her hip-length curtain of inky hair was piled atop her head in a messy bun, and she wore ECRA+ cooling under-eye gel pads. She was one of the most naturally gorgeous women Eva had ever encountered, if not *the* most.

"Lauren," Ireland called out to the AI assistant, "lower volume."

The breezy SoCal reggae piping through the surround sound speakers dropped to a conversational level.

Entering, Eva crossed the small foyer into the living room,

which boasted soaring ceilings, wide and tall windows, and prewar embellishments. Over the years, the adjacent guest apartment to her and Gideon's penthouse had offered a haven for friends and family in transitional periods of their lives. Her best friend Cary had lived in it a couple of years before his marriage. Chris, her father-in-law, had stayed there for a spell while he searched for a permanent home after his divorce. And then Ireland had settled in when she'd started at Columbia. The place now reflected the young woman's tastes and style—it was as cheerfully fierce as Ireland herself.

Her cat, a massive white Maine Coon named Blizzard, dozed on a sunlit shelf attached to a wall papered in a black and white photograph of a NYC building. Disguised as three-dimensional fire escape landings and stairs, the many artfully arranged cat hammocks and ladders were fun features Ireland had added.

"You checking up on me about Mom?" Ireland asked, putting her bowl and remote on the coffee table before sitting down with crossed legs. "Or the asshole ex?"

"Both." Eva sat on the other end of the white couch. "But I'm going to guess you're not fazed. Gideon said you wouldn't be, but still..."

Ireland smiled. "You're the best, you know that? Always looking after everyone, making sure we're all okay. You've done so much for our family. I think that a lot, but don't say it enough."

Deeply touched, Eva demurred, "It doesn't need saying but thank you."

"As to how I'm doing... I don't give two shits about Graham Teller. I would've handled it differently, but not necessarily better." Ireland gave an offhand shrug. "He's not the first to see me as a superhighway to success, but he's the last. And karma will deal with him eventually."

So, Gideon was right about how his sister was taking it. Good. Still, Eva wasn't going to stop working on his collaborative skills. "Yes, I believe that, too."

"And I talked to Mom this morning. She sounds better than she has in a long time. She loves being a wife to influential men. She loves planning, hosting, and socializing. She's an asset to any businessman, and Daniel will be lucky to have her. Once he sees her in action, he'll kick himself for not proposing sooner."

"My thoughts exactly." While Eva had only attended one of Elizabeth's glamorous parties before the Vidal marriage collapsed, she'd been impressed by everything about the event. And in the years since, she'd seen Elizabeth work the room at social gatherings and noted her charismatic poise. She didn't respect her mother-in-law fundamentally but could acknowledge her talents.

"I met someone."

The blurted-out change in subject raised Eva's brows. "Oh? Tell me more."

"He might be perfect." Ireland's smile lit up the already light-flooded room. "He plays the trumpet like he was born to it, but—get this—he's not a professional musician! He's tremendously talented and so, so sexy onstage, but it's just a hobby."

Eva grinned at her delight. "I take it that's a selling point."

"For me, it's a huge one. I can't help being attracted to musicians. No matter how hot he is, I couldn't be with a guy who didn't love music." Making a face, Ireland continued, "But musicians who want to make a career out of it are a problem for me. They find out who I am—or they already know—and I'm not a woman anymore. I'm just a golden ticket."

"They're idiots," Eva snapped, angry on her behalf. She'd been there when Ireland's tender heart had been broken the first time. That guy, too, had used her. Stringing her along on the side while blaming Gideon for the secrecy of their relationship—all the while, he'd been dating other girls. "What you do for a living is the least interesting thing about you."

Ireland reached over and squeezed her hand. "Thanks. I was beginning to wonder what the fuck is wrong with me that I'm only good for what I can do for someone. Alina thinks I pick the wrong guys, but I think I just attract them. Then, I met Ronan."

Just saying the man's name noticeably altered Ireland's mood from frustrated to hopeful.

"So, what does this perfect guy do for a living?" Eva asked.

"Leveraged buyouts and the occasional hostile takeover. And he's got to be successful at it because he's got this swagger to him. He's an alpha because he's earned it, you know what I mean?" Ireland smiled. "He also happens to be the most gorgeous creature I've ever seen, and he's so fucking sexy he raises my body temperature when I'm around him."

Ireland grabbed her phone off the sofa's armrest and swiped at the screen. She flipped it around to show a picture of an extraordinarily handsome man sitting at an antique desk with a lithe black cat stretched across the far edge. "That's Ronan with his cat, Marie Laveau. He's from Louisiana. His hair's longer now. A bit longer than Gideon's and crazy thick. I want to touch it so bad. I swear, I didn't know a man could check every box on a wish list."

"He's certainly a looker," Eva agreed. The kind of guy who turned heads and short-circuited a woman's common sense. While Gideon's face had been carved to perfection by enamored angels, Ronan was all devilish, sultry temptation. The sparkle in his eyes, the natural come-hither curve of his lips. And that hair... "He looks... mature."

Ireland laughed, and there was such a lightness about her. Her stunningly blue eyes were feverishly bright, and her cheeks flushed pink. Eva had seen that look on her own face before—when she'd first crossed paths with Gideon.

"Older, you mean," Ireland said. "He'll turn forty on Christmas. What a birthday, right? But he's mature in the other sense, too. Eva, you have no idea how wonderful it is that he's figured himself out, who he is and what he wants. There's nothing I can do for him, nothing he needs me to do for him. And that feels so amazing."

Eva kicked off her sandals and tucked her legs, wrapping her arms around them. "The only thing sexier in a man than confidence is a sense of humor."

"Oh, he makes me laugh!" Ireland's face took on a dreamy expression. "He's impossibly charming—suave, really, and it's effortless for him. He's a Southern gentleman all the way. He's got the faintest hint of a drawl when he talks. It's like music, actually. That's why I love it so much!" She looked astonished by the realization. "The way he speaks is melodic. I could listen to him all day."

It was startling to see Ireland finally excited by a romantic interest. Eva wasn't sure the men in their family were ready for an additional source of testosterone, let alone from a man of Gideon's age. A man in his early thirties, like Christopher Jr., was still malleable and easier to ruffle. A man of forty was another animal entirely. "How did you two meet?"

"Right place, right time. I was still pissed at Graham and hating anything with a penis. I told Ronan I wasn't interested, and he wasn't on the prowl either, so it was just sharing a table in a crowded club at first. I think he was a little wary, and who could blame him? He has to be getting hit on every five minutes."

Eva's brows lifted. "You just met him *last night*?"

"After work. Then we went to dinner at this amazing Cajun

restaurant. I'll have to take you. Everything was delicious! He's close friends with the owners, and we stayed with them for hours after closing, just talking and laughing over wine."

Leaning forward, Eva lowered her voice. "Is he here?"

"God, I wish!" Ireland pouted. "The sexual attraction is off the charts. He's like catnip to me. I invited him over, but he wants me to know him better first since I told him I have a terrible track record with men."

"He turned down an offer to hit the sheets with you? With *you*? Are you sure he's straight?"

Ireland broke into peals of laughter. It took her a minute to catch her breath enough to speak. "You're good for my ego, sis. But no, he's definitely into me. I mean, he flat out looked me dead in the eye and said, 'I want you' in that smoked whiskey voice of his."

"Oh boy." Eva went on alert. Gideon had been as blunt about his lust for her in the early days of their eventual relationship. She knew exactly how devastating it was to be faced with a gorgeous, successful, supremely confident man who was honest about his craving for you. It was a powerful turn-on, and for her, it had caused the first crack in her meticulously built defenses.

Whoever Ronan was, he warranted a closer look because a man like that could either anchor you or set you adrift.

"Can you imagine?" Ireland flushed prettily. "So direct and assertive. Aggressive even. Like swoon, right?"

"I'd like to meet him. Will you be bringing him to the masquerade on Friday?" Preparing her husband for the first-ever occasion of meeting his sister's boyfriend might take a little finessing. Although the charity event for their Crossroads Foundation should keep Gideon on his best behavior. She hoped.

"Oh… I haven't even considered asking him. Ronan's not

based here, and it's too soon to talk about the logistics of seeing each other once he's finished his business in the city."

"Maybe we could schedule a lunch or a quick drink?" Eva pressed. "You've met his friends. Introduce him to us."

"Um. Well... he doesn't know who I am," Ireland confessed, rubbing her thigh absently.

"Huh?"

"When I realized I was just a random woman to him, I gave him my middle name. I didn't want to ruin it by being me. You know what I mean?"

It took Eva a long moment to process what she'd heard. "Oh, Ireland."

Ireland looked down at her clasped fingers.

The slump of her shoulders pained Eva. With a deep sigh, she reached forward to set her hand over her sister-in-law's. "I get it. You come into a relationship with a big, wonderful package of protective family members and a high-powered career, and you need to be wanted despite those things, not because of them. But how far can you go pretending to be someone else before you've gone *too* far?"

"I'm not sure." Ireland shrugged awkwardly. "I'm just counting on intuitively knowing when."

"Your latest ads will be plastered all over the city starting Monday," she warned, "when the body lotion campaign kicks off."

"Crap. I forgot about that." Ireland groaned. "If I could go back and do it differently, I would. I just didn't want to be used again, but in hindsight, I realize he's taking on that same risk himself. He's wealthy, and for all he knows, I could be eyeing him as a sugar daddy."

"Have you looked him up?"

"As soon as I got in the cab home last night, but nothing

came up. There are other men with his name, but I couldn't find any information specifically about him. But then, not everyone names their companies after themselves, like our family tends to do."

"True." Even the ECRA+ line was eponymous, with the EC standing for Eva Cross. "How did you get the picture you showed me?"

Ireland's smile was both fond and sheepish. "We traded cat photos."

"What's his last name?"

Pausing, she wet her lips. "You know, I think I'll keep him to myself for now."

"You're protective."

"Not of Ronan. My sense is that he can take care of himself just fine. But of this thing we're doing? Yeah. I want to let it breathe and give it a chance to grow."

Eva nodded, then smiled for good measure. Ireland had enough meddlers in her life and didn't need another one. Then again, there were ways to pick up information without necessarily meddling… "When are you seeing him again?"

"Today." Ireland's expression brightened. "A picnic in Central Park. Can you believe I've never done that? I'm looking forward to it."

"Well, keep me posted, will you? He sounds very exciting."

"Oh my god, yes! I've been dying to talk about him. If Alina were in town, I'd've been at her door in the wee hours of this morning. Ronan's just… He's raised the bar. *And* my expectations. I want someone who *sees* me, who wants to *know* me. Someone who asks questions and cares about my answers. You have that with Gideon."

"I do. And it's life-changing and wonderful to be someone's priority. I want that for you more than anything." But Eva was very protective of the ones she loved and knew all too well that sometimes, when something—or someone—seemed too good to be true, it was because they were.

Ireland turned back and forth in front of the full-length mirror in her bedroom, examining the white linen romper she considered wearing. It was a warm day in the city, in the mid-eighties and moderately humid. She'd tried a half-dozen outfits so far, but the romper looked like the winner since she would worry less about giving someone a view while sitting and possibly lying on a blanket in the grass. Suspended from thin straps on her shoulders, it hung loosely—like a shift dress—to the tops of her thighs.

"What do you think, Bliz?" She looked at her cat's reflection in the mirror. "You're going to say white, aren't you? You know I can't wear white exclusively like you do, right? I've got to switch it up sometimes."

Blizzard gave her a bored stare, then began cleaning his right front paw.

Ireland's phone began ringing, and she dived for the bed where she'd tossed it. She was slightly disappointed that it wasn't Ronan.

"Hello, brother," she greeted Christopher as she returned to the mirror. "How's it going?"

"Good—soon to be great once we herd the hellions." The exasperation in his voice was partially explained by the sound of her niece and nephew's excited voices in the background. "We're heading to the Museum of Ice Cream."

"*Ice cream!*" the kids screamed with joy.

"Yum. Have a scoop for me."

"You're welcome to join us," he offered, which set off a litany of *Auntie Ireland!* calls from Lorenzo and Serena.

"I wish I could, but I've already made plans. Count me in if you go again and give me more of a heads-up."

"Yeah, yeah. Nat and I just came up with the idea this morning. Hang on. Let me move where it's quieter." The kids' voices grew distant as he walked away from them. "Listen, I talked to Dad about Mom's news, and it turns out he's known for a while, so it wasn't a surprise. Guess she found the ring or the receipt—I can't remember which—and knew the proposal was coming, so she warned him."

"Oh." She frowned. "Well, that's good, I guess."

"And now that she's remarrying, he won't be on the hook for alimony anymore. So, it's good all around. They're both happy."

"Sure. It's all great," she said absently, sitting on the edge of the bed. The memory of her father crying by himself was still fresh and raw enough that she was uncomfortable sharing it with anyone, even her brother. "Thanks for checking in with him."

"You could've asked him yourself," Christopher admonished.

"Sure. The man who tells me nothing? You got more out of him than I would've."

Chants for ice cream broke the brief quiet on the other end of the line. "I've gotta go before they mutiny. Say good-bye, everyone."

Ireland and the kids called out to each other in unison, then the call ended. She sat there for a long minute with her phone in hand, her mind replaying the scene in her dad's office. It wasn't all that unusual for her father to react strongly to a song; it's what made him so great at his job. And that attuned ear had been passed on to her, so there was no question he'd lied to her. If not about her mother, it was something else.

She checked the time.

Looking across at the mirror, Ireland figured she was ready to go. Sure, she could spend another hour dithering over which earrings and shoes to wear, but she'd go with her gut on those, just like she was going with her gut about her father.

She texted Ronan.

Hey. I might be a little late, but I'll be there.

He replied almost instantly.

However long, I'll be waiting.

Rushing, because she hated to lose even a moment that she could be spending with him, she jumped up and finished getting ready fast. She swiped sunblock, a hat, and sunglasses into a raffia bag. Then she shoved her feet into flat sandals, kissed Blizzard on the top of his head, and darted out the door.

Ireland's foot tapped impatiently as she rang the after-hours bell at the Vidal Records offices, even though it only took a few seconds for the guard to let her in.

"Good afternoon," Eady said, pulling the door open. "This is the busiest Saturday we've had in a while. We've got a full house today."

"That's why I'm stopping by," Ireland fibbed cheerfully because she already felt guilty. If any of her family noticed her name in the log, having a valid reason for visiting the offices over the weekend would help hide her true intent.

Not wanting to chance running into anyone by taking the elevator, she took the stairs. With every story climbed, Ireland's guilt began to morph into irritation. She wouldn't have to be underhanded if her family bothered to share information with her.

The pervasive sense of desertion on the third floor was strange and unwelcome. With the overhead lights off, the wide reception hallway between the executive offices was dimly lit, and the space was eerily devoid of the music and conversation that normally enlivened it.

Crossing over to her father's office, Ireland locked the door behind her. Moving swiftly, she woke his computer by shaking the mouse and then typed in his password, a blend of Christopher's name and birthday with her name and birthday. As often as they both warned their father to have multiple passwords for his logins, he stuck to what he knew best.

Since she and her father had left the office shortly after she found him, everything on his monitor was precisely how it'd been the night before. It only took a moment to see what he'd been listening to.

"Changes" by Black Sabbath was a sad song about divorce but was not an unfinished new song by any stretch of the imagination.

Ireland rocked back in her father's desk chair and drummed her long acrylic nails on the desktop. Maybe he'd lied to Christopher, too, downplaying how he was taking the news of his ex-wife's remarriage. But he'd been awfully detailed about that lie.

With a sigh, she pushed back from the desk. It was something she could work out later when she didn't have the sexiest man alive waiting to spend the afternoon with her. Monday was soon enough to confront her father.

But she paused at the sight of the partially opened desk drawer.

She pulled it the rest of the way open, finding the papers he had swiped into it when she'd sat in the chair across from him. Right on top was a lined piece of paper with handwritten notes; beneath it, partially obscured forms and a formal letter on business letterhead.

Ireland would know her father's penmanship anywhere, and the names listed were also recognizable, especially her own. Extracting his notes, she confirmed that they were a rundown of the company's handful of private shareholders and how much stake they had.

Years before, Gideon saved the company by getting their mother to convince Chris and Christopher to take it public. The infusion of capital facilitated the turnaround, but eventually, when Gideon sold his stake back to the family, her father took Vidal private again. Still, he'd listened to Gideon's advice and brought on investors who'd serve as a brain trust to keep the company healthy after his poor business sense had led to near insolvency.

Most shareholders had either a checkmark beside their share percentages or were struck through with a line. A company—McCaffrey Holdings—had both a checkmark and a question mark. Her and Christopher's stakes of ten percent each remained unmarked, as did their mother's fifteen percent. Their father's stake wasn't included.

Since the letterhead beneath the list was from McCaffrey Holdings, she read that next. It appeared to be a reply to something her father had sent earlier, concisely relaying that they'd be happy to discuss their shareholding position at his convenience. And underneath that was unexecuted loan paperwork from three banks that had yet to be filled out.

Ireland frowned. Was Dad methodically buying back interest in the company?

Assuredly, Vidal was better and stronger than it had ever been. Their recent upgrades to the recording studios and the availability of suites at the Vidal Hotel for those who were recording had proven very popular with their artists. While the suites were an exclusive perk for their signed talent, indie artists also booked time in the studios.

Still, she wasn't so sure that making the company entirely family-owned was the best decision for Vidal.

Unless her father was planning to retire or actively considering it. If so, he'd want to give her and Christopher a blank slate, free from the encumbrances of his past mistakes.

Returning the papers to the drawer in the same order and disarray as she'd found them, Ireland turned to the keyboard to search her father's calendar. There. Monday afternoon. A meeting with McCaffrey in the conference room.

She made a mental note to call Christopher after he'd put the kids to bed. If he'd known about this and not said anything, they would be having a conversation requiring his full attention.

In the meantime, she had a golden god waiting for her to show up late yet again.

As had happened the night before, Ireland's gaze locked on Ronan Boudreaux from a distance like a heat-seeking missile. He was simply a man who caught the eye, like glass glinting in the light. This time, she was on foot and could slow her steps to study him at her leisure.

They'd arranged to meet at the 72nd Street entrance to the Park on 5th Avenue, and he lounged there, half sitting against the

Inventor's Gate with his long, tanned legs crossed at the ankles and his hands thrust into the pockets of his khaki shorts. Sunlight burnished his golden skin and reflected off the copper mirror of his aviator sunglasses.

He wore a white linen shirt lightweight enough to reveal the shadow of his tattoo. The sleeves were rolled up to his elbows, the collar left open, the tail untucked. His feet were sheathed in braided leather loafers, and a large picnic basket sat beside them. The luxurious strands of his hair drifted softly in a gentle breeze.

At first glance and to the unobservant, he appeared relaxed as he spoke to a fit brunette in running shorts and sports bra. But Ireland noted his reserve, that distance he'd enforced when she had first met him. He was there, right there, but unreachable. And he wasn't as insouciant as he appeared, subtly moving his tawny head as the woman spoke with animated gestures. Ireland was sure he was scanning his surroundings, vigilantly watchful.

The jogger turned slightly and pointed, a momentary distraction that allowed Ronan to survey the street. He caught sight of Ireland standing in the shade of a building, and his mouth curved in a very male smile. Withdrawing his hand from his pocket, he coaxed her with a crook of his finger.

Everything inside her bloomed into breathless, heart-pounding chaos.

She started toward him. It should be impossible for a smile to overwhelm a woman. How would she survive his kiss? Thus far, he'd only held her hand, maintaining a physical distance even as he revealed himself in far more profound ways. It was maddening and intriguing and made her crave so much more.

Butterflies in her tummy slowed her steps, and it seemed like forever before she reached him. She hoped it felt endless to him, too, and that he suffered a little because of it. That would be only fair.

"...and I highly recommend Lombardi's for pizza," the brunette told him. "It's in Little Italy, of course. Lots of great Italian joints down there, but—"

"Here she is," Ronan interjected, straightening as Ireland drew abreast of them. The jogger stopped talking, her head turning as Ireland stepped into view.

"Hello," she greeted the woman, who sized her up.

"Thanks for all of the excellent advice." Ronan caught up the handles of the picnic basket. "Enjoy your day."

"Enjoy your picnic." The brunette's smile reached her eyes for Ronan but dimmed for Ireland, who couldn't blame her.

As they turned away, he drew Ireland into his side and murmured, "More than worth the wait."

Her breath left her in a rush as he tucked her lightly against him. His body felt like sun-warmed granite, impossibly hard and taut with muscle. She slipped her arm around his lean waist and realized there was no softness to him. The smell of his skin was so delicious; she fought the temptation to nuzzle him.

Ronan kept her exhilaratingly close as they entered the park with his arm around her waist. They strolled Terrace Drive, passing the Morse statue and people reading or chatting on the row of shaded benches. Ahead, two dog owners traveling in opposing directions paused to let their pets sniff each other with eagerly wagging tails.

"I should probably be coy and not say how excited I am to be with you again," Ireland told him, her hand at his waist sliding lower to hook into his back pocket. It didn't escape her that they looked like they'd deliberately coordinated their attire.

"Should I not tell you how little I slept because I couldn't stop thinking about you?"

"No, you should absolutely tell me that." She also noted that walking with him gave her a certain level of anonymity because he drew attention away from her. It was really quite lovely. "Did you toss and turn and get tangled in your sheets?"

"I wrecked the bed," he drawled.

Heat flushed her skin at the images that filled her mind. "Tell me you sleep nude—but only if it's true."

"You'll discover that yourself."

Tilting her head, she looked up at him, grateful for the shield of her oversized sunglasses. "When?"

"When we're both categorically certain you won't regret it."

"Maybe you're worried *you'll* regret it," she countered.

His reply was a sardonically arched brow.

She pouted. "I shouldn't have told you about my man embargo."

His laugh was so vibrant and warm that the sound drew looks as they walked through the ever-crowded Bethesda Terrace and around the fountain. "I'm flattered you want to break that embargo for me, but regardless—I don't take risks when I can't afford to lose."

"Most men would view getting me in bed as the win."

"That's the reward. Getting you to *stay* there, now that's the win."

Her pulse fluttered wildly. "Maybe I'm terrible at it. Maybe you'll be one and done."

"Don't worry," he soothed. "I'm good enough for the both of us."

Ireland laughed so hard she tripped over her own feet.

They followed the shore of the Lake until they reached the Bow Bridge, then slipped through the row of benches onto the grass. Other picnickers were there; it was considered the most romantic spot in the Park. At the picnic with the most elaborate setup, an unaccompanied man with a crown of curly brown hair stood as they approached.

"I'll be nearby if you need anything," he said. Then he walked away, leaving behind the extravagantly arranged picnic, including a galvanized bucket filled with champagne on ice, two lap trays with place settings, plump seating cushions and pillows, and an exuberant royal blue bouquet.

"Wow," she breathed. "You sure know how to impress a date."

"Playing to win," he reminded with a debonair grin, supporting her with an outstretched hand as she kicked off her sandals and kneeled onto the oversized blue and white striped blanket.

Ronan set down the basket he carried and joined her, tucking a velvet floor cushion between his back and the trunk of the tree that shaded them. He sighed, long and slow, and his muscular body visibly relaxed. "God, it feels good to be surrounded by trees instead of concrete."

She stretched out beside him, resting her elbows on a cushion and propping her chin with her hands. She studied the way he'd tilted his head back, and though she couldn't see it through his mirrored lenses, she suspected he'd closed his eyes.

"You need big cities to make your fortune," she murmured, "but at heart, you're a man who prefers the wild."

She sensed that he'd opened his eyes to look at her.

"You're starting to know me, *cher*."

But she wanted to know more. "Any marriages for you? Any engagements? Divorces? Children?"

"*Non*."

"Are you not into serious relationships? Do you get bored? Prefer variety? Like the hunt more than the capture?"

He pulled his sunglasses off and hooked them onto his open collar. His gray eyes were piercing. "Time is a luxury I've enjoyed too little of. I could say I've been focused on my goals—that's true, in part. The more honest answer is that marriage and children weren't included in those goals, so I never pursued them."

"Oh." There was a sudden tight pinching in her chest.

He ran his fingertips down her arm. "And you?"

"I've never been with anyone long enough for it to become serious."

"That's incredible to me."

Ireland shrugged artlessly. "To be fair, I tend to check out of relationships fairly quickly."

"Hmm. Why?"

Tossing her sunglasses aside, she rolled toward him and tucked the pillow behind her head. She ran her foot along the length of his bare leg. "Not knowing what I wanted?" she speculated. "Looking for the wrong things?"

Ronan held his silence.

"Actually..." She realized she wasn't being as forthright as he'd been because she wasn't being truthful with herself. "It's simpler than that. My parents were crazy in love. My brothers are both madly in love with their wives. And since that's ultimately what I want, I can't risk being tied up with the wrong guy and unavailable when the right guy comes along." She gave a wry laugh. "Of course, that's assuming he'll want me back."

Rubbing the strands of her messy bun between his fingers, he murmured, "I can't imagine a man alive who wouldn't give everything to have you."

Her breath left her in a shaky rush, and she looked up at him, amazed that he affected her no less when viewed upside down. "You're the most dangerous kind of flirt, Ronan Boudreaux. You spin a woman around until she forgets which way is up."

His mouth curved in a lazy smile. "Is that what's happening? Are we spinning? It feels like falling."

She tensed against those maddening butterflies. They multiplied every hour she spent with him; until now, it felt like she could hardly contain them all.

Ireland grasped for a safer topic in an effort at self-preservation. "Where's home for you?"

"Primarily New Orleans, but I sometimes escape to a smaller place I keep in Lafayette Parish."

"In the bayou?" she guessed.

"Yes. It's peaceful." His accent deepened as his voice took on a dreamy quality. "Feels like there's no one else on the planet but you."

Shimmering images of towering trees cloaked in mist filtered through her mind. It was another world entirely from the one she lived in. "I think being in the middle of nowhere might frighten me a little."

Reaching over her, Ronan grabbed the champagne bottle. "You're as ferocious as anything out there."

That made her laugh, and she sat up with her legs crossed.

"Where do you live?" he asked, peeling off the foil hood and loosening the muselet.

She pointed up at her building on Fifth Avenue. "There."

"You're pointing at the sky. Are you all the way up at the very top? Like Rapunzel?"

"Why else would I keep my hair so long?" She grinned as she collected the champagne flutes from the lap trays. "So now you know—in case it ever crossed your mind—your wealth appeals to me only because you don't need mine."

His laugh was full-bodied with delight. "See? Ferocious."

She made a purring noise.

Leaning forward with a grin, Ronan pressed his lips to her bare shoulder, and a shiver of delight radiated from the spot of connection to her nape. Unfamiliar yearning filled her. The desire to feel those lips against hers was so unexpectedly strong, almost a deep ache. But she wouldn't make the first move. She positively refused to. He'd set the rules; now, she needed him to break them.

He straightened, his strong hands cradling the heavy bottle. He gave it a few masterful twists, expelling the cork against his palm with a soft hiss and setting it aside. "I assure you I can more than afford to pamper an expensive, luxurious woman such as yourself without any assistance from you or anyone else."

"I'm not expensive."

"*Cher.*" He shot her a chastising look and began to pour into the flutes she held steady for him. "You're the kind of woman who'll take the soul of the man who loves you. I'd say that's damned fucking expensive."

"Well…" She was speechless for a minute. Then, "What will *you* take from the woman who loves you?"

He winked at her and shoved the bottle back into the ice. "Everything."

Ireland stuck the tip of her tongue out at him and passed him a flute. They toasted, and she sipped the crisply chilled golden liquid.

She savored the flavor, the feel of the warm summer breeze as it caressed her skin, and her delightful and impishly seductive companion. There'd never been a more perfect afternoon.

"Tell me more about Jules and Claudette," she urged. "Do they work with you?"

"Yes." Settling against the tree, Ronan beckoned her to join him. When she turned around and leaned back, he adjusted her comfortably into the crook of his arm, her head nestled against his shoulder. "Claudette finds the businesses that suit our needs, and Jules tracks their performance."

"And you?" She nestled deeper against his incredible hardness, enjoying his steady warmth at her back. "What's your job?"

He nuzzled her temple. "I sniff out where they're bleeding."

"Of course you do," she murmured, and he'd be good at it.

"Are you hungry?" he whispered behind her ear, making her shiver. "There's fried chicken, cornbread muffins, red beans and rice, salad, peach cobbler, and iced tea—all from Valentin and Genevieve."

If anyone had told her the recitation of a menu could be a turn-on, Ireland would've laughed at the ridiculousness of it. Now she knew better.

"It all sounds amazing." She turned her head to rest her cheek against his chest and breathed him in. "But I just want to stay here for a while."

Ronan wrapped his arm around her waist. "Stay as long as you like, *cher*. I'm not going anywhere."

Eva tried to slow her steps so that she didn't tug on her husband's hand, but she was growing impatient and starting to feel like her attempt at non-meddling was fruitless.

"If I'd known you had this much energy," Gideon said, his other hand holding Lucky's leash, "I would've gone for Round Two before letting you out of bed this morning."

"Fiend," she chastised absently as they crossed the Bow Bridge. "You act like two orgasms don't count as two rounds. And we haven't taken our time in the Park since forever."

When they reached the dappled path on the other side of the Lake, she turned right, taking them in the opposite direction from their home. Behind them, their security detail began crossing over the bridge.

"Are you planning on surveying the entire eight hundred forty-three acres?" he asked.

When he said it like that, her goal really did sound ludicrous.

She slid a sidelong glance his way, but when she caught his teasing smile, she found herself staring. God, he was gorgeous. And it was totally effortless for him. He was dressed casually in shorts and a white V-neck T-shirt, with black wayfarer sunglasses shielding those brilliantly blue eyes. A breeze swept through his inky hair, and her synapses fried momentarily.

With effort, Eva shook it off and looked away, returning to her furtive search of the grassy area to her left. "Stop distracting me, ace."

"What exactly am I distracting you from?"

Oops. She scrambled for something to say. "I'm planning a seduction in my head if you must know."

"How intriguing. Let's discuss."

"It's not a surprise if I tell you about it in advance," she muttered, startled by the number of picnickers dotting the grass. Suddenly, her task seemed herculean.

"Give me a hint, then," Gideon cajoled, then his voice changed. "Lucky, heel," he ordered gently.

It was a command her husband seldom had to give, but then Lucky changed from pulling on the leash to darting diagonally in front of them, straining toward the grass.

Eva looked to see what was drawing him and spotted Ireland. Frantically, she scooped him up before he gave away their presence.

"What's gotten into him?" her husband wondered.

"He probably smells food," she improvised, trying hard not to stare as they walked past the tree that had previously hidden her sister-in-law from view. Instead, she looked at the lake and exclaimed, "Look at the swans!"

When Gideon's head turned, she took a good long look at Ireland and her man Ronan. As impressive as he'd been in the photograph, he was much more so in the flesh. As Ireland had said, his hair had grown since the picture had been taken and the length suited him, deepening her initial impression of a man who dressed with sophistication but was, in fact, a little untamed. She was hyperaware of men who leaned toward being dangerous. It was a self-protective instinct she'd honed.

"The swans aren't going to distract me from your seduction plans," her husband pointed out with a laugh.

As Lucky wriggled in an effort to run to his owner's sister, whom he adored, Eva tightened her grip. He chuffed in protest, his tail lashing like a whip.

"Here. Let me take him," Gideon offered, collecting Lucky and lifting him high. "You're not starving, dawg."

Eva snuck another side glance. The stunningly gorgeous couple on their luxurious picnic could have been shooting an advertisement for a high-end lifestyle brand; they looked so perfect together. Tucked together against the tree, they seemed oblivious to the many people around them. Ireland was breathtakingly lovely, her expression soft and dreamy as she snuggled tighter against the man who had so clearly—and swiftly—captivated her.

But the look on *his* face, the cool steely-eyed antipathy that Ireland couldn't see, alarmed Eva more.

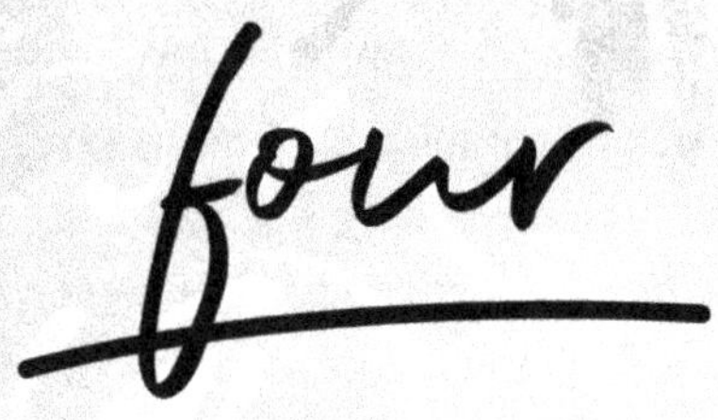

"HE'S ON HIS WAY UP."

Here we go. Ireland's hand tightened involuntarily on her phone as her excitement became almost unbearable. "Thanks, Edwin."

Ending the call, she realized how nervous she was and laughed aloud at herself, startling Blizzard. He gave a deep yowl, blinking his icy blue eyes at her with visible displeasure.

"Sorry, Bliz." She walked over to where her cat lay sprawled across the back of the sofa and gave him an affectionate rub behind his ears. "I'm having a moment."

Had she thought of everything? Missed *anything*?

Glancing around the living room, she double-checked for any stray socks or slippers she might have kicked off and forgotten about. She'd put away the magazines featuring her interviews and/or ECRA+ advertisements and all the framed photos of her family members.

When she and Ronan had parted ways the prior evening, she'd felt a sharp sting in the middle of her chest that warned of a growing vulnerability. Then—and now—she realized adopting another identity was actually fortuitous. It created a barrier, a shield to protect herself. “Lizzie” had nothing to lose and could take risks Ireland Vidal couldn’t.

Thankfully, she no longer had to resist the urge to call down to the lobby reception desk—yet *again*—to triple-check that the staff hadn’t forgotten that *she* was Elizabeth Duffy when a dangerously gorgeous, smooth-talking Cajun came calling on a resident with that name.

The kitchen was spotless, the breakfast she’d ordered was in the warming drawer, and two place settings waited on the large island that doubled as her dining table. Instrumental jazz piped softly from the speakers embedded in the ceiling.

She rushed to her bedroom—*again*—to stand in front of the full-length mirror and give her appearance yet another studious appraisal. Pivoting, Ireland assessed her front and back views. She’d spent too much time twisting her hair into a sleek chignon and on her makeup, aiming for sophistication rather than her usual bare minimum. But the wide-legged linen trousers and matching fitted vest in a warm cream hue were undeniably elegant, which was a plus.

When she exited to the living room, she left her phone on her vanity table and closed the door behind her. She convinced herself that she was prepared until the doorbell rang, and she jumped at least a foot in the air—an unwelcome and jolting reminder that she was strung tight with anxiety and anticipation.

Blizzard gave the door a baleful, curious stare as she rushed past him.

“Be nice!” she admonished, pausing at the door to take a deep breath and tug at the hem of her vest. She touched a hand to her hair, then dropped it. Closing her eyes, she willed her nerves to calm, achingly aware of Ronan standing just on the other side. It wouldn’t do to answer too quickly, after all. She may have worked herself up after inviting him over, but he didn't have to know that.

When she found her center, Ireland turned the knob and pulled the door open…

…and the sight of Ronan Boudreaux in her apartment's small elevator vestibule stole the breath she'd worked so hard to steady.

Sunlight shafted through the narrow window between the elevator and her front door, drenching his tall, broad-shouldered frame in a golden glow. The roguish mane of hair she longed to touch held a dazzling range of tawny hues and framed his sculpted features. A pair of silver aviators hung from the open collar of the gray dress shirt he'd tucked into jeans so lived-in they draped his long, strong legs. His alligator boots—a different pair than last night's—were equally worn but polished to a high shine. He was elegantly informal and still; seeing him felt a lot like taking a hit to the chest while sparring at the Krav Maga studio.

Ireland had never known such heated yearning. He was so savagely beautiful that looking at him was a uniquely pleasurable torture. And inside of the striking packaging was a man who fascinated her. Dazzled her. Challenged her to want more.

Abruptly, the unrelenting agitation she'd been besieged by all morning began to ebb. Ireland sighed with relief. The bright smile she'd initially feigned softened into sincere delight. Ronan was the most exciting man she'd ever met, in myriad ways, but his effect on her was conversely soothing and warm.

"Well, hello, gorgeous," she greeted him.

His returning grin was wicked. "Morning, *cher*."

Backing up, she waved him in.

"Not quite yet," he murmured, settling into the threshold by propping his shoulder against the jamb. His legs crossed at the ankles, and he slid his hands into his pockets. "I prepared myself for the sight of you, but here I am, still gathering my wits."

"I don't believe that for a minute," she shot back, resenting that he could hold himself back so effortlessly while exuding a silent demand she seemed hardwired to respond to. "You're not a man who ever loses his edge."

"Jules argues that you've certainly softened it."

"Does he?" Her smile widened. "Your charm's wasted on me, you know. That pretty face of yours already bowls me over. And the boots, of course."

"Of course." His eyes sparkled in a way that softened the sharp, sly intelligence she'd seen in them from the first. Then his gaze slid behind her and lowered. "You must be Blizzard," he said, his smile shifting from flirtatious to amused. "And you're territorial, I see. Message received."

Ireland turned her head to see what Bliz was up to and gasped at the sight of her majestic cat sitting primly on the floor with the strap of a black lace bra dangling from between his teeth. "Oh my god! Give me that!"

Face hot, she darted for the scrap of lingerie. The mischievous Maine Coon swatted at her with his giant paw. "You little shit!"

Ronan's rich, deep laughter sent waves of heated awareness through her. Served her right for not checking between the sofa cushions, but still. Ugh!

She lunged toward Blizzard, but the cat darted away. Ronan caught her by the hips and pulled her back against his hard body, which was shaking with hilarity. She felt and heard him kick the door shut behind them but was arrested by the feel of his arms around her.

Nuzzling behind her ear, he inhaled slowly and deeply. It was animalistic, the way he scented her. Her heartbeat quickened even as her skin warmed with arousal. She shivered when he briefly caught the shell of her ear in his teeth. There was something essentially untamed about Ronan Boudreaux. She was drawn to that quality in a way she'd never been to anything, which could make a future between them impossible.

"This is a matter best handled between him and me," Ronan drawled, his fingertips flexing restively on her hips.

She pouted. "I'm mortified."

"Admit you planned that to drive me crazy."

"Does it?" She tried to turn in his embrace, but he held fast. "If so, I totally plotted that."

Laughing again, Ronan released her and backed away. The sudden loss of his heat caused goosebumps to race up her arms. She faced him, noting the casual way he distanced himself with a retreating step as if she were a bomb ready to explode. She caught his gaze and held it; her head tilted slightly in inquiry. He looked away first, searching for Blizzard and then moving toward him.

Ireland crossed her arms. "Are we ever getting to the point where we greet each other with lewd kisses and frisky groping?"

He shot her a glance over his shoulder. "Are we in a hurry?"

The words might've stung if they hadn't been delivered in that lyrical drawl.

"Aren't we?" she challenged, watching as he approached Bliz with a confident and unhurried stride. "You're not a New Yorker, and I'm rooted here, so... Are you worried that I can't handle something short and sweet?"

He held his hand out to Blizzard and let the narrow-eyed, bra-carrying traitor sniff him. "I think you can handle anything," he said smoothly. "Which I appreciate far more than your beauty."

She might've been dangerously close to losing her cool if he'd teased her. But he was straightforward and solemn. And Bliz seemed to like how Ronan smelled as much as she did and shoved his big head under the Cajun's palm in a demand for behind-the-ear rubs.

All of which turned her frustration into resignation.

With a sigh, Ireland walked into the kitchen. She didn't lie to herself or see only what she wanted to. Ronan Boudreaux wasn't merely an exciting distraction from worries about her parents and Vidal Records, even if she wanted that to be true. No, the man was a deep-seated craving, a gnawing hunger that grew more unbearable the longer it went unappeased.

He retrieved her bra from Bliz and folded it neatly before putting it on the end table. Facing her, he half sat on the back of her couch next to the now docile, affectionate cat. "I thought you sounded a bit subdued this morning. And I feel a bit underdressed. Tell me what you're taking seriously so I can catch up."

She gripped the edge of her marble countertop and shook her head. "I bought this outfit with family brunch in mind. It's not formal or anything."

"Aren't you formal with your family?" he queried, massaging Bliz's back in a way that made Ireland envious. "That's been my impression."

"I—" she began, then paused, her mouth closing slowly. Had she been too candid during their long discussions about everything that came to mind?

When she'd been lying in bed thinking about him, she realized she'd talked more with Ronan than she ever had with anyone besides Alina. Blanketed in the anonymity of an assumed name, had she been bolder than wise, or was he just insightful? Perhaps it was both. She was so comfortable around him, which was insane, considering how powerful the sexual tension between them was.

But maybe she was more affected by that inexorable pull than he was. Ronan was always so cool and collected, his actions as unhurried as his manner of speaking. Maybe it was no problem for him to take his time with her because he didn't feel the same driving urgency.

And didn't that feel shitty?

Everything she'd planned to say suddenly seemed like it'd be too much. Not because she was afraid to scare him off with worries that she was moving too fast or entertaining unrealistic expectations. If being honest about her feelings was enough to cool Ronan Boudreaux's jets, he'd never survive the first bladed look from Gideon. And she spent enough time and energy around her family overthinking what she said and tempering how situations affected her; she sure as hell wouldn't expend the effort for anyone else.

What really gave her pause was the sense that Ronan was intrinsically uneasy in a metropolis like New York City. You'd never know it to look at him now, lounging with the ease of a lion at rest, strength evident in every line of his delectable body. He was a man completely comfortable in his skin. But she would never forget how he'd melted into a long, deep sigh when they picnicked in Central Park. And she'd initially found him performing in Jazzie's because he needed the escape of music to center himself amid Manhattan's frenetic pace.

Something more than transitory just wasn't in the cards for them. He lived a life without romantic entanglements. Speed dating on the road worked perfectly for his lifestyle, even if she could catch more than his fancy.

"You don't have to weigh your words with me," he coaxed, as ever seeming to read her thoughts. "I gather you don't feel comfortable expressing yourself to your family, but I can handle you and anything you can throw at me."

She frowned, bemused and concerned. "Ronan… If I gave you a bad impression of my family, that was a mistake. They're overprotective, sure. But that's only because they love me and want good things for me."

"Do they choose their clothes to make an impression on *you*?" he countered.

"Don't we all dress to impress in one way or another?" She shrugged, resigned to how things were. Her brothers had their power; she was still establishing hers. "I'm not the only one who makes an effort."

"But I'd wager you're the one to do it most often," he rejoined, his gaze challenging her to deny it.

His keen insight was often startling. She loved how *seen* she felt with him. But she didn't even know if she'd see him tomorrow. A day with him was enjoyed as a singular, separate event from the rest of her life.

Her mood darkened again. "You and I are moving at different speeds," she said curtly. "And maybe that answers the questions I had. Are you hungry? Should we start with mimosas?"

"Let's start with your questions." Straightening, Ronan moved to the opposite side of the island. He somehow looked even more gorgeous assuming command, his lips still sensual even while unsmiling. He seemed unreal at times, nearly too perfect to be anything other than a fever dream.

"And now you're scowling," he noted, amused. "And still breathtakingly gorgeous anyway."

He remained standing, his hands sliding into his back pockets. The pose showed off the power of his biceps and shoulders, along with the leanness of his hips. Did he do that on purpose? Did he realize the effect it had on her?

Ireland turned to the fridge to pull out the freshly squeezed orange juice she'd ordered and a bottle of Cristal. "Are you baiting me?"

"Possibly."

She arched her brow at him as she set the bottles down. "Why?"

"So I can recognize you. You've disguised yourself this morning."

"Bullshit."

His brows lifted.

Planting her palms on the marble, she glared at him. "Stop playing with me."

"I haven't even started." The sudden heat in his gaze startled her and knocked her off balance.

Up to that moment, he'd flirted outrageously but playfully. While lust burned within her, he'd barely registered at a simmer. That teasing glimpse of fire was acutely frustrating, taunting her with the man she wanted but wasn't sure she could ever have.

"Am I too young for you? Is that the problem?" she snapped. "Not worldly enough for your comfort? Are you worried I won't be able to let you go when you leave, and I'll become inconvenient?"

His jaw tightened, then his words came clipped and fast. "You're already inconvenient, and I don't think that highly of myself, *cher*."

"Yeah, well, *I* think of you. Pretty much nonstop since we met."

"The captivation is mutual, so we're not moving at different speeds. At least in that regard."

Irritated, she turned to open the cupboard where she kept her stemmed glasses. "Something you said, which I brushed off at first, really struck me as important last night."

"Oh…?"

"You said we wouldn't become intimate until you were sure I wouldn't regret it." Setting the flutes down, she watched him pick up the champagne. "And I've wracked my brain trying to figure out what that means. Then I realized *you're* the only thing that could make me regret being with you. You would have to do something or say something to hurt me or make me lose respect for you. So, you don't think I can handle whatever we're doing here?"

His expression didn't change, his gaze fixed and steady on her face even as he unwrapped the foil. "We're already intimate. We were talking about fucking in that conversation. Two very different things."

Her lips parted. *Fuck*—and all of its various derivatives—was a hard, crude, occasionally insulting word, and the Southern gentleman he'd been thus far wouldn't have used it with her. But Ronan wasn't that man now. He was harsher than she'd seen him before, less controlled. And so much sexier that she gritted her teeth against the urge to hurtle over the island and kiss him senseless.

She swallowed hard and nodded. "We were, yes."

"And when we met, I asked you how far you wanted this thing between us to go, and you replied that you were worried you'd regret me. Do you recall saying that?"

She blinked in surprise. "Uh… I didn't remember that, no."

The stern line of his mouth softened. "What were you expecting to regret?"

Ireland pressed a hand to her forehead. "You've got me all mixed up now."

"Take your time," he said, lifting the lid on the island's built-in countertop trash can and swiping the cork, muselet, and foil into it. "I'm not going anywhere."

She grasped for that because she wasn't confused at all about the logistics. "But you will. When?"

"When am I going somewhere?"

"Home, specifically. Don't be coy."

"Not coy. Cautious." He caught her gaze. "You want to charge headlong into bed with me, and we're absolutely going to get there and stay there for a damned long time. But you've got doubts, questions, concerns, so we'll get them sorted now before they get in my way later."

"How much later?" she asked.

Ronan began to pour. "Are you asking if I have a timeline for how long I'll want you?"

"No. Damn it." She finished each mimosa with a modest splash of orange juice, more in his than hers. "When are you resuming your normal life away from this city and me? Is that clear enough?"

He watched her with those stormy eyes as he accepted the flute she handed him. "Geography has never stopped me from getting to something I want."

When his fingers brushed hers, it sparked a primitive awareness. It was an ache that could not be soothed. "Do you always answer questions with slippery evasions? Because it's starting to piss me off."

The air around Ronan became charged.

"*Merde*, you sound like Jules! You don't understand your own power," he growled, "and it infuriates me that no one close to you has pushed you to see it. You're worse than a Gulf hurricane —at least I can prepare for those."

"That's another non-answer."

"I'm scheduled to leave tomorrow."

"Oh." The sting of dismay was an acutely unwelcome surprise.

"Unless there's a chance of seeing you again."

Ireland gaped at him. Maddeningly, she warmed to him in a way that had nothing to do with her desire for his body. She looked down into her flute as she lifted it to her mouth, afraid to reveal more than she already had.

She hated feeling gauche and too eager.

He was older, more experienced, less emotive. And worse, her own demons tormented her—Ronan had never made her feel unequal. Undeveloped, maybe. Untapped. And she adored that he saw something in her she wasn't sure was actually there.

But she could work on it. She could fake it until she made it a reality.

"We could maybe work something out," she managed to say with some elan.

He shot her an arch look. "Glad to hear it."

"So… you'll leave Tuesday?"

"I'll leave when you want me to or when I'd rather be somewhere else than with you."

She fidgeted with the stem of her glass. "I see."

"Do you?" He crossed his arms, his biceps thick beneath his shirtsleeves. "I'm treading carefully with a woman who tires of men quickly and has recently sworn off my gender altogether, but you question your desirability *first*? That's ass-backward, *cher*, and damned infuriating."

"Well…" She didn't know how to respond to that.

His exhale was an incredulous huff of laughter. "Incredible."

She licked a drop of mimosa from her lower lip and watched his features harden. He was edgier than he'd ever been, his emotions closer to the surface but still firmly in check. She liked him this way.

A lot.

To be so attuned to someone was both foreign and thrilling.

Could she break through that cage he kept himself so securely locked in? It was a challenge she couldn't walk away from.

Setting her glass down, Ireland started to round the island, moving leisurely if cautiously.

"I'm really not very worldly," she admitted, her fingertips trailing across the cool marble countertop. "I've never had the opportunity to take on a man of your caliber before."

"You're flawless." He followed her with his eyes. "Faultless. Far out of my league. That you don't know that is a crime. I've set the pace out of an abundance of caution because when this is over, it'll be over for both of us. I won't be left with an *envie* for something I can't have."

"You don't fit the mold of anyone I've ever met." Ireland stopped on the opposite side of the corner from him. "Who knows what could happen? Just because I haven't wasted time with the wrong guy—"

"*I'm* the wrong guy," he said flatly, his eyes dark.

Her lips pursed, then twisted in thought. "Why would you say that?"

"I'm an immoral man. I believe the ends justify the means without exception."

She knew his sultry charm was as much a mask as her studied calm. She knew because he'd wanted her to know. Beneath his polished exterior was the child who'd stolen food to survive and spent considerable time on the streets.

"Will you hurt me?" she asked bluntly.

Ronan stared at her, silent, for the length of a breathless minute or two. Then he replied, "Not by design, no."

She, too, paused to consider, then nodded. "I don't plan to hurt you, either—if I even can."

He shook his head. "You're too reckless. Too wild. It's why I want you and why you want me, but it's not wise."

Her chin lifted. "We've spent a lot of time together in the past two days. Talking. Sharing. Revealing things about ourselves that are—as you said—more intimate than if we'd spent the time fucking. You wanted me to know you, and I know enough to want to know more. Isn't that how anything worthwhile begins?"

"I can't say."

"Then I guess we'll have to take our chances." She eased toward him, moving into his space. His scent, warm like whiskey and faintly smoky, like a fine cigar, was as earthy as the man and equally intoxicating. She wanted to melt into him, press her nose to his throat, lick the salt from his skin. He made her feel fluid and languid, longing only to wrap her limbs around the heat and hardness of his powerful body. The fierce attraction bubbled like champagne inside her, spurring a wild, unfettered need.

He unhooked the sunglasses from his collar and set them down on the island, the faintest of invitations to get closer to the virile body she thirsted for. "You never answered my question about those regrets you anticipated."

Ireland didn't hesitate to be honest. After all, she already had the weight of using her mother's maiden name to crawl out from under. "Regret—singular. And that would be wanting too much."

"That's not typically a problem for you."

"No," she agreed. "But then, you're not a typical man."

He caught her hand in his when she reached for him. "How easily you tie a man into knots." His mouth curved against her knuckles as he pressed a kiss to them. "You're a dangerous woman."

"Isn't that what you like about me?" She linked their fingers. "You know, I have this impractically romantic notion of being in the bayou with you, miles from civilization, wearing nothing but a sheen of sweat that's somehow sexy, sipping bourbon on the rocks as I watch an elegant egret flying over the water."

His smile fled, his gaze on her face taking on a predatory gleam. His jaw tautened with a hunger she recognized intimately because she also felt it.

"And what am I doing?" he asked gruffly, stroking her knuckles with the pad of his thumb. "Something filthy, I hope."

"You tell me." She pushed forward, freeing her hand to rest atop the heat and hardness of his chest. The pounding beat of his heart was revelatory, betraying how she affected him. The rhythm was familiar, and she was amazed when she realized why: it matched the cadence of the silent demand emanating from him, the ferocious animal attraction she could not deny. "Or better yet, show me."

Ronan circled her wrists with his fingers, then gently urged her hands down to her sides, then behind, to the small of her back. He held her captive with one hand, his other reaching up to the gold comb she'd used to secure her hair. "May I?"

She swallowed, her mouth dry. She tried to answer but ended up nodding instead. The heavy strands of her hair dropped in a rush, and she moaned in relief, her scalp tingling.

"I want you just the way you are." He nuzzled her temple as he deftly wrapped her hair around his forearm, fisting the mass at her nape. "Don't change yourself, tigress, to suit me or anyone."

The rush of air that left her took all the tightness in her muscles with it. She sagged into him, her breasts growing sensitive at the feel of his torso against hers. Nuzzling him in return, her eyes closed, her fingers flexing with the need to touch him. His single-handed hold on her wrists was too light to be legitimately restraining, but she wouldn't break it, just as she wouldn't urge him to a faster pace than he was comfortable with.

It was compelling, the withholding of his body from her. Did he know that? Was he exploiting her hunger to his advantage? Why wait? Unless he wanted something beyond sex...?

He was the flawless one. Ireland was awed that she'd found him, this contrary and complicated man. The warmth of his body proved he was real, but it still seemed impossible. Too good to be true.

Her lips parted, and she sought his mouth, kissing the corner of it, licking the seam. His low, pained groan vibrated against her.

"If I have a taste," he said huskily, brushing his lips across hers with enflaming lightness, "I'm afraid I won't be able to stop."

"Why stop?" she whispered, straining to deepen their contact but held back by his hand in her hair.

"I ask myself that question every few seconds."

"It's okay," she breathed, teasing his lips with a flick of her tongue. "I'm not going anywhere, either."

Ronan broke with the power of a breached levee, crushing her against him, his lips sealing atop hers. He cupped her head in his hand, angling their mouths to fit tightly together. Between them, she felt his arousal, the heft and hardness of his cock straining against her lower belly. The ache inside her intensified with fierce need, her whimper a sound she'd never heard herself make before.

Ronan's answering growl poured into her, weakening her knees. His tongue swept deep, stroking along hers, fucking her mouth with dominant precision.

He held her weight effortlessly, kissing her with consummate skill, tasting her with lush deep licks. She was captive in his arms, limp and trembling, completely at his mercy. She moaned, shivering violently, overwhelmed by the riot of sensations gripping her body.

But her lips were moving, her tongue tangling with his. He tasted like brown sugar, lust, and bourbon, a melding of equally energizing and intoxicating flavors. How had he hidden such rampant male need? Restrained it? Now, it was like fire, licking across her senses until she burned with it.

She wanted to taste him all over, to lick the inky spikes of his tattoo sleeve, and to run her mouth over his golden male skin until she found the paler flesh untouched by the sun. Her clit throbbed in time to her galloping heartbeat, and she grew wetter by the second, so aroused she wanted to scream at the torment of it.

The kiss was the most erotic act she'd ever engaged in, the melding of their mouths so unrestrained that they were devouring each other, their lips sliding against each other wetly, their tongues twining and caressing. Her hands were freed, and she thrust them into his hair, humming with delight to finally feel the thick strands that felt like rough silk. He cupped her buttocks, lifting her, holding her as she wrapped her legs around his lean hips.

Tightening her thighs, Ireland rose above him, arching his neck back so that she took control. She rubbed against the hardness of his erection, thrilling at the rumble of warning that vibrated from his chest. Ronan was leashed, barely, and the thought of further breaking his control was electrifying.

Minutes. She was mere minutes from having what she desperately needed, and she wanted to rush yet also to savor.

The sound of the doorbell was like a torrent of ice water.

Feeling crampy, bloated, and cranky, Eva leaned her head against the headrest of the Bentayga and closed her eyes. She hated menstruating, and that hate was making her bitter. Or was she just moody? The way her emotions shifted lately, she couldn't say for sure.

If she'd referenced her period calendar, she would've scheduled lunch with her best friend on a different day and stayed home, curled up with her husband and a bottle of wine. But the thought hadn't entered her mind until now. Irrational wishfulness, maybe? Or just negligence.

So here she was, in the back of the Bentley while Gideon was probably working in his home office, although she hoped he'd take her advice and invite Ireland over for breakfast. Her sister-in-law craved Gideon's personal and private attention but rarely initiated getting it.

"Hey, sweetheart...? You okay? You look pale."

The concern in her father's voice opened her eyes, and she met his gaze in the rear-view mirror. She sighed. "Time of the month."

Victor winced. "Ah. I'm sorry."

"Yeah..." She looked out the window. "Me, too."

Was he regretful for the same reason she was? Of course, if the person who threatened them were known and imprisoned, there would be no lingering doubts about Gideon's safety or hers. But she couldn't put off the passing of time any more than she could stop the hidden yearning that hollowed her. Soon, the choice would be out of her hands. She wasn't getting any younger.

They pulled up to the valet stand in front of Tableau One, and it was easy to see why there was a crowd in front of the restaurant's large bay windows. Cary Taylor—former model, entrepreneur, and influencer extraordinaire—was indulging the line of people wanting to take pictures with him. And they wouldn't be disappointed with what they walked away with. As stunningly beautiful as he was in person, Cary looked even more unreal in photographs, having been blessed with the rare photogenic quality only top-tier models could lay claim to.

Her father rolled down the driver's side window to speak to the approaching valet. "I'm just dropping off. Won't be more than a minute."

Nodding, the valet stepped back. With the car still running, Victor did a thorough visual sweep of their surroundings before opening the door and unfolding his tall frame from behind the wheel.

Everything about him screamed law enforcement, despite having left the job a dozen years prior when her mother was murdered. That was the impetus for him to move to New York and take over the responsibility of keeping his only child safe from the dangers of being married to one of the wealthiest men in the world.

That Gideon was also the child of a notorious Ponzi scheme orchestrator who'd ruined lives only widened the threat. So many of Geoffrey Cross's victims held Gideon unfairly accountable, believing his present success had to have somehow been built upon their stolen funds, despite the work of the Department of Justice, which recovered a significant amount of the losses, and Gideon's personal contributions to righting his father's wrongs.

For some, everyone with the last name Cross should pay the price for Geoffrey's misdeeds. It was impossible to gauge how many truly dangerous enemies they had, making it imperative to investigate every possible hazard.

Her father came to her door and opened it, his black suit jacket concealing a holstered firearm while still showcasing his broad, muscular shoulders. There were social media accounts dedicated to photos of him, and while he cringed at the avid attention paid to his good looks, Eva was proud of him and found it amusing.

He blocked the door, shielding her from the paparazzi who made it a habit to linger at Tableau One for the many celebrity sightings. They camped out on the other side of the street, but with Cary in fine form, it was likely one or more had taken the opportunity to meld with the crowd.

"What are my chances of running in without being photographed?" she asked.

He gave her a wry smile. "You're one of the most recognizable women in the world. What do you think?"

Eva sighed and steeled herself, gathering her purse and shifting to make as quick a getaway from the Bentayga as possible. She'd long ago accepted that her marriage weirdly fascinated the world, and people couldn't seem to stop talking about it. She understood why Gideon was so phenomenally popular—she wasn't alone in recognizing that he was the handsomest and sexiest man on the planet. And she put up with the intrusive attention because it came with him, and he was hers. All things considered, it was a small price to pay to share her life with him.

But fuck, if it wasn't a terrible burden some days.

"Ready?" Victor asked, a tremendously supportive presence for her as always.

"As I'll ever be." She slid onto her feet into the small space between the shield of the door and her father's body. That she struggled with him protecting her with his life was something she'd learned to keep to herself because it angered him when she mentioned it.

I go first, he'd once told her bitingly. *And if I go keeping you alive, I go happy. Got it?*

Tucking her under one arm, her father pushed his way to the entrance with the other, ushering her inside.

He paused in the vestibule, holding the inner door open for her. "Text me when you're ready."

"You should be home sleeping in with Shelley!" she shot back, unable to resist.

The level look he gave her before exiting to the street said a dozen things at once. He used to take the weekends off, working as a team with the other members of their security detail. That he hadn't yet returned to that schedule was probably the most significant indicator that her security was still elevated.

"Your table's ready," the hostess said with a bright smile, gesturing for Eva to follow her. The restaurant was co-owned by Gideon and the flagship for one of his oldest and closest friends, celebrity chef Arnoldo Ricci. The brightly lit interior was a haven, and Eva breathed a sigh of relief.

It was probably too much to hope she hadn't been captured in a salable photograph. Even if a paparazzo hadn't been lucky enough to snap one, someone waiting for a picture with Cary might have. When they saw him in public, it was expected that she wouldn't be too far away. Cary could go unnoticed when he wished to. When he was seen, it was because he was with her.

She could write the ledes and comments that would accompany that photo because she'd seen them regurgitated countless times.

Is that a baby bump?

She's getting fat because her marriage is over. She doesn't want a baby, so Gideon Cross is ready to move on.

She's had some work done. Look how swollen her face is.

She's definitely putting on weight.

Whoa! Someone went overboard on fillers.

She's finally pregnant!

Eva had read it all, and it never stopped. The fascination with whether she was pregnant, whether childlessness was negatively impacting her marriage, whether Gideon was cheating on her or unhappy, whether she had an overreliance on cosmetic procedures... The surgeons who weighed in on what work she'd had done were so ridiculous she couldn't believe the press amplified their bullshit. Gossip sites and tabloids posted lies constantly. And photographs of her and Gideon graced covers on every magazine rack everywhere all the time. Not every cover, but at least a couple. All. The. Time.

Sliding into her usual booth in the back, Eva released her

breath in a rush, relaxing the stomach muscles she'd pulled in, which had only aggravated the cramping of her uterus. She wished she genuinely didn't care what people said about her, but of course, it affected her. And she felt a responsibility as Gideon's wife to do him proud, not that he ever held her to any standard. He genuinely found no flaws in her. Still, she knew he hated how the public picked her apart, that he couldn't understand it, and felt helpless to stop it.

It was another ten minutes or so before Cary extricated himself from his fans and made his way to their booth. Eva took advantage of the time to order a bottle of crisp white wine and their favorite brunch dishes. Then she texted her husband.

What are you cooking Ireland for breakfast?

She was surprised when he didn't reply with his usual alacrity, her brows pinching together. Hopefully, he was too busy with his sister and not something unexpected with work. Gideon managed his conglomerate with a chess master's acumen, always dozens of moves ahead of everyone else with the endgame already in mind. When something caught him off guard, it was trouble on an unforeseeable and significant scale.

"Hey, baby girl!" Cary leaned into her side of the booth and pressed a quick kiss to her temple before taking the seat across from her. He was an exceptionally handsome man, his glossy sable hair precisely cut in his preferred style: trimmed on the sides and nape, longer and artfully mussed on top. He was carelessly elegant in a simple black crew neck T-shirt, tailored slacks in tan, and cognac loafers.

He studied her for a heartbeat before his megawatt smile twisted into sympathetic ruefulness. "You plugging?"

"My god, Cary!" she protested. Groaning her frustration, Eva shoved her phone back into her purse. "Is it that obvious?"

He shrugged. "Not really. I just know what it means when your chin breaks out, and you wear a shift dress. Your face is a little puffy, too."

"Great." She took another sip and shook her head, remembering how her husband had come up behind her while she was slathering serum over her face and said in all seriousness, *How you become more gorgeous by the day never ceases to amaze me.* "You, however, look drop-dead gorgeous, as always. I can't believe you were able to get through all those people outside."

While most male models never stepped out of obscurity, he'd been thrust into the tabloid spotlight overnight when she pulled him into Gideon Cross's orbit with her.

"I didn't." The sparkling mischief in his emerald eyes was trademark Cary Taylor. "I begged off on your behalf and told them if they came to Trey's adoption drive this weekend, they could get their photo with me plus swag and maybe a new best friend as awesome as mine—but with a tail!"

A laugh burst out of her, breaking through all the bullshit that had been floating around in her head. "No one can spin a situation around to best advantage better than you."

"Gotta hustle. You taught me that." He tipped his wine glass toward her in a silent toast. "And I've got a husband who wants to save the world's animals—or at least the ones in the Greater Five Boroughs. Anything I can do to help him with that keeps him happy, which keeps me happy."

"That is how marriage works," she agreed, her smile reflecting her joy at seeing him so happy and healthy.

Cary radiated a vitality that made her memories of the sullen, self-destructive teenager she'd first met seem like a completely different person. Where once, most people would've considered them both destined for failure—in work, in love, and in life—they'd managed to hold each other up and drag each other through rough spots that might've undone years of intense and painful therapy. Together, they'd found the soulmates who helped heal them, but while they both had spouses now, there were still things they shared only with each other. That was the nature of best friendship—nothing could replace it.

"You're both coming to the masquerade on Friday?" she queried, sitting back as the runner set their meals in front of them. She thanked her with a smile.

"Wouldn't miss it." Cary snapped his napkin open with panache and draped it over his lap. "You know I never skip a chance to see Trey in a tux—or strip him out of one."

She laughed, her body incrementally relaxing with each passing moment. "We still haven't found a bachelor who can draw the high bids you did."

Their annual fall masquerade and bachelor auction was the largest fundraising event of the year for the Crossroads Foundation, which Gideon had established to help other sexual abuse survivors via advocacy, shelters, and legal support. While their personal experiences with childhood trauma were known only to each other, their therapists, and select family members, the foundation's work was covered extensively by the press, and their events of all sizes and persuasions always sold out.

"I'd say I'm sorry," Cary replied between bites, "but I'm too damned happy being married to sound genuine about it. You know, you could switch it up to a bachelorette auction and put Ireland up there. She'd bring in Fort Knox level bids and could probably wheedle more out of the winning bidder during their date."

She snorted, her fork hovering over her baked eggs and sausage. "As if Gideon would ever. In his mind, every man her age is as debauched as you two were. I told him the winning bidder would likely be Richard's age, considering how high the bidding would go, but he doesn't like that idea, either. And really, since she's taken over emceeing the auction, it's never been more fun, so I'd hate to lose her."

"Has your man never seen that girl spar on the mat at Parker's studio?" He shook his head. "I've seen her rock the clock in guys twice her size."

"That's a good idea, actually." She made a mental note of it. "I should bring him with me sometime when I know she'll be there. Still, I think he's more concerned with her poor choices than he is about her ability to defend herself physically. I worry about the same thing, to be honest."

And Ireland's new infatuation, whose phenomenal attractiveness was the kind that screwed with a woman's common sense, was a threat to take seriously. Eva trusted her instincts. She was seriously debating whether to set Angus on the hunt for information but felt hypocritical after the hard time she'd given Gideon.

Angus had been with her husband since childhood, serving as both chauffeur and security, as her father did presently. The wily Scot had made the transition from day-to-day security to top-level investigations years back. He'd said retirement wasn't for him, and she and Gideon were both grateful to have him on hand whenever the need arose. She especially appreciated that Angus trusted her when she asked for his discretion, knowing she would only keep something from Gideon for the best of reasons.

"Another thought," Cary went on, swallowing hurriedly, "would be changing it from a bachelor auction to a 'Hot Lunch' and throwing your man into the mix. He'd rake in truckloads of moola. Think of how many would bid for the chance to present their big idea to Gideon Cross while he's a captive audience. Sure, a hopeful lady might shell out and get her heart broken, but it could just as soon be an entrepreneur with a great idea."

"Cary!" She stared at him with wide, delighted eyes, her thoughts racing. "That's genius. We could tease it a bit in conversation during the event and see what the initial reaction is. We really have to think of something new. We had so many hot bachelors to choose from when we started, but most everyone's off the market now."

"Time's a-changin'!" he singsonged while digging into his pocket. He pulled out his phone and began swiping. Then he held it out to her.

She took it and looked at the picture he presented. A strange chill swept through her body, countered by the sudden heat in her face. There was a violent recoiling deep inside her, in a place she avoided looking because it was too dark. Too cruel. Too ugly.

Her voice shook as she asked, "Why are you showing me a pregnancy test?"

His laughter was as bright and happy as the sun. "Trey and I are pregnant!"

Her thoughts scattered into incoherence. "Huh?"

"Our surrogate is having our baby, silly."

The entire room tilted. Her eyes widened as she looked at him, her emotions rioting. A million thoughts and words spun through her mind and filled her mouth, but she couldn't give voice to any of them. Tears stung the backs of her eyes.

"Isn't it the craziest, most wonderful thing?" He sat back, beaming. "I'm so fucking relieved to tell you finally. Trey was all twisted up about letting anyone know that we were even *hoping*. He said women keep pregnancy news to themselves for several weeks, so we should do the same." His laugh was threaded with wondrous delight. "Whatever. Happy hubby, happy chubby."

Eva's hand trembled so badly that she dropped the phone as she attempted to set it down. The abrupt thud rattled her already shaken nerves. How she managed to curve her lips into a wide, watery smile was a goddamned miracle. "I'm so thrilled for you, Cary. Thrilled for you both. Congratulations! You have to catch me up on everything."

Grabbing his phone back, Cary started swiping again. "I've actually kept notes, so I don't leave anything out." He paused, his happiness dimming along with his smile. "I haven't told Tatiana yet. I don't know how to have that conversation."

"You should call Dr. Travis." She dug deep for composure. "But I'd say how you handled telling her about your engagement is worth repeating. Just give her a call, tell her you have something serious to discuss—so she's mentally prepared—and then go to her place and give her the time with you to process it."

"Yeah, well..." His shoulders drooped. "That was before she asked me to be a sperm donor, and I turned her down. It's been really awkward between us ever since."

Leaning forward, Eva set her hand over his. "Building a family with your husband is your right. You're kind to think of her and her feelings, but don't let her—or anyone—steal your joy."

Not even me. And it killed her to have that concern. She couldn't stand the thought of being the kind of person whose misery tainted the happiness of her loved ones.

"How's everything so far?" their server asked as he stopped by their table. "How are we doing on drinks?"

Looking up at him, Eva saw how his smile tightened at the edges and knew her face revealed too much. "We need a bottle of champagne!" she pronounced too loudly. "We're celebrating!"

"That's great!" He looked relieved. "I'll grab the wine menu."

Ireland froze as the ringing of her doorbell reverberated, her body stiffening.

Ronan's forehead rested against hers, his eyes squeezed shut. His big body was taut and quivering, fighting against his abrupt restraint.

Or was she the one trembling?

"*Maudit!*" he growled.

She didn't need to know the curse he'd uttered to understand what it meant. Unwrapping her legs from around his waist, she tried to separate, but he held her securely. Her blood was so hot she felt feverish, and her pulse raced at a gallop. Their panting breaths mingled between them, both hovering on the precipice between control and abandon.

The doorbell rang again, and she jolted, her nerves stretched to the limit.

Was it Eva?

God help them both if it was Gideon.

She debated ignoring whoever was out there. But if it was her brother or sister-in-law, they knew she was home. The family location sharing app they all used would betray her.

Ronan set her down and away from him, his face flushed and eyes dark as coal. "Are you worried it's the guy from Friday night? Does the desk downstairs still have his name?"

Blinking in confusion, Ireland tried to puzzle out what he was saying. "The guy from—Oh, Graham? No, he was never on the permanent list." She ran trembling hands over her hair, then her clothes. "And I'd fuck him up if he showed his face here."

He huffed out a laugh and raked both hands through his hair. "Of course you would."

What the hell was she going to do with him? Eva showing up wouldn't be so bad, but Gideon would take one look at both of them and see that they'd been fooling around. Knowing her brother, the interrogation would begin immediately. Hell, he'd even grilled Alina when they first met, albeit charmingly and to the director's delight.

"I'm going to need a minute," Ronan said as knocking commenced.

She seized that opportunity. "You can go in my room through that door over there. My bathroom's in the back. Could you take my bra with you, please? Just leave it on my bed."

He arched a brow, then reached forward and cupped her jaw, his fingers resting lightly on her pulse. "You good, *cher*?"

Setting her hand over his, Ireland forced herself to focus on him alone and give him a genuine smile. "Yes. Frustrated. Maybe a little irritated. But I'm happy with you."

"Okay." He pressed his lips to her forehead, then strolled away, catching up her bra before entering her bedroom and closing the door behind him.

Thank god she'd straightened up in there, too, and made her bed. She'd been hopeful they'd end up there, naked and sweaty and satisfied.

Rushing to the door, she pasted on a bright smile and pulled it open with a flourish. "What's the rush on a lovely Sund— Oh my god, Alina!" she squealed, throwing her arms wide with relief and joy. She hugged her best friend hard, possibly too hard. "What are you doing here?"

Alina laughed, and they spun together in a tangled embrace. "I caught an earlier flight. I don't know what I've done to earn such a warm welcome, but *hello*!"

Ireland whispered in her ear, "I've got a man over, and I thought you might be Gideon or Eva."

"Ah." Alina pulled back, revealing amused brown eyes. Dressed in an elegant and comfortable lounge suit in green cashmere, she looked fresh for having recently endured a transatlantic flight. Even with the comforts of first class, dry plane air did a number on most people. "So, you're happier about not seeing them than you are about seeing me. Got it."

"It's an equal mixture of both, I promise you." Ireland shut the door and gave a happy sigh. "And I'm thrilled you'll get to meet Ronan. I need someone I know and trust to tell me what I'm missing because he's too perfect to me."

"No," Alina scoffed sarcastically.

"You think I have terrible taste, but—"

"I *know* you have terrible taste. And how that's possible with Gideon Cross as an examp—"

"Call me Liz," she hissed urgently as the bedroom door opened behind her, "not Ireland."

"What?" Alina frowned, then lifted her gaze, and her eyes widened. Her face suddenly softened with something akin to awe and wonder.

Ireland spun on her heel, her long hair swirling around her like a cape. "And there he is! Ronan, this is my best friend and partner in crimes, Alina Rurik. Alina, this is Ronan Boudreaux!"

Ronan approached to greet her, every inch the Southern gentleman but there was no mistaking his vibe. He was so inherently sensual and earthy, with poise that told a woman he knew exactly how to blow her mind in bed.

"Alina, an unexpected delight."

She watched as her best friend went googly-eyed at the faint drawl.

"Uh, hi." Alina stretched forward to shake his hand as if she couldn't wait for him to close the distance. "It's nice to see you. Um, *meet* you."

He smiled, and Ireland felt it low in her belly. Did Alina feel that same simmering response? Or was she uniquely susceptible to his charms?

"I'll head out and let you two catch up," he said, moving into her space and taking her hand in his with easy familiarity.

When he took a step toward the door, she held him back. "You don't have to leave!"

"I didn't mean to interrupt!" Alina protested. "We weren't supposed to get together until tomorrow. I should've called first."

"We'll switch days, then." His smile was all charm and warmth.

Ireland pouted. "What about breakfast?"

"Are you hungry, Alina?" he queried.

"I could eat."

"Problem solved." He gave Ireland's hand a soft squeeze. "I appreciate the efforts on my behalf, *cher*, but we've agreed that I have travel arrangements to cancel. Walk me out. It was a pleasure, Alina. I look forward to seeing you again the next time."

"Oh, yes," she said, grinning. "Same. Do you have any brothers or close cousins you could bring with you?"

Ireland waved that off with a laugh as she followed Ronan into the elevator vestibule. "You're canceling your flight? Not just postponing it?"

"Does that scare you?" He pushed the call button, then turned into her, unlinking their fingers to pull her into his embrace instead.

"You're the one who can't skip out of here fast enough," she countered, leaning into him so they were pressed together. "Do *I* scare you?"

Ronan held her with the faintest of curves to his lips. "I've already admitted that you do."

"Alina will want to go home and sleep off her jet lag soon. Will you come back? Or maybe I could come over?"

The rumble of his deep laughter tightened her nipples. "I'm going to enjoy wearing out your inexhaustible energy. The challenge is as tantalizing as you are."

"That's not an answer."

His hand lifted to her face, the backs of his fingers caressing her cheek. "No, we won't be seeing each other again today." He pressed the pad of his thumb against her kiss-swollen lips, then stroked the curves, effectively silencing her protest. "Trust me on this, *cher*."

She nipped him with her teeth, smiling when he hissed at the sting. "Dinner tomorrow?" she asked, even as she planned to call him later and change his mind about today.

"How about lunch? Do you have time for that?"

Her gaze narrowed. "Why do I think you're trying to avoid the possibility of hitting the sheets together?"

Cupping her buttocks in his hands, he tugged her up against the length of his cock. The feel of his arousal reignited her own. She rubbed shamelessly against him.

"There's no avoiding it," he said, his gruff voice exciting her. "We just have some things to discuss first, and you'll need to behave."

"What things? And yes, to lunch. And to dinner. I'll bring an overnight bag to work with me."

Ronan was laughing when the elevator dinged its arrival. Cupping her nape, he folded over her, kissing her with such savage intensity she felt dizzy with it. His lips were so firm yet soft, the stroke of his tongue silky yet dominant. That he could make such a simple act so searingly erotic made her weak in the knees.

And then he straightened, releasing her and backing into the elevator. “Have a good day, tigress.”

How she wasn’t puddled on the floor confounded her. “What things?” she repeated. “Just tell me now. And we’re on for dinner, too, right?”

His wink was the last thing she saw as the doors slid closed. She tried to thrust her hand between them, but not in time. She slapped at her frustrated reflection in the outer brass doors. “Damn it.”

Instantly, Ireland felt drained, sapped of all the energy Ronan brought with him. She heaved a frustrated sigh and returned to her apartment, typing her code in the numerical lock. It whirred open, and she stepped inside, finding Alina sitting on the couch with Blizzard and a mimosa in hand.

“Holy fucking sexy beast!” her best friend exclaimed, twisting to look over the back of the sofa at her. “I leave for a few weeks, and you somehow find good taste in men!”

“Gee, thanks.” Ireland went to the kitchen to retrieve her flute.

“That guy is the ooey gooey caramel version of the Gideon Cross hot fudge sundae.”

“Please,” Ireland groaned, “do not compare Ronan’s sex appeal to my brother’s. Ick.”

Alina laughed. “Catch me up. Spare me no details. And for god’s sake, tell me he’s a maestro in bed.”

“I wish I knew,” she lamented, settling into the couch.

“What? *What?*”

Ireland sighed. “Buckle up, buttercup. I’ve got a story for you.”

It was nearing three o'clock before Alina started yawning. "I'm going to hit the bathroom, then head home. I'm dead on my feet."

"I'm surprised you lasted this long." After changing into a tank top and shorts, Ireland had brought out a couple of ECRA+ skincare masks, and they'd finished the bottle of champagne while catching up on the episodes of their favorite shows that they had fallen behind on.

"It's only eight in the evening in London," Alina grumbled. "I shouldn't be this wiped, but flying isn't what it used to be, or so I'm told. It's been shitty as long as I've been alive." She disappeared into Ireland's bedroom.

There was a half-bath off the living room, but the litter box was in there, so Alina used the master bath to avoid the shock of Blizzard slinking through the cat-shaped cutout in the door while she was in the middle of relieving herself.

"Hey!" Alina called out. "When did you take this picture, and can I have a copy?"

"Huh?" Ireland unfolded from her cross-legged position on the couch and went to her room.

Alina stood in the hallway that led to Ireland's closet on one side and the bathroom on the other. Ireland came to a stop behind her, easily looking over her best friend's shoulder because she was six inches taller. On the wall was a collection of framed photos showcasing what she held most dear: past trips with Alina, Blizzard looking majestic, and group shots with her brothers and parents.

Her best friend pointed to one of her and Gideon at a Vidal party taken in the last year. "That is a prime shot of your brother, and since you're in the picture, too, it wouldn't be at all weird for me to frame it by my bedside."

"Oh, stop already." Shaking her head, Ireland headed back

the way she came. She stopped so abruptly she tripped over her own feet. "Shit. Damn it."

"Come on. It's a harmless crush."

"Not that." Ireland turned around and stared, horrified, at the artfully designed gallery wall. She'd spent a whole weekend arranging the matching gold frames into the perfect configuration, which made it even crazier that she'd forgotten all about them. "Ronan was in here. He could've seen these."

"Shit," Alina agreed, her nose scrunched.

Wouldn't he have said something if he'd seen them? Maybe he didn't because Alina was here. But then they'd been alone for a bit while they waited for the elevator. Was seeing her with the ultra-recognizable Gideon Cross why he'd rushed to leave? He'd recognize them as siblings. Everyone did.

"You really need to tell him who you are," Alina told her. "Better if you bring it up than wait for him to do so. You've got an understandable reason for not telling him. I'm sure he'll see that."

"I don't know. It might not be an issue if we'd just been hanging out for a few days, but we've been so honest with each other about so many personal things. He might feel like his trust in me wasn't reciprocated. Oh, god. That's probably what he wants to talk about. And he didn't agree to dinner." Closing her eyes, she groaned. "I've screwed this up already."

"I'm sure he didn't see them," Alina assured her. "He didn't seem at all turned off by it if he had. I wouldn't worry about it. Just give him a call and tell him."

We just have some things to discuss first.

Not worrying was easier said than done.

Ireland's call to Ronan's phone went straight to voicemail—again. The first time, she'd merely said, *Tag, you're it.* The second time, she told him, *I just wanted to hear your sexy voice.*

This time, she sighed and bit the bullet. "Hey, you. This is the last time I'm calling, I promise. It's just that I have a black-tie event on Friday night and was hoping you'd agree to be my plus-one. In the spirit of transparency, you should know my entire family will be there, too, but it's a party with hundreds of people, games, auctions, and entertainment, so we'd have fun. Anyway, I'm going to be optimistic and put your name on the guest list. Just remind me, if I forget, that it's one of the *things* we're discussing tomorrow. Have a good night, handsome. Sweet dreams."

She killed the call and clutched her phone, anxious and a little bit scared. Was Ronan avoiding her? He'd never not taken her calls or answered her texts. And getting sent straight to voicemail meant his phone was either off or he was doing it deliberately. He just didn't strike her as the type to ghost someone. He came at things too directly.

Whimpering, she closed her eyes and let her head fall against the back of the sofa. She hadn't been twisted up over a man in years, not since she'd fallen for a douchebag in high school. A vibrating alarm inside her made her want to hop in a cab to the Vidal Hotel. Maybe he was in Jazzie's, dazzling an audience of captivated women like her. She'd love to see him play again, hear him sing again, and yes… feel his hard body plastered to hers again.

"Ugh." What she should do was take these horrible feelings of unease and inadequacy as a sign to ghost him instead. She could cut him out of her life cleanly if he didn't know who she was. The doormen could tell him there was no resident named Elizabeth Duffy, and he'd never get past them to prove otherwise. He wouldn't know where else to look for her if he hadn't seen the photos in her hallway. And since he wasn't from New York, he'd have to leave eventually, perhaps even immediately, once he couldn't reach her.

She'd block and delete his number and eventually get over this silly infatuation.

Her phone rang in her hand, and she was so wound up she dropped it on the floor. Scrambling for it, she shot from the pits of despair to the heights of hope, only to be painfully disappointed when she saw her mother's face on the screen.

Heaving a forlorn sigh, she answered, "Hey, mom."

"Hey, back," Elizabeth Vidal greeted her. "I hope I'm not interrupting a fun night out."

"No, I'm hanging with Blizzard tonight."

"How is that gorgeous creature? Please don't say he's gotten bigger."

Ireland laughed, which eased some of her tension. "He's full grown now, so no. He's as ginormous as he'll ever be."

"Thank god for that. You'd have to move into a house if he got any larger. Listen, I don't mean to keep you, but you and I need to go over some things. Could we get together for lunch tomorrow?"

More *things*? Her nose wrinkled.

"Uh... I have plans." At least she hoped she still had plans. Even though she didn't know what time or in what place those plans might materialize.

"This is important, Ireland."

She sighed inwardly and stared up at the ceiling. Of course, wedding planning would be at the top of her mom's list of immediate tasks, and she wanted to participate as much as possible. "I kept my schedule mostly clear tomorrow because Alina was due back from London. But she got home today and came over so I could stop by in the morning…? Would that work for you? Say nine?"

"Yes, that's perfect. See you then, darling. Bye."

"Bye."

Hanging up, Ireland tossed her phone onto the coffee table. It added insult to injury that her mom had no trouble finding adoring men while Ireland struggled to do the same. She was thrilled for her mother, no question. She just wished she was the same woman who'd so blithely declared on Friday that she was swearing off men. Unfortunately, the woman she was today was stupidly pining for one.

And she didn't like it. Not one bit.

GIDEON WATCHED HIS WIFE SPREAD CREAM CHEESE ONTO a mini bagel and knew something was wrong. He'd thought so the day before, but Eva had perked up over chocolates and a heating pad—he had acquired a few strategies over the years to help him feel less useless when she was menstruating—and he'd set the concern aside. But it was a new day, and his usually energetic wife was subdued and distracted.

She was dressed for comfort in wide-legged slacks in cherry red and a loose sleeveless tunic in cream silk. Ruby earrings he'd once given her as an anniversary gift winked at him between strands of her blond hair. And the full, lush lips she'd wrapped around his cock this morning were now slicked with bright red lipstick.

Coming up behind her, Gideon slid his arms around her waist and felt her jump slightly in surprise. He could rarely startle her—she was as attuned to his presence as he was to hers. They both instinctively knew when the other entered or exited a room, sight unseen.

If he'd needed proof that her thoughts were tangled up in something, he had it now.

He pressed a kiss to the top of her head, breathing in her familiar beloved scent. Her proximity grounded him immediately, silencing the noise and worry in his mind. When she leaned into him, he sighed inwardly with soul-deep contentment. They could handle anything life threw at them as long as they were aligned.

"Something's bothering you." He nuzzled her temple as Lucky lay down with front paws on his oxfords. "Something that came up during your lunch with Cary?"

"It's uncanny how you do that," she muttered in what sounded like a complaint.

"You do the same to me," he reminded. "Then you worry at it like Lucky with a bully stick until you find out what it is. It's how we work."

"I know. I just don't have the words now." Eva turned her head to press her cheek to his, hoping he would leave it at that for now.

But, of course, he didn't. "Are you worried about Cary?"

"No, it's nothing like that. He's doing great." She breathed measuredly in and out, fighting irritation at being forced to talk about something she wasn't ready to. She spoke in a rush. "They're expecting their first child. Maybe their only child, actually. I don't know if there will be others, but there's one on the way."

"That's exciting. I'll text him my congrats."

She nodded and started to pull away. "He had some great ideas about the masquerade. I'm going to run them by the team, see what we can do."

Gideon held fast. "Which of those two very different things is the problem?"

"I didn't say there was a problem. I've just got a lot on my mind. It's Monday, and I've got a week of work to sort out in my head."

"I can read between the lines." He urged her to face him, his hands lifting to brush her hair back from her breathtaking face. He'd studied her at length over the years: the curve of her brows, the symmetry of her wide gray eyes, the shape of her nose, and the plumpness of her lips. She was noted for looking like her mother, but he saw her father in her, too. "Since you've been around the block with the masquerade for a few years now, I'm going to say your best friend having a baby has you thinking thoughts you should be sharing with me."

Shrugging wearily, Eva slipped her hands into his open jacket and held him by the waist, the warmth of her touch taking a bit to sink through his waistcoat and shirt to his skin. "I've learned that thinking big thoughts and making big pronouncements needs to wait until I'm not overly emotional on my period."

"How about a little clue, then?" He kissed the tip of her nose.

She was silent for a long while, staring at his tie clip, then, "A couple without a uterus between them get pregnant before me. There's some irony in that."

Gideon heard the tremulousness in her voice, and his heartbeat quickened. "Sounds more like frustration."

While he technically knew it was impossible for his wife to be happy every minute of every day, it was his primary goal. It seemed only fair since she was the sole reason he was happy. He'd been content before her, even satisfied, but knowing joy didn't happen until she happened.

"Separate situations at play, of course," she murmured, unnecessarily fidgeting with his waistcoat buttons. "No one's threatening them."

He went very still. "Is someone threatening you?"

Eva looked at him with incredulity. "Gideon… come on. Things have never returned to normal since we started receiving those letters."

There was no mistaking the blend of accusation and irritation in her husky voice. He moved his hands from her hips to her wrists, gripping them with firm pressure. He watched her eyes darken and her lips part, her focus narrowing on him.

"We have a new normal," he said evenly, attuned to every nuance of her expression. "If that's made you feel less secure, you should've said something before now."

She scowled. "Don't make this about your ego."

A flash of anger gave an icy edge to his reply. "Say that again."

"I'm sorry." Her eyes squeezed shut. "I didn't mean that."

"Oh, I think you did."

"Argh!" She tried to pull away. "I told you I didn't want to talk about it, and now we're fighting, which is the last thing I want to do. Ever. But you just had to push."

"Apparently so, as it seems you have a lot you haven't been telling me." Gideon pulled her hands up to his chest and pressed her palms against him, his grip on her wrists light but unbreakable. He couldn't bear it when she attempted to distance herself from him, largely because she did so only when she was angry or hiding something. "You need more time to find the words, so we'll table this discussion until dinner. But answer me this: have you made any decisions based on the thought that I can't keep you safe?"

She looked up at him with those big gray eyes that could peer into his soul, and he realized she had. The sudden knowledge was wounding, and he backed away from her in instinctive self-defense.

Eva felt a spurt of panic as her husband physically and

emotionally retreated. A smooth mask descended over his features, and she couldn't bear it. "Gideon, you—"

"No. Now I need time." He pivoted and walked away, speaking to her curtly over his shoulder. "I'll be in my office. Let me know when you're ready to leave."

Her eyes stung as she watched him depart. There was so much she wanted and needed to say, but she didn't trust herself not to fuck it up further.

It took a heroic effort for Ireland to finish winging her eyeliner before answering her phone. The fact that Ronan's face was on the screen made it even harder. She briefly considered letting the call go to voicemail, but that was the type of game she didn't have time or inclination to play.

"Hello, handsome," she greeted him coolly.

"Good morning, *cher*. Did you enjoy your time with Alina?"

"I did. I would've told you so last night if I could've."

"And I would've been delighted to hear about it if I could have."

Her gaze narrowed as she studied the symmetry of her eye makeup in the mirror. Wearing eyeliner on a workday wasn't usual for her, but then she'd been holding out hope that Ronan was still planning on seeing her. "Really? What tied you up? Or, more to the point, *who* tied you up?"

His voice came low and amused. "Your jealousy is unwarranted. You've ruined me for other women. I don't even see them anymore; I'm so blinded by you."

Her huffed laugh was wry. "One: I'm only possessive of things that are mine. Two: You're the most outrageous flirt. I can't take you seriously."

"You're a weakness," he said artlessly. "I've mastered self-denial, and I have no vices aside from a fondness for sex, but I can't seem to resist you. And I know you, tigress. You'd set your mind to changing mine, and it was necessary to avoid the temptation."

Ireland watched her reflection alter, her eyes and expression softening. She made a frustrated sound. "Okay, that's a pretty good excuse as far as excuses go," she admitted. "So, what did you do?"

"I blew up all my best-laid plans," he told her cheerfully. "Claudette is enjoying it all immensely, but Jules is less entertained. He's used to me doing what he expects me to. It's probably good to shake him up a bit. He's too easily bored, and then he gets into trouble."

"Can't have two mischief-makers." She began to put on her mascara. Thankfully, ECRA+'s Out All Night line of makeup had insane staying power because it sounded like she might be having an all-nighter with the golden god, after all. The thought alone made her so excited her feet began to tap. "Although someone once told me that being bad is much more fun than being safe."

"Sounds like a bad influence."

"Oh, I hope so!" Her smile was so wide the sight of it embarrassed her.

Ronan's laugh swept over her like a heated caress. "What time will you be free for lunch?"

"That depends."

"On?"

"If we're also having dinner together. If so, then I'm free any time after eleven-thirty. If not, then any time after five works better."

The sound of his amusement was as much music to her ears as his drawl. “Anywhere in particular you’d like to eat?”

“Let me think about it. I’ll text you some ideas.”

“*C’est bon.*”

Ireland held her tongue until she couldn’t any longer. “I missed you last night. That’s stupid, I know. But it sucked. I didn’t like it.”

The other end of the line was silent for a long moment. Then she heard him sigh. “A better man would apologize, but I won’t because I’m glad I didn’t suffer alone. See what kind of man I am?”

“An honest one? At least, I hope you aren’t stringing me along. It wouldn’t be necessary, considering how obvious I’ve been about wanting to have sex with you. It’d be cruel.”

“*Cher*…” He exhaled harshly. “I’ll be waiting for your text. Waiting for you.”

They said good-bye, and Ireland sat on her vanity stool for too long, staring at where Blizzard was sprawled diagonally across her king-sized bed. Her thoughts twisted and wandered, constantly circling back to Ronan. “He can’t be the real deal. It’s impossible to just stumble across sex on legs with a heart of gold. For one, such a man doesn’t exist. And two, you’re the only truly perfect male, right, Bliz?”

Blizzard rumbled and stretched to his full incredible length.

Glancing at the clock on her bedside table, Ireland jumped to her feet in alarm. “Oh, hell. I’m late. Gotta run.”

In under five minutes, she was out the door with her black Birkin slung over one forearm and a muted gold overnight bag gripped in her other hand. She ordered a rideshare pickup on the way down in the elevator. After her parents divorced, her mother moved from their former Dutchess County estate to a condo in Gramercy Park. Her father moved to the Upper West Side near

Christopher and his family. Aside from her mother, who'd secured the purchase of a magnificent brownstone as part of the divorce, they all lived in buildings owned by Cross Industries.

It took just over thirty minutes to travel the five miles in morning traffic, giving Ireland time to review her to-do list and weekly reminders.

"Crap," she muttered under her breath, remembering that she'd meant to call Christopher to talk about Vidal and whatever moves her father might be making to secure more of the company's privately held shares.

This time, she actually put the reminder on her phone, setting it for later in the afternoon between lunch and dinner. But she'd see about talking to him in the office if he was around when she finally got there. While most of the staff were in the offices all day, she and Christopher often ran all over town.

Once she reached her mother's place, she was greeted with a warm, strong hug at the door.

"I was beginning to wonder if you forgot," Elizabeth said over her shoulder, still squeezing her. "Oh, it's good to see you!"

Ireland grinned and hugged her back just as hard. Because she was in heels and Elizabeth wore ballet flats, she was slightly taller in the embrace, but they were nearly identical in appearance, from the color of their eyes to the sleek length of their hair. Her mother had initially resisted graying, but the fight against silver when your hair was pitch black was too time-consuming. Now, she sported bright white streaks around her hairline and a scattering of tinsel throughout, a natural pattern that looked salon-worthy.

"You act like you don't see me every other week," Ireland teased.

"It's never enough." Pulling back, Elizabeth studied her,

brushing her hair behind her ears. "You must have a big day ahead by the look of you."

"A big *date*," she corrected, admiring the off-the-shoulder sweater her mother had pulled on over silk slacks in the same deep amethyst hue.

"Really?"

The surprise on Elizabeth's face was so pronounced Ireland laughed. "I do spend time with men, you know. I'm not a twenty-nine-year-old virgin."

"Of course I didn't think that." Shutting and locking the door behind them, Elizabeth followed her daughter into the living room, noting the small duffel bag Ireland was carrying. "Is it a destination date?"

"Huh? Oh, no."

Elizabeth waited for more information, and when none was forthcoming, her interest sharpened. "Aren't you going to tell me about him?"

"Not yet." Ireland dropped her bags onto one of the taupe armchairs and passed through to the kitchen. Her mother had decorated the home in Parisian shades of cream, gold, and robin's egg blue—a palette that flattered her and was soothing to guests. The air was fragranced with notes of citrus and peonies, with the faintest note of coffee that made her mouth water.

Grabbing a mug out of the cabinet, Ireland put it beneath the spout of the coffee machine and selected a mocha latte. "Want something?" she asked, as sounds of building steam and grinding beans filled the air.

"I'm well-caffeinated at this point." Elizabeth settled onto one of the barstools at the island. "Why be so secretive about your date? Is it someone I know?"

"No. It's just that tonight is our first overnight together.

Things might look different in the morning, and then talking about him would be moot."

Her mother's brows raised. "Are you worried he might disappoint you in bed? If so, don't even take him for a trial run."

"No. God, no, that's not a worry whatsoever. My sex drive redlines the minute I lay eyes on him. And his smile is so wicked it's nearly orgasmic." Ireland shrugged sheepishly. "I've never been so hot for someone, and maybe that kind of heat burns out fast."

"Hmm..."

"Maybe we'll wake up agreeing that we've scratched that itch into oblivion. Then we'll just be acquaintances who tangoed together once."

And there was part of her that hoped for that resolution. A wild, incendiary night followed by a good-bye as smooth and warm as his drawl. No more pining or hoping or worrying.

"But he might be my date on Friday," Ireland admitted cautiously, refusing to feel optimistic about that possibility. "If so, you'll get to meet him."

"Well, I'll be dying of curiosity until then."

But Elizabeth was more than curious. Gideon also hadn't brought any romantic interests around the family aside from the two women he'd been engaged to, one of whom he married. Elizabeth loved Corinne, but the temperature of her relationship with Eva was frostier. She prayed that Ireland would follow Christopher's example instead and make sure her partner fit in with the family before committing to anything permanent. Or semipermanent, as the case may be.

Ireland kicked off her heels and leaned forward to rest her elbows on the island. "So... what are you thinking about for your big day?"

"Oh, no. We're not digging into wedding planning yet. Your

brother has to negotiate the prenup first." Elizabeth waved a careless hand. "Can't have Daniel thinking of me as a *fait accompli* before Gideon gets that finalized."

Blinking in surprise, Ireland straightened slowly. "Mom, if you've got any concerns, you shouldn't—"

"Of course there are concerns. I have a remarkable ability to find men of means who can't manage their money properly. I'm too old to keep hitting rock bottom and starting over."

Knowing what her mother had been through in her previous marriages, Ireland admired her strength and resolve, even while regretting the past circumstances that led to such cynicism. "Do you love Daniel?"

"I wouldn't marry him otherwise. And he adores me. Falling in love has never been my problem."

Ireland offered a quick, relieved smile. "That's the most important thing."

"I wish that were true, but enough about me and the wedding. There's plenty of time for that yet. We need to discuss what you're going to do."

Confused, Ireland frowned. "What *I'm* going to do?"

Elizabeth's posture straightened, and steel slipped into her tone. "I hate bearing bad news, but forewarned is forearmed. Your father has squandered the fresh start Gideon gave Vidal."

A chill swept through Ireland; then she immediately realized the news wasn't wholly unexpected. She'd known something was really wrong, even if she hadn't acknowledged it. "What do you know?"

"Everything," Elizabeth said matter-of-factly. "I learned a crucial lesson from Gideon's father: always be aware of the finances. So, I made sure I had access to everything when I married your dad. That's how I knew when to bring Gideon in to fix Vidal the first time it got into trouble; I saw that rapid intervention was necessary."

Fighting sudden queasiness, Ireland asked, "How bad are we talking here?"

"Enough that sharks have scented blood in the water. Your father took out a loan to upgrade the recording studios, and he's about to default. He was required to maintain specific levels of capital and liquid cash, and he's fallen below the threshold for both."

"By how much?"

"Too much. He shouldn't have done it."

Ireland winced. She'd marveled at their new state-of-the-art studios but had never considered the cost. Her father insisted modernization was necessary to attract the young, fresh artists who were independent. *We've got to offer advantages to signing with a label...*

"So..." she began, "what do the boys think we should do? What's their plan?"

"I haven't told them."

"*What?* What do you mean...?" Aghast, she gaped at her mother. "Why not?"

"Gideon's already saved the day before. I won't ask him to do it again. If you want to ask, go ahead. And Christopher was active in the company when your father ran it into the ground before and did nothing to stop it. I chalked it up to his youth and inexperience, plus he was estranged from Gideon then. But now he hasn't any excuses left for allowing it to happen a second time."

Blinking back tears, Ireland asked, "Shouldn't I have known, too?"

"How could you?" Elizabeth's eyes were flat chips of ice.

"They keep you in the same box Geoffrey kept me in, locked safe and happy away from all the sordid money stuff."

"Still… Shouldn't I have refused to stay in my lane?"

"Now that you know better, you can fix it," Elizabeth said calmly. "I'm selling my shares. It doesn't make sense to be part of my ex-husband's family business now that I'm marrying Daniel. It's time for a fresh start without the headache of micro-managing Chris's bad fiscal sense."

Ireland's exhale was shaky and took her dangerously close to sobbing uncontrollably. She held herself together by a thread. A roaring in her ears made it hard to think or comprehend. She wanted to call her kind, dear father and ask him what to do. Not being able to lean on him hurt more than anything else. "I understand. You've…um…You've done so much already."

"You're going to buy them from me, Ireland."

That statement rocked her to the soul. Her breath came quick and fast.

Elizabeth's almond-shaped nude nails tapped a rapid staccato on the countertop. "You own ten percent. When you take over my shares, you'll have twenty-five. With Christopher backing you with his ten, you'll have a majority position together, but you'll have the power."

"What about Dad's?"

"He's going to lose his shares. They were collateral for the loan. You may also lose all the new equipment in the studios if you can't work out something with the lender. You'll need to act fast."

Ireland realized belatedly that her head was shaking back and forth. She stopped the movement, her fingers whitening where they wrapped around the counter's edge. "Run Vidal without Dad? I…I don't know."

She'd always figured her father would leave the company one

day because he was done with it and ready for someone else to steer it into the future. Christopher would step into his shoes, and she could decide then what she wanted to do. Maybe she would realize the business ran in her blood and stay. Or maybe she'd start something new with Alina. She'd never seriously contemplated alternative careers, and suddenly, the future yawned wide before her, an unknown and frightening void.

"Ireland," her mother said bitingly, snapping her back to attention. "Your father and brother weren't thinking of you when they dragged you into this mess; you can't think of them now. If you don't want Vidal for yourself, for god's sake, don't sink your money into it! You can sell your shares and do something else with your life."

Unbidden, she thought of Ronan, and her panic eased ever so slightly. She was planning to tell him who she really was during lunch anyway, and once she did, she could ask for his advice. This situation was in his wheelhouse.

But she suddenly grasped how scary that option was. God help her if she ever *needed* him and came to depend upon him—a man who'd proven capable of walking away and avoiding her calls. Better to lean on Gideon, even if she sincerely hated having to approach him with anything unpleasant. Her brother would take on the burden without a single word of complaint. But her mother was right: he shouldn't have to.

"You'll need to decide," Elizabeth stated firmly. "And soon. I want to divest my shares before they're worthless."

Over an hour later, as Ireland left her mother's and slid into the back of a waiting rideshare, she knew she was in some stage of shock. Still, she and her mom had managed to discuss all sorts of mundane topics at length, although she could hardly remember any of them. Chatting about nothing had given her mind a brief reprieve, but she didn't have time to bury her head in the sand. She had to know what they were up against to make an informed decision about what to do.

Her purse vibrated against her hip, and she jumped, her nerves stretched to the limit. She dug for her phone, pulling it out in time to catch the incoming call. The photo of Ronan and his black cat on her screen was possibly the only thing—aside from Alina—that could make her feel anything remotely pleasant.

"Hey," she answered breathlessly. "I'm sorry. I was supposed to text you. I…uh…I got tied up and forgot."

"What's wrong?" Ronan asked sharply. "You sound upset."

"Nothing," she answered reflexively, then caught herself. She groaned. "Everything. I'll fill you in when I see you. Are you at the hotel? I can meet you there, and we'll decide where we're going."

"Yes, I'm at the Vidal. When will you get here? I'll meet you downstairs."

It was disconcerting hearing her name spoken in his voice. "I'm on the way now. I'll share my trip, so you'll know when I'm close." With a few quick taps in the app, she did just that.

"*C'est bon*." A moment later, he added, "I see you."

"I can't wait to see *you*," she replied with feeling.

They hung up, and Ireland let her head fall back against the headrest. It felt strange and disorienting not to be aimless, which made her realize that she'd always been precisely that. She had always done what was expected of her. Now, she had choices to make and a direction to set. Was she even capable of leading when she'd always followed?

At least her mother thought she was.

She replayed their conversation in her mind, picking through the minefield of information for anything that might help her decide what to do. She and Christopher had to talk, but when? She'd always presumed he would take over their father's role when the time came, but she'd also believed he was capable of doing so. Was he not? Was he too much like their father in that regard?

If Christopher couldn't be trusted to run it, was it up to her to hold it together? Until when? When his children took over? That would be damn near a lifetime commitment.

Straightening with a gasp, Ireland fumbled for her phone again, and speed-dialed her mother.

"Well, that was quick," Elizabeth answered.

"I've been thinking about what you told me."

"Good. You should be."

Ireland glanced into the cab beside her at the traffic light, her gaze briefly meeting that of the suited businessman in the backseat who was also on his phone. "You said the *sharks* had scented blood. Is there more than one loan?"

Was it even *possible* to save Vidal? She held back a groan.

"No, there's just the one loan. I was referring to one of the other shareholders, who somehow caught wind of what was happening. They approached me with a generous offer, which has grown more attractive the longer I resist selling to them."

Ireland sat bolt upright, her pulse leaping back into a frantic rhythm. *The list and documents she'd found in her father's desk drawer…* Her nausea returned. "Who was it?"

"McCaffrey Holdings. I was going to suggest them to you if you decide to sell because they're willing to pay."

"Jesus. Thanks. I've got to go." Hanging up, she slid forward in the seat. "I'm changing my destination in the app," she told the driver urgently. "It's just a couple of blocks from where I was originally going."

He looked at her in the rearview mirror. "No problem."

She remembered checking her father's calendar. He was meeting with McCaffrey—she checked the time on her phone—*now!* Panic tightened her throat.

"Get me there as fast as you can," she said huskily, "and I'll tip you double the fare."

He flashed his teeth in a wide smile. "You got it."

Ronan waited in the lobby of the Vidal Hotel, standing in front of the floor-to-ceiling windows overlooking the entrance driveway. His back was to the lobby, his posture such that it discouraged anyone from approaching him. His blood thrummed steady and hot in his veins; the anticipation of seeing the woman he'd spent the past few nights dreaming about was now at a fever pitch.

Behind him, the noise was astonishing. The music pumped through the Vidal sound system was set at a louder volume than most hotels and leaned heavily toward rock. The driving beat of frenetic drums forced guests almost to shout to be heard, and tourists passed through in surging waves, pouring in from Times Square at all hours of the day and night.

It was not his preferred type of lodging by any stretch, but Jules had enjoyed a steady stream of companions in his room since their arrival. Claudette was merely amused that Ronan had chosen it. She was perceptive, that one. She knew him well enough to reason what he didn't say.

His left hand was in the pocket of his dress slacks and his

phone was in his right. He watched the screen as the little black car steadily followed the line on the map leading to the hotel. Ten minutes to arrival. Scarcely any time at all, considering how interminable the morning had been waiting for her. But her voice on the phone had been strained and hurried, and now he was concerned. He would continue to worry until she was with him again.

The screen blinked as if it glitched, and suddenly, the destination on the app was not the Vidal. His gaze narrowed as he studied the map, noting that the new destination was within walking distance away. He almost called her to see if everything was all right but found himself spinning through the revolving lobby doors instead. At this point, he'd much rather see her than hear her voice. His concern was now suppressing his excitement.

"What are you up to, *cher*?" he murmured to himself, noting the approximate location of her new destination on the app before sliding his phone into his pocket.

He wasn't the only person in a business suit passing through Times Square, but they were in the minority. Tourists clogged both the roads and sidewalks as they gawked at the massive digital billboards and performers wearing dirty Elmo, Cookie Monster, Barney, and similar costumes. The smell was unpleasant, the ground littered with trash. Bourbon Street was also malodorous and dirty, but at least the architecture was lovely. Times Square was garish in every way.

He reached 48th St. and turned, his pace quickening when he spotted the woman he sought unfolding from the back of a black town car, her hair a silky curtain that enveloped her. She was dressed in a short column of black material, the fit loose and the shoulder straps thin. Her sleek legs were miles long and strong, her calves and thighs flexing with lithe muscle.

Ronan noted the small duffel bag in her hand and smiled grimly, accelerating his pace to catch her. Her gaze raked over and past him, as he weaved through the cars crawling through the densely trafficked area. Then her attention shot back to him, her eyes widening with surprise.

"Ronan!" She turned toward him when he reached her but was too stunned to react when he caught her close and lowered his mouth to hers. The moment their lips made contact, she surged into him, her free hand clutching his lapel as she kissed him back with such eagerness it stole his breath.

He pulled away only because they were on a crowded street.

"How did you—" Realization dawned in her eyes, the shade of blue one he'd only ever seen in Caribbean waters. "Oh! I'm sorry. I should've called to explain. I work here and have to take care of something urgent."

Cupping her jaw in one hand, he committed every nuance of her extraordinary face to memory, especially how she looked at him at that moment.

She covered his hand with hers and nuzzled into his palm. "I'm glad you're here. I have so much to tell you. Would you mind waiting for me?"

"As long as it takes."

Her smile was like sunshine. Catching his hand, she pulled him behind her, but he lengthened his stride to get the door for her.

"Hey, Charlie," she greeted the guard as he gained his feet behind the desk. "Can you hook Ronan up with a badge, please?"

"Of course."

Ronan slid open the wallet attached to his phone and handed the guard his driver's license and a business card.

She smiled at him but was visibly anxious and uneasy. Her wide, mobile mouth was pinched at the corners, and her expressive eyes were dark and sad.

He squeezed her hand when she attempted to pull away from him. "Let's go up together."

"I'm late for something important, or I'd wait. It won't take Charlie long to get you checked in." She pushed onto her tiptoes to press those lush lips to his in a brief kiss. "I'm going to surprise you today. Just trust me, okay?"

"*Cher*—"

But she was walking away, already miles from him in her mind, and no longer heard him. The elevator doors opened instantly when she pushed the call button, the car already on the ground floor.

He followed, calling after her again, but she was gone. Exhaling harshly, he tried to shrug off the tension tightening his body. The scent of her perfume lingered, taunting him.

He wanted her beyond reason, with a deep-seated hunger that was maddening. He'd called her inconvenient, but she was a much bigger problem than that simple word implied. He was operating blind, having blown up all of his meticulously crafted plans, and his lack of guilt for making that choice was a dire warning.

"Like a tornado, isn't she?" he said to Charlie.

The guard's smile was fond. "Been that way her whole life," he agreed, his gaze on his monitor as he typed. It seemed interminable before he handed over a badge in a clear sleeve. "Wear that at all times. Head up to the third floor. Reception will direct you where to go."

"Thanks." Ronan clipped the badge to his jacket pocket and took the stairs at a dead run. He was conditioned to strenuous exertion, yet his heart hammered in his chest. He broke through the door on the top floor and skidded to a halt just in front of reception.

Ronan assessed the space in a single sweeping glance, noting that the meeting in the glass-walled conference room had arrested his tigress the moment she'd exited the elevator. She stood utterly still, her lips parted and eyes narrowed beneath a confused frown.

"*Cher*," he murmured, approaching her cautiously from behind.

Her head turned toward the sound of his voice, but her gaze remained fixed on the three people seated at the conference table as he took her hand in his.

He caught the attention of the dark-haired man and woman who sat facing a fellow with silver-dusted auburn curls whose back was to the elevator. That man noticed when their focus shifted to someone behind him, and he spun his seat around to face Ronan.

There was a moment of utter stillness in everyone, then the man's face contorted with mottled rage. He bolted from the chair and shoved through the glass doors into the reception area.

Ireland sidestepped to shield him with her body despite the tableau in front of them.

Incredible.

"Dad!" She dropped her duffel on the floor and lifted her hand, still gripping Ronan with the other. "Calm down."

"Get out of the way, Ireland!"

Ronan raked him with a derisive head-to-toe glance, cataloging the round brass glasses, wrinkled khaki slacks, green cardigan, and scuffed loafers. A harmless-looking man despite his fury, but his looks were deceiving. "You know my face, *non*?" he taunted with an icy smile.

"Let go of my daughter!"

The receptionist stood behind her desk. "Should I call security, Mr. Vidal?"

"Yes. Do it now."

"Hey!" Ireland's voice took on a note of steel. "We're all adults here. We can sit down and figure this out rationally."

She turned toward Ronan in what felt like slow motion, looking first at him and then down at the badge he wore. The color bled from her face as her lips read silently: *Ronan McCaffrey.*

Her hand went slack in his. It would've slipped from his grasp if he hadn't been holding on. Regret became a sharp ache.

Rubbing her suddenly cold fingers between his, he spoke softly so only she could hear. "As I said, *cher*, we have things to discuss."

seven

"WHAT THE HELL IS GOING ON OUT HERE?"

Ireland glanced at Christopher as he exited his office and entered the reception area. She decided in an instant that she was already up to her neck in bullshit, thank you very much, and wasn't sticking around for more.

The elevator dinged behind her, and she turned on her heel, smiling rigidly at the tiny pop singer with teased blond hair and minuscule blue latex dress who exited the elevator with an entourage of half a dozen people.

"Hey, Ireland," Chantal greeted her.

"Hey, superstar," she replied, catching the woman's hands and spinning with her so that Ireland's back was to the elevator again. "We have to catch up soon."

Then she walked backward into the car and hit the button for the ground floor.

"Ireland!" Ronan and her father barked in unison.

How she resisted flipping off the former and sobbing over the latter was beyond her.

She watched Ronan snatch her abandoned overnight bag up from the floor outside the elevator as the doors slid shut.

There was a great deal she didn't yet understand about what was happening, but she was catching up quick. The blows had been coming swift and hard all morning: the talk with her mother, seeing Ronan on the street outside Vidal, finding Jules and Claudette in the McCaffrey meeting with her father, and her father's fury, which she'd never imagined him capable of. He was such a mild-mannered and inherently soft-hearted man who so rarely raised his voice that she couldn't remember the last time he had done so.

And Ronan. Ronan *McCaffrey*. Dressed in a blue Glen plaid blazer with a white dress shirt, solid blue tie, and navy slacks, his business style was distinctly Southern and classically elegant. She loved it madly, as she adored everything about him.

There was a sharp pain blooming and spreading through her chest.

How? *Why?*

She exited into the lobby and waved at Charlie as she passed him, her stride lengthening as she pushed out onto the street. She didn't think twice about her destination and plunged into the stream of pedestrians headed into Times Square.

Ronan waited a heartbeat for the group of people who'd exited the elevator to step between him and Chris Vidal, Sr., then he spun on his heel and slammed through the stairwell door, racing down with Ireland's bag in hand. There was shouting behind him. Whether from the two Vidals or his own siblings didn't much matter. His concern was the look on Ireland's face when the pieces started falling into place for her.

The stunningly fierce tigress of a woman who'd sworn off

men but given him a chance was wounded now, and while her father was ultimately responsible, Ronan had to shoulder some of the blame. He'd known this moment of revelation was imminent, that he had only a matter of hours in which to make a lasting impression that might leave him a chance of redemption.

Tossing his badge at Charlie with a barked apology, Ronan burst onto 48th St. and glanced from side to side, searching. Spotting Ireland heading toward 7th Ave, he lunged through a small gap in the stream of shopping bag-laden tourists in pursuit.

"Wait a damned minute!" Drawing abreast of her, he slowed his pace from breakneck to matching her catlike stride.

Her head swiveled toward him, and he saw the same icy look on her face that he'd seen Friday night when she'd shredded the guy in the bar.

It sliced deep.

And she didn't slow, her endless legs crisscrossing with sleek, feline grace. He pivoted to walk forward at her side but continued having to weave through the flood of pedestrians to keep up, clutching her duffel bag against his chest so it didn't drag him down.

"What the hell was that back there?" he asked, fuming.

"You can't be asking *me* that."

He shot her an arch glance. "Is 'Lizzie' a separate personality from 'Ireland?' Because the woman I met Friday came spoiling for a fight and enjoyed the hell out of it."

She stopped so suddenly that the woman following behind her almost bumped into her back. "You think I should've started yelling at you with the situation being what it was? Are you a masochist, *Mr. McCaffrey*? Do you target family businesses for the thrill of having multiple people screaming at you at once?"

"Yell at *me?!*" He moved to face her and urged her to one side, outside the flow of foot traffic. "Your father is the villain here.'"

"You don't know my father.'"

His smile was tight and cool. "I know him better than you do. Why didn't you confront him?"

"How I deal with my family is none of your business."

"What the hell have they done to silence you?" he snapped. "You're a completely different person when they're involved."

Her beautiful eyes narrowed. "You don't know *me*, either."

She stepped down into the bike lane and then around him, resuming her hurried pace on the sidewalk. Ronan cursed under his breath and turned to follow, then stopped so abruptly he tripped, shocked into immobility.

Ireland was everywhere he looked, stories tall, plastered on every building he could see.

And she was completely naked.

Against a tan background, she strutted back and forth in nude stilettos, her hip-length hair plastered strategically across her bare body by a firm breeze—and expert CGI. She moved with graceful abandon, lifting her arms high and spinning like a dancer, her willowy figure strong and sexy.

It was a body lotion ad, he grasped through a haze of white-hot need, watching as she dropped gracefully into a crouch and blew a kiss at everyone watching her. And since the company she represented had staged a takeover, multiples of Ireland circled the digital billboards of Times Square in unison, a sex goddess exploiting her power to dazzle her adoring followers.

Ronan shook off the stupefaction and realized he wasn't the only person standing motionless on the street, watching Ireland move with seductive confidence and utter delight. But he damned well better be the only one doing so with an erection.

"*Pour l'amour de dieu*," he growled, adjusting his cock in his slacks before stepping into the bike lane to chase her as quickly as he could manage with a hard-on and a crush of gawking people everywhere. God help anyone who recognized and approached her...

The urgent ringing of a bike's bell warned him to hop back onto the sidewalk just before a courier cyclist whizzed by.

Ireland was heading toward the hotel. Ronan's lips curved with grim relief once he realized her destination. Throwing her over his shoulder and hauling her there wouldn't help his cause, but he'd been resigned to doing it if necessary to say what needed to be said.

He caught up to her just as she spun through the revolving doors into the lobby. She stopped on the other side, waiting for him to join her.

"You forget how to walk?" she asked with one brow arched and her arms crossed.

"Don't." He caught her by the elbow and urged her toward the bank of elevators, adjusting his grip on her bag in his other hand. "If you're naked, I'm staring, and I won't apologize for it."

"Naked?" She frowned. They stopped behind the mass of people waiting for the next elevator car. Leaning toward him, she whispered, "Is my dress see-through?"

He gave her a level look. "Did you not see yourself walking laps around Times Square selling lotion?"

Her eyes and mouth opened wide. "I forgot about that! How'd it come out? Did it look okay?"

His teeth clenched as his mind replayed the memory of her splendid body moving with joyful, aggressive sexuality. His blood heated again, and he growled, "'*Okay?*' No. Not even close. There's actually no word that covers how perfect every inch of you is."

Ireland's mouth curved in a smug smile, then she shifted her gaze from him to watching the floor numbers change. The older woman in front of them turned her head and gave Ronan an approving nod.

They were able to get into the third elevator car, and Ronan pulled Ireland into place in front of him, his arm slung around her waist. Turning her head, she shot him a strident look, but he just nuzzled her temple and breathed her in, absorbing the fragrance of her perfume blended with the scent of her skin. Closing his eyes, he was no longer crammed into the back corner of a packed elevator car, he was simply holding the woman he desired intensely. The strain in his shoulders eased enough to be bearable. It was the first time he'd ridden an overflowing elevator without hating it.

When they stopped on his floor, she reached a hand back for him and led him out with her. But once they were free, she shook him off. "I can carry my bag," she said.

"I know." Extending his hand, he directed her to walk in front of him. "5100."

An odd tingle raced down Ireland's spine. "Really?"

"Why would I lie about my room number, *cher*?" Ronan took his phone out to unlock the double doors to the three-bedroom suite.

She knew exactly what to expect when she entered the room because she'd designed the signature suite herself. Her father and brother had also designed suites as part of the branded feel Gideon wanted for the flagship property. Each had a distinctive style, with her father following the 70s styling of the Vidal offices and Christopher reminiscing with an 80s theme. Ireland had wanted to evoke a different feeling than nostalgia.

She'd wanted indulgence.

So, she stepped into a very familiar sprawling space filled with sumptuous fabrics and overstuffed furniture. The windows were covered in sapphire sheers framed by puddled velvet drapes in the same hue. Day or night, the rooms were drenched in simulated dusk thanks to strategic mood lighting in the coffered ceiling.

The suite was an amalgam of all the things she loved and couldn't implement in her own place. A big, white, long-haired cat shedding on dark fabrics? No, thank you. And she wanted her family to feel comfortable when they stopped by.

Did Ronan like the inherently sexy suite? The thought of him living and sleeping in it stirred heat inside her.

"Can I get you anything?" he asked as he dropped her duffel into a chair and shrugged out of his suit jacket. He loosened the knot of his tie and unbuttoned the top button of his dress shirt on his way to the bar. "Water, soda, juice? Something stronger?"

Ireland set her Birkin down next to her overnight bag and then plopped herself into the thick cushions of the silver velvet sofa. Kicking off her shoes, she tucked her legs and draped her arm along the back of the couch. "Sparkling water, if you've got it. Did you know who I was when we met Friday?"

He straightened from bending down to the minifridge behind the tufted gray silk bar, untwisting the cap of a blue glass bottle and grabbing a hobnail drinking glass before strolling toward her with sultry sexual grace. He reminded her of a lion on the prowl, loose-limbed and formidable even at leisure. "Yes."

"And yet you acted like you didn't."

"I wasn't sure if *you* were acting." He poured for her, deposited the bottle and glass on the coffee table, and then settled into the matching sofa across from hers. Reaching down, he unzipped his sexy-as-sin crocodile dress boots. He pulled off his socks so he was barefoot, too, draping them over the boot shafts before tucking them under the couch.

Such a simple act shouldn't feel so intimate.

"What do you mean?" she asked, forcing her mind to stay on track.

Sitting back, Ronan widened the spread of his knees and began working on unbuttoning and rolling up his sleeves. "I don't believe in coincidences or serendipity. You were in the same space as me, in a fine temper, and I had to think that was by design."

She mustn't stare at the sizeable bulge between his legs. She definitely should not feel a growing ache while doing so. Licking her dry lips, Ireland forced her gaze upward and found him staring back with knowing amusement. She cleared her throat. "When did you realize I was clueless?"

"By Saturday afternoon, I started to believe you had no agenda."

"No way it took that long," she contested. They'd been together until the early hours of Saturday morning, enjoying the food and company of Valentin and Genevieve.

"Buying out the other Vidal investors didn't happen overnight. It was unimaginable that you didn't know what was happening. You'd also given me a false name, were vague about your career, asked me intrusive questions, suggested some conflict with your family, and were actively seducing me. What do—"

"I was not!" But the observation she protested wasn't the one that stung.

His half-smile was a blatant challenge. He finished tugging off his tie and tossed it over the armrest, his entire body seeming to shrug off tension along with it. He wore his civility with such confident ease, yet the truth was that it suffocated him.

"*You* were seducing *me*," she countered, her fingers drumming on the sofa back.

"I am, yes." He smiled when she bristled. "I knew I had a very limited window in which to show you who I am before the situation with Vidal came to a head."

"And you didn't think being honest about that and your name was a better tactic?"

"I could ask you the same."

She studied him for a long moment, cataloging the flagrant invitation of his virile body. His arm draped over the armrest, his fingertips stroking channels into the metallic velvet. His right hand lay atop his thigh, near his groin. And his charisma…it lured her so irresistibly it was an effort not to go to him, straddle him, and take what she so recklessly wanted despite everything.

He looked so at home in the space she had meticulously designed, and the sensual décor complemented him, made him even more sinfully attractive—the king of the voluptuary's haven she'd created.

"I was protecting myself," she said finally. "I wanted you to like me for me."

"I do. Very much." His gaze shifted from warm to heated. "And my motivation was the same."

"Hmm." She looked away, still trying to align what she knew with how she felt. "So why not take me to bed and win me over that way?"

"You know why."

Pursing her lips, Ireland unfolded from the sofa and padded barefoot to the nearest window. "Am I supposed to give you points for not taking me to bed under false pretenses?"

"Yes, damn it." The shift in his voice revealed that he'd stood, too, and then followed her. "It's the hardest thing I've ever done, and I don't say that lightly."

She faced him with a tight smile and narrowed eyes. “But you did it for you, Ronan. To claim gallantry at the very moment your deception became known. What’s the difference if you fuck me as a Boudreaux or a McCaffrey? Or have me now versus yesterday?”

“I assessed which would give me the greatest probability of tomorrow and the day after. And I’m prepared to grovel as long as necessary.” He stopped in front of her and extended his hand. “Ronan McCaffrey Boudreaux.”

After a brief hesitation, she accepted the introduction, marveling at how strongly affected she still was by the sexual attraction between them. She was used to losing immediate interest when a relationship slid sideways to any degree. But the moment her skin touched Ronan’s, her lips parted on a sharp inrush of air, her fingers flexing involuntarily against the sudden surge of electricity.

“Ireland Elizabeth Vidal,” she said, her voice betrayingly husky.

Lifting her hand, he kissed her knuckles. When he straightened, his gray eyes were stormy. And watchful.

She pulled her hand back and walked around him, knowing it was up to her to decide the next steps. Should she insist they return to Vidal and get the mess sorted out? She didn’t have to look at her phone to know there were missed calls from her father and maybe Christopher, possibly even Gideon, if they’d elected to drag him into the fight.

Better they do that than she.

Her hands fisted at her sides. There was really no point in going back. Ultimately, it was up to her and Ronan to find the way through the crisis.

She looked around the living room as she crossed it, noting the two closed doors on each side that led to the second and third bedrooms. The primary suite's double door entrance was wide open, and she went to it, intending to pause on the threshold but lured deeper inside by Ronan's scent. She felt him following, felt that ineffable pull between them.

Before her was the massive round bed that had been custom-made to realize her vision. It had a curving headboard anchored by crescent-shaped nightstands that nestled against the sides of the bed. A ruched silk coverlet in vivid sapphire pooled onto the top of a raised dais. Above, on the ceiling, hung a mirror of equal size to the bed.

Ronan came up behind her, close enough for her to sense his warmth but not near enough that they touched. His proximity set off a low and deep trembling inside her, so she moved away. Reaching the edge of the dais, Ireland turned and looked at him propped casually against the jamb, his hands in his trouser pockets. His relaxed posture was misleading. His gorgeous face had the taut, focused look of a hungry predator biding his time before pouncing.

She climbed the short steps. Had she come to the bedroom just to remind herself of its decadence, or had she led him here because the gnawing craving for him had become unbearable?

Grabbing the hem of her linen dress, she yanked it over her head before she answered that question. She heard his harsh exhale, then felt the searing heat of his gaze as it slid over her.

But he didn't move.

She held his covetous stare as she slid her thumbs under the delicate lace of her panties and pushed them down her legs. Stepping free, she faced him again completely naked.

"I'm not airbrushed now," she murmured, turning around with arms wide. "Disappointed?"

"Delirious," he corrected, moving to grip and stroke the bulge of his erection through his slacks. "I didn't quite believe we'd actually get here."

"Would you like me to go?" she teased, trying for worldly in the hopes of masking the chaos inside her.

"I'd like you to come," he said gruffly. "Around my tongue, my fingers, my cock. Until I've wrung you out."

Her nipples tightened into hard points. "Then stop staring and take your clothes off. Let me see you."

His sinner's mouth curved in a smile that didn't soften his piercing focus. "If you want to use my body to pleasure yours, I'm at your service. Any time. Any place. Except for right now, when you'll have to come over here and take it."

"Why? I'm right here by the bed."

"And far too tempting for what little restraint I have left. Come set the pace, *cher*."

Ireland bit her lower lip and threw caution—which she exercised so little of anyway—to the wind. She descended the short steps and closed the distance between them, wishing she'd kept her heels on for visual impact. When she stopped in front of him, she took a moment to relish the unusual feeling of being petite next to his tall frame. Without her stilettos, she was at eye level with his collar. She watched as his tanned, strong throat worked on a hard swallow, betraying his reaction to her.

Placing both hands on his chest, she felt the heat and strength of his body and the elevated beat of his heart through the material of his dress shirt. Her fingers flexed, finding hardly any give. She surged onto her tiptoes, pressing her nose into the crook of his neck. He absorbed the sudden press of her weight with a hoarse laugh, his hands catching her hips to steady her.

Nuzzling, Ireland breathed him in with a soft hum of delight. The scent of his skin was familiar now and as decadent as the rest of him. The fragrance—smoky, intoxicating, and sexy as hell

—was wickedly alluring for a man with no vices. It resonated inside her, making her feel safe and highly attuned to him.

She licked the salt from his skin in a long, slow lap. He shivered violently and cursed, his hands gripping her too tightly. His erection was like steel against her lower belly. Her low laugh was exultant.

"I'll have you again," he said gruffly. "If you want mercy when that happens, you'd best show some now."

"Your threats have the opposite of their intended effect, you know."

He caught her face in his hands, his thumbs sweeping into the hollows beneath her cheekbones. The contradiction of his tender touch and imperative desire moved her. "I can't decide if you're a punishment or a gift."

"Maybe I'm a little of both."

Her fingers went to his shirt buttons and began undoing them. His big, warm hand claimed her breast and squeezed, plumping it. She didn't have much to play with, not enough even to have worn a bra under her dress, but Ronan didn't seem to mind, his gaze openly lustful as his thumb circled her nipple.

Parting the halves of his shirt, Ireland revealed him to her gaze and tightened her thighs against the sudden ache between them. Golden skin stretched taut over slabs of rigid muscle. His abs were so perfectly defined she traced them with her fingertips, making them leap beneath her touch as he laughed and twisted away.

"You're ticklish," she said with wonder, finding that endearing.

Ronan's eyes glowed with an inner fire that lit her up inside.

"I'll have you know I'm a champion tickler," she warned.

He caught her wrists and pressed her palms against his chest.

"I've ways to torture, too. Tread carefully, or you'll discover what they are."

"Oh, I hope so," she breathed, reaching for him again but using more pressure, her fingers sliding into the neatly trimmed hair.

His dry laugh was both amused and resigned.

He was so physically superior to any other man she'd known previously. The lankiness of men her age had seasoned into broader shoulders and thicker, heavier muscles. But more than the obvious—and delicious—physical maturity was the sheer animal attraction he radiated. It intoxicated her, made her a creature of wants and needs without rational thought.

Still cupping her jaw in one hand, he outlined the curves of her lips with his thumb before pressing between them. She caught him between her teeth, stroked the tip with her tongue, then suckled firmly and rhythmically.

"It won't be now," he murmured, his eyes on her in the filthiest of stares, "but soon, I'm going to fuck this sassy mouth and slick your lips with my cum."

His coarseness intensified her desire, and she whimpered, suddenly thirsty and so hot that perspiration misted her skin. She nipped him, and he yanked his hand back with a muttered curse. Beyond aroused, she couldn't stop herself from pushing his shirt off his shoulders, restraining his arms with it, and rubbing her body against his.

"*Dieu*, give me strength," he groaned.

She caught his lower lip between her teeth, her hands busy pulling his shirt the rest of the way off. He caught her up and took her mouth, the kiss so ferocious she was bent backward over his arm, yielding and pliant in his embrace. He grabbed her butt and squeezed, pulling her into the hardened steel of his cock.

Hands in the mass of his hair, Ireland held on and drank him in, the taste and feel of his lust overriding any possibility of shame or inhibition. She felt free in the most dangerous way, no expectations, no rules. Just raw need and the man who encouraged it.

"Fuck me," she muttered into his mouth, "before I lose my mind."

He softened the kiss, nibbling and licking. "You won't regret this?"

"Not even a little. Although you might. I'm a little wild about you if you haven't noticed."

Straightening, Ronan lifted her feet from the floor and walked toward the dais. She wrapped her legs around him, debated her next move, then gave in to the instinct to press her wet pussy against the flexing ridges of his abs. He stopped midstride, capturing the length of her hair around his forearm. He pulled gently, snaring her attention.

"You're more than a little wild, *cher*. You're feral and merciless."

"You like it," she gasped, thrusting against the silky line of hair leading down to his penis, marking him with her scent. More, *she* liked it. She'd never been so brazen.

"You have no fucking idea." He lunged toward the bed, taking the short steps in a rush.

They shifted together as they fell, her Krav Maga training and his quick twist enabling them to land on their sides. Their bodies came together in a tangle of passionate need. She clutched at him, her fingers caressing the hard muscles bracketing his spine. Her legs twined with his, her lips open to the skilled stroking of his tongue. When she reached frenziedly to open his slacks, Ronan pushed up onto his knees to give her more room to work, still hunched over her in the searing wild kiss, his hands wandering all over her body as if to learn every inch of her by touch.

Ireland moaned in protest as he pulled away, but he only reached down to yank his fly open so roughly the material ripped. The sudden loud tearing was a shock to her senses… and like a match to tinder. A violent tremor wracked her body, her lust instantly at a fevered pitch. She reached for his cock, feeling the velvety soft tip as it strained above the waistband of his boxer briefs. She growled when he rolled away from her to reach for the nightstand drawer.

She followed, wrapping herself around his flexing back like a vine. Her lips slid over the sharp talons of ink covering his shoulder and the length of his arm, her hands traveling down his sides and grabbing his devilishly fine ass. He was hard there, too, leanly muscular from head to toe.

"*Merde*," he growled, "you're a menace!"

She almost laughed, but her lips and fingers had run over scars, some faint, others thick and uneven. Pulling back to look, she gave him space to rise onto his knees instead. Ronan held a condom wrapper between his teeth as he shoved his ripped trousers and boxer briefs to his thighs, his cock straining high and hard against his lower belly, the broad head wet with excitement.

A shiver moved through her at his size, startling even though she'd fantasized that he would be extravagantly perfect everywhere. He deftly rolled the condom on without looking, his gaze on her. His chest had a fine sheen of sweat, and his breathing was fast and rough.

Ronan Boudreaux was like a thoroughbred stallion, and she couldn't wait to ride him. "Hurry up already and give me that big, beautiful cock!"

Laughing softly, he folded over her and pressed his damp forehead to hers. “You’re robbing me of the preliminaries.”

“Tease.” She tilted her head back to lick his lips, her hands pulling at him to lower his strong, solid body to her but unable to move him. “Sadist.”

He cupped the back of her knee and widened the spread of her legs, sinking his hips between them. She squeezed his butt, hurrying him, moaning when he took himself in hand and rubbed the crest of his penis between the slick folds of her pussy.

More. *More!* Thrusting her hips up, she took the first inch with a breathless cry.

He groaned as his entire body went taut as a bow. “Grab the headboard,” he ordered, his voice so gruff it took her a second to understand him. “*Asteur!*”

She’d barely managed to press her palms flat against the lacquered mahogany before he thrust deep and hard, possessing her to the hilt. Her cry was thready, her fevered body absorbing the shock of entry, her pussy so wet it gave no resistance. Stretched tight around the thick, unrelenting hardness of his penis, she panted beneath him, eyes wide and unseeing. She was so close to orgasm it was a screaming tension inside her.

“Oh my god,” she gasped, her hips moving in involuntary tiny circles, her body seeking the relief she needed so desperately. She’d never been with anyone so well-endowed, and the feeling of utter fullness was like a drug in her veins, sliding through her in heated pulses of delight that echoed in the rhythmic squeezing of her pussy around his cock.

“Stop moving,” he said hoarsely, his lips moving against her throat. He held his weight aloft with one hand planted on the bed while the other pinned her hips down. “Give me... a second.”

“Ronan…” His name came out slurred, her senses overloaded with the scent and feel of him. The crisp hair on his chest abraded her stiff, aching nipples in the most delicious way, and she couldn't stop moving, too restless to be still. "Please."

He circled his hips, and they moaned in unison.

"*Bon dieu*, you're tight as a fist." He rubbed his cheek against hers. A stream of Cajun French poured from him, and she grasped enough to understand that he praised her. *Tu es magnifique… exquis… merveilleux.*

Wrapping her legs around his hips, she spurred him with her heels, finally taking in their reflection in the mirror above. She saw the scars she'd felt and touched them again, Ronan quivering as her fingertips learned their shape and texture. His ruined slacks were bunched beneath his magnificent ass, the cheeks clenching and releasing as his body urged him to move. That he fought the need to thrust made no sense to her lust-addled mind, and then that became clear, too.

"Let go," she coaxed, pressing kisses to his temple. "I'm your tigress. I can take you."

"Ireland…" The sound of her name in his richly decadent voice affected her powerfully.

And then he moved, withdrawing from her in a heated glide. His following thrust was as smooth as his charm but shattered her. She began trembling and couldn't stop.

Ronan hummed, slid a hand beneath her hip, and lifted her. His subsequent withdrawal was as easy as the first, but his surging drive was hard and fast. Her back bowed as pleasure sizzled through her, her orgasm hovering on the precipice.

"Not just wild," he noted with hoarse, strained amusement. "You like a hard ride."

She watched, dazed, in the mirror above them as his entire body flexed on his next forceful thrust. The stroking of that big cock was sublime. The sight of him still partially dressed excited her further. It became a struggle to hold on to him, her arms and legs refusing to cooperate. "It's y-you," she told him, her voice breaking. "I've never been this hot for it before."

He kissed her, a lavishly erotic plundering of her mouth that revealed how close to the edge he was. Shifting again, he gripped her by the nape and adjusted the angle of her hips.

Then he started to fuck with all the power of his muscular body.

Her abrupt climax was so violent she seized with it, her body straining into his hold. Her pussy tightened on his driving cock, then pulsed around him in greedy ripples. His feral growl increased her pleasure, the orgasm rolling through her in waves. And he didn't stop.

Possessed by his utter domination of her body, she could only cry out as he nailed her into the bed, his hips swiveling as he thrust, displaying an athletic carnal skill that pushed her too swiftly to the edge again.

"Ronan… wait…" she gasped, overwhelmed.

But he just changed his angle and tempo, finding a spot inside her that set her off like an explosion. She screamed as the orgasm burst through her, the sensation multiplying as he growled with triumph and targeted that sensitive place with his hammering drives, stroking it over and over with the heavy crest of his thick erection. He watched her, his gorgeous face flushed and glistening, eyes dark and hot with lust, learning what worked for her by gauging her responses.

It felt like hysteria. A frenzied madness. Sweat poured from them both, their bodies sliding fluidly against each other. The flex of his muscles against her, the knowledge that he was using every bit of his strength to rut into her with savage need, was the most carnal experience of her life, and watching him fuck her seared into her memory.

She was too hoarse to cry out when the next climax hit her

if the previous one ever ended at all. She trembled with the surfeit of sensation, her fingernails scraping across his skin. Ronan tensed, his gaze losing focus. Then he tossed his head back and roared, the sound of his pleasure so raw and feral her pussy tightened possessively around him. His climax was as violent as hers had been, his hips pounding his cock into her as he emptied, his neck straining against the power of his release.

His teeth ground audibly as the orgasm tore through him, but gradually, his desperate cadence began to falter, then slow. The rigid tension of his body relaxed, and he moaned her name, wrapping his arms around her before he fell panting onto his back with her tucked against his side. His chest lifted and fell beneath her cheek as he gasped for breath, his big body quivering.

They lay like that for long minutes, her arm slung around his waist and his around her shoulders. He moved away only once to toss the condom in the bedside wastebasket, and the effort clearly cost him. Then he tugged her close again. The tremors felt like aftershocks, both of them twitching until Ireland laughed.

"You know… it could be argued that it was always going to be the fuck of the century because of the delayed gratification, and now that we've wrecked ourselves, it'll never be that good again."

Ronan turned to her and pressed a kiss into her tousled hair. "Are *you* making that argument?"

"I'm just saying." Her fingertips circled his nipple, and she smiled as it hardened. "We'll have to do it again to prove them wrong."

"That's a given, *cher*." His head fell heavily into the pillow.

"Why wait?"

Raking a hand through his lion's mane, Ronan laughed

breathlessly. Then his gaze met hers in the mirror above them. She gave him a come-hither look.

Growling, he rolled over her again, and she broke into laughter, holding him off with both palms on his chest. “I’m kidding! I’m kidding!”

He snarled into the crook of her neck, and she tickled him, forcing him back until she straddled him.

“I’m going to need a minute,” she told him. “And lunch. I’m starving. You should feed me.”

Ronan sat up, and they were face to face, with her arms and legs wrapped around him. His smile made her feel a little tipsy. “Okay.”

She pressed a quick kiss to the tip of his nose and stretched toward the bedside phone. “You’re too easy, you know that. I can’t believe you can go again already.”

His hand caressed the length of her back, and she felt his lips against her skin when he replied, “It’s you.”

Closing her eyes, she enjoyed a secret smile. *Yeah, it’s you.*

Sharing a corner of the suite’s dining room table with Ronan, Ireland watched him pop a slice of the sushi roll she’d ordered into his mouth and smiled when his brows lifted in obvious enjoyment.

She gestured at him with her chopsticks. “See? Told you.”

He wiped his mouth with a napkin. “I believed you.”

Sitting cross-legged in the dining chair, she took in the sight of him. He wore only well-loved jeans, the top button undone because he’d pulled them on after the doorbell had rung. Before that, he’d been sprawled half on top of her, alternating between lush kisses and worshipful attention to her breasts. Her nipples were sweetly sore from his gentle suckling and teasing tugs of his teeth.

Ronan made her feel like a goddess. Like she could do anything, be anything. Solve anything.

"My dad takes his sushi very seriously." She took a quick drink of iced green tea. "He insisted on a sushi restaurant here at the hotel, then talked his favorite local sushi chef into making the move here. And now Chef Sato has a host of awards to his credit and has global recognition thanks to the many guests who've discovered him. My dad has an unbelievable gift for finding talent and amplifying it."

Nodding, Ronan continued to eat with an unusually closed expression. He had an appetite, which she chalked up to how hard he'd worked in bed. She'd hoped, dreamed, and fantasized that the wildness she sensed in him would be fully revealed during sex, and she was so, so glad to have been right.

She sighed. "I know you don't agree with how my family kept me in the dark about this whole situation, but once you get to know them, you'll see how great they are." She flashed him a bright smile and teased, "They raised me, and you like me, so they can't be all bad."

He reached over and took her hand, lifting it to his lips. "I adore you."

"I need you to know that I will help you fix this mess. I'm really good at what I do, and what I don't know I can learn. I'll be a helpful partner, I promise."

His nostrils flared, and he set his chopsticks down. "You're talking about Vidal."

"Of course, silly. What else? As far as I know, we don't have any other messes." She frowned. "Do we?"

"No, we do not. A bit of a locational problem for now, but

that's easy to resolve. Why would you want to 'fix' Vidal? You participated because it's expected of you."

"Well…it's always been there," she hedged.

Ronan shifted in his seat to face her. He was so incredibly beautiful sitting there in just his jeans. So open and accessible in exactly the way she'd yearned for him to be. Yet there was still so much to learn. She wanted to ask him about his scars and the meaning of his tattoo sleeve. The tribal design was a tornado of dangerously sharp objects spiraling down from the ubiquitous talons on his shoulder like layers of hell: razor blades, concertina wire, flames, and knife tips—all rendered in deep liquid black.

"You're a woman of high passions, and that's the most passionless defense you could make." His jaw tightened. "You want to save it for your father, not for you."

"What does it matter, really?" Leaning forward, she set her hand on his knee. "We'll get to work together. And I can't wait to see you in action. I expect it'll make me horny."

But he didn't smile as she expected him to. Or tease her as he so often did.

"Or do you have people who take over from here?" she asked. "Will you not be involved?"

"No, I'll personally be the one to dismantle it and sell off the parts."

Ireland blinked at him. "That can't be the only solution. There has to be a way to save it."

"I don't want to save it, and neither do you."

Confused, she shook her head. "That's not true."

"It is," he insisted. "That's been obvious to me for some time."

"What are you talking about? We never even discussed Vidal."

Impossibly, his expression became even more closed. His growing remoteness stung.

She pushed back from the table and stood. "So, you don't want to go to the trouble of fixing it. Well, I do."

He caught her hand and held it as he stood, too. "Your father owes me a large debt, Ireland. This is how he pays."

"I'll pay you! And if I don't have enough, my brother is Gideon Cross, and he'll pay you."

"Money won't buy your father out of this."

Ireland looked at his implacable, austerely gorgeous face, and her heart sank. "Explain, please."

"You need to ask him."

She tugged her hand free. "Ask someone who hasn't told me anything thus far? Ask *that* guy? Why won't *you* tell me?"

Ronan set his palms down on the tabletop. "Because it's his story to tell."

"Bullshit. That's bullshit. So, you don't care at all what I want? Or what I think about all of this?"

"I already know what you think of it, Ireland, and you're relieved, even if you don't want to admit it. You've fulfilled all of their expectations. Your conscience is clear. I'm buying you out—take the money and do what *you* want. You're free."

Shaking her head, she backed away from him. The end of Vidal would devastate her father. She was still haunted by finding him crying at his desk, struggling alone with this massive problem. Christopher couldn't know, or he would've attended today's meeting.

"Ireland." Ronan moved to follow her.

"No. Don't." Pointing a finger at him, she ordered, "Stay right there. You waited until I knew your name to fuck me, but your agenda was okay to keep hidden? Was screwing me part of your revenge? Are you going to throw that in my father's face?"

Anger tightened his mouth. "You fucked me believing I'd take the hit for your father's colossal mismanagement. Are you having regrets now? Was saving Vidal a condition to having sex with you?"

She pressed a hand between her breasts, massaging the sudden pain that pierced her. "I can't believe you just said that."

"It doesn't feel good when someone you care about insults your character, does it?"

The door to the second bedroom flew open, and Jules ran headlong into the room. Skidding to a halt, he looked at Ireland, then his brother, eyes widening as he took in their appearances.

He whistled. "You'd best get dressed, *beau-frère*. I've been keeping her daddy waiting around on you, but then he got tired of her not answering his calls and looked up where she is on some app he's got. He was marching toward the hotel when I saw him last. I had to sprint through that madness out there to get here first."

Ireland was already darting for her shoes.

"Wait a damned minute, *cher*," Ronan snapped. "We're not done talking."

She slung her duffel over her shoulder. "I heard what you had to say."

"*Maudit*, you're too old to run when your daddy doesn't like your choices!"

Thrusting her arm through the handles of her Birkin, she skirted Jules with a nod of greeting and farewell and hurried toward the door with shoes in hand. "He's not the one I'm running from, asshat."

She sensed Ronan lunging for her without seeing it. When his hand caught her biceps, she shifted to the side, tucked her elbow close, and spun, sending him stumbling back with a palm strike to the abdomen. Then she was out the door.

The ding of the service elevator set her running down the hall in the opposite direction, toward the guest elevators she'd ridden up in. She heard Ronan's door open as she turned the corner and braced herself to hear him shout her name. Instead, she heard her father.

"McCaffrey! Is my daughter in there?"

Ireland stabbed at the elevator button, then dug into her purse for her phone. She texted her mom.

I'm buying you out.

Then she texted her dad as she stepped into the elevator.

Hey, I'm at the offices. When you get back, let's work out our battle plan.

EVA HEARD THE KNOCK AT HER DOOR AND GLANCED OVER to find her husband entering her office. As she always did, she paused, arrested by the sight of him—the way Gideon moved with powerfully seductive self-assurance, how he looked in his bespoke three-piece suits, the rakish fall of dark hair framing a face so stunning every thought in her brain scattered. And those eyes, a piercing aqua blue, saw through all her protective layers to the woman she was inside.

Her lips curved in delight and welcome, even as she felt a sharp pang of guilt for her earlier thoughtless words. He responded to her joy at seeing him, his sensual mouth lifting in a warm smile.

"Hello, ace," she murmured, rocking back in her desk chair. "You're a sight for sore eyes."

"Am I now?"

"Always." She stood and ordered the office AI to opaque the glass walls separating her office from the sea of cubicles. "Come here."

His smile widened. "You know we have a meeting in five."

"We'll be there on time. I just need a minute." When he

reached her, she urged him around so her desk was behind him. "Now, half-sit on the edge so you're not so dashingly tall, please."

He gave her a quizzical look but complied.

"Now spread your legs," she said, "so I can step between them."

Moving into the space he created for her, Eva draped her arms around his neck and pressed herself into him, humming approval when his arms encircled her. She rested her cheek against his lapel and closed her eyes, savoring his warmth and scent. His hands stroked up and down her back, gentling her. The tension in her shoulders eased, and she sighed heavily. An instant later, she felt the same transformation in him, his muscular body relaxing into their embrace.

"Hmm." He nuzzled the crown of her head. "I needed this."

She offered her mouth to him, and he took it. His lips sealed over hers, and he kissed her with all the tender passion in his soul.

"I've been thinking..." she murmured between kisses. "Let's fly down to the Outer Banks after the masquerade and spend the weekend unplugged."

"Yes," he agreed with zero hesitation.

"I'll be over my period by then."

His laugh was everything she needed to shake off her cloudy mood. "Even better."

They'd somehow managed to keep their Outer Banks house a secret from the world at large. *How* was something she marveled at every time they were there. Without ever discussing it, they'd both never mentioned it in interviews. And while they'd renewed their vows there with friends and family in attendance, word of their sanctuary had never been leaked. Of course, they left the house infrequently. It was stocked with provisions before they arrived, and while they walked Lucky on the beach and surrounding streets, they very much kept to themselves.

Pulling back, she cupped his magnificent face in her hands. She loved him so much, almost beyond bearing. She wanted every single piece of him she could have, even as she acknowledged how greedy she was to want more. "Okay, we can go to the meeting now."

Gideon gave her hips a soft squeeze. They both knew there would be more to unpack later at home, but they'd learned to connect even when they were apart on an issue. Neither of them was at their best when they weren't solidly aligned. Reaching the point where they could disagree and not feel like the end was imminent had been a significant turning point for them both.

Taking her hand in his, he straightened. Fingers interlaced, they walked out together, heading to the elevator to reach the next lowest floor where Cross Industries' advertising and marketing teams were located. In short order, they entered the reserved conference room, where familiar faces greeted them with easy smiles. That was something Eva took pride in, the camaraderie they'd built with their employees over the years. Gideon could still scare the hell out of someone—and did, if warranted—but working with her had revealed his softer side. For many, the first time they'd ever seen him smile was at her.

The man leading the meeting, Mark Garrity, stood when she walked in, and they exchanged affectionate grins because they were friends. She'd started her career in New York as his assistant at an independent advertising agency, and he'd been a great boss, generously sharing his knowledge. Gideon appreciated his work and hired him, and over the years, Mark advanced up the ranks to lead Cross Industries' advertising team.

But while time had passed, Mark hardly seemed to have aged. There were a few strands of silver in the tight coils of his hair and closely cropped goatee, but his dark skin remained smoothly unlined.

Flanking him were Jeanette and Edita, the two female directors in charge of their liquor brands. They'd been with the company for over a dozen years, and Eva took pride in that longevity, too.

They all settled into their seats, with Gideon and her on one side and the team on the other.

"Before we get started," Mark began, opening his leather portfolio and pulling out a folded piece of construction paper. "I'm supposed to give you this, Eva."

Taking the makeshift card from him, she opened it to a child's drawing of three stick figures encircled with unadorned Christmas trees. Her fingers traced the crayon marks, feeling the texture of the wax raised from the thick paper beneath. In her mind's eye, she saw Janessa Garrity-Ellison bent studiously over the drawing. The little girl would tackle the task with the utmost seriousness.

The inner void Eva felt so keenly was filled to overflowing in Mark. She could see and feel it, which only made her yearning more acute.

"A budding talent!" Gideon said warmly, looking over her shoulder.

Mark beamed with pride. "Janessa drew that for you when I told her we were having a meeting today. You, me, and Gideon. When I asked her about the trees, she said they make people happy, and she wanted that for us."

"It's lovely," she managed, her voice huskier than usual. She refolded the paper and tried to regain her composure. "And a very sweet thought. Thank her for us, please."

"Of course. Now, down to business." Mark flipped open the cover of his tablet. "I have to start by saying that rebranding

Kingsman Vodka feels like coming full circle. We even have the same faces around the table, although some of us have changed which side we're sitting on."

The memory of that long-ago first meeting was still fresh in Gideon's mind, and he smiled. Even then, he'd had a robust advertising and marketing team at Cross Industries but had chosen to hire Mark's agency—and Mark in particular—to get himself in front of Eva. She'd become his obsession but wanted nothing to do with him. Those early days had been rough, and he appreciated finding the humor in them now. He'd never desired anyone or anything so fiercely—or so provocatively out of reach.

Glancing at Eva, he reached for her hand and linked their fingers.

"Now see that chemistry right there," Mark began, jerking his chin toward them, "is why it was necessary to test creative featuring you both."

Eva's grip tightened before she let go to steeple her hands together on the tabletop. "I expressly asked you to exclude us."

"I know, and initially we did, but feedback from early round testers was that your absence from the campaign was glaring." His fingertips tapped the screen of his tablet, which was mirrored on the large wall monitor. "So, we threw something together just to keep respondents focused on the options in front of them. And when I tell you this creative outperformed the rest, I mean it wasn't even close."

The mockup exploded across the wall, taking over the screen entirely. Gideon studied it, silently noting the strain in his wife's voice. A photo of him and Eva on the red carpet had been altered so that the blindingly white camera flashes of the paparazzi were now glittering stars and diamonds against an inky velvet sky. The precious gems sparkled across the vivid image and piled around a towering Kingsman vodka bottle and a handblown martini glass in the same glorious emerald hue as Eva's dress.

"Testers loved this," Mark said, "to put it mildly. The top descriptors were luxurious, top shelf, and sexy. They selected a higher price point for the product and, better still, felt the price was justified. In comparison, the other ads had descriptors like energetic, fun, and colorful."

Gideon huffed out a laugh, thinking his wife could advertise tap water and make it sexy. But when he looked at her, she wasn't smiling, and there was a furrow between her brows. She withdrew her hand from his.

Mark's mouth quirked thoughtfully from side to side. "You don't like it."

"It's a striking image," Eva said flatly. "I just don't understand why you can't use models in the same concept."

"We tested creative with models," he explained, swapping out the mockup with a rotating slideshow of other options. "And actors and musicians. But consumers know this is a Cross product and expect to see you. Dwayne Johnson is in the ads for Teremana. George Clooney is in the ads for Casamigos. It's what works."

"They are very specifically *celebrities*," she argued.

"So are both of you," Jeanette said with a smile.

"We're not," Eva retorted. "We're business owners. And as you all know, we didn't create Kingsman. We bought the brand, as we've bought hundreds of other brands. We can't be expected to be the face of everything."

Concerned by his wife's growing agitation, Gideon moved his chair imperceptibly closer to her.

Mark frowned. "Of course not. For instance, I wouldn't suggest a campaign with you and the GenTen gaming system. But we're launching an ultra-premium vodka. Lavish.

Sophisticated. Elegant. Buzzwords also used to describe you, Gideon, and your lifestyle. Consumers want the fantasy of drinking what you drink and sharing that part of your life."

"I don't want to share my life!"

Everyone froze except Gideon. He pushed smoothly back from the table and rose to address the room.

"You've given us a lot to think about," he said mildly as if ending the planned hour-long meeting after fifteen minutes was not unexpected. It was his company; no explanations were required. Concern for Eva overrode every other consideration. The discussion was triggering her; therefore, it needed to end.

Without looking at him, she stood, too, because they were always a united front. But she continued speaking. "There have to be limits to what people can take from us. I refuse to contribute to the media's fetishization of Gideon and our marriage!"

"So, we're all agreed on revising our approach to this campaign," he said, filing away Eva's response for closer examination later. "We excel at exploiting unexpected angles to boost sales. It's one of our strong suits."

Mark was on his feet, having stood when Eva did. "Yes, it is. Thank you. We had some other ideas, which I worried were a little avant-garde—a remnant of working with too-cautious brands, I'm afraid. I'll assemble a deck and get back on your schedules as soon as possible."

"Great work," Gideon assured him as he slid his arm around his wife's waist. To support her and soothe himself.

"You'll be pleased to know," Mark went on, "that the social chatter for the new ECRA+ campaign is extremely robust. The billboards featuring Ireland launched today here in the city, Philadelphia, Chicago, and Los Angeles, as well as Vancouver, Montreal, and Toronto."

“Not my favorite campaign,” Gideon said drily.

Eva snorted and bumped her shoulder into him. “Ireland looks amazing. The ads are striking and unforgettable.”

“Obviously not in our liquor wheelhouse,” Edita said with a cautious smile, “but the ads definitely worked on me as a consumer. I contacted the ECRA+ team this morning to snag a bottle of lotion.”

“What more could we ask for?” Gideon urged Eva toward the door with a hand at the small of her back. “Thank you for your hard work on both campaigns.”

“Appreciate that.” Mark shot Eva a concerned look. “We’ll regroup and do great work on the Kingsman campaign, too. And quickly. We won’t lose momentum.”

Edita and Jeanette both nodded their agreement. The two brunettes gathered their folders and notes, then pushed their chairs back to stand. Gideon walked with his wife to the elevator vestibule and pressed the call button.

“Don’t say anything,” she warned, holding Janessa’s card at her side.

His brows lifted. “You’ll be doing the talking, angel. Over dinner. For now, why don’t you take the rest of the day off. Go home and cuddle Lucky.”

“I have meetings.” She stepped before him into the car.

“Anything that can’t be canceled, I’ll manage. We’ve covered for each other many times.” The doors closed, and he cupped her face in his hands, his thumbs running lightly beneath her eyes. “Did you hide these dark circles with makeup this morning? Did you have trouble sleeping?”

“No.” When he just gave her a level look, she straightened and rolled her shoulders back. “I’m not lying. I slept like the dead. And I didn’t have dark circles this morning, so maybe I’m low on iron. I probably just need steak for dinner.”

"Done." He leaned down and kissed her forehead as the car slowed. Taking her hand, he walked adjacent to her out of the elevator. "The day's closer to the end than the beginning. I'll be home before you can miss me."

"I miss you the moment you leave my line of sight," she said tiredly.

He smiled at her, but inside he was quiet and focused. Eva was not herself. Figuring out why and handling it was his top priority because he wasn't himself without her.

Once Ireland reached the Vidal offices, she checked the family location sharing app to see where her father was. When she found that he was still at the hotel, she took a quick sink bath in his office bathroom and changed into the clothes from her overnight bag.

How swiftly things had changed. It felt almost like whiplash. Less than an hour before, she'd relished the scent of Ronan on her skin and the thought of her scent on him. Now, the only fragrance she wore was her perfume. Still, her body wouldn't let her forget how close they had become before it all went to hell. She tingled all over, especially between her legs. If he'd been who she had believed him to be—a breathtaking stranger with effortless charm and wild animal magnetism who wanted nothing but her—they'd be making love again at this very moment.

But that was never the case when it came to the men she was attracted to. She hated that she couldn't seem to learn that lesson.

Exiting Debra Sherman's office—Vidal's chief legal officer—Ireland caught sight of her father stepping out of the elevator.

"Dad," she called out, snagging his attention. He walked

hurriedly toward her, meeting her on the threshold of his executive suite.

"How do you know Ronan McCaffrey?" he asked without preamble, urging her inside and closing the door behind them.

"I don't." She sat in one of the visitors' chairs and crossed her legs. She'd changed into a teal silk set comprised of wide-legged slacks and a fitted vest, a decision she regretted now because the material was too sensual against skin with heightened sensitivity. Making love with Ronan had felt like shedding a protective layer. She was exposed now, tender, and far too vulnerable.

"You were holding his hand, Ireland. You went with him to the hotel." While he avoided being more specific, she could see the deeper question in his gaze. He may not have found her *in flagrante delicto*, but he'd seen Ronan in a very suggestive state of partial undress.

"I met him very recently. And the name he gave me was Ronan Boudreaux. So, again, I don't actually know him."

Her father moved to sit behind his desk, so she almost missed catching his flinch when she said Ronan's name. "Are you romantically involved?"

She arched a wry brow. "He wants to destroy the family business, Dad. What do you think?"

"Was he your date Friday night?"

"You're focused on the wrong thing," she deflected. "He wants Vidal because of *you*. I'm irrelevant."

And she refused to dwell on that or how she felt about it. Not now, when there was so much to be done in so little time.

Pulling off his glasses, her father tossed them onto his blotter and massaged his temples. "I've never met McCaffrey—or Boudreaux... whatever his name is—before today."

"He says you owe him a debt that money can't repay. What is he talking about?"

"Hell if I know." Her father's hands dropped to his lap. "He's a total stranger to me."

"He said it was a story you needed to tell me," she insisted.

He gestured helplessly. "I knew a Boudreaux once, a lifetime ago. It's a very common Cajun surname, but the resemblance between the two is striking. Uncanny really, so I suppose it's possible they're related. The man I knew was attractive and charming. He came from an esteemed and wealthy Southern family and used all those advantages to avoid consequences. His lack of empathy and remorse made him dangerous, and after talking with McCaffrey face to face, I can tell you they're of the same ilk. They both have soulless eyes."

She tried to reconcile the Ronan her father saw with the one she'd thought she knew. Ronan was so vital, such a vibrant and warm man. To think of him as soulless was impossible…unless she acknowledged that the man she'd spent the weekend with was merely an invention. It pained her to admit that with her dating history, it was more than possible that she just couldn't see Ronan for who he really was.

"You need to stay away from him, Ireland," her father said urgently. "That handsome exterior is hiding a rotten core. You have to trust me on that."

"Doesn't need saying," she said tonelessly, "but he owns a big chunk of Vidal, so that may not be possible."

"He doesn't own enough. I'll deal with him. Just keep your distance until I do. He's not to be trusted."

She studied him intently. "You seem very sure of someone you've just met."

"He revealed his character when he deceived you. If he has nothing to hide, why was he hiding?" Without his glasses, Chris Vidal, Sr. looked older in a way she'd never noticed before this past weekend. The lines in his handsome face appeared deeper, his mouth thinner, his eyes reflecting inner turmoil and sadness. The hits had been coming fast and hard for him, too, with her mother's engagement news and now McCaffrey's takeover attempt.

"How are you going to deal with him?" she asked.

"We need to pay off the note he's holding. Some weeks back, Brett Kline sent me a demo of a song Six-Ninths is working on. It's good, honey." His expression brightened. "Really good. It's just what we need right now."

"You're kidding."

He sat forward and put his glasses on again. "They performed at a festival this past weekend, but they'll be flying in soon to record it. We'll release the single right away and add it to a new album later."

Gripping her head in both hands, she groaned. "Please tell me you're just grasping at straws and that you haven't been banking on a new single from Six-Ninths to save the company."

"I don't understand your reaction."

"Seriously?" She gaped at him. "Six-Ninths is a one-hit wonder. They haven't been relevant in ages." When he just stared at her as if confused, she went on. "Their recent albums have barely covered their expenses. They've been mimicking midlevel rock bands for years. Their NFL playoff halftime appearance made headlines for how boring it was. Do I have to go on? Because I can."

"It only takes one song to make a comeback," he said resolutely.

"Dad." Ireland bent forward, her hair flowing almost to the floor as she rested her elbows on her knees and linked her fingers together. "I have to ask you something, and I really need you to think hard about the answer. Do you see a future for Vidal beyond you or only within the span of your lifetime?"

He scowled. "What kind of question is that? It's a family business."

"Then why do you keep making decisions that jeopardize the future of this company?"

His breath left him in a rush as if she'd knocked the wind from him. "That's not fair, Ireland. Growing a business has inherent risks."

"Yes, *managed* risks. Which should never lead to the brink of disaster not just once but twice." She held his gaze, sharp and direct. "Vidal needs you, Dad. Needs your gift for spotting and working with talent. But executive decisions are not your forte. You have to acknowledge that if you envision your grandkids working in these offices someday."

He sat motionless, his jaw taut.

"Maybe you've felt like you have to handle that end of things," she went on, "whether because you're the parent or you don't think your kids are ready for the responsibility yet. Whatever the reason, you're about to lose your shares, and I can maneuver into the majority position by acquiring Mom's and aligning with Christopher. So, will you step aside and let me fight off McCaffrey? Because if you want to keep forging ahead on your own, I'll ask Christopher to buy me out and leave you both to it."

His brows lifted. "You have to be in charge or you're leaving? That's your ultimatum?"

"No. McCaffrey wins, or we do. Those are your choices."

"You don't think I can fend off the takeover?"

She shook her head and forced herself to be brutally honest. "Not without Gideon's help, no. And I hope you don't go that route because he's got a bazillion businesses to run, and Vidal is my only focus."

His fingertips drummed restlessly into the blotter. "And Christopher agrees with you?"

"He'll have to agree, or we'll be out of business. He's too much like you. He won't be the change Vidal needs to recover and rebuild."

Her father gave her a long, studious appraisal, and then his eyes and nose began to redden. "When did you grow up?" he asked hoarsely.

Today. But she didn't say that aloud.

Pushing back from his desk, he stood and faced the windows, his fingers linking behind his back. She'd spent her lifetime seeing him in this space. She had memories from when she was so small that the heavy wood desk dwarfed her, the desktop inches above her head. She remembered hiding from Christopher in the kneehole and putting toys in the drawers for her dad to find.

Framed on the walls were photos of her father with legendary performers and music industry figures, along with magazine cover stories and articles about him. Chris Vidal, Sr. had built a sterling reputation for his unrivaled ear and history of signing talent who set trends rather than followed them. And beyond that acumen, he was widely regarded as a good man with a kind heart. She'd always been immensely proud of him and still was. Whatever flaws he might have, he was still the best father she could ever ask for.

His heavy sigh weighed on her heart. "You're right about Christopher, I'm sorry to admit. He does love the business, though. As much as I do."

She hated hearing the despondence in his voice. "We're just shuffling jobs. You can focus on the talent, and I'll handle the business."

He faced her. "I've never doubted that you're capable of

doing much more here at Vidal. But you don't love it like we do. I've struggled with that for years now, Ireland. It's why I've structured our workloads the way I have, hoping that if you're having fun, you'll stick with us. The task you want to take over is hard, heartbreaking work."

"Dad…" She tried to find the right words. "No, I don't love it to the same extent, but that doesn't mean I don't love it."

Standing, she ran her fingertips along the worn and nicked edge of the desk. "I remember when this desk used to be Pop's and all the clutter he had on it—the guitar strings and picks, the levers and valves, the scraps of piano wire. I remember Mom and Nana working together to turn this old storage space into offices while Christopher and I built forts out of the empty boxes."

Her father's mouth quirked with a melancholy smile.

"I love my family," she went on, "not entities or things. You've got to believe me when I tell you I'll fight harder for Vidal because *you* love it. More than I ever would for myself."

"I don't want you fighting on my behalf. I don't want you to have to fix my mistakes." Rounding the desk, her father gripped her shoulders and held her gaze. "You should be doing what you love."

"Oh, I'll love waging this war," she told him with a sharp-edged smile. "But you decide. Right now. Because if this is the route we're taking, I have homework for you to get started on."

Settled in the sitting area of his office, Gideon reexamined the half dozen notes in protective plastic sleeves strewn across the coffee table. It had been a couple of years since he'd last studied them at length, but their familiarity made them no less disturbing.

Around him, Raúl Huerta, Victor Reyes, Chase Kwon, and Angus McLeod—the top-level supervisors of his security team—waited quietly. Only Angus was dressed casually in jeans and a gray Henley. The other men wore black suits tailored to hide their sidearms.

The notes were disturbing at first glance before a single word was read. Photos of him and Eva, haphazardly cut out of magazines, had been disfigured by a red Sharpie and razor slashes. Individual letters had been pasted into words that formed malevolent rhymes.

Four blind eyes. Enucleated twice.
How will you run? Can't wait for
the fun.

Twinkle, twinkle—I'm not far.
Know exactly where you are.
Up above the world so high,
You'll be in a gutter when you die.

Blood is red,
Your eyes are blue.
Will she cry real tears
when I eviscerate you?

The last had been found under the Bentayga's windshield wiper. The others had been left with the reception staff at various Cross Industries-owned businesses around the city and even with the lobby staff at the penthouse. All were delivered by couriers who had no knowledge of what they were delivering, and no fingerprints or genetic material was left behind to trace who the author was.

"The last arrived—what…two years ago?" he asked tensely, his fury a deep chill inside him.

"Just about," Raúl confirmed, his dark eyes raking over the items on the coffee table.

"Could be he's incarcerated," Victor offered. "Or he self-destructed."

"You're sure it's a man?" Gideon asked, studying the faces around him.

"More than likely, lad," Angus said, the music of Scots threaded through his voice. "Removing the eyes. Disemboweling. The Glasgow smiles carved into the photos. All knife injuries. Not typically a woman's choice of weapon, especially against a man of your size and strength."

Nodding, Gideon straightened. "Since it's been some time since the last contact, could we dial back security?"

"I wouldn't recommend it," Chase interjected. "Why take the risk?"

He was the most recent addition to the team, having joined them several years before. He'd worked his way up to swing shift supervisor, and his relative youth brought a different energy to the team.

Gideon explained. "You're all doing exactly what you should, but the heightened security is making Eva feel anxious, not secure."

"Since when?" Victor asked, frowning.

"I don't know. But it's become an issue."

"It's a risk to lower our guard," Chase repeated. "This guy's smart. His language is educated. He may be waiting for you to feel comfortable enough to give him an opening."

"I can talk to my daughter," Victor offered. "Help her see the necessity of it."

Gideon raked a hand through his hair. "We'll be discussing it this evening. If I need reinforcement afterward, I'll let you know. In the meantime, let's find a way to keep her secure without making her feel like she's constantly under threat."

"But you are," Raúl said frankly. "You have round-the-clock security because there are threats, even beyond this wacko."

And that was the problem Gideon didn't know how to fix. He'd made enemies. His father had made enemies. Plus, there were those who fixated on him and his wife for reasons ranging from infatuation to ransom. Being so prominently in the public eye made them targets. "I don't know the solution," he admitted grimly. "But we need one. Eva isn't feeling safe, and that's unacceptable. Can we make security a little less visible to her without compromising it?"

His phone line beeped on his desk, then his assistant Scott's voice came through the speaker. "Ms. Vidal is here."

Gideon turned his head to look at the reception area outside his office and saw his sister standing by Scott's station. Pulling his pocket watch from his vest, he realized Ireland was right on time for their six o'clock meeting. He paused to admire the photo of his wife inside the case, then snapped it shut.

When Ireland had called to see if he could fit her in, he'd suggested they meet at the penthouse. But it was business, she said, and she didn't want to bring that home with them. Since she also expected to work late, they'd agreed to meet after hours. He hadn't anticipated spending so much time reviewing the damned notes. He'd somehow managed to put from his mind how deeply unsettling they were.

"We'll work on it," Angus said, standing. There was significantly more silver than red in his hair these days and more lines on his craggy face, but his biceps strained against his sleeves, and he still radiated vitality and strength.

"Thank you."

They all stood. Raúl gathered up the notes and slid them into a file. Then, they moved in unison toward the door. Ireland watched them through the glass, admiring how the four men carried themselves. Deadly predators, all of them. Casual attire couldn't disguise Angus McLeod's lethality. And Chase Kwon's boyishly youthful features and flashing smile weren't enough to distract from the trained economy with which he moved.

They filed out of her brother's office, each giving her a fond smile.

She stopped Angus before he walked away. "I was going to call you later," she murmured. "There's someone I'd like to know everything about. No detail is too small."

"Of course. Who is it?"

"I'll text you." She glanced at where her brother waited, holding open the glass door for her. "Please keep this between us. And thank you!"

"Havnae done anything yet, lass." He winked before continuing on, and she thought, not for the first time, that he was undeniably sexy for a man in his mid-sixties.

Taking a deep breath, Ireland approached her brother with a sunny smile. "Thanks for fitting me into your day—or evening, as the case may be."

"I'm always available to you." He let the door swing shut behind them and gestured toward the sitting area. "What do you need?"

Ireland studied her brother as he settled into the sofa across from her. His suit jacket hung on a coatrack behind his desk. His waistcoat hugged his lean torso like a second skin, while platinum cufflinks, matching tie clip, and the fob of his pocket watch caught the light at random intervals. Unlike Ronan, Gideon was thoroughly comfortable in his urbanity. She couldn't ever remember seeing her brother with his sleeves rolled up or his tie loosened.

She was like Ronan in that way. Her style was a little edgy and unorthodox—except when she was shopping with her family in mind. And while Gideon's confidence was dynamic and aggressive, Ronan's was smoothly nonchalant. It was a polished facade that hid a man whose morals were as gray as his eyes.

"I feel like an idiot asking this," she began, "but I don't know the extent of my assets. I know I own a bit of Cross Industries shares—thank you very much for gifting me some on my birthdays—and I have a ten percent share of Vidal, but I don't know how much that's all worth."

"I'm happy to tell you." He moved to stand.

"Wait. I just want to know if I've got what I need to buy Mom's fifteen percent stake in Vidal."

Gideon resettled into the sofa. "You want to take a controlling interest in Vidal?"

She nodded, having decided before she arrived that she wouldn't say anything about McCaffrey Holdings, which would also hold a twenty-five-percent stake in the company if the loan defaulted and they exercised their lien on her father's shares.

"The shareholder agreement gives your father right of first refusal," he noted. "So, he declined to buy them. That surprises me."

Ireland hadn't known that, but her father must have. But he hadn't brought it up or used it to get in her way. "He's ready to focus on the creative side exclusively," she lied. "And Mom wants me to have her shares. She won't sell to Christopher."

Her brother winced. "Ouch."

"Tell me about it," she muttered, digging into her purse. Her phone screen was lit up with another incoming call from Ronan and the sight of his face twisted her into knots. She'd had to silence her notifications earlier because of his efforts to reach her. "I'm not looking forward to explaining what I've done, but I'll handle it as soon as everything's finalized. I'm hoping the sale can be done quickly because I won't be able to keep it under wraps long."

"Sales of private shares can be done at any time, barring any conflict with the shareholder agreement."

"Great." Reaching across the table, she held a folded piece of paper out to him. "This is the amount I'd need to buy Mom out. Do I have it?"

Accepting the paper, he sat back and opened it. "I'd have to run the numbers to confirm—"

"I'm not asking you to verify the amount. Just tell me if I can afford it."

His brows shot up. "Well."

"Don't take it like that. I'm just saying I didn't graduate summa cum laude because of my good looks. I know how to run a debit-to-equity ratio calculation." Of course, she'd fudged the numbers because Vidal was so upside down, and she wanted to pay her mother fairly, more so because McCaffrey Holdings' most recent offer had been so generous.

"I am going to need your help," she went on. "You're a mastermind and I'd be stupid not to tap your experience even if I do really hate adding to your workload. So let me handle the stuff I can. There will be plenty for you to do when the time comes."

His mouth quirked in a half smile. "Okay. Yes, you can afford it. You have many times that amount in your cash reserves. You won't have to sell off anything. You can assume control as soon as the wire transfer is completed and you have a signed shareholder agreement."

Her sigh of relief deflated most of the tension in her body. "So, first thing in the morning. Great. Could I conceivably have enough to pay off Vidal's debt?"

His amusement sharpened into calculation. "Not knowing how much we're talking about, I can't say. But why would you want to do that?"

"Oh, you know." She waved a careless hand as if the company wasn't failing due to its debt. "Having a clean slate when I get started."

"Don't do it. Once you start pouring your personal wealth into a company, you're both in trouble. Buy the shares, get the company in a position to sustain itself, then make it profitable. If it fails—and I'm not doubting your ability, just observing that the music industry is facing extreme challenges—you're going to be just fine."

Staring at him, she chewed on her inner lip and debated arguing. Paying Ronan off and getting him out of her life was such an attractive possibility that she ached to make it reality. If she never saw or heard from him again, she'd never risk doing something stupid.

It was the height of irony that her feelings for every other man she'd been with had turned on and off as easily as flipping a light switch. But Ronan, the gravest threat yet, was proving harder for her to shake off. All afternoon, she'd been fighting the urge to call him and attempt to change his mind somehow.

You could have me if you'd just pick me over Vidal! But he'd already made his choice, and he'd done so when she'd been sitting right in front of him, still warm and pliant from sharing his bed.

In the end, she had to take Gideon's advice because he was right, and she knew it. If she couldn't save Vidal without transfusing her own money into it, then it couldn't be saved, and she had to accept that. All she could commit to was trying her best.

"You're right," she agreed. "Thanks for keeping me straight."

Her brother's smile was so warm it thawed some of the chill left by Ronan's betrayal. "I'm proud of you for taking this step. It's a big deal to take control and bigger yet that you want to."

Ireland smiled back, feeling a little more settled. Yes, circumstances had forced her hand, but she was making a major shift in her life no matter the reason.

"Do you want me to schedule the wire transfer?" he asked.

Gathering up her purse, she stood. "I feel bad asking you to do that. It's way beneath your pay grade."

Her brother stood, too. "It's not a problem."

"Thank you." She rounded the coffee table. "Knowing that's handled without me screwing up an account number or something is a relief, and I appreciate it."

He draped an arm around her shoulders and pulled her into a side hug. "I'm about done for the day. Want a lift home?"

"No, thanks. I'm going back to the office for a bit. Lots to get done before tomorrow morning."

Gideon pressed a kiss to her forehead. "I'll have Raúl take you back."

She rolled her eyes. "Fine. But only because you won't let me say no."

"Don't work too late, either," he called after her as she pushed through his office door.

"Hey." She stopped on the threshold. There was a reason her brother was at work late after Eva had already left. His competitive drive was fierce, and closing deals satisfied it. "Think you could use a warehouse in Queens?"

He gave her a thoughtful look. "Possibly."

"There's a family clothing business using the building now,

but you could move them to another of your properties that would suit them better. They're getting forced out, so if you went in with an offer to relocate them, I'm sure you'd be more attractive. I figure if someone else wants it, there has to be potential."

"Where did you get your information?"

She gave an offhanded shrug and smiled inwardly at the bright acquisitiveness in his gaze. "I overheard it in a bar. The guy was an asshole, so I'm happy to foil his plans. You'd have to move fast, though. Sounded like he almost had it in the bag."

His smile was sharply amused. "Thanks for the tip."

"Anytime, bro." Ireland whistled on the way to the elevator.

GIDEON ATE HIS DINNER AS QUIETLY AS POSSIBLE IN THE wingback chair beside the sofa where his wife lay sleeping. Eva had fallen asleep with the television on, a throw blanket pulled over her bare legs, both hands tucked beneath her chin as she slept on her side. Her face was scrubbed clean—he could see the smattering of freckles on her nose—and her voluptuous figure was draped in one of his t-shirts.

Lucky sat at his feet, hoping for a bite of the steak he'd cut into pieces in the kitchen to keep the noise down, but there was a circular imprint in the blanket by Eva's tummy that told him the beagle had previously been curled up with his mom.

Being the early riser in their marriage, Gideon spent time every morning just watching over Eva as she dreamed. It was a privilege he never took for granted, the joy of watching her eyes blink open and then focus on him. There had been a time when having someone share his life seemed impossible. He'd never dwelled on being alone, but he had been. Intrinsically so.

But the moment he'd first spotted Eva outside the Crossfire Building, he'd felt a deep, almost primordial recognition. She was a stranger then, but he somehow knew that she carried the missing pieces of his heart and soul inside her. He would never admit to being superstitious, even though he required a specific pen to sign his name, but he believed Eva had been his from time immemorial and would always be his. He'd learned to trust that feeling, to believe that nothing could separate them. The fears he'd once harbored about losing her had been put to rest long ago… It was irrational to have those fears again now.

He set the plate on the floor, and Lucky made short work of the remaining chunks of steak, his tail wagging with joy.

Gideon clasped his hands behind his head and leaned back in the chair.

Not that Eva would ever leave him by choice. But reviewing the ominous notes had reminded him that there were those who would take Eva from him, given the chance. His wife was his only vulnerability, and he couldn't hide that when he looked at her or spoke about her.

How could he have grown complacent about the risks? He, of all people, knew how dangerous their enemies were. Once it had been made irrefutably clear that Eva's safety could only be assured if her stalker and rapist were dead, Gideon had planned and carried out Nathan Barker's execution himself.

Watching her now, he accepted that easing back on their security wasn't an option, especially when the men he entrusted with their lives didn't recommend it. He and Eva would just have to talk it out. His wife was a reasonable woman; she would see the necessity of it and understand that while danger was ever present, it was being managed, and her safety was assured.

Gideon heard her breathing change and watched her twitch as consciousness returned to her.

A moment later, she blinked rapidly, then smiled sleepily at him. "Hey, baby. I didn't hear you come in."

"Lucky knew you were sleeping and stayed quiet, didn't you, boy?" He rewarded him with a quick rubdown.

Eva yawned, her back arching as she stretched. "What time is it?"

"Almost eight."

"You got home late. Did taking over my meetings bog you down?"

He shook his head. "I met with Ireland after hours."

"Did you?" Her smile was like the sun.

He was so relieved to see her genuinely happy that he decided to delay the discussions about their security and Ireland's power move. Eva's voice had been in the forefront of his mind while he smiled through Ireland's excitement, knowing his wife would caution him against being heavy-handed. But he didn't see the harm in digging a little deeper into the fiscal fitness of Vidal Records, and so he would.

Eva sat up, her blond hair a sexy tousled mess. She took him in, noting he wore only black silk pajama pants. His hair was still damp from the brief shower he'd taken before seeing to dinner. "I was going to cook that steak for you."

"It's the thought that counts." He stood to go into the kitchen. "Want anything?"

"I'm good. God, I'm tired. As soon as I suck you off, I'm passing out."

Gideon paused midstep, his pulse accelerating. "Come again?"

Her slumberous eyes held wicked amusement. "Okay, okay. I'll suck you off twice if you insist. I've been thinking about it since we took that moment for a hug. I wanted to drop to my knees, unzip you, and make you come in my mouth. You know I love it when I open your fly to get to your delicious cock, but you're otherwise dressed from head to toe. The idea that if someone saw you from behind, they'd never know what I was doing to you."

Giving up any idea of cleaning up after himself, Gideon set his plate on the kitchen island and pivoted back to the living room. They'd discovered a new kink together early in their relationship: the fantasy of exhibitionism drove them both wild. Their reasons were primitive. He wanted to mark her, own her, possess her, while she loved being claimed by him, dominated by his desires, used for his pleasure—and they wanted everyone to know. That his wife often visualized sex with an audience was even more exciting than anything he could dream up.

He'd found ways to indulge their shared hunger without risk of exposure: two-way mirrors, smoked glass, behind closed doors in crowded spaces. As much as the fantasy excited them, the reality was that he treasured his wife too much to ever expose her vulnerability and passion to anyone.

He scooped Eva up from the couch, and she shrieked with laughter as he carried her down the hallway to their bedroom.

"Keep laughing, and you might find yourself missing work tomorrow, too," he warned because his wife's period never stopped them from exploring inventive ways to pleasure each other.

"I'm already missing work tomorrow." She wrapped her arms around his neck and kissed his cheek. "It's Aunt Katherine's birthday."

There was no hitch in his stride, but her words exploded like a bomb in his mind. Katherine was her mother's twin, so it was Lauren's birthday, too. Lauren, the woman he'd known by the alias "Monica," whose face was so like Eva's he could envision how his wife would look at the same age. Lauren, who'd been murdered on the red carpet in front of her daughter and husband, with her security detail and Gideon's nearby.

Maybe Eva's recent moodiness was tied to the date. Had he missed signs in previous years? How was that possible when every nuance of her emotions resonated so empathically inside him?

Entering the bedroom, he planted a knee on the bed, then the other, setting Eva down gently. Her arms stayed linked around his neck, keeping him with her. She took his mouth, her tongue stroking along his. Her soft moan of enjoyment hardened his dick, and he sank into her embrace.

Everything he needed was in his arms. Tomorrow, they'd work on making her feel safe there.

"Can I just say how terribly disappointed I am that Mr. Smooth & Sexy turned out to be an epic jerk?"

Alina panted as she helped Ireland move the heavy wood desk into its new location. Paint fumes made labored breathing even more difficult despite the open windows but Metallica promising vengeance through the room's built-in speakers kept them motivated.

Setting the desk down with a thud, Ireland blew a sharp breath to get a rogue piece of hair unstuck from her eyelashes. "You can, but it won't change anything. You'll still be disappointed, and he'll still be an epic jerk."

"I mean, the way he looked at you… It made me melt," Alina said. "Not just because he was obviously hot for you but because he was so gentle with you, too. Was he tender in bed?"

"No." The memories Ireland wished she could avoid flooded her mind, and she abruptly overheated for a different reason than moving furniture around. "Though not for lack of trying," she conceded. "I was too impatient."

And she was a woman who usually needed heavy petting and her own fingers on her clit to orgasm during sex. But Ronan's desire, confidence, and searing sensuality were perfect foreplay for her. He turned her on just breathing.

Alina's mouth twisted with regret. "Gorgeous, sexy, well-hung. Of course he's an asshole."

Ireland stood back and studied the desk's new placement against the newly painted wall. While she knew it was necessary to take over both her father's office and her grandfather's desk to solidify her new position from the get-go, the reality of it weighed as heavy as grief. She'd called Alina, crying, worrying that she was doing everything wrong already and would only make things worse.

And Alina had come through as always, showing up with Chinese takeout, a can of pale blue paint she said matched Ireland's eyes, and a huge tote bag carrying drop cloths, paint brushes, rollers and a pan, along with a framed photo of the two of them, and some tchotchkes.

Gotta make the space your own, she'd said.

In short order, they'd painted the wall at one end of the room, then decided that rather than the desk being the first thing visitors saw when they entered her new office, they'd move it further in and shift it ninety degrees. Except for the desks, everything from her old office had been relocated to the new one, and all of her dad's stuff now occupied her former space.

While Ireland expected the transition to be rough on her dad for a bit, she thought it'd be good for him to use her glass desk. His job would be a lot lighter now and expressing that visually could help solidify that for him and the rest of the Vidal team.

The phone rang, and she spun, searching for and finding it on the floor where the desk had previously been. "Shit. Did we check if there's a phone jack on this side of the room?"

"Uh… Didn't think about that."

Ireland hurried over and grabbed the receiver, noting that the call was coming from the security desk downstairs. "Hey, Jimmy."

"McCaffrey's on his way up."

She froze. "Wait! What?"

"I told him you weren't here, but he said he'd see for himself. He's on the permanent list so I couldn't stop him."

"How is he—?" But she realized Jules or Claudette must have seen to that detail while they were here. Or else it was routine for shareholders to be on the list. When she and Ronan had stopped by together that morning, he'd followed her up to the offices much quicker than most visitors.

"Damn." She hated the little—okay, big—thrill she felt because Ronan was trying so hard to get to her.

"He's real pissed, Ireland. Want me to come up?"

The prickle of awareness between her shoulder blades told her it was already too late. She turned slowly around. "No, that's okay," she said, her gaze locking with one of tumultuous gray. "I can handle him. Thanks."

Those stormy eyes were narrowed on her as she reached down and dropped the receiver into its cradle. Ronan filled the threshold of her dad's—*her*—office. He was wearing a blend of the day's outfits: the dress shirt from the morning paired with the jeans he'd pulled on for lunch. Of course, the collar was open, and the sleeves rolled up. Of course, his hair was a luscious, luxuriant mane. Of course, he was gorgeous and roguishly sexy and everything she hadn't known she needed.

The sight of him sparked fierce joy, desire, and anger in equal measure. She was now intimately familiar with his leanly muscular body. As badly as she'd craved him before, the hunger was worse now that she knew what sex with him was like.

"You know," Alina began, coming to stand beside her with militantly crossed arms, "I was really pulling for you, Ronan. I thought maybe you had something more to offer than a pretty face, but you're just another idiot who's too stupid to realize you landed a goddess."

"Not true." Ronan's voice was clipped with fury. "I realized what I had in front of me from the first. For no other reason would I have gotten myself into this *misère*."

Alina made a little *aww* sound and shot a questioning glance at Ireland.

Ireland scowled and flipped him the bird.

"Very mature," he shot back. "Equal to avoiding my calls all day."

"I don't want to talk to you."

"Tough." He glanced at her father's name plate on the wall outside the door, which she hadn't yet swapped out. His jaw tightened. "What are you doing, *cher?* Do you even know?"

"Fuck you. You don't get to come in here and tell me I'm incapable."

"That isn't at all what I said." His tone was too controlled, his temper honing the edge of his drawl. "You're choosing something you don't care for over someone you do. Why?"

She stood silently for a long minute, her jaw clenched. "Did you really think I'd choose you over my family?"

"I thought you'd choose freedom over the cage, but you're too used to the leash."

She inhaled through the pain his words inflicted, her nostrils flaring. Alina reached over and took her hand.

"Just proves you don't know me as well as you think." Squeezing Alina's hand, she released her. "Excuse us for a minute, Ali."

"Are you sure?" her best friend asked skeptically.

Ronan answered. "There's no place safer for her than with me."

Ireland stalked up to him. "Get out of the way."

He stepped aside and swept his arm outward with mocking gallantry. She stomped barefoot across the hall to her former office and spun to face him as he closed the door behind them.

"Okay." She gestured impatiently with her hands. "Say whatever you need to get off your chest, then leave me in peace."

Ronan's intense focus unnerved her as he approached, stopping mere inches away. The scent of him enveloped and irrationally soothed her. "I apologize for the hurt and anger you're feeling now. My involvement with Vidal was years in the making by the time we met, so pissing you off was inevitable. But I've hurt you, too, and I'm sorry for it, Ireland."

She bit her lower lip to keep it from trembling. She wanted to yell that she didn't care and that he didn't have the power to wound her. But she couldn't form the words. "You told me you wouldn't hurt me. And you could've avoided doing so by walking away from me at Jazzie's or asking me to leave your table."

The regret on his face affected her more than she cared to admit. "Neither of those things were possible until I knew what you were up to. Once it became clear that you truly didn't know who I was, it was too late—I couldn't stay away from you."

"You didn't seem to have a problem staying away last night."

"Does that still sting, *cher?*" The look in his eyes made her throat tight. "It cost me more than you know. And today has also been rough for me. Having you in my bed and then losing you immediately after... Not being able to reach you, to hear your voice, to explain—"

She stumbled back when he reached for her. "Don't touch me. Your apology doesn't change anything. You want me to choose you over Vidal, but you've chosen Vidal over me."

"Neither of us is choosing this fucking company! We're both

taking care of our families, nothing more. And I refuse to allow them to come between us!"

Ireland was astonished by his vehemence…and stirred by his passion. "You can't think we could still be together after this."

His gray gaze held a dangerous fire. "Why didn't you answer my calls?"

"I told you. I didn't want to talk to you."

"Why not answer and tell me that?" His words came clipped and fast. "Why can't I touch you?"

"Because it's business now. You need to keep a professional distance."

"*Tête dur!* This is as personal as it gets. You forget I've seen when someone's pushed you too far. You want to be eye to eye when you tell a man he's nothing to you." Ronan spread his arms wide. "Well, here I am. Tell me we're done, and you never want to see me again. Tell me you haven't been remembering all day how it feels to have my cock inside you, my lips on yours, my sweat on your skin. Tell me you never want my hands on you again."

"Fuck off. You're the one who ruined everything!" Blinking through bitter tears, Ireland turned her back to him and walked to the window, her arms wrapped around herself. The day felt endless. She was so tired. Enough of this. *Enough.*

"Say it, Ireland, because I can't. Touching you is all I want to do."

She sensed him following her, coming so close that she felt his warmth. She heard his slow, deep inhale and knew he was breathing her in, scenting her like a lion would its mate.

"Did you ask your father about me?" he murmured, so near that his breath stirred the strands of her hair.

Her reply was equally hushed. "He says you two met for the first time today. That you're a stranger. Is he lying?"

There was a long pause.

"Answer me!" she demanded, turning to face him and brushing against him in the process.

They both froze. His hands clenched as if he fought the need to reach for her.

She longed so deeply to feel his heat and strength. The desire remained unrelenting. "Is my father lying to me, Ronan?"

"*Non*," he bit out between clenched teeth. "But he's not being truthful, either."

"That makes zero fucking sense. You need to stop playing games and tell me everything."

"Did you make the same demand of your father?" His tongue slid along his full lower lip, his gaze intent on her mouth. "I won't spare your father the duty of telling you the truth."

"*Why?* Why not explain this vendetta so I understand why it's so damned important to you?"

More important than me.

His frustrated growl rumbled between them. "Your father is using you against me, don't you see that? He's put you in front of him as a shield, forcing me to get through you to reach him."

Ireland cursed under her breath and skirted him, intent on leaving, but he followed, his palm slapping flat against the door above her head so she couldn't open it.

"Don't make me hurt you," she warned, her hand on the knob.

"Too late."

Facing him, she pressed herself flat against the door, but it was a futile effort to evade him. His other hand lifted to join the first, caging her in with his sinfully sexy body.

"You can't turn me against my father," she told him, "and Vidal isn't only his. It's mine and my brother's, too. You'll eventually return to where you came from and forget us, but family is forever."

He rested his forehead against hers. Even that chaste contact was too much, her body shivering. The attraction was inexplicable. Irresistible.

"I'm nothing but hunger and need." He nuzzled her temple, his deepening accent another layer of persuasion. "I have me an *envie* for you, *cher*, and it's eating me alive. I need to taste you, touch you everywhere...until I know your body as well as my own. Tell me how I can have you."

Squeezing her eyes shut, Ireland fought his relentless seduction and the silent demand for her surrender that radiated from him.

"You and I," he went on, his voice hushed, "we're different people with each other than we are with everyone else. You're burying the Ireland I know to be the daughter and sister your family knows. They can have that side of you. I just want the part of you that's mine."

She was surrounded by him, by his scent, his lust. He made it hard to think, to endure.

"I won't expect you to go easy on me," he murmured, "just because I've made you come until you beg me to stop. What we do to each other outside of business hours is for us alone. They can't have all of us, *cher*. We've already given pieces of ourselves to each other that we can't take back."

"It doesn't work that way, Ronan." But her body didn't care that they stood on opposing sides of a battle line. She yearned. Passionately. Despite everything.

"Who says it can't?" His lips brushed hers in a feather-light kiss. "Are you afraid you won't be able to fight for Vidal if you're sharing my bed? Am I getting under your skin? Or is it that you know this company is lost already, and denying me is your only avenue to revenge?"

She shoved him away, needing air not scented of him. "You haven't even considered the possibility that I'll win. Screwing me excites you when it's part of a larger victory. Will you still have a hard-on for me after I've ruined all of your plans?"

Ireland reached for the doorknob, but he stayed her by gripping her biceps. His gaze was bright and hot as he stared down at her.

"Wanting you and wanting your father to suffer are two completely unrelated things for me," he said tersely, his color high. "Time will prove the truth of that, and I can wait. Until then, remember what I told you: anytime, anyplace. No explanations or expectations. Call me, and my body is yours to use at will."

Yanking the door open, she glared at him over her shoulder. "Please hold your breath until that call comes."

She marched back to her new office, her teeth grinding as Ronan's taunting laughter followed her.

It was still dark when Eva woke, but the rising sun wasn't far off. Turning her head on the pillow, she found Gideon still asleep, a rare occurrence. She studied him, her sigh of contentment too quiet to wake him or Lucky, who slept flat on his back by Gideon's calf. The top sheet and light coverlet were tangled around her husband's lean waist, and with one arm draped over the top of his head, his magnificent chest was fully revealed to her gaze.

At any other time, she'd reach for him, running her hands

and mouth over him until he came to vibrant life in her arms. But not today.

She slipped out of bed, placing a finger across her lips when Lucky flipped onto his belly to watch her. She rubbed the top of his head before heading into her closet to gather her clothes for the day, then she went to one of the guestrooms to shower.

Her hair and makeup took the most time. It had taken hours of examining photographs of her mother—and a lot of help from Cary—to get Monica Stanton's look right. She was grateful that she could go through the process in utter quiet and alone, allowing herself the time and grace to experience the chaotic range of emotions that always assailed her on visitation days.

When she was transformed, she grabbed her purse and the gift bag she'd left in the foyer and silently left the penthouse. She took their private elevator to the garage, where she requested their Aston Martin DB12. Taking off without security was a stupid thrill, but she felt rebellious enough to enjoy it.

Truth was, it was awkward when her dad drove her, knowing that his trained observation skills didn't miss how she styled herself into a likeness of her mother, the love of his life. She knew it was hard for him to wait in the car for the hours she was there, knowing that the twin of the woman he'd adored was so close, yet he'd never get to meet her. Katherine feared men with such vehemence that she was never exposed to them at all; her caregivers and doctors were all women.

The distance to the exclusive residential treatment center in Dutchess County was less than two hours, and Eva eagerly anticipated the rare opportunity to slide into the driver's seat. Commuting had been a daily necessity when she'd lived in San Diego, but she'd dreaded driving then due to the heavy SoCal traffic. Years of being chauffeured everywhere had given her a new perspective on the underappreciated freedom of getting yourself where you wanted to go.

The sun lit the sky when she pulled out of the parking garage onto 5th Ave. Manhattan was already thrumming with activity despite the early hour. Pedestrians hurried along the sidewalks as cabs weaved between livery cars and private vehicles sporting rideshare app stickers. There were dogs of various sizes and breeds every few feet, their owners taking them out before heading to work for the day.

Her love affair with New York had matured differently from her love for Gideon, which remained fresh and new because they continued to learn and grow together. Some of the things she'd once found romantic about the city were less delightful now, but the love remained, perhaps more solid because she acknowledged the flaws she'd once glossed over.

Turning up the volume on Sabrina Carpenter's "Bed Chem," she settled into the thrill of driving the DB12. The powerful car reminded her of Gideon—sleek, sexy, and exhilarating.

As if she'd thought him up, an incoming call interrupted the music.

Hitting the phone button on the steering wheel, she answered, "Good morning, ace."

"Maybe for you. I woke up without my wife. Where are you?"

The question was unnecessary; he knew where she was. He could check the location sharing app or the tracking signal from the car and had probably done both after realizing she'd left on her own. But he wanted her to tell him, and so she did. "Merging into Highway 1."

His heavy sigh was like a shout because she knew it meant he was frustrated, likely irritated, but was restraining himself from saying so. "I had Raúl scheduled to drive you."

Of course he had. Gideon Cross never missed a trick. He would've known and anticipated sparing her and her father the discomfort of visiting Katherine together. There were countless reasons she loved her husband more with every passing moment, but his thoughtfulness ranked at the top of the list.

"I wanted to drive." Eva checked her blind spot, speeding up to change lanes in front of an eighteen-wheeler. "And whether it's my dad or Raúl, it's distracting knowing someone's just sitting around waiting for me. I wanted to spend time with Katherine without looking at the clock."

"Then I would've driven with you. I could've gotten some work done in peace."

Her heart skipped a beat. How lucky she was to have him. He had the weight of the world on his shoulders most days but was always willing to set it aside for her, even if he suffered for it later. "That would've set you back days in your schedule, and we're heading to the beach house this weekend. I want you to relax, knowing that you won't be buried in work when we get home."

"Angel…" He paused. "I want you to feel free to do whatever you want. But…"

"…but I can't do any of it alone," she finished.

His pause before answering revealed the care he was taking to choose his words. "You have to think of the security team as a second set of eyes, freeing you to focus on whatever makes you happy. We don't have to be vigilant when they're with us."

She wanted to tell him that their security wasn't a problem, the *need* for it was, but how could she? She would never change who he was, and she loved their life together. The risks were inherent, and she'd accepted them when she accepted his marriage proposal. She just hadn't factored in the true cost of being hunted relentlessly, and she had only herself to blame for that.

"I understand," she said, because that was easiest. "I'm sorry I'm making you worry."

"I'm sorry you're feeling hemmed in. I'm working on a fix for that but keeping you safe is of paramount concern to me and always will be."

An idiot merged into the lane in front of her, then immediately slowed down. Cursing silently, she slid into the next lane and drove around them. "I want you safe, too, so I get where you're coming from."

"Let's not discuss this on the phone, especially while you're driving. Please be careful. Come home safe, and we'll discuss it then."

"Okay, baby. I love you madly. I didn't mean to upset you, although I knew you wouldn't be happy with me just taking off."

His rueful laugh gave her more than a twinge of guilt. "I'm always happy with you. I love you, too, angel mine."

They ended the call, and Eva finished the drive in relative peace, although the concern in Gideon's voice haunted her thoughts. Just a few weeks ago, she'd been content. Then, a random chat with a stranger in her doctor's waiting room and the routine updating of her medical chart had upended everything.

- *Total number of pregnancies: 2*
- *Number of living children: 0*
- *Pregnancy outcomes/deliveries – Miscarriages: 2*

And an unexpected question that hit her hard:

- *Are you planning to get pregnant in the next year?*

She hadn't known that a medical questionnaire could traumatize her. How had the twelve years of her marriage just flown by? She'd focused on spending a lifetime with Gideon and how many years they would share. But some milestones had expiration dates, and being confronted with that reality on a standardized form suddenly made that achingly clear.

Eva pulled into the familiar long driveway dappled by a canopy of stately old trees flanking each side. The serene drive to the exclusive mental health facility where she'd moved her Aunt Katherine after her mother's death was her last chance to fortify herself for the hours ahead.

A former mansion of the Gilded Age, the main building still contained many of the trappings of luxurious wealth. Expansive rooms were warmed by fireplaces, framed by elaborate molding and cornices, and filled with elegant furnishings. Cottages were spaced out across the sixty acres of the property, each serving as a private residence for a patient.

Katherine had several full-time staff members looking after her because of her childlike emotional state. She'd locked away her trauma in some dark corner of her mind and couldn't remember it, but certain situations could trigger her, so she was insulated from any possible cause of stress. Even the shows and films she watched and the books she read were vetted to ensure no violence was depicted.

Parking in the circular drive, Eva got out of the car and retrieved the gift bag from the backseat. She was momentarily startled to catch her mother's reflection in the car's window, then remembered herself. That quick shock was fortuitous when the front door opened, and Katherine stepped out to greet her because she was more prepared for the blow of seeing the mirror image of her late mother, which hit her with the same brutality every time.

"You're early today," Katherine said as Eva ascended the two wide, shallow steps to her. She threw her arms wide in welcome. "Happy birthday to us!"

"Happy birthday, Kathy." Eva smiled through the sting of tears and embraced her aunt, the sensation so very similar to being held by her mother.

Eva's birthday was many months away, in February, but Katherine didn't know her as Eva; she saw only her sister Lauren. A possible self-defense mechanism, her doctor said. Meeting new people was frightening for her, and it had been decided that learning of her sister's death might shatter her fragile emotional and mental states.

However, Lauren's letters to her sister had been filled with mentions of her daughter, so Katherine knew about Eva. Because of that, Eva talked about herself in the third person, which gave her the freedom to say things she might not otherwise have the courage to. She also kept up the handwritten letters her mother had been so religious about sending, and the correspondences were like journal entries, snapshots of her life, and the fictional activities of her late mother.

Pulling back, Katherine gripped her by the shoulders and studied her. "No fair. You don't age."

"My husband takes good care of me," she said, examining Katherine as closely in return.

Different circumstances and lifestyles meant Katherine was no longer exactly identical to her sister, who'd used a variety of cosmetic surgeries and treatments to maintain her youthful appearance. Katherine was aging naturally and had a minimal skincare routine, which Eva knew from the itemized list of expenses she received monthly. Barefaced and living as serene a life as possible, her aunt was radiant and lovely. Thankfully, she also still spoke with a rural Texas accent, which her sister had trained herself to drop. Eva couldn't imagine how she would feel if Katherine not only looked like her mother but sounded like her, too.

"I'm glad you found a good one," Katherine said, linking their arms and pulling her into the cottage. "I think they're very rare."

"I couldn't agree more."

They entered the light and airy living room and settled together on the pretty floral loveseat. Katherine loved pink flowers, so a designer had been brought in to transform the cottage into her dream. Taking agency over the space had helped her make the transition to New York, which had nevertheless been a rough adjustment for her. She required routine and familiar people and places, no surprises, and very little change.

Katherine blended the past and present in unique ways. In her mind, she and Lauren were both still teenagers, but Lauren was also married with a daughter old enough to be married herself. These two vastly different eras in a lifetime existed concurrently in Katherine's mind.

"Good morning, Mrs. Stanton."

Eva turned her head to find Katherine's housekeeper carrying over two glasses of orange juice on a tray. "Good morning, Penny."

"And a happy birthday to you both," she said, smiling at them. "I made a hummingbird cake for the occasion."

"Did you, Penny?" Katherine's face lit up. "That's my favorite!"

"Must've been a good guess, then."

"Oh, stop. You knew that."

"Might also have a lemon cheese layer cake sitting around, too," Penny added, giving Eva a wink.

Eva returned a grateful smile. She personally leaned more

toward chocolate, but having a slice of her mother's favorite childhood dessert had become an annual birthday tradition she cherished. It was a detail about her mother she hadn't known before. So many things she hadn't known because her mother had reinvented herself with every successive husband.

Katherine grabbed her hand. "Catch me up on everything. How is Richard? And Eva and Gideon? How is their adorable dog?"

"Richard is... well, he's Richard. He should retire but says he wouldn't know what to do with himself. Gideon and Eva work nearly as much. I tell them to live a little or give me a grandchild to spoil, but..." She shrugged helplessly. "I guess they're happy with Lucky."

"You? A grandmother?" Katherine's smile wavered, and shadows entered her blue eyes. "I don't know how you aren't crazed with worry over Eva, let alone wanting to bring a baby into this dangerous world. A dog can guard you, at least. They should just get another one and save themselves a lifetime of worry."

Katherine's unwittingly accurate assessment of the situation was a painful surprise.

Eva's hand went to her tummy before she thought about it. She dropped it back into her lap. "It's difficult when a woman feels the urgency of her biological clock. Eva's thirty-six now, and fertility declines after thirty-five."

"Well, maybe the decision's been made for her, then. I hope I never feel that urge. I don't think I will. I'm happy living here, far from all the evil and crime. Thanks to you. And Richard, too!"

Catching up both of her aunt's hands, Eva gave them an affectionate squeeze. "I'm so happy to hear that you're happy. That's all I've ever wanted for you."

Katherine's grin was childishly joyful.

Eva chose to focus on celebrating the day. When she was with her aunt, her mother felt so beguilingly near. It was bittersweet, the balance between what she had and what she ached for, but she was grateful nonetheless.

"YOU LOOK LIKE HELL."

Ronan glanced up from the article he was reading at the dining table and shot an arch glance over the top of his glasses as Jules sauntered into the living room.

"*Bon matin* to you, too," he growled, rubbing a kink in his neck. His mood was foul and made worse by the *envie* he had for chicory coffee that could not be satisfied, just as his hunger for a stubborn, unreasonable tigress was also not being appeased. Yet another sleepless night did nothing to sweeten his temper.

"Did you sleep on the couch?" Jules stared at the pillow and blanket tossed haphazardly on the flattened sofa cushions. He was dressed in a sleekly tailored suit the color of turmeric. While the color was striking—Jules preferred it when everyone noticed him entering a room—it was saved from being overwhelming by classic lines and quietly luxurious accessories.

"I didn't sleep at all," Ronan shot back. "And I'm damned tired, so don't test me today."

His brother's laughter conveyed biting amusement. "I never thought to see the day a woman tied *you* into knots. When Scarlett couldn't do it, I figured it couldn't be done."

"*Ah, but Ireland Vidal's millennial* joie de vivre *is captivating for a GenX old man like our* beau-frère, non?"

Claudette entered the room, not looking the least bit guilty for eavesdropping. Unlike Jules, her style was so understated as to be almost severe—wide-legged slacks in navy paired with a champagne silk shell with a bow at the throat. She wore her dark hair in thick, loose curls over one shoulder, and pearls hung from her ears.

Both of his half-siblings were now so far removed from the neglected, malnourished children they'd once been. They were now thriving, which helped dispel the lingering nightmare of what had happened. Ronan was profoundly grateful that they'd beaten the odds and had been placed together with a foster couple who genuinely cared for their wellbeing when he'd been unable to see to it himself.

"I'm not old," Ronan groused, his mood darkening further. He tried not to dwell on Ireland's youth. The woman could decide for herself which men she dated. There were many reasons he was unsuitable for her that ranked higher than his age.

"Let him have fun, Jules," Claudette went on. "A last hurrah."

"What's fun about cold showers and sleeping on the couch?" Jules challenged. "Care to explain it to us, *beau-frère?*"

"We are *not* talking about this, Jules." Ronan returned his attention to his tablet, silently damning the spirits for putting Ireland in his path. She was a curse; he knew that now. A bane. A damned *trevail.*

Her visit had left him with a bed that smelled so erotically of her perfume and sex he couldn't sleep in it. He'd never smelled anything as delicious as her. The need to bury his mouth between her long sleek legs and tongue her sweet pussy was so strong it was a torment. He wanted his hands and mouth on every inch of her silky skin. He wanted to take her body in every filthy way possible. He wanted to wallow in a bed with her for days, gluttonously feasting on her tempestuous passion until he'd had his fill and craved no more.

Jules snapped his fingers in front of Ronan's face. "Earth to Ronan. Come in, Ronan."

Embarrassed to be caught daydreaming, he pulled his glasses off and tossed them on the table. "Shut up, *couillion!* I have a lot on my plate at the moment."

"Which usually makes you cool and precise, not hotheaded and grumpy." Jules pulled out the chair next to him and grabbed a mug from the coffee service Ronan had ordered after abandoning sleep. "We're meeting with Elizabeth Vidal at nine."

Ronan sat back. "We should've had her commitment long before the meeting yesterday. We've shown our hand before the showdown."

"The loan defaulted at 12:01 a.m. yesterday," Claudette reminded, joining them at the table and waving off the steaming mug Jules attempted to slide her way. "Owning Elizabeth's shares will expedite things, but we've got the company by the throat either way. Elizabeth can string us along all she likes, but from now on, we have no incentive to offer her more and should consider offering less."

"So cutthroat, *petite sœur*," Jules teased with a grin. "I expect we'll wrap things up this morning. Elizabeth is wily and has to know that we've reached the ceiling of what we'll offer for her shares." Jules sipped his coffee and winced. "*Sacre bleu, c'est terrible.*"

Drumming his fingertips on the table, Ronan felt rushed by

the ever-accelerating timeline. Once they controlled Vidal Records, there were a million reasons to return to Louisiana and only one reason to stay—a reason who presently wanted nothing to do with him.

Putting his mug down in disgust, Jules sat back. "Depending on how long you think you'll be panting after her daughter, you might be relieved to know Elizabeth's beauty hasn't faded in the slightest. She's still a smoke show. I'd have a go at her if she were at all receptive."

"You have a go at every woman who's receptive," Claudette said impudently.

"He's not known for his discernment," Ronan agreed.

Jules's brown eyes took on a hard, chilling light. "Well, I'm not the prodigal son of the illustrious Boudreauxes forced into making a high society match for respectability. That's your fate, *beau-frère*, and I'm grateful to leave high-maintenance women like Scarlett Claiborne to you. I'm just a Robicheaux, the irrelevant son of a dirty cop who had the devil's own heart and a cesspit for a soul. I enjoy proving that I'm just as much a scoundrel as they say."

"You can set down that cross you bear at any time," Ronan drawled.

Snorting derisively, Jules tossed a careless hand. "What would be the fun in that?"

"Indeed." Ronan flipped the cover of his tablet closed. "I'm going to work in the Vidal offices today."

"Is that so? To rub salt in Vidal's wounds," Jules queried, "or to try for another round with his delectable daughter?"

"I said we're not discussing this."

"You know, her mother gets this look in her eye when I mention her ex-husband. No man wants a woman wearing that look while thinking about him." Jules caught himself before picking up his mug again. “Ireland had the same look when she realized who you are. You can’t trust her. If I were you, I certainly wouldn’t want her anywhere near my dick.”

Pushing back from the table, Ronan stood. “You’re not me.”

“You’re taking this far too seriously, Jules.” Claudette tore into a croissant from the breadbasket. “Ronan loves a challenge, and women tend not to offer him any. Let him enjoy this one who will.”

“She wasn’t a challenge before yesterday!” Jules said crossly. “He could’ve spent the weekend fucking her out of his system before she even knew what was happening. All these months of mooning over videos of her, Googling hundreds of pages deep to find the most obscure information about her, insisting on staying in this specific hotel room in the armpit of New York… This isn’t a game, *petite sœur*. He’s obsessed and putting everything we’ve worked so hard for at risk!”

Ronan gathered up his belongings. “I researched all of the Vidals, not just Ireland. I could leave nothing to chance.”

“You can lie to yourself, but I’ll never believe it, so save your breath. I bet you can name every man Ireland Vidal has dated but haven’t a clue who her brothers have hooked up with.”

“Her brothers have been married for years,” he dismissed. “A romantic interest can cause *travails*, and Ireland is the kind of woman a man fights tooth and nail for. It was important to assess all possible interventions.”

Jules’s smile was icy. “*Mon dieu*, no one can bullshit like you. But the clock is ticking. We’re just about done with this city. I meet with the Lees tomorrow about the warehouse in Queens. Should’ve been today, but they wanted to postpone the inevitable, so I gave them an extra day. I expect we’ll be enjoying Marcelle’s café au lait before the end of the week.”

The thought of Marcelle and the comforts of home was

unequivocally appealing and always would be. Claudette and Jules had wanderlust and were often elsewhere, mainly for McCaffrey business but occasionally for pleasure. Ronan was more rooted and usually felt out of sorts to an uncomfortable degree while on the road. Playing music could quiet the noise of being *other* and out of place, but Ireland could silence it entirely.

How would it feel to have her with him in places where he always felt settled? Would he need to take her home to break the spell holding him captive to her? It would take more luck than he had to convince her to travel with him anywhere when she was avoiding him entirely.

But she'd once imagined being in the bayou with him. Perhaps she could be made to imagine it again. He could scheme and would. He'd warned her that he was an immoral man for whom the ends always excused the means.

"Let's get everything wrapped up tight," he said as he headed toward his room for his jacket and satchel. "Call me when you get the agreement signed by Elizabeth Vidal."

Ireland rubbed her damp palms over her denim miniskirt and paced the smaller of the two meeting rooms, the one that could be used as the living room set of a television show. Outfitted with deep-cushioned sofas, a squat coffee table, and a faux fireplace with a television mounted above it, this was where the informal meetings took place rather than at the conference table.

The glass-walled meeting area was directly outside the elevator and opposite the main conference room. It was the most neutral location to tell Christopher that she'd become the majority shareholder as of—she checked her phone—fifty minutes ago. Her mother had signed the shareholder agreement electronically mere moments after the wire transfer was deposited. Within twenty-four hours, Ireland had gone from the beginning of a dizzying romance to its shocking end, from having little say in the business to controlling it.

The elevator doors opened, and she felt a spurt of anxiety. It worsened when Christopher stepped out, whistling, one hand tucked into the pocket of forest green dress slacks. He wore a charcoal dress shirt with a soft sheen and a tie that was a lighter gray shot with a diamond pattern in the same hue as his slacks. A messenger bag was slung across his lean torso. Unlike Ronan and Gideon, Christopher seldom wore blazers or jackets during the warmer months.

Her brother's mahogany hair was darker than their father's but just as wavy. Objectively, she knew he was a very attractive man. Her high school friends had always dissolved into infatuated giggles whenever he entered the room.

Christopher saw her through the glass as she moved to the open doorway of the meeting room, and he gave her a bright smile that pricked her heart a little. While she'd always been a little afraid of Gideon's commanding presence and emotional reserve, Christopher had been her playmate, schoolmate, and friend her whole life. She loved him wholeheartedly.

"Hey," she called out, her hands wringing together. "Can we chat a minute?"

"Absolutely. I was going to hunt you down. What the hell was the uproar yesterday?" Pulling the strap of his bag over his head, he joined her in the room.

She shut the glass door. "Dad didn't tell you?"

"He took off after you did, with whomever he was conferring with yesterday. And an off-site meeting with a music director ate up my afternoon."

Gesturing for him to sit, Ireland did the same. She had little energy to be angry at their parents for leaving the disclosures to her. She'd learned long ago that her mother demanded the appearance of perfection from her children and spouse. Reality could be tumultuous as long as the surface was serene to anyone who might look. There was no way that Elizabeth Vidal was interested in a conversation with one of her children that was likely to get messy.

As for their father, Ireland was coming to realize that she needed to spend more time with him and learn more about who he was beyond the role of parent.

What was most important now, though, was making the role reversal between her and their father as frictionless as possible for her family and their staff. While it would've been easier for her if their parents had shouldered some of the responsibility for their choices, it was better if Christopher heard everything at once from her rather than in bits and pieces from multiple people.

And now that running Vidal was her responsibility, uncomfortable meetings were something she needed to get good at. Conceivably, her father thought the same, and that was why she was left to handle her brother.

"Vidal is in serious trouble," she said bluntly. "One of our shareholders is attempting to take us over."

A confused frown replaced her brother's smile. "What? No way."

"McCaffrey Holdings has been quietly buying out the other investors. I'm not sure if Dad was aware of what was happening before it was too late or not."

The confused frown turned into a scowl. "Why does the name McCaffrey sound familiar?"

"Did Dad discuss the funding for the overhaul of the recording studios with you?"

Christopher's face blanked, then his eyes widened. "Oh, yeah. They financed the loan. They're a private equity group."

"Is that what Dad told you?"

"Yeah."

"And you didn't look into it?" she asked, keeping her tone as smooth and even as possible.

"Why would I?"

"Because Dad almost bankrupted the business before. Maybe he's not so good at making financial decisions."

Her brother's gaze narrowed. "You're blaming Dad?"

"I'm saying you and I have been riding in the backseat, assuming Dad's following directions, despite him getting us lost before. We should've been paying attention to where we were going. I'm as much at fault as you."

"Wait a minute." He bristled. "You're accusing *me* of something?"

"That came out wrong." She took a steadying breath and gathered her thoughts. She'd rehearsed this conversation dozens of times to prepare and couldn't remember half of it now. "It doesn't matter how we got here. I'm not looking for anyone to blame. What's done is done. Dad's meeting yesterday was with McCaffrey Holdings, and that's why things got so heated. The loan defaulted first thing yesterday morning, and McCaffrey is taking ownership of Dad's shares."

Christopher snorted and shook his head. "Don't get worked up, okay? I'm sure everything's fine. We'll either pay off the loan or refinance it. Dad must've just forgotten the date. He's a little scattered sometimes, you know that. And with Mom's news, he might have been more distracted than usual."

She wanted to point out that Christopher himself had said that their mom remarrying wasn't a problem for their dad, but she would never argue. "We can't afford to pay off the loan. It didn't just fund the new studios. Dad also needed to cover wages, bonuses, and tour support. We haven't been profitable for a few years now, and there has been a persistent shortfall. And we financed with McCaffrey because no other lender would extend the amount of credit Dad wanted. We weren't going to be good for it, and everyone knew it, especially McCaffrey."

She'd learned they had been hemorrhaging money since shortly after Gideon pulled out, which drove home how vital it was to properly manage a business's expenses. Christopher had chafed under Gideon's cautious approach to spending, saying it was "miserly" and hampering the company's ability to grow. Ireland had secretly agreed, not knowing any better.

Stupid. She couldn't stop kicking herself for being so willfully blind.

"You must have misunderstood what Dad was saying," Christopher said, pale beneath his summer tan. He stood. "I'll talk to him and get this sorted out."

Her hands were so tightly linked in her lap they were bloodless and hurting. "I know you didn't intend to insult me, and I'm trying not to take offense. Please sit down. I'm not done explaining the situation."

He lowered back onto the sofa. "Hey, I'm sorry. I'm trying to calm you down, but I'm a little wigged out right now, so I'm blundering through it."

"I get it. I went through the same shock and disbelief, and I'm still trying to shake it off."

Out of the corner of her eye, Ireland saw the elevator doors open. When Ronan stepped out in a tan business suit with a leather satchel in hand, her heartbeat quickened with unwanted joy. Then, the apprehension kicked in. Having him show up ready to work was nothing but a bad sign for her. He headed toward the reception desk with his seductively unhurried stride, then suddenly turned his head and found her as if he knew instinctively that she was nearby.

Their gazes locked. For a heartbeat, they just looked at each other, so many emotions flickering across his face. And likely hers. Then Ronan's mouth curved in that slow, easy smile that made her pulse leap because it revealed so clearly that he was happy to see her. She could only stare back, longing for and resenting him in equal measure. He winked at her, and it struck her suddenly that he must not yet know about her mother's shares.

Then again, neither did her brother.

"So, what else do I need to know?" Christopher prodded just as she refocused on him.

Everything in her recoiled against saying anything that might cause pain or anger. It went against her ingrained nature to disturb the peace in her family. "Well… with Mom gearing up to marry Daniel, she mentioned wanting to cut all financial ties with Dad. So" —she said the rest in a rush— "I've bought Mom out."

Christopher stared at her unblinking for an endless minute. "What do you mean you bought Mom out?"

He had to have understood what she'd said. He just couldn't believe it.

"I've bought the shares she was given in the divorce," she restated. "I now own twenty-five percent of Vidal. McCaffery had been courting Mom, trying to buy the shares from her, which would've given them the majority. This way, McCaffrey and I are even. And you're the tiebreaker."

His gaze narrowed dangerously. "So, Dad is out? That's it?"

"Yes, although I suggested he continue working with our

artists because we need his magic touch, and he's agreed. We worked out an appropriate salary, although if we don't find a way to start making money, we won't be able to afford him."

"You've taken a majority position and made Dad an *employee?* Am I hearing that right?"

Ireland rubbed at her increasingly upset stomach. She'd hardly slept or eaten since leaving Ronan's hotel suite, only picking at the orange chicken Alina had brought her for dinner. Her stomach was an acidic mess, with a pot of coffee being the only thing she'd had so far that morning. "It's the only way to keep Dad here," she said simply.

Sitting back, Christopher ruffled his hair absently, his thoughts clearly running through everything he'd learned. "When did you find out about all of this?"

"Sunday morning." She looked at Ronan as he moved away from the reception desk and headed toward the conference room. He settled on the far side of the conference table, with her in his direct line of sight. Knowing he was watching her increased her nervousness to an unbearable degree. She hadn't forgotten that reading lips was one of his talents.

"Two days," Christopher snapped. "You've known about this for *two days*? And I'm just now hearing about this?"

She wanted to point out that she'd felt precisely what he was feeling after discovering the entire family—except possibly their mother—had known about Graham for days before she was told. However, her primary focus was keeping them all connected and working together rather than against each other. Her childhood had been fraught with ruptures in the family, a pervasive sense of bitterness and resentment, all glossed over by her mother's need to keep up appearances.

Ireland could only shrug helplessly, unable to accuse their father of failing to keep them both in the loop.

Christopher leaped to his feet, filled with restless energy that worsened her anxiety. "You guys all saw the deadline coming and didn't tell Gideon or me? You just let this McCaffrey group seize Dad's shares?"

"Gideon has already bailed us out before." It felt like she was vibrating inside, so violently she might rattle into pieces where she sat.

"So what?" he countered angrily. "Way better—*waaay*—to have family running things than some outside outfit! Now we're relying on some equity group with no clue about the music biz to get us back on track?"

The room tilted a little as Ireland looked up at her brother with a pounding heart. "McCaffrey doesn't want to turn Vidal around. They want to shut it down. Permanently."

He stared at her with the kind of hot, mean look he used to reserve for Gideon. "Are you fucking kidding me?" he yelled, drawing the attention of their receptionist. "We had the chance to shut these guys down, but you all just decided to hold the door open for them? What the hell were you thinking?"

"Christopher—"

"Dad couldn't afford to buy Mom's shares, so *you're* sweeping in to save the day? Is this supposed to demonstrate that you're ready to step up? Or have you been thinking that you can run things better this whole time?"

"I'm trying to save the company for you!" she argued, her throat so tight and dry it ached. "For your kids and—"

"You could've told me what was happening and let me help!" He threw up his hands, and the violent motion made her recoil back onto the sofa. "We'd be solid now. *I* have zero problem talking to Gideon about saving this company. Running a business doesn't mean you do it all yourself. You have to ask for help when it's needed!"

It was so painful to look at her brother's furious face that Ireland's gaze dropped to the floor. "I'm not afraid to ask Gideon. But he's got his own problems. If you and I can't save Vidal, maybe we're not meant to have it."

"Jesus Christ!" He stood over her, casting a shadow that deepened the chill inside her. "So, you're good with letting the company go under rather than ask your brothers for help? Wait until Gideon finds out about this. As pissed as I am, how do you think he's going to react?"

"I hope he respects my intentions."

"Really? What was the point of buying Mom's shares if you're unwilling to do everything possible to save Vidal? Whatever you think you're proving, you're missing the mark by a mile!"

"I'm not trying to prove anything," she said curtly, staring at the laces on his chestnut oxfords. "I'm trying to keep the company afloat."

"Sounds like you let that chance expire," he said bitterly, his hands on his hips. "And why? Because you think I've screwed up somehow? That I'm not doing my job? Or is that I'm just not any good at it?"

"I didn't say anything even remotely like that!"

"You might as well have! And despite what you think, I could've dealt with McCaffrey on Sunday before the clock ran out. Negotiated some sort of extension. It's not in anyone's interest to let the company fold. That's basic business 101."

"It's not business for them," she explained faintly, holding back tears.

"The hell it isn't! No one lends money hoping they won't get it back. And if they've acquired twenty-five percent, they stand to lose much more than just the loan. You and I evidently have issues to sort through but let me deal with McCaffrey for now. I'll set them fucking straight."

"*I'm right here to be dealt with.*"

At the sound of Ronan's dangerously calm drawl, Ireland turned toward the door and found him standing on the threshold. His grip on the brass handle was white-knuckled.

Her pulse accelerated into a panicked rhythm. A confrontation between Ronan and her family was inevitably layered. He was the first man she'd ever been involved with to stand in the same room with both her and the people she loved. That he was also their enemy made the encounter even more fraught with danger. She was torn between opposing desires: to stand in front of him protectively and to battle him head-on.

Christopher pivoted to face him. "Who are you?"

"McCaffrey." Ronan's gaze was dark and flat. "You can direct your anger at me moving forward, but you'll be waiting a moment for that. Ireland, may I have a minute of your time?"

"It's not—" she began.

"Why don't you just deal with me," Christopher interrupted.

"I look forward to it." Ronan's half-smile was glacial. "But Ireland wields the power here, and I'll speak to her first."

She gave him a pleading look, desperate to avoid a fight between the two men. She didn't think she could bear it.

"I don't like your tone," Christopher retorted.

Ireland winced. "Christopher…"

"You won't like anything about me," Ronan said flippantly. "Ireland?"

She stood on shaky legs but rolled her shoulders back and lifted her chin. "Come with me, Mr. McCaffrey."

"Whatever you need to say, you can say to both of us." Christopher's arms crossed. "It seems the three of us are the last remaining shareholders."

Ronan stepped aside to let Ireland pass. "You'll have my undivided attention when I'm good and ready to give it to you.

Best you don't anger me more than you already have before then."

She walked toward her office, her stride steadying as her tensed muscles began to ease with movement. Her heartbeat hammered in her chest, the dread of another confrontation spiking her adrenaline.

Ireland wields the power here. He must know now. Her mother had told her about the meeting with Jules and Claudette, which would've started almost an hour before Christopher and Ronan had arrived at the offices.

She turned into her executive suite and moved toward her desk, needing to put the substantial piece of furniture between them. Even after leaving the windows open all night, the room still smelled of paint.

"Wait, *cher*," he murmured.

The sound of the door shutting and locking turned her around. The dark circles beneath his beautiful eyes provoked something akin to triumphant regret. And wasn't that just the way it was with him? Her feelings had been chaotic from her first sight of him onstage at Jazzie's.

She held her ground as Ronan approached cautiously as if she were a skittish mare. Then his arms opened. She stumbled back, her eyes wide. "What are you doing?"

His mouth was a hard, disapproving line, but his gaze was soft with remorse and sympathy. That look, and all the emotions it conveyed, blurred her vision with tears.

"You've worn yourself down to the bone," he chastised softly. "Did you get any sleep last night?"

"You're looking a little ragged yourself," she shot back.

"And feeling that way, too. So this hug is as much for me as for you."

She lifted her hand to ward him off, but he just caught it in his, the chaste touch electrifying.

Her tone was biting. "Are you seriously trying to comfort me when you're the reason I need comfort in the first place?"

"Consider it penance," he cajoled.

He pulled her slowly toward him, closing the short distance between them. Ireland could've resisted the physical pull, but the maddening attraction was undeniable. His arm slid cautiously around her waist, giving her time to protest further. When she didn't, he enfolded her, cradling her against his warm chest.

The tears came, hot and stinging. She slipped her cold hands under his jacket, rubbing the hard muscles of his back to absorb his heat. He shivered without protest and gripped her more firmly. He nuzzled her hair, inhaling deeply. She felt the tension leave him in a slow ebb as his hands caressed her, soothing her as she quaked with sobs against him.

Burrowing into him, she cried silently, her exhaustion profound. The tears flowed unchecked, draining the anger and frustration until she was limp against him. Ronan supported her with ease, and as the storm inside her passed, she felt the movement in his chest…

…and realized he was singing to her—in French.

Ireland tilted her head back and caught his soulful gaze. His voice, even barely above a whisper, was like moonlit magic—deep, mysterious, and incandescent. It touched an unfamiliar and unreached place deep inside her. "What is that you're singing?"

Catching her face in both hands, he brushed the tears from her cheeks with his thumbs. "It's an old Cajun song," he murmured.

"About what?"

“A man whose woman leaves him for her family.”

She gave him a dry look.

His wicked smile ruined his innocent shrug. “Ah, I’ve amused you. *Ça c’est bon.*”

“Please don’t be charming,” she said guardedly, pulling away.

“How can I help it?” He caught her by the elbow, suddenly serious. He waited a moment, letting his somberness penetrate so she could steel herself for what he’d say next. “Your mother’s shares are worthless. You shouldn’t have wasted your money, *cher*. I was prepared to take the loss, are you?”

Her chin lifted, and she used his words. “How could I help it?”

Ronan’s harsh exhale was long-suffering and resigned. “And your father left you to explain everything to your brother.”

“With great power comes great responsibility. Isn’t that how the saying goes?”

“That might explain why your father no longer has power,” he said wryly.

“Ronan…”

He held up both hands in surrender. “Not another word about him.”

Giving him a narrow-eyed glare, she walked around him to the bathroom and turned on the light, wincing at the sight of her reddened nose and eyes in the mirror.

He appeared in the door's opening, leaning insouciantly against the jamb. “I want you to know that my body—which, I’ll remind you, is available for your use at any time—can also serve this purpose. You may not find the comfort you need from your family when you need it.”

She favored him with a level look. “The only reason a man tolerates a crying woman he’s not related or married to is to get in her pants.”

“Two birds, one stone.”

Snatching the hand towel off the bar, she spun and snapped it at him. He jumped back, laughing.

“Get out!” she ordered.

“Fine.” He paused at her office door with his hand on the knob, all teasing gone. “You good for now?”

She studied him, realizing how easily he could recenter her. He was wholly civilized now, wearing a jacket and tie, his sleeves buttoned at the wrists. His hair was slightly tousled from his hasty backward retreat, and the effect of it against his polished urbanity was sexy as sin.

“Yes. I’m better.” It was on the tip of her tongue to thank him, but it seemed wrong to do so.

“I’m not the problem,” he pointed out somberly. “I’m merely the result of the problem. It’s an important distinction I ask you to keep in mind.”

The doorknob rattled in his hand; then someone pounded on the door. “Ireland! McCaffrey! Why is this locked?”

Ronan opened the door, and Christopher stumbled in with his fist raised mid-thump. Catching himself, he glanced around, finding Ireland standing several feet away in the bathroom.

He paused, seeing the ravages of crying on her face. “Are you okay?”

“Yeah. I’m just tired.”

His nose twitched, and he turned around, taking in the almost unrecognizable room she and Alina had painted and redecorated. “I can see why.” He faced her with angry color on his face. “You move quick.”

“Your mistake,” Ronan drawled, “is in thinking she wants any of this. She’s doing it all for you. And you haven’t even the grace to be grateful.”

Christopher's fists clenched at his sides. "What do you want, McCaffrey?"

"Why don't we discuss that out here and let the boss see to more pressing business?"

Her brother marched out the door, his shoulders stiff, and Ronan shot her a last look before following.

Eva smiled through the windshield and waved good-bye to her Aunt Katherine, who waved back from the cottage's doorway. Then she stepped on the gas and circled the drive.

Her phone rang, and she hit the button on the dash to answer. "You have the most impeccable timing, Mr. Cross," she said by way of greeting.

"I live to please you, angel mine." The slight rasp in his smooth, cultured voice was both familiar and exciting. "Swing by the main building, please, and pick me up."

She blinked, then her brows lifted. "You're here?"

"Seems like."

Heaving an exasperated breath, she tightened her grip on the steering wheel. "You are the most obstinate man, you know that? How long have you been here?"

"Not long."

Yeah, right.

Following the drive, she turned onto the main entrance road and drove toward the turreted mansion. In short order, she circled the large fountain and pulled into the porte-cochère. One of the arched double front doors opened, and Gideon stepped out with a briefcase in hand. Her heart skipped with joy at the sight of him.

She'd missed seeing him get dressed that morning. His sense of style was flawless and watching him swiftly and without inner debate select the various pieces of his attire and accessories was her favorite way to start her day. Sometimes, she was so turned on by observing him clothe his magnificent body that she undressed him again and made them both late for work. She'd even added a small coffee station and seating area in their massive walk-in closet so she could ogle him and caffeinate herself simultaneously.

Today's suit was a black pinstripe, and he wore her favorite cerulean tie, the colors playing off the inkiness of his hair and those magnificent eyes. When he bent to smile at her through the passenger window, she found that her throat was so tight it ached. His smile faded instantly.

Instead of opening the door, he put his briefcase on the car's roof and came around to the driver's side. She was already unbuckling her seatbelt and pushing the door open when he reached her.

"Hey," he murmured, easily absorbing the blow of her throwing herself into his arms. "I've got you."

She clung to him, the emotional toll of the day suddenly too much to contain. One of his hands cupped her nape beneath her hair, and the other held her by the hips, his lips at her temple as he gave her all of his warmth and support.

"You always know when I need you." She sniffled. Her eyes were dry and burning, her emotions too complicated to be expressed through tears.

"I would hope that's all the time, not just occasionally."

She gave a watery laugh and pressed grateful kisses to his cheek. "I should scold you for not listening to me."

"Oh, but I did. You're right that we need to take some dedicated time just for us, but the weekend is too far away." He cupped her jaw in his hand and held her gaze. "Let's go to the beach house now."

The sudden longing that assailed her almost weakened her knees. "I wish we could! But the masquerade is Friday, and there are a million little things to manage before then."

"I've already spoken with the foundation's events team, and they assure me that everything is well in hand, and they can take it from here."

She gave him an indulgent look. "You do understand that you're you, and they'd never tell you that they didn't have things under control."

"That's because they're paid to run things smoothly, not to run my wife ragged." He pressed his lips to her forehead. "The jet's ready and waiting, the flight crew is presently spoiling Lucky, and I turned my phone off the minute you pulled into sight. We'll fly back Friday morning for the masquerade and out again that night. Or possibly Saturday morning if seeing me in a tuxedo has the usual effect on your libido."

"You can't blame me for your hotness, ace."

His mouth curved. "I'm absolutely not complaining."

Catching her lower lip in her teeth, Eva debated all the reasons they couldn't just take off on a whim.

"We haven't played hooky in a while," he contended. "And think of how many trees we'll get planted to offset our carbon emissions."

"That's a truly terrible argument," she grumbled.

"But was it effective?"

She kissed him, long and slow and deep. "You alone are all the incentive I need to do anything."

"Are you driving, or am I?" he asked, his lips moving against hers.

"I am. I've missed it." Pulling back, she brushed a wayward

strand of hair away from his magnificent face. “Did you get any work done?”

He smiled. “Ireland gave me a heads-up about a building she thought I might have a use for. I had the acquisitions team look into it, and she’s right about its potential. It also has the side benefit of a new tenant in a recently vacated property.”

“So, it was a productive day for you.” She placed her hand over his heart. “I’m glad because I’m really happy you’re here.”

“Angel, with you is the only place I ever want to be.”

*IRELAND TURNED IN A SLOW CIRCLE. THE FORMER VIDAL offices, now emptied of furniture, looked like a dystopian wasteland. The ever-present music that had once enlivened the air had been silenced. The space seemed cavernous, the open windows creating a whistling breeze that echoed throughout. Cords dangled from the walls and lay like snakes on the carpeted floor, having no equipment to connect to. Torn bits and pieces of paper were scattered on the floor, along with one of her business cards—*Ireland Vidal, Chief Executive Officer & Shareholder*—and a pen with her name engraved on the barrel.*

That was all that was left. What she had set in motion could not be stopped.

She dashed away hot tears but could not control her bitter laughter and moaning sobs, her emotions swinging wildly between joy and despair.

A warm arm slid around her shoulders, spooking her.

"You did all you could, sweetheart," her father murmured.

She looked at him, catching his half-smile. Then she saw through his glasses to the sheen of wetness in his eyes.

"I'm so sorry, Daddy!" she sobbed, both heartbroken and relieved that she'd failed.

"Don't be. Now you're free to do what you want."

That was the most terrifying thing of all. "I don't know what that is."

"You'll figure it out." He slid his fingers beneath the edge of his glasses and swiped at his tears.

"What will you do?" She turned to face him and found herself alone, his warmth and touch disappearing as if he'd never been beside her. "Dad?"

An inexplicable breeze blew the ripped-off cover of a magazine across the carpet to hug her feet. Bending down, she picked it up and unfolded it, seeing her most recent headshot staring back at her.

WHAT WENT WRONG AT VIDAL RECORDS?

The cover line screamed at her with an audible banshee's shriek. Bright red tears leaked from the glossy paper and saturated her photograph with a garish mask. She threw the cover away before the stain reached her fingers, and it floated to the floor, promptly sinking into the viscous redness that suddenly saturated the carpet.

Rivulets of crimson wept from the holes in the walls left by picture frame hangers. Horrified, she stumbled back toward the elevator, trying to evade the relentlessly creeping flow of red...

Ireland bolted upright in bed with a gasp, her heart hammering in her chest. A fine sheen of perspiration covered her skin, and she threw the covers off with a curse.

Blizzard's disgruntled growl had her clawing the blankets back to unbury him. "Sorry, Bliz!"

He looked at her with flattened ears, then stood and stretched before jumping off the bed.

"Blizzard! Come back. I'm sorry!"

He sauntered out to the living room with a furiously flicking tail.

She flopped onto her back with a groan. But the spot where she'd been laying was feverishly hot and damp. She pushed the covers off again and got out of bed, looking at the AI unit on her bedside table for the time.

"Damn it! It's not even midnight," she complained, raking a hand through her hair.

The nightmare clung to her like a possessive lover. She grabbed her white silk kimono from her vanity stool and yanked it on, still so fucking tired and now wide awake.

She knew the dream meant nothing, even as she replayed it over and over in her mind. Christopher's harsh words had tapped into her fear that she would be the death of the company. Maybe she'd already killed it by not asking Gideon for help. Maybe there was nothing else she could do to save it now.

Following Blizzard's initiative, she left the bedroom and went to the kitchen, the tiles cool on the hot soles of her feet. It was inexplicable to feel a bone-deep chill while simultaneously being overheated. She poured a glass of orange juice and gulped it down.

The thought of Gideon being angry with her was stressing her out, too. In her master plan, her big brother would understand and even respect her for not involving him, but…what if he didn't? Was he going to be furious instead? Would he view it as a rejection of him and his expertise, as Christopher did?

"Ugh." She rolled the cool glass over her forehead. The same repetitive thoughts had driven her half-mad before she'd escaped into a fitful, exhausted sleep. When she'd left work at the end of the day, she had briefly considered going to Parker Smith's studio to burn off the adrenaline and anxiety with a good, aggressive sparring session. But she knew it wasn't wise to keep pushing herself while running on lack of sleep.

Here, cher. *Something so delicious you won't let it go to waste.*

Even in memory, Ronan's alluring voice affected her. He'd startled and moved her when he came to her office with lunch from Valentin's—a cup of gumbo and half a muffuletta sandwich. She hadn't been paying attention to the hour, too engrossed in bank statements and outstanding invoices.

It wasn't that Ronan was the only one to think of her. The largest bouquet she'd ever seen had been delivered shortly after her conversation with Christopher and included a note of congratulations from Gideon. Not long after, her mother had couriered over a monogrammed leather folio from Tiffany & Co., and her father had settled into one of her visitors' chairs and slid a Montblanc pen across her desk that had her name engraved on it. Even Christopher had brought her a cup of coffee when he saw that she was struggling to keep her eyes open.

And while Ronan's thoughtfulness, consideration, and attentiveness were unique traits in her history of boyfriends—Alina said she intimidated most guys because she was a ballsy babe with her shit together—that wasn't what gave the Cajun the ability to slip under her defenses and beneath her skin.

No, what got to her was that he should want her to wear down. She was all that stood in the way of what he wanted. The more tired she was and the less she took care of herself, the more mistakes she would make.

He was acting against his own interests. And after too many romantic entanglements with men who had self-serving agendas, that selflessness made him something special.

She set her empty glass down on the counter, remembering how Ronan had noticed what she was reviewing when he brought her lunch and had returned a few moments later with some of the documents she hadn't been able to locate that were in his possession.

It was the worst sort of mindfuck that the man responsible for everything going wrong in her life was also the person determined to support and care for her while she struggled through it.

A soft brush against her calves drew her attention down to Blizzard, who'd apparently decided to forgive her—or maybe she was just too pitiful. She scooped him up and draped his forelegs over her shoulder, his long feline body approaching the length of hers.

"I told you he was too good to be true," she murmured, stroking her hand down Blizzard's long back. "I thought maybe he was Prince Charming, but he's actually the bad guy. So, your title of Perfect Male remains unchallenged, Bliz."

Blizzard began purring, the soft rhythmic rumble the only sound in the otherwise quiet condo.

Ronan sat on the couch and stared at the television; his view repeatedly interrupted as Jules paced back and forth in front of him. Not that he was actually watching the disaster movie playing on the large flatscreen on the wall. He had enough disasters of his own to deal with.

"*Merde*, Jules! Either sit or find a woman to burn off that energy."

Jules glared at him as he marched past. "How can you be so calm? That woman strung us along for months!"

Setting his elbow on the armrest, Ronan propped his head in his hand and yawned. "Elizabeth Vidal was never a sure thing."

He was tired. He'd spent an hour in the hotel gym, half the

time running full bore on the treadmill and the other half on the weight machines, hoping to wear himself out enough to finally sleep. But until he was certain Ireland wasn't going to do something incredibly hardheaded, such as go back into the offices, he was keeping his eyes open. He'd asked the lobby guard at Vidal Records to notify him if she came in but had walked over around nine to check for himself—just in case.

"I don't like being played!" Jules's volume was nearing a yell.

"It was always a gamble," Claudette agreed, her legs tucked at the other end of the sofa. "Which would she choose: to screw over her ex-husband or protect the careers of her children? Perhaps we thought she'd choose revenge because our parents never put us first."

Jules snorted and paused to point his finger at her. "None of that talk. Let's focus on getting this wrapped up before something else goes wrong. We'll start liquidating tomorrow."

"Not yet," Ronan said.

"*Pardon?*"

"A few extra days won't hurt us. It'll get done."

Jules stared at him with a hard expression. "You're holding off for her."

Ronan stared at the television. "If you're referring to Ireland Vidal, then—"

"Who else? *Mon dieu*, you piss me off!"

"Ireland is going through the finances now. It won't be long before she understands the hopelessness of the situation."

"And then what?" Jules threw up his hands. "She'll forgive you and spread her legs again? Is that the new plan?"

"Don't be ugly, Jules," Claudette scolded.

"*Désolé* but we've spent years working toward this moment, and now that we're finally here, he won't act. He's paralyzed by lust and can't see straight."

"Will you shut up about that already?!" Ronan barked. "I'm sick of hearing you complain about Ireland."

"*Beau-frère*, I haven't begun to complain." Jules's tone took on a dangerous edge. "This is no longer just about you. I went to goddamned law school to further this goal. Claudette became a fucking accountant!"

"And I will be forever grateful to you both. I couldn't have gotten here without you, and I never forget it. I never will."

Jules's wide, sensual mouth compressed into an obstinate line. "We committed *our lives* to getting you this revenge, and I won't let you jeopardize everything because you're thinking with your dick!"

"That's enough!" Ronan slashed his hand through the air. "You came along for the ride because you get off on tearing things down. We're finally at the part you enjoy, and you'll have your kill. We can give Ireland a little time to reach her own conclusions, that's all."

"She and her brother were always going to be collateral damage," Jules argued. "That was never a problem for you before you met her."

"What do you want me to say? That I like her? That I regret having to hurt her? Both are true. She can't stop what's coming. Give her time to make peace with it."

"But why? What does it matter? We could be home with the Vidals buried and left behind us. If they hate us afterward, it means nothing." Jules's gaze narrowed with incisive consideration. "Or are you hoping for more time with the daughter of the man you're destroying?"

"It is rather romantic, isn't it?" Claudette smiled. "Like the Montagues and Capulets."

"Oh, please. Ronan can't lose Scarlett over a woman he has no possible future with. Ireland Vidal is not leaving this place, and our dear brother gets the *frissons* here! And that's the least of their problems."

Ronan's phone lit up where it lay on the coffee table, and Ireland's photo filled the screen. Scrambling for it, he answered. "*Oui, cher.*"

"You're the reason I can't sleep," she accused in that voice he loved. Assertive yet smooth, with the softest of rasps, it was as sexy as the rest of her. "You've given me carte blanche with your body. It damn well better make my insomnia worthwhile."

He was on his feet and moving. "I'm on my way. Give the doorman my name."

"Which one?" she asked caustically.

"Whichever you prefer. See you soon." He hung up and shoved the phone into his back pocket.

"Are you fucking kidding me?" Jules yelled. "She calls, and you go running? We're in the middle of a conversation!"

Ronan went to his room, shoved a string of condoms into his front pocket, and slid his feet into loafers. Then he headed toward the exit. "Don't wait up."

"*Pour l'amour de dieu!*" Jules called after him gripping his head in both hands. "*C'est fou, gros bête!*"

The door swung slowly closed, and Jules stared at it in utter amazement. He turned to his sister. "Can you believe this? I don't recognize him."

Claudette eyed the door thoughtfully. "Perhaps a night with her will do him good. Their liaison on Monday was too short to satisfy the *envie* he has. He's too noble sometimes, and that little chivalrous streak won't allow him to admit he's using the woman for revenge."

"Do you really think so?" Jules dropped gracelessly onto the sofa beside her.

"He's like you, Jules. Women are a pleasant diversion. What makes this one so special? She's a Vidal."

He slouched, petulant. "We're so close to having what he's long wanted. He could finally put this all behind him and try to be content for once. He deserves peace more than anyone."

She draped her arm across his shoulders and gave him a comforting hug. "Imagine if Scarlett was to hear of this somehow? Ireland Vidal is photographed on the street all the time. If Ronan is with her..."

His handsome features hardened. "I won't let her ruin everything. If I have to, I'll do what our brother can't."

Studying Jules, Claudette noted the obstinate line of his clenched jaw. He was the impetuous one among them. Bold, brash, and unafraid of consequences. Mostly, they used those traits to their advantage. They knew to be wary when Jules got that look in his eye.

"Don't get any stupid ideas, Jules," she admonished. "Ronan has never failed us. He won't start now."

Ireland turned her phone off after receiving the doorman's heads-up that Ronan was on his way to the elevator. How many times had she reconsidered her decision to invite him over? At least a hundred. She'd had his contact card open on her phone screen since they'd hung up, but she couldn't seem to hit the button to make the call.

It had been easier to avoid him the night before when she'd been rushed to get things finalized. Now, she was awake and frustrated by fatigue, but thoughts whirled ceaselessly in her mind. Mixed in with the mental chaos were taunting, tempting memories of Ronan. It felt like the worst betrayal that the man targeting her father—for a reason neither of them seemed willing to tell her—was the same man whose presence made her feel alive in new and compelling ways. She was being selfish, indulging herself with him, her defenses weakened by her self-doubt and the soul-deep weariness that felt like a smothering weight.

Perversely, she wasn't too tired to be excited. Her breathing was quick, her pulse quicker. He still turned her on, still lured her with a heady attraction. It infuriated her that the yearning was so insistent, which gave an edge to her desire. The near-feral sex they'd had should have been enough to satisfy her for a while, but she only wanted him more now.

Opening her front door, Ireland tried posing herself on the threshold in a way that would drive Ronan wild. She rested her forearm against the jamb above her head and adjusted the white silk of her kimono to bare her leg. Then she fluffed her hair and widened her neckline. She bared one shoulder, then covered it again. Then she tried leaning her back against the frame and bending her leg to brace herself.

But when the elevator's soft chime signaled its arrival, she found herself paralyzed, lamely standing in the doorway.

The car doors slid open, and Ronan appeared, his breathtaking face wearing the hard, hungry look of a man whose base needs were driving him to the edge. Their gazes locked and communicated so much in the mere blink of an eye—wariness, anticipation, desire, and the sensual joy of seeing someone whose presence was a wild thrill.

While she was frozen with indecision, Ronan was determined, and he ate up the distance between them with his long-legged stride. He caught her up in a crushing embrace, lifting her feet from the floor. His mouth sealed over hers in a greedy, demanding kiss.

Wrapping her legs around his waist, Ireland held on, kissing him back with the same voracious need. His groan echoed in the small vestibule, the sound so searingly erotic a shiver swept through her.

Everything rushed by them as he carried her into the condo and kicked the door shut behind him. All the lights were off, the sole illumination coming from the moon shining through her large, uncovered windows.

He took her straight to the bedroom and lowered her to the bed, toeing off his shoes before stretching out beside her. Their legs twined, his well-worn jeans soft against her bare legs. It was all so fast, mere seconds from his arrival to falling into bed together. There was no time to think or second-guess. His lips moved across her cheek, and then he buried his face in the crook of her neck. He breathed her in with a long, slow inhale and nuzzled deep.

Then he stopped moving at all.

After a few moments, Ireland lay confused. "Ronan?"

"A moment, *cher*," he murmured. "Just to hold you."

Slowly, she felt his big body relax. His hard planes and valleys settled against her slight curves as the fine tension drained from his long frame.

It took her a bit more time to loosen up, her mind arguing that she shouldn't draw any comfort from the man who tormented her. But she couldn't stop the easing of her tight muscles. It was an involuntary reaction to the feeling of being... *enough*. With Ronan, she didn't feel like she needed to be more, do more, give more. She wished she knew what he drew from her in return.

Ronan Boudreaux was either her dream man or a nightmare, and she was drained by the effort of figuring out which was true. In the end, it didn't really matter. He would always be the enemy of her family. She had him now, and if she did her job right and fought off his takeover attempt, that was all she would ever have.

And *why* was she even thinking of anything beyond the next hour or so?

Her fingers slid into his hair to hold him to her as she burrowed into his embrace and followed his lead, allowing his opulently seductive scent to permeate her senses and soothe her agitated nerves. It felt so good to be held after the upheaval of the past days, and she permitted herself to enjoy it. She'd thought she wanted hard, grinding sex and knew he could—and would—give it to her. But this moment of reconnection before such wild intimacy had been needed, too. He'd apparently known that, but she was just now catching on.

Ronan's warmth, their companionable silence, and the steady thrum of sexual affinity between them served as a balm for her raw emotions. He was a highly sexual creature, one who radiated such hot male animal energy, and yet he was content for the time being just to be close to her, one thick biceps pillowing her head and his hand curved possessively around her butt cheek.

Her fingers traced the sharp objects that formed his tribal tattoo, then she ruffled the rough silk of his hair. She closed her eyes, but sleep was far from her mind. Ronan was too exciting, even when he was doing nothing.

Eventually, he pulled back and looked down at her. He searched her expression with a thorough once-over.

Had he held himself back so she could come to grips with her choice to invite him over?

"No regrets," she whispered, able to confirm that because of his actions—or inaction, as the case might be. He could've used her body in countless ways since they'd met if that had been his aim.

"*C'est bon.*" His bright smile and gleaming eyes were radiant in the moonlight slanting across her bed. "*Bonsoir, cher.*"

His casual attire made him look younger than his age. Lying in bed together, dressed as they were, felt almost adolescent, as if a boyfriend had snuck into her room on a school night. She'd never had that experience. Her family was intimidating, and their former Dutchess County mansion hadn't been the kind of residence that lent itself to secretive trysts. In so many ways, Ronan delighted her, her mysterious magic man.

"Hi back." She gently twirled a thick strand of his hair around her fingers. The darkness was more than a shield... it separated them from who they were during the day.

"I'm glad you called."

Her smile was rueful. "I won't lie; I kicked myself for doing it. But it's not so bad now."

"Not so bad?" His grin gave her butterflies. "I'll have to work on that."

"Why don't you start here?" She grabbed the end of her kimono tie and pulled it loose.

Heat flared in his gaze. Lowering his head, he pressed his lips to hers, his tongue licking along the seam. She reached for his waist, but he abruptly rolled away.

"Hey!" she protested.

"I'm taking my clothes off this time." He moved with impatience, standing and reaching behind him for the neck of his T-shirt to yank it up and over his head. Every muscle in his back and arms flexed with the aggressive movement, giving her a delicious eyeful of how beautifully powerful he was. She briefly saw the scars again, some thin and silvered, others puckered and pink. One looked like a nasty knife wound that had been sutured without finesse.

She wanted to ask him about them but held back. Too much

intimacy would not be good for her when it came to him. Better to keep in mind that his past and future weren't hers to know and never would be.

Still, she was reminded of how dangerous he was despite always feeling so protected by him. She saw the same hypervigilance in Gideon's security detail, the kind of awareness that came from living with threats and fighting for survival. How her mild-mannered father could do *anything* to incite the fury of a man like Ronan was impossible to grasp; her mind just couldn't do it. Maybe it was all a terrible mistake.

Tossing his shirt onto her clothes chair, already piled high with her garments, Ronan faced her. "And I won't hurry, either. If you misbehave and rush me like last time, I'll tie you to the bed."

"Really? I'd like that." And she knew she would, emboldened by him, despite never having trusted anyone to restrain her. He was the cause of all the upheaval in her life, and yet, in moments alone with him, there was an ease between them, a sense of safety.

"Then we'll add it to the list." His teeth flashed white in the dimly lit room as he pulled a string of condoms out of his front pocket and tossed it on the nightstand. He pulled his phone out of his back pocket, turned it off, and set it down.

"What list?" she asked, her voice made husky by the quantity of condoms he'd brought with him. If he kept to his previous ratio of three orgasms for her to one condom for him, she was in for a wild night. Her blood heated, and her breathing quickened.

"The one with all the things I want to do to your enchanting body, *cher.*"

Rolling to her side, she propped her head in her hand to watch the show.

He shoved his jeans and boxer briefs to the floor in one swift, forceful movement. Then he straightened and stepped out of the puddled denim and cotton, shamelessly erect.

And why wouldn't he flaunt himself? She'd never seen a more perfect male body. Ronan could even, maybe, put a bit of weight on; his ripped physique was all golden skin and taut muscle without an ounce of extraneous flesh. He was like a rogue lion in need of a mate to look after him.

And his cock… Her mouth watered. It was hard and thick, curving upward to nearly touch his navel.

Her thighs tightened against the empty ache between them. "Enchanting. I haven't heard that one before."

"Enchanted. Bewitched. Possibly cursed. Whatever it's called, I couldn't get to you fast enough. Jules thinks I've lost my mind."

He returned to the bed and pulled her effortlessly into the middle. She barely caught a warning glimpse of the feral gleam in his smoky eyes, and then he lowered his head and took her mouth in a slanting, tempestuous kiss. His shift from cautiously playful to ravenously lustful was instant and unmistakable, and it set her on fire. She could taste his need; it deepened the lush intoxication of his seductive flavor.

His hand slid into her kimono and cupped her breast with proprietary aggressiveness. The shock of his warmth against her cool skin made her breath catch.

"I love the sounds you make when I touch you," he said hoarsely.

"I love when you touch me."

His agile fingers finished untying her kimono sash, and then he parted the silk as if he were unwrapping an expensive gift. The icy illumination of the moon detailed every curve and hollow of his muscular body. The flexing of his biceps was brilliantly defined by light and shadow as he plumped her breast with gentle kneading. She grew heavy and taut within his grasp, her body blooming under the fierce heat of his lust.

"How is it possible that you're more beautiful every time I see you?" he murmured, more to himself than to her.

Lowering his head, Ronan blew a cool stream of air across her nipple, making it pucker. He smiled with purely male conquest before bathing it in a long, savoring lick.

She moaned as his mouth wrapped around her, drenched the taut peak in wet heat. His cheeks hollowed as he suckled delicately, the lazy drawing pulls radiating through her body and echoing in her womb.

He licked across her cleavage to her other nipple, lavishing it with the same unhurried, focused attention. His hair hung around his face as his working mouth sucked rhythmically, his low groan vibrating through her.

She began to writhe against him, her hands stroking over every inch of him that she could reach. It felt almost desperate, the need she had to memorize how he felt beneath her questing fingertips. Her ferociously carnal desire heightened all of her senses, making every contact sizzle with near-unbearable pleasure. "Ronan…"

Lifting his head, he adored her body with gleaming eyes and tender hands. "*Dieu,* but you're delicious."

He whispered something in French as his fingertips stroked a featherlight line of fire between her breasts to her belly. Then lower to gently comb through the triangular patch of trimmed hair above her denuded labia. "I've lain in bed, stroking my dick, imagining tonguing your pussy until I'm drunk on you. That I haven't had my mouth on your cunt every day since we met has been driving me insane."

His gruffly voiced words swept like warm water through her, heating her from the inside out. When he parted her and stroked a finger across her slit, she arched off the bed with a hiss of shocked delight. Holding her gaze, he slid his finger into his mouth, his jaw working as he sucked her flavor from his skin. His sensual hum made her so hot she pushed up onto her elbows and shrugged out of the white silk.

"Sweeter than pralines," he murmured, his tongue gliding along the seam of his lips as he savored the taste of her.

He moved to straddle her, his powerful thighs settling on either side of her hips. Pulling her close, he kissed her passionately, his chest hot and lightly furred against her tight, tender nipples. She wrapped her hands around the fiery steel of his upthrust penis, her head tilted back in supplication as he fucked her mouth with lushly erotic thrusts of his silky tongue. She whimpered as her body began to tremble with unappeased need, her fists working in tandem to slide up and down the impressive length and girth of his cock.

Ronan growled into her mouth as he swelled within her grip. A thick wash of precum leaked from the wide head, and she massaged it in with her thumb, using the lubrication to quicken her pace.

"Stop," he ordered hoarsely, "I'm too close already."

She slid her thumb into her mouth, tasting him as he'd tasted her. The rich and darkly compelling flavor exploded across her tastebuds, sending a wave of tingles across her skin. She moaned, and his gaze heated further, his features tightening with ferocious desire. Her pussy grew slick with a surge of arousal.

"Let me suck you off," she whispered.

"*Non*. It's my turn to taste now."

"We can share a turn."

His thumb stroked the plump curve of her lower lip. "When I take your mouth, I'll be selfish with it. Right now, I want you wet, *cher.* I want you slick and hot when I fuck your pussy with my tongue."

Goosebumps raced over her skin, and he noticed, his slow smile promising dizzying delight. With his arm curved around her for support, he urged her onto her back with a filthy kiss. His hand slid between her legs. His knowledgeable fingers parted the plump lips of her pussy and stroked teasingly over the slitted entrance. The touch was like fire, sizzling across her nerve endings. She gasped into his mouth, and he nipped her lip with his teeth, a tiny tell that revealed the edge of his control.

Massaging her slit with two fingertips, Ronan spread the slickness of her desire up to her clit and rubbed, taking her to the very edge of orgasm. When her body tightened in anticipation, his touch moved lower, and he thrust inside her. She arched off the bed with a sharp cry, the feeling of fullness what she needed and yet not nearly enough.

His other hand slid beneath her head and supported her with his big palm, holding her steady as his fingers began to fuck her fast and hard, thrusting into her pussy in rhythm with his tongue strokes into her mouth. She grew slicker, hotter until she was audibly wet as he pumped his fingers into her, curling the tips so they rubbed over and over the sweet spot inside her. The orgasm was sharp and unbelievably intense, her channel clenching and releasing in ecstatic ripples. His growl of triumph made her shiver, the room darkening around them as her vision narrowed.

Then he was sliding away, his body losing all contact with hers. Ireland made a weak sound of protest, her senses overloaded, and then his broad shoulders were widening the spread of her thighs. She had an instant to register the feel of his hair brushing across her sensitized skin, and then his hot mouth was flowing over her clit, his tongue fluttering with maddening speed.

"Oh, god, Ronan." It was too soon; she was too sensitive.

The sound he made was practically a snarl, his mouth eating her with ravenous greed. Her hands fisted into the comforter, her hips lifting into the heat of his lushly carnal licks. He shoved his hands beneath her, cupping her butt in both hands as his head tilted and his tongue speared into her slick opening. She tensed, every muscle screaming as the wicked pleasure of his mouth drove her to the edge of madness. His tongue plunged in and out of her pussy, his throat working as he swallowed. He drank from her as if he'd been starved for the taste of her, elevating her hips to his mouth so that he could shove his tongue as deep as possible.

Ireland thrashed under the relentless pleasure, her thighs splayed wide as he tongued her with taut focus. Her next orgasm hovered tantalizingly within reach, and she whimpered, desperate for a release from the shattering ecstasy of his ravenous mouth. He moved one hand to massage her pulsing clitoris, and she tightened around his thrusting tongue, her pussy convulsing, trying to pull him deeper. She screamed his name when the climax broke, flooding her senses with fierce, addictive pleasure.

And he didn't stop, his lips forming a tight circle around her slit as he sucked her slick juices. Then he moved to her clit, lashing at it until she tried to push away weakly. Her low, soft moan as she came again made him growl with unmistakable exultation.

Dazed and spent, she offered no resistance when he pulled away and flipped her onto her belly, his tongue licking the sweat from the curve of her spine. He stretched away from her, and she heard a condom tear away from the others. Her pussy was throbbing in time with her racing pulse, wet and swollen from the avid attentions of his voracious mouth. When he gripped the back of her thigh to bend her knee and open her again, she jolted, so sensitized even his quiet shushing to calm her was too loud.

Ronan spooned behind her, fitting his larger body to hers. He took himself in hand, notching the broad head of his cock into her drenched slit. Gripping her waist with a steely forearm, she felt the coiling of his strength, and then he thrust deep, shoving the rigidly thick length of his penis in her to the wide root. The sound he made was one of pure animalistic indulgence, a guttural groan that almost made her come again.

Packed full of incredibly stiff cock, she moaned and squirmed against him, plastered to his torso by his weight and the grip he had on her hip. He linked their left hands together, stretching their arms above her head.

"*Mon dieu*," he gasped, his hips hunching against her bottom as if he couldn't stop himself from moving. "Your cunt is like heaven. Shoving my cock into you is all I can think about."

"Please..." It was all she could say, the stretching of her sensitive channel so sublime her thoughts spun incoherently. The heavy tip of his penis rubbed deliciously inside her, stroking with tantalizing pressure.

"Yes," he hissed, blanketing her back in the fiery heat of his sweat-slick chest as he began to rut furiously into her with all the power of his thickly muscled body.

Ronan took her like an animal, holding her captive beneath him as he fucked her ruthlessly, his heavy scrotum slapping against her clit in a frenzied cadence. Her orgasm seized her, her body no longer her own. It spread through her in waves, surging higher as he rode her clenching pussy with urgently deep thrusts, grunting every time he hilted inside her. She milked him hard in climax, her sheath tightening and releasing until she thought she'd die from the pleasure of it.

His teeth caught the muscle between her shoulder and neck, like a lion mating, and the feel of that soft bite was like an erotic wildfire in her body. She came again, burying her face into her pillow to silence her frantic cries, and this time, he came with her, pounding his impossibly hard penis into her melting, trembling core. His groan of release vibrated against her skin, drawing out into a sound of desperate need.

It was base and primal, unmistakably possessive, and she loved it in a way she'd never suspected she could or would.

Gasping, Ronan kissed the spot where he'd gripped her with his teeth. Then he rolled to his back, breathing hard, his sudden withdrawal leaving her empty.

"Come here," he husked, coaxing and pulling her over to drape his body.

His heart pounded beneath her ear as she struggled to breathe with her cheek against his chest. Her entire body felt full of electricity, her skin carrying a charge that made the tiny hairs stand at attention. The smell of Ronan's hardworking body was intoxicating, so delicious she pressed her nose against him.

His hands stroked up and down her back, his eyes closed as his body began to recover from its strenuous exertion.

Her stomach growled.

One of his eyes opened and focused on her. "Don't tell me the last thing you ate was lunch."

"Okay," she murmured sleepily, her limbs growing heavy.

"Oh no, *cher*." He shook her gently. "No sleep until we get some food in you."

She yawned. "I'm too tired to eat."

"This won't be the only time I ride you hard tonight." He rolled with her cradled in his arms and looked down at her with his hair a wild tangle around his stunningly gorgeous face. "You need the calories."

"I need sleep. *You* need calories."

He paused in the act of getting out of bed, twisting back toward her from his seat on the edge. "*Pardon?*"

"You're too lean," she told him, curling onto her side. "I think you're leaner now than when I met you. You're not eating enough."

He studied her with a slight smile, reaching over to run his hand through her hair. "You sound like Marcelle."

"Hmm."

He gave her a playful swat on the butt and stood, laughing at her grumbled protest as he pulled off the condom, wrapped it in a tissue from the box on her nightstand, and tossed it in the wastebasket by her vanity. "Get up, tigress. I'm certain there's something in the kitchen I can whip together."

"I doubt it."

"Messy and can't cook." He bent and kissed her. "My dream girl. *Allons.*"

Moaning in protest, Ireland dragged herself to the edge of the bed and sat up.

"You make that sound again, *cher*, and you'll get your wish to be flat on your back in that bed."

She could tell he wasn't making an empty threat because his cock had visually expressed its interest. She started to moan to get her way…

He put his hand over her mouth, laughing. "If you won't behave for you, do it for me. I'll need the energy to keep up with your insatiable demands."

Nodding her acquiescence, she grinned when his hand fell away. Then she stood and swayed on her feet, her legs weak.

Ronan caught her and gave her a measured look. "Is that from lack of food, or was I too hard on you?"

"You were perfect." She pushed onto her tiptoes to kiss his

jaw, relying on his support. "You could even go harder if that's what drives you wild. I love it when you lose control."

"*You* drive me wild." He reached for her kimono on the bed and handed it to her, then grabbed his jeans and pulled them on, only partially fastening them. Slung low on his hips, the softly draped denim revealed twin dimples just above the curve of his magnificent ass and the most outrageously defined abs she'd ever seen. The way those hard muscles arrowed down to his hefty penis made her want him all over again.

Taking her by the hand, he led her to the kitchen.

In short order, Ireland had another glass of orange juice in front of her, and Ronan was flipping an omelet with caramelized onion and sharp cheddar cheese.

"Do you like cooking?" she asked from her seat at the island, taking the opportunity to memorize every scar on his back. There were at least a dozen by her count and three that looked traumatic.

"I don't mind it. When I go to the bayou, I fend for myself. At home, I have Marcelle, and she fusses over me as you just did. She makes sure I eat regularly and often."

"Have you not been eating enough in New York? We're kinda known as one of the great cities for foodies."

He shrugged, sliding the omelet onto a plate and setting it before her. "I lose track of everything when I'm working. A lot of moving pieces to stay on top of. It wasn't easy to get… here."

From the way he picked his words, she understood that he meant it hadn't been easy maneuvering her father to the brink of insolvency.

My involvement with Vidal was years in the making by the time we met…

"A big strapping guy like you forgetting to eat?" she teased, agreeing that it was best to avoid discussing why they shouldn't be together like this.

He cut off another pat from the stick of butter and dropped it into the pan. "I've been told that food restriction is common among those who grew up not knowing when their next meal would be."

She paused in the act of chewing, startled then anguished. Despite everything, she cared for Ronan. It hurt to imagine him so young and vulnerable. "I didn't know that," she admitted faintly.

Pouring the last of the scrambled eggs into the melted butter, he faced her to put the bowl in the sink. He gripped the edge and held her gaze, dazzling her with the utterly masculine beauty of his body. "I can eat with you, though. I've found that being with you makes some things easier for me."

Ireland's face went slack, shocked by his revelation and how it tightened her chest.

His mouth curved wryly, and he returned to cooking as if he hadn't just dropped a bomb on her.

She drank her juice, her throat so tight it hurt to swallow. It took so long to pull herself into a semblance of calm that Ronan was digging heartily into his finished omelet before she could continue talking.

"So, when this is all behind you, will you slow down and work less? Maybe take better care of yourself. Have you killed your great white whale?"

The lusciously sensual curves of his lips compressed into a thoughtful line. "I haven't really thought of what would happen after."

"Isn't that the goal of revenge? To get on the other side of it and live the life you envisioned for yourself once the scales were evened?"

His nostrils flared on a deep inhalation. "I never looked that far ahead."

"I guess it's time you did," she said quietly, forking another bite into her mouth.

Ronan nodded and resumed eating.

His subsequent thoughts took him far from her, just as life soon would.

IT WAS A GORGEOUS DAY AT THE SHORE, THE SKY A VIVID cloudless blue. Seagulls hovered and dipped playfully, their raucous cries carrying on the soft, warm breeze. Eva lay between her husband's legs on a deck chaise with her back against his bare chest. His hand was under her oversized T-shirt, drawing circles on her belly. Lucky lay by their feet, his chin resting on Gideon's ankle.

She reached for the flute of champagne on the end table beside them and took a sip, searching for the easy equanimity she usually felt when they were in the Outer Banks. Instead, the now inescapable sense of driving impatience haunted her.

When did the three of them stop being enough? Inexplicably, she was still completely happy yet aware that something vital was missing. She took another big sip and set down the flute.

Gideon held an e-reader in his other hand, enjoying the latest installment of the police procedural series she'd introduced him to in the early days of their relationship. The couple in the series —a mogul and his cop wife—were childless, too, but by choice.

"I can hear your thoughts spinning," he murmured. "What's on your mind?"

She hummed evasively instead of answering.

His attentiveness was only one of the many qualities he possessed that would make him an exceptional father. When you had Gideon Cross's focus, it was absolute and laser-sharp, making you feel like no one else existed for him. A child would bloom under his care, just as she and Lucky had.

Earlier, she'd watched Gideon playing with Lucky on the beach, throwing a small piece of driftwood for their beloved beagle to fetch. She'd stood on the main deck, coffee in hand, and imagined children playing with them. A dark-haired, blue-eyed boy and girl. Then, two girls—one with lustrous dark hair and the other with beautiful auburn ringlets. Then, a tow-headed boy alone, joined later by a smaller sibling perched on Gideon's hip. The mystery of what a child of theirs would look like begged to be solved.

Heaving out her breath, Eva turned her head to rest her cheek against her husband's chest. A sudden wash of hot tears took her by surprise, the sadness rising so swiftly that she was taken under by it. She pressed her hand over his, stopping the gentle motion of his fingers over her skin. His palm was warm against her stomach, while the salt breeze that ruffled her hair was a cooling counterpoint to the sultry humidity.

"Do you ever think about our baby?" she whispered.

His abrupt stillness reverberated through her body. His chest lifted and fell beneath her, and a hot tear slid from her lashes to wet his skin. He immediately set his e-reader down to wrap her in his arms.

"Yes," he said tenderly, his lips to her temple. "Of course I do."

It was excruciating, knowing that her body had failed to nurture their child. They hadn't been trying to get pregnant and had both been startled—and yes, more than a little frightened—

to realize they were expecting. But the excitement began to grow, and they started envisioning the future.

To this day, no one else knew they'd ever been pregnant. They'd needed time to come to grips with the changes ahead before sharing the news, and then she'd miscarried.

"We never talk about it." She curled onto her side against him, careful not to dislodge Lucky, and placed her hand over his heart. "We talk about everything, but not that."

And because they weren't talking about their baby, no one was, and that was killing her slowly.

His chest lifted and fell against her shoulder. "I… I don't know how."

And she didn't, either. Their couples' therapist, Dr. Petersen, had suggested a few options for grief and fertility counseling, but they'd never pursued it, and she couldn't say why. The loss remained a raw wound, made more profound by the years since in which they hadn't tried to get pregnant or even discussed trying.

There was nothing physically wrong with her. She had miscarried her rapist's baby when she was fourteen, but that wasn't a contributing factor to her miscarriage in adulthood. Still, she was afraid to try and fail again. She was also scared of *not* trying and living with regret forever.

"It was terrifying for me," he admitted quietly, his hands running up and down her suddenly cold arms, using friction to dispel the goosebumps. "You were suffering, and I was helpless. You know I don't do well when you're sick or just not feeling well, and that was…"

His words trailed off, but the memory was evoked. For months afterward, she'd had nightmares of his bloodless face and haunted eyes. She remembered how he'd trembled violently as she'd lain wrapped in a blanket in his arms, hemorrhaging, his voice shattered as he'd tried to comfort her on the way to the hospital.

His trauma had affected her more than her own. Gideon was always so self-possessed and attuned to her that he often knew where her head was at before she did. He led, and she followed.

When he was lost, a yawning unknown opened in front of them that petrified her.

She swiped at her wet eyes. "Have you decided you don't want children?"

"I..." He paused. "It's not for me to make that choice. It's your body, angel. What you're willing to put it through is ultimately your decision."

Sitting up, Eva shifted on the chaise to face him. His careful reply almost seemed rehearsed. "That's bullshit."

His mouth was a grim line. "It's not."

"We're a team," she argued. "A decision like having children is one we make together. It's not just up to me." There was a vibrating fear in the pit of her stomach. "But you don't want kids, do you? You've never wanted any."

"I've never said that."

But then, he didn't have to. She saw it in the way his gaze broke from hers and dropped to Lucky. The entire family used to tease him because even the mention of babies sparked a visible fear. Then, one day, the teasing stopped, as if the family collectively decided that the time for choosing parenthood had expired.

"You're everything I need, Eva. I'll be more than content if it's just you and me forever. That doesn't mean I'm not open to more."

"Open to it, but not necessarily wanting it." She pushed onto her feet, feeling raw and vulnerable.

Gideon caught her by the wrist. “Don’t pull away. Talk to me.”

“What more is there to say?”

“Do *you* want to try again?”

She shrugged lamely, her throat tight. “What does it matter if you don’t?”

“Damn it, I didn’t say that!” His eyes took on the hard, icy light that signaled his growing temper. “I’m afraid for you. Afraid for us if something goes wrong again. You, our marriage, and your happiness are what’s important to me. If you’re not happy, let’s address it.”

“What does that mean, Gideon?” she asked wearily, so tired of her inner turmoil. “You’ll do it for me? Having a baby is something we should both want equally.”

“I don’t know how else to say this,” he snapped. “It’s not about whether I want a baby. It’s about not wanting to gamble with your safety! Yes, a child would be…amazing. But I can live without having one. I absolutely cannot live without you. If it’s one or the other, my choice will always be you.”

“But you could have both! Did that ever occur to you?”

He gestured helplessly. “Pregnancy has risks.”

“Aren’t we at risk every day?” she countered. “Isn’t that why there are security guards nearby even now? I’m more worried about keeping a child safe than I am about childbirth!”

He stood, too, bristling. “Why is this coming up now? Because Cary’s expecting? Or have you wanted to try again and haven’t said anything?” Abruptly, his face was transformed with astonishment. A stiff breeze whipped his hair across his face, and he shoved it impatiently out of the way. “This is about our security. This is why you’ve been upset about it. Damn it!”

In frustration, she threw up her hands and marched over to the deck railing. There was no point in bringing up something that couldn't be changed. But she couldn't bite the words back. "How do we raise a child under lock and key?"

"Eva..." He came over and embraced her from behind. "I grew up with security. Angus has been with me practically my whole life. When it's what you know and have always known, you're just used to it. And I promise, any child of ours won't be the only one going to school under the watch of a bodyguard."

She shook her head. "There's a big difference between being used to armed guards and having a vital need for them. If we're not safe, our children won't be, either. Losing a fetus was devastating. How would we ever survive losing a child?"

Eva felt his rapid, shaky breathing. But in the end, he stayed silent.

She knew she'd wounded him, and it hurt her equally. Protecting those he loved was one of Gideon's tenets and protecting him was one of hers.

But her unrelenting restlessness was telling her it was time to face the reality of their situation and the choices it left them with.

Ronan hummed as he stood before the full-length mirror in his bedroom and began knotting his tie. He was physically fatigued, his body aching from Ireland's hard use following the hour he'd spent in the hotel gym, and he couldn't remember ever feeling better. Energy vibrated through him, and his mind was sharp and alert. Which left him able to clearly see that while he'd known what needed to be done yesterday, today, everything was complicated by Ireland.

Just thinking of her made his blood heat, which should not

be possible after the night they'd had. He was a man who'd had his share of women. And he'd indulged in a period of hedonistic debauchery after a period of forced abstinence. Still, he'd never had a more searingly carnal experience than the night he'd spent in Ireland's bed.

There was a strange alchemy between them, something that unleashed every elemental need without shame. She was untamed in his arms, her hunger for him as voracious as his for her. How many times had he woken to the urgent tugging of her mouth on his cock? Three? Four? He couldn't come enough for her.

It's you. I've never been this hot for it before. And he knew she'd been as honest about that as she was about everything. She was visibly startled by some of the ways she responded to him and how much she could take, and the more he indulged his erotic obsession with her, the more abandoned she became. The pleasure he took in her willowy, glorious body was what made her so greedy, and her greed made him crazed with lust. It was a cycle that had now spun him completely around.

He adjusted the drape of the navy silk around his neck until it lay against his shirt at the perfect length.

But hadn't he known, instinctively, that she would be different? He'd been captivated the moment he'd caught sight of her in Jazzie's club. As photogenic as she was, nothing could prepare a man for the living, breathing woman. Watching her ferociously sexy stride, hearing her full-bodied laughter, catching the mischievousness in her stunning blue eyes... Some primal need had stretched awake inside him, a bone-deep recognition that he had met his match.

Ireland Vidal saw him in ways no one else did. She saw the feral child he'd been and the savage he'd become to survive. She somehow recognized that he would never be entirely civilized, and she accepted that about him, was even attracted to that quality because it gave her the freedom to be unbridled. Other women were turned on by the unease his wildness instinctively evoked, the perverse attraction some women had to dominant men, but Ireland's lust for him was about affinity, not fear.

She held her own. When they were in places that made him uncomfortable, she calmed him. She made him laugh in moments alone and asked questions that made him see things from new angles. She brightened his day with her utter *joie de vivre*. And his desire for her was as much instinctual as physical. He'd never expected to find a connection like they had, and now he must decide what he was willing to do to continue exploring it.

"So...?" Claudette asked from the doorway. "Are you cured?"

He tightened the Windsor knot at his throat and dropped his arms to his sides, sliding his hands into the pockets of his tan slacks. "I don't understand the sudden interest in my personal life."

"*Beau-frère*," she began, her voice a lush slow drawl, "pretending that you're not acting differently won't work."

His mouth curved in a fond smile. She knew him well—and he knew better than to reply.

She wore a trim, fitted business suit of soft green, the skirt ending just a few inches above the knee. The matching jacket hugged her small waist and flattered her svelte figure. She'd wrapped her thick hair into an elaborate coil at her nape and wore small gold hoops in her earlobes.

Her gaze narrowed slightly as she studied him. "She's under your skin, isn't she?"

"So what if she is? That doesn't change the fact that we've succeeded in separating Chris Vidal from his life's work."

"That wasn't the goal, though, was it?" she prompted. "You weren't going to stop until that building was gutted and another business was established there. That was the result you promised your father. Are you moving away from that now?"

It took him a moment to answer because he hadn't yet dedicated himself to weighing the options. "I haven't decided."

"But you're considering abandoning the plan? How serious are you about this woman you've just met, who has no connection to your life or roots?"

He crossed his arms. "I don't have an answer. Whatever this is between Ireland and me, neither of us wants it, and at the same time, it's all we want."

Her dark eyes were flat. "What am I to take from that?"

"I don't know, Claudy," he admitted. "Some fires burn so hot they flame out quickly. Maybe that'll happen here. I can't say." It felt like he and Ireland were locked into a fierce mating heat. Surely, they'd eventually be able to actually *sleep* together. They wouldn't fuck for hours at a time forever…

"Why not go home?" she suggested. "Leave the closing to Jules and me. We aren't at all conflicted about what needs to be done."

"I've thought about that."

She waited for him to say more, and when he didn't, she prodded, "And…?"

"I'm still thinking about it."

"Jules isn't taking this well," Claudette warned. "You're both father and brother to him if you don't know. Your approval is all he wants, and not knowing where your head is at has been hard for him to deal with."

"He's too focused on Ireland." Ronan moved to the bed and collected his suit jacket from where he'd tossed it earlier. "The steps and goal haven't changed; it's just been slowed down a little."

"Maybe there's a little jealousy involved," she conceded. "We're not used to having to share you."

As if on cue, Jules shouted from his room, and the sound of glass breaking shocked them both.

"*Maudit*," she muttered, turned to face Jules's adjoining door, which was ajar. "What now?"

Ronan shrugged into his suit jacket as he walked over to where she stood. He was eager to get to the Vidal offices. How would Ireland be with him at work? When he'd awakened her with coaxing good-bye kisses, she'd gifted him with a sleepy smile that had obliterated his plans to leave. Before he even processed what he was doing, the fly of his jeans was open, and he was between her lithe thighs, fucking his relentlessly hard dick into the tight silky depths of her exquisite pussy. She'd come apart for him, her long nails digging into his ass as she begged him for harder, deeper strokes.

Merde, he needed to stop thinking about her before his unruly cock embarrassed him.

"I can't fucking believe this!" Jules yelled, his voice getting louder as he marched into the main living area from his bedroom, his face mottled with fury. His suit today was a bright blue, his dress shirt a lighter shade, while his tie blended the two hues with soft green arrows. He held his phone in one hand, his grip white-knuckled. "Did you tell that bitch about the Lees?"

Ronan's features hardened. "You'll want to rephrase that, brother."

Jules' jaw worked for a moment as if he had to physically restrain himself from speaking. Then he bit out his words one by one. "Did you tell Ireland Vidal about the Lees's building?"

"*Mais non*. We don't talk about work."

"Do you talk at all?" Claudette asked sardonically.

He looked at her, unamused.

"Are you leaving your phone unlocked around her?" Jules asked crossly.

Ronan spoke calmly. "Can you just lay out what the problem is?"

"Remember that meeting Claudy and I had scheduled with the Lees this morning to wrap up the purchase of their building? They've informed me that they've accepted a better offer—including a new location for their business—from Cross Industries, and they signed the contract last night. That's why they put us off yesterday. The Cross team was putting together the paperwork."

Ronan went very still, his mind racing. Had he mentioned their plans to Ireland in passing? He couldn't recall.

"Do you know how many hours Claudy and I invested to get the Lees to the finish line and for what?!" he shouted. "The Clairbornes have a wire transfer ready to send us that we'll never see now! Scarlett's family was counting on us getting that warehouse for them! We're losing millions on this deal, not to mention what we've dumped into Vidal that we knew we'd never recoup."

"This is a disappointing development, I agree, but Cross becoming a complication is something we anticipated happening long before now."

"*Disappointing*?" Jules gripped his head in both hands, melodramatic as usual. "A week ago, this news would've made you scarily dangerous. Now? You shrug and say *c'est la vie!* Who cares that the family we're supposed to run into the ground is costing us *millions!* It doesn't feel like we're winning here, *beau-frère*. Can't you see that?"

Ronan took a steadying breath before answering, agitation

beginning to build. "I'm heading over to the offices now. I'll talk to her."

"Is that code for 'I'll fuck her and not care that she's a treacherous cunt?'"

Lunging forward, he caught Jules by the lapel and rammed his fist into his brother's jaw. The blow sent Jules back but Ronan's grip on his jacket kept him from falling. Then Ronan shoved him away so that he sprawled on the floor.

"Watch your mouth," he snarled.

With a roar of fury, Jules pushed up and rushed forward to tackle him. Ronan shifted his weight, caught his brother in the stomach with his shoulder, and hurled Jules into the sofa.

"Stop it!" Claudette ordered. "We're not turning against each other!"

Jules sat up, pushing his hair out of his face with an impatient hand. "He's not on our side anymore, *petite sœur*. We no longer have a common enemy."

"That's not true," Ronan shot back. "But I won't have you speaking of Ireland with disrespect. She doesn't know the history. Without that context, we're the enemy, and she's fighting for her family."

"Why haven't you explained it to her?" Claudette frowned with confusion. "If she cares for you, perhaps she could be an ally. Wouldn't that serve us best? It would sweeten her *envie* for you, *non?*"

"Because the truth will hurt her." Ronan raked a hand through his hair and gripped the back of his neck, frustration tightening his shoulders.

Jules's handsome face was twisted with disgust and rage. "You're more worried about her feelings than you are about the damage she's caused!"

"I don't blame her. That doesn't mean we're not fighting back. We always knew there was a high probability her brother would get involved, but for whatever reason, Chris Vidal didn't lean on his former stepson when it could've delayed the inevitable."

Pushing to his feet, Jules glared at him. "And we agreed that getting in and out of this claustrophobic city as fast as possible was the best way to avoid a pissing match with a man who can afford to ruin us!"

"Jules is right." Claudette gave Ronan a sympathetic look. "Sorry, but he is. We planned this to be quick and clean so that our time as an active threat was limited."

Everything in Ronan vehemently resented having his hand forced. But his siblings were right: his indecision could be costly, and while it was a price he'd been contemplating paying for his own sake, it was unfair to expect Jules and Claudette to suffer for it.

He growled. "*C'est tout*. I'll do what needs to be done."

Ireland was humming as she strolled into her office. She probably shouldn't be in such a good mood, all things considered. She should be dead on her feet, for one thing. There'd been times during the night when she and Ronan had slept but only in brief intervals.

It was as if their bodies couldn't bear to be separated. Even being tucked up against him in slumber wasn't enough to satisfy the near-desperate desire that drove them both to their limits. If he wasn't waking her with his strong, skillful hands and ravenous mouth, then she was waking him. They'd been burning through borrowed time, which had made her determined to wring every bit of pleasure she could from him.

Walking to her filing cabinet, she typed in the code and dropped her purse in the drawer where she stored it. Then she went to her desk and woke her computer by wiggling her mouse.

God, her body throbbed. Her breasts felt heavy, and her pussy was swollen and tender. Just washing herself in the shower had proven that she was so hypersensitive even water felt like a caress.

Ronan's desire for her was so raw and insatiable that it shattered all her inhibitions. She'd never felt sexier or bolder. She surrendered control to him completely because there was never even a twinge of unease, discomfort, or shame. He could use her body in any way he desired, and she loved it all because what drove him crazy was her pleasure. She couldn't orgasm enough for him, and the more she climaxed, the more feral he became until he was fucking that magnificent penis into her like he'd die if he didn't.

The most potent aphrodisiac was being the object of an extraordinary man's sexual obsession. She was addicted to the feeling of being everything he wanted yet couldn't get enough of.

She moaned and squirmed in her chair, forcibly pushing the memories from her mind. She was so hot just remembering how Ronan had taken her that she pressed her fingers hard between her legs, trying to ease the throbbing of her clit.

The knock on her open door startled and embarrassed her, even though her grandfather's old desk hid where her hand had been. She blushed when her eyes met her father's.

"Good morning, boss," he greeted her.

Rolling her shoulders back, Ireland managed to smile in return. The sensual haze Ronan had left her with began to ebb. "Good morning."

“Brett, Darrin, and the rest of the Six-Ninths crew will set up later today to start recording tomorrow,” he told her as he walked in and sat in one of her gray velvet visitors’ chairs. He wore a cream cardigan today, over a light gray shirt and darker gray dress slacks.

She could see his excitement and feigned her own. “I saw that they’ve reserved Studio One for the next week. That’s great!”

“It will be,” he assured her. “I sent you the demo. Have you listened to it?”

“Not yet, but it’s on my to-do list, I promise.” She tapped her fingers on the desktop. “I have a question for you. Where is the licensing money for Vidal Hotels going? I can’t find it.”

He nodded. “We don’t actually receive it. It didn’t sit right with me that the hotels would bear our name but not truly be owned by us. So, I asked Gideon to use the money to purchase shares in the venture. Every payment buys more shares.”

“And we’re reinvesting the dividends,” she guessed, which he confirmed with another nod. “Okay. That’s good to know. And a good plan.”

“I’m glad you approve. I did try, Ireland.” His wry smile faded as he sobered. “The terms of the McCaffrey loan were unusual, as I’m sure you’ve discovered, but he’s a shareholder and stood to lose a great deal of money if Vidal failed. There was no way to know he was willing to lose millions to see us go under.”

Guilt settled over Ireland like a shroud. How was it possible that she could take such pleasure from someone causing her family such turmoil? What was *wrong* with her?

“Now I have a question for you,” he said evenly, but his piercing gaze meant he was in full-on dad mode. “Christopher told me that McCaffrey insisted on speaking with you privately and behind a locked door. Is he intimidating you, Ireland?”

She shook her head. “No, he’s always a gentleman. He saw

that Christopher was reacting to the changes here in a way that was upsetting me, and he removed me from the situation so I could pull myself together."

Her father nodded thoughtfully. "Do you like him?"

"Dad." Her face was hot. "We're not talking about this."

"Do you trust him?" When she opened her mouth to protest again, he rushed on, "Can *I* trust him?"

Closing her mouth, she frowned at him. "What do you mean?"

Christopher walked in without knocking, looking sharp in monochromatic burgundy. "Here you are. Get this." He waited until he'd taken the chair next to their father before continuing, the two men looking so similar and yet uniquely themselves. "Gideon left town with Eva yesterday and is apparently now completely off-grid until Friday. No one from his office can reach him, and all of my calls to either of them go straight to voicemail."

Ireland rocked back in her chair, her gaze narrowing. "Why are you trying to reach Gideon?"

He shot her a look. "Why do you think? McCaffrey thinks he's hot shit, but Gideon will destroy him."

An anxious knot tightened in her gut.

"We've decided not to approach Gideon with this situation," their father said.

"No," Christopher corrected, "*you two* decided that. *I'm* going to fight tooth and nail."

"We have other avenues, Christopher," she argued, standing and walking to the door to close it.

"Like what? A new single from Six-Ninths?" Christopher snorted. "I know Dad's counting on that but come on."

Their father shook his head. "You haven't listened to the demo, either."

Christopher gave Ireland a sardonic look. “I don’t have to be a fan, Dad, to sell the shit out of them. I’ll give it my all, I promise you.”

She settled back in her seat. “You’re both forgetting about London Grant.”

Both men perked up, studying her avidly. London Grant was a young actress/singer who’d skyrocketed to prominence as a supporting character on a teen-focused musical television show. Her reps had leaped to capitalize on her growing fame by shopping her to all the major record labels. Ireland had heard about London’s ambitions and pursued the chance to sign her.

Her father spoke first. “I thought her team was aiming for a bigger label.”

“They were. But they’re ambitious. They want her everywhere—school supplies, fashion collabs, and even home goods. Once I learned that, I suggested something that put us over the top: branded hotel suites in Vidal Hotels. Similar to the suites we all designed.”

Christopher whistled. “Holy shit.”

“She’ll bring the added benefit of helping the hotels appeal to a younger demographic. And” —her smile widened with excitement and pride— “I reached out to Chantal because she’s presently recording and asked if she’d be open to a duet with London so we can launch her faster. Turns out Chantal’s sister is a fan of London’s show, so it was an easy yes for her, and London’s favorite song is one of Chantal’s, so she’s thrilled.”

“Maybe our luck has changed,” her father said with a brighter smile than she’d seen in days.

“We’ve got a songwriter working with them now,” she continued. “Hopefully, we can get them in the studio before Chantal’s session time expires. Then London and I will discuss some producer options for her debut. We launch her with care, and it'll pay off."

Her phone rang, and she saw that it was her assistant. "Hey, Matt."

"Hey, boss." There was more than a hint of amusement in her longtime assistant's voice. He was getting a kick out of their changed circumstances, not knowing the gravity of the situation. "Mr. McCaffrey would like to see you as soon as you're available."

Her traitorous body heated at the mere mention of Ronan's name. "I'm in a meeting now," she said.

Her dad stood. "I can let you go. Just wanted to check in, and now, with all this good news, I'm energized to get some shit done."

"Fuck yeah." Christopher pushed to his feet. "I'm fired up, too. I'll start making some calls about the new Six-Ninths single. See what kind of support we can pull together."

"Listen to the damned demo!" their father told them, rocking back on the heels of his sneakers.

"Never mind," she told Matt. "You can send him in."

"Will do."

Her brother and father filed out. Her dad paused on the threshold and stared hard at Ronan, forcing him to enter the room sideways. The two men's height and overall body size were so different, her father almost looked small, but the ferociously stern line of his mouth made her nervous.

Ronan squeezed past her dad with his jaw clenched.

Her father's gaze narrowed at Ronan's back, then he continued out. Ronan stared after him with a scarily intense glare.

"Hey," she called out, standing to draw his attention. "What do you need?"

It took him another long second before he turned his head toward her and finished entering the room. He walked up to her desk, looking mouthwateringly delicious in a simple combo of navy slacks and tie paired with a white dress shirt with tiny navy stripes. The fall of his hair around his face was so sexy that her thighs tightened. She wanted him to come close enough that she could smell him, but kept to her side of the desk because she didn't trust herself not to forget that her door was open.

His hands went to his hips, and he gave her an uncompromising look. "You told your brother about my warehouse in Queens?"

She blinked at him. "Um…"

He growled low in his throat. "I forgot I even told you about it, but you didn't. You've cost me a pretty penny, *cher*. Jules is damn near apoplectic about it."

She shrugged with feigned nonchalance. "All's fair in love and war."

His eyes took on a hot gleam. His breathing began to pick up, rapidly becoming heavy. With a taut hungry look, he closed the remaining distance to her desk. His voice was muted, for her only. "You've made a lot of *tracas* for me, *cher*. You're nothing but trouble from head to toe. Certain destruction for any man, and yet all I want at this very moment is to tongue-fuck your sweet cunt until you scream for the whole office to hear."

Ireland swallowed hard past a sudden lump in her throat, fighting the urge to round the desk and press her needy body against his. He should be furious, and maybe he was, but there was a gleam of pride in his eyes and the slightest hint of indulgence in the firm curves of his mouth. Not to mention the lust pumping off him in heated waves.

"I don't think my daddy would like that," she whispered

huskily, provoked by his amorous gaze, sinful drawl, and the temptation of his splendid body.

"I'd fucking love it," he told her gruffly. He rolled his shoulders back and stepped away from her, his eyes dark. "And hey, if Jules stops by today, stay out of his way."

She licked her dry lips. "You're the one I need to stay away from."

He backed away with a cocky smile. "Good luck with that."

THE FEEL OF LUCKY'S WARM, WET TONGUE ON HIS CHIN woke Gideon. Grabbing the beagle's velvety body, he hugged the dog close and rolled to his side, careful to be quiet so as not to disturb his sleeping wife.

Initially, Lucky's determination to awaken him from nightmares was startling, but he'd become used to it over the years. And truly, cuddling the dog helped to slow his racing heart as reality pushed the dreams back into the distant corners of his mind.

Sometimes, the nightmare was still vivid when he woke, and it was especially so tonight. A blend of memory and his fears, he was left with an icy knot of terror in his gut and cold sweat on his skin. Snuggled close, Lucky licked at the salty perspiration, happy to receive his owner's grateful petting.

Gideon silently extricated himself and the beagle from the bed and looked down at Eva. She was curled toward him in a fetal position, her face soft and carefree in slumber. There was none of the tightness around the lips and eyes that he'd observed in recent days. She was always breathtakingly beautiful, but somehow more so while sleeping. He woke before her regularly just to enjoy the sight of her at peace, secure within the safety he provided.

A baby.

He shivered as the night's chill further cooled the sweat on his skin. The clock told him it was just after three in the morning. Lucky became restless in his hold, so he set him down, grabbed his pajama pants from the bench at the foot of the bed, and tugged them on. They headed out of the room together.

The sweeping view of the Atlantic outside the expansive windows was now a luminous blackness, the moon revealing the edges of the clouds above and the white crests of the tumultuous waves below. It was easy to imagine they were at sea, separated from the world by hundreds of nautical miles. The feeling of remoteness was a charming feature of the oceanfront property they'd fallen in love with.

Nothing else in the world existed when they were here, and he couldn't be happier. They unplugged—no phones, televisions, or AI assistants—and he needed nothing more than Eva's company. She was endlessly fascinating to him, her mind so nimble and her heart so big. She nurtured and protected those she loved, and he was damned lucky to be among that number.

But she wanted more. More of him, of *them*. And being intimately familiar with that yearning himself, he understood how she felt.

Entering the kitchen, Gideon grabbed a glass and got cold water from the fridge. Lucky whined at the folding glass doors leading out to the deck. He headed that way, keying in the disarm code on their alarm system before unlocking and pushing aside one pane so they could both exit. It was warmer outside than in the house, the humidity lending a sultry quality to the night breeze. Lucky ran ahead to the stairs and down to the sandy shore below.

Gideon grabbed their favorite piece of driftwood off the stair railing, leaving his water glass in its place, then followed him down.

The sand was cool beneath his feet, the world leached of color by the silvery light of a waxing moon. The waves surged and retreated rhythmically against the shore, the crashing waves creating a soothing cadence. Lucky danced in circles, eagerly awaiting a game of fetch. Pulling his arm back, Gideon whipped the driftwood stick down the beach, smiling at Lucky's joy in chasing it.

Hadn't he imagined playing with a child on the beach and then, later, multiple children? He had memories of playing at the shore with his father and cherished them.

In the early days of his marriage, he'd been afraid of fatherhood, positive that he wouldn't be any good at the job. It had taken over a year of therapy to manage the nightmares that had made sleeping with his wife dangerous, and the healing was ongoing. He still had bad nights, but Lucky was his literal dreamcatcher, and he'd addressed a lot of the trauma that had made his subconscious a menace in the first place.

As his life stabilized around Eva, possibilities opened up. Making a family with his wife became a new tentative dream. When she'd told him she was pregnant, she had been noticeably scared, which had tempered his excitement. It *was* too soon, they'd agreed. There was still so much to accomplish as a couple before they'd be ready to share each other with children. But excitement and joy had quickly overtaken the doubts and apprehension.

He sighed and accepted Lucky's stick, throwing it again as he walked out from under the house into the open. The stars glittered profusely, seemingly a completely different sky from the one he slept under in New York. That sky was gray with only a scattering of stars, while this sky was inky blue and a field of sparkles.

When Eva awakened, he would tell her they should start trying. He was going to convince her that he wanted to, which he did, and he would find a way to put the memory of their previous miscarriage behind them.

The wind whipped through his hair as he followed Lucky's paw prints. He took the stick when it was brought to him and threw it again.

He and Eva would mitigate the risks as best they could. He'd ensure she got lots of rest, wasn't on her feet too much, had no stress or worries whatsoever, and overall, had the most peaceful and restful pregnancy achievable. She wanted their child, and he would do everything in his power to grow their family safely and in good health.

When Lucky returned to him again, Gideon turned to throw the stick toward the house, and they started back. Now that he had the beginnings of an actionable plan, he was keen to tell Eva and get started.

He laughed at himself for his sudden eagerness. He was already technically putting the effort in. He made love to his wife at least twice a day, often more, a frequency which shocked their therapist but was as necessary to them as breathing. Sex was how they bonded, allowing them to express the love that words were inadequate at communicating. And Eva was presently taking the placebo pills in her birth control pack while on her period, which meant she was already weaning off the hormones.

They were ready to begin trying.

So…

Throwing the stick one last time, he went to the bottom of the stairs and started up. The salt breeze ruffled the hair at his nape, and a sudden chill coursed down his spine, spreading goosebumps in a prickling wave across his skin. He paused mid-step, struck by a growing uneasiness. Lucky ran past him up the stairs and reached the top, then stopped suddenly, his body crouching as he began growling low in his throat.

Tilting his head, Gideon listened intently for any creaking on the deck above him.

He'd left the door open…

Spurred by icy terror, he raced up the stairs and ducked low when he reached the deck, making himself a smaller target. Lucky launched into frenzied barking. The house was still dark, the folding door still open. Darting into the house, he jabbed the silent alarm button below the security system panel, alerting the team on his way to the interior stairs, which he took two at a time to reach the bedroom.

He ran in, stumbling around the bench to reach Eva. Dropping to his knees, he felt for her almost blindly, his hands finding her soft, warm body.

She woke with an audible start, turning toward him. "What?" she asked huskily. "What's wrong? Did you have a nightmare?"

Relief made him giddy, his heart pounding so hard he felt dizzy. Through the open bedroom door, he saw the downstairs and deck lights coming on as the security team swept the house.

With a rueful laugh, he sat on the edge of the bed. "I think I psyched myself out," he admitted.

The landing light came on, and Raúl filled the doorway.

"I need to clear the room," he said, flicking the switch on the wall and entering with gun drawn. He moved efficiently through the space, checking the bathroom, closet, and even under the bed. Meanwhile, outside on the uppermost deck, a male silhouette passed by their closed curtains.

Eva sat up, hugging the blankets to her chest. "What's happening?"

He ran a sheepish hand through his hair. “I took Lucky out, and the breeze hit me wrong. Felt like someone walking over my grave. Then he wigged out about something, and I reacted.”

“Better safe than not.” Raúl retreated to the doorway and shouted down, “Clear!”

“I’ve got something,” Chase yelled back from outside.

All three of them tensed. Raúl headed down swiftly. Gideon stood, grabbed Eva’s silver kimono from the bench, and handed it to her. He shrugged into his robe and belted the black silk, then took his wife’s hand and led the way down to the living area.

Their team of three men—Raúl, Chase, and Rizwan—stood on the deck with Lucky sitting at their feet. The group had clustered at the top of the staircase to the beach, and it took him a moment to follow Lucky’s gaze and understand why.

The lethal crossbow bolt was black and, against the weathered gray siding, almost invisible. The vicious tip pierced the side of the house, its shaft a nearly straight line.

Chase glanced at them briefly. “Stay indoors.”

Sliding an arm around Eva’s waist, Gideon urged her to move inside with him. Settling her on the couch, he kneeled in front of her. “I’m going to start a pot of coffee for the team. Can I get you anything?”

She looked at him with blank, haunted eyes, and he saw the hopelessness there and something far more painful he recognized from when her mother had died: grief. Her silence was like a scream to him, her petite frame sagging under the weight of resignation. She’d already believed they weren’t safe enough to have a child; now, that belief was established as truth.

Gideon moved into the kitchen and started working on the coffee, repeatedly lifting his gaze to watch the team work. Through the open folding doors, he heard them clearly.

Raúl took photos of the bolt with his phone. “We’ll check the security recordings, see when it was shot at the house.”

“From the trajectory,” Chase said, “we’ll determine where the shooter was.”

“Must’ve been fairly close for accuracy,” Raúl said, almost to himself. “Way easier to hit the glass than this relatively small patch of siding between them. Thirty to fifty yards. Maybe a bit more distance if the guy’s an expert.”

Rizwan shined a flashlight around and beneath the Adirondack chairs nearby. “Got something else.”

Withdrawing a vinyl glove from a cargo pocket, Raúl crouched. He straightened with what looked to be a tube of black duct tape in his gloved hand. Bringing it into the house, he joined Gideon in the kitchen. The others followed.

Jaw clenching, Gideon knew with sickening certainty that they’d received another menacing note after two years of silence —delivered courtesy of the bolt.

He quickly wiped off the breakfast bar with a bleach wipe and watched grimly as Raúl tugged on another glove. Eva joined them, sliding onto one of the barstools. Her eyes were big and dark, her lips white. She clutched the lapels of her robe in a fist at her throat, her other arm hugging her waist.

Underneath the tape, a transparent sheet protector filled with black paper uncoiled as Raúl gingerly spread it open on the counter. Gideon’s jaw tightened with growing fury, a chilling rage spreading through him. The modus operandi was horrifyingly familiar. There were the Glasgow smiles carved into recent paparazzi photos of him and Eva. There were the mismatched letters crudely cut from headlines. And there was the twisted children’s rhyme.

He took his wife to the sea, sea, sea

`To see what they could see, see, see`
`But all that he could see, see, see`
`Was her body at the bottom of the sea,`
`sea, sea!`

Eva shook her head mechanically, tears streaming down her face.

He turned his back on the malevolent taunt and focused on his wife, whose state of shock was his primary concern at the moment.

All the excitement he'd felt such a short time ago felt like something from a dream, and the plans he'd hoped to share with her were now trapped in his dry, aching throat. An unknown menace, dark and perverse, once again shadowed the cautiously optimistic future he'd envisioned.

The feelings of being unsafe and violated were made worse by their location. Their beach house had always been their safe place and now that was taken from them.

"I'm okay," she told him hoarsely as he helped her back to the sofa.

But she wasn't. And neither was he.

Ireland awakened to the feeling of freefall, her entire body jerking in alarm. Heart pounding, she lay there a moment, willing herself to calm. Blizzard stretched out a meaty paw and placed it on her leg, extending his claws just enough that she felt their prick against her calf.

"Listen, buddy, I'm not happy about being awake, either!" she groused.

She'd gone to bed early, the lack of recent sleep catching up with her, but she kept waking intermittently. A glance at the clock told her it was just past four. She debated just getting up. A cup of coffee, a shower—if she took her time, she could stretch it out and get to the office around six. Early, but so what? There was so much to be done; she could use extra hours in the day.

Reaching for her phone, she frowned at the notifications of missed messages. Yes, she silenced her phone at night, but no one ever contacted her anyway. She opened her messenger app and was delighted to see Ronan's name with a new notification. She would never admit it, but she'd nearly locked her phone in the half-bath to prevent herself from calling him.

There was also a text from Angus, sent just after nine. She made herself open that one first.

> Let me know a good time to stop by tomorrow. I'm available all day.

She chewed on her lower lip. Did it mean anything that he wanted to talk face-to-face? A text or even an email would save him trouble. But maybe that's just how he liked to give his reports and was most comfortable with that routine...? If there were anything of an urgent nature, surely he wouldn't delay telling her.

What did she hope to find out? That Ronan was as perfect as he seemed so that he could be an even bigger regret? The sexy, charming, talented, intelligent, phenomenal-in-bed, wealthy, musical dream man who got away. Or was she hoping a skeleton in his closet would be a dealbreaker for her, freeing her from his spell?

She opened Ronan's message.

> Invite me over

She exhaled through the surge of heat that flared throughout her body. She could hear his voice in her head, saying those three words to her in his melodic drawl, as seductive as sin itself.

He'd followed up with another message a couple of hours later.

Please

The last message was a few hours old, but she felt the intense craving behind it. That a man as magnificent as Ronan Boudreaux was jonesing for her rather than easily scoring a hookup... God, it turned her on to be so explicitly wanted by a man like him.

They should be staying far away from each other. What was *wrong* with them? She expected his family disliked her as much as her family disliked him. He had the exact same reasons as she to keep his distance.

What was this strange alchemy between them that was so irresistible? The only time she felt like herself anymore was with him, and yet she was unrecognizable in his presence—bolder, more aggressive, and yet more submissive, too. She felt emotions for him that frightened her because she didn't understand them, yet when she was with him, she was fearless.

This invite expires in 20 mins

She stared at her reply for a long time. *Don't send it.* Just because she half-hoped he was unconscious and wouldn't see her invitation until too late, didn't mean it wasn't going to still be there on his phone when he woke. Then he'd know the weakness she had for him. She'd been so proud of herself for successfully resisting the urge to call him, which took more effort than she would like to admit.

But she was lonely and had been for a long time. Plus, she was making herself miserable, constantly thinking she was doing everything wrong. She was tired of her spinning thoughts. More than all of that, though, she wanted to be with Ronan. He saw what she needed and gave what he could. And the man fucking owed her that much for all the bullshit he was putting her through.

Ireland sent her text with the invisible ink effect to lessen her future embarrassment.

On my way!

His shortcut reply came so fast that she blinked at the screen in disbelief.

"No way," she said aloud, still shocked. Blizzard gave a little warning growl of disapproval. Many people had cats who knew what it meant to be nocturnal, but not her. Blizzard started demanding that she move into the bedroom around ten o'clock, and as far as she knew, he spent the whole night taking up half her bed. And he became pretty grumpy if his beauty sleep was disturbed.

She added Ronan to her visitors list via the building app, then set her phone on the charger again. Sliding out of bed, she stretched and berated herself for being selfish. She could hardly look her father in the eye when Ronan's name inevitably came up.

How could she ever explain that being with him made her happy in a way she'd never known? That even as he was destroying their familial legacy, he was supporting and encouraging her, and taking pride in the very accomplishments that were setbacks for him? Not that she would ever have to defend her actions.

The path she and Ronan traveled together inevitably forked, and the split loomed closer by the hour.

Ronan roamed the elevator like a caged beast, his gaze locked on the numbered display that ticked off each floor as the car raced to the top. He'd been pacing most of the night, strung out from wanting Ireland.

What had she done to him? When he was with her, he felt... peaceful. And it was a damned miracle that he recognized what she made him feel because he'd never known peace previously.

But there was a price: everything became increasingly discordant within hours of leaving her. He worried about her. Where was she? Was she taking care of herself? Was she safe? And did he enter her mind, even briefly? It enraged him that the fates would put a once-in-a-lifetime woman like Ireland Vidal in his path and make him the villain in her story.

But of course, he didn't have the morals to be the hero.

And she was actively trying to distance herself from him, which stirred a primitive and possessive reaction so fierce he couldn't restrain it.

When the elevator began to slow, he stopped pacing directly in front of the doors and pushed through them the second they began to open. A flash of red snagged his attention, and he found Ireland waiting for him in the vestibule, restlessly pacing just as he had. The bold crimson of her kimono was like a matador's cape. He charged toward her, yanking his T-shirt off and tossing it aside. She met him partway, throwing herself at him with a soft cry.

The feel of her in his arms brought instant clarity. The pounding beat of her heart was the tempo he'd been missing. He had always been slightly off-key with the world, a burden on those he loved and who loved him.

But he'd found a rhythm with Ireland.

Pulling her long, slim body as close as possible, Ronan took her mouth with avid hunger and pressed her against the nearest wall. The taste of her, minty and warm, and the feel of her supple body, so strong and utterly feminine, licked like fire across his senses. He groaned, the sound filled with relief and torment.

She wrapped her arms around his neck and thrust her fingers into his hair, holding him where she needed to take control of the kiss. The thrusts of his tongue were near frantic. His frenzy drove hers until she was trying to crawl up his body, her legs and arms tightening around him.

The look in her eyes when she'd watched him exit the elevator haunted him. Her initial joy shifted to regret and then guilt. Yet her desire for him burned through it all—but for how long?

He thrust his jeans-clad leg between hers, supporting her as he fumbled with the tie of her kimono. She caught his tongue with soft suction, drawing on it rhythmically, reminding him—as if he could ever forget—of the heady feel of that voracious suction on the head of his dick. He shuddered hard and thrust the silk open, growling when he filled his hands with her tits. He squeezed them, his finger and thumbs finding and teasing her taut nipples until she began to rub her pussy against his thigh.

"*Mon dieu*," he muttered into her mouth. "I thought you weren't going to call me."

"I didn't."

He couldn't stop kissing her. His hands stroked every inch of skin he could reach, proving to himself that he was with her, and she was his, at least for now. "I cursed you. Damned you to hell."

"You should've left your table to me at Jazzie's."

"I fucking should have."

She was equally frenzied, yanking open the button fly of his jeans to get to his straining penis. She whimpered at finding him commando. He was so aroused she had to pull his cock away from his belly, the rigid hardness pumped with thick veins. She traced them with her talented fingers, rubbing the precum that wept from the sensitive tip with the pad of her thumb. His brain and body seized at the exquisiteness of the sensation, his breathing quickening into panting.

For a long moment, he could only quiver helplessly as she stroked and fisted his aching cock, the pleasure of her touch so potent he gritted his teeth against the urge to spew his cum all over her pretty pink tits.

He knew damned well she would welcome him losing control that way. There was nothing they did together that was wrong or dirty or shameful, nothing that needed to be negotiated or explained. They were so attuned to how their bodies served each other's pleasure, he was certain neither of them would ever find this freedom with anyone else.

His ardent mouth moved over her face. "I went down to Jazzie's tonight. For once, playing music was no help."

"I'm sorry."

Her tone was sincere, and he didn't doubt it. If anyone could understand what losing the comfort of an instrument truly meant to a musician, it was Ireland. Their shared love of music was one of their points of connection.

"So, I flirted with a beautiful, sexy woman," he went on, "and took her to my room."

Ireland's body went stock-still; even her breathing stopped. A harsh sound that was almost a sob escaped her, and she released his cock, pressing her palms to his stomach to try pushing him away. Malicious triumph filled him. If she felt jealousy, she felt ownership.

Good.

Gripping her hips with flexing hands, he pressed his damp forehead to hers, his chest working with heavy breaths. "She tried to kiss me, and I threw her out." He barked a bitter laugh. "You've unmanned me. I only want you."

"Ronan…" She surged into him, catching him with a hand at his nape as she kissed him with everything she had—covetously, possessively, angrily.

"I have to have you," he muttered against her trembling lips.

Then he sank into a crouch and buried his nose in the silky patch of curls just above her hairless labia. He inhaled deeply, the lush female scent of her intensifying the need that drove him so hard. Nuzzling her, his tongue dipped between her folds, finding her slickly aroused. Her head fell back against the wall with a soft thud, desire sweeping across her body in a flush of soft pink.

Sliding his hand behind her knee, he draped it over his shoulder, opening her up to his long, slow licks. Her flavor drove him wild. He'd imagined finding her in the Vidal offices, sitting her atop a desk or conference table, and sliding up to her succulent cunt with a rolling desk chair so he could tongue her to orgasm.

Like he was determined to do now. Swirling his tongue around her clit, he moaned and fisted his eager cock, which would have to wait its turn to feel her incredible pussy wrapped around it. Right now, he was locked into her honeyed flavor, avidly rubbing the flat of his tongue over her from cunt to clit. Her fingers slid into his hair, finding and massaging the sweat-damp roots, holding him against her soft folds as if it were even possible that he could pull away. Spearing his tongue, he teased the tiny slit that seemed too small to take his rampantly hard dick but could not be a more perfect fit.

She cried out and began rocking against his working mouth, riding his tongue as he speared into her with voracious thrusts, feeling the delicate muscles of her tight channel grasping to hold him. Later, he would spread her wide on the bed and settle in to feast, but impatience drove him now, the hours he'd spent waiting and hoping for her to reach out to him still too fresh in his mind. He groaned as he tilted his head to try and get deeper, the scent and taste of her so intoxicating he felt drunk on her.

"Ronan!" She gasped his name when he circled her clit with his lips and then suckled it, the tip of his tongue massaging the hood. She bucked against his mouth, her hands gripping the back of his head. Her thready cry when the orgasm hit her was like music to his ears, and he growled with masculine victory, surging onto his knees to better support her weight as she trembled and shook, her cunt pulsing and clenching around his driving tongue.

He continued licking her for long moments, gentling her as she twitched with aftershocks. Only when she was utterly relaxed did he wipe his wet mouth on her inner thigh and slide her leg from his shoulder.

He stood, holding her steady with his hands on her hips. She was flushed all over, her eyes dark and dilated in the dimly lit vestibule. He held her gaze as he pushed the kimono off her shoulders with one hand, then he raked her with a head-to-toe glance, thrilling at the sight of her beautiful body lush from orgasm and still hungry for his. His dick felt like a heavy club between his legs, and he was mere moments away from shoving it inside the hottest, tightest, sweetest—

"*Malhereux!*" he bit out, his eyes squeezing shut.

"What?" Her hand cupped his face, and he leaned into her touch.

He looked at her. "I was in such a hurry to get here... I forgot to bring protection."

Her eyes were luminous, her face so stunningly perfect it hurt him to breathe. "I have some, although I'm sure you need a bigger size than I have."

"There are other ways to satisfy, *cher*," he pressed his lips softly to hers, "some of which we've already enjoyed together."

She gripped his waist and arched her body sinuously against him, a temptress bent on his destruction, and he succumbed willingly, even gratefully. "I need your cock inside me," she breathed, her lips on his jaw. "And your cum."

Ronan's palm hit the wall abruptly for support, his cock swelling so rapidly that his knees weakened from the sudden rush of blood to his already engorged dick. "*Merde*," he growled, his thighs quivering with the need to drive hard and fast into her before she changed her mind.

"I'm on the pill." Her voice was a whispered temptation. "And I've never had unprotected sex."

"Neither have I," he bit out, his entire body straining toward her. His hand at her waist slid around her, pulling her tightly to him. She was cool against his feverishly hot skin, the antidote to the craving that afflicted him.

He'd felt this way with no one else and had, in fact, feared an unwanted pregnancy so intensely that wearing a condom had always been a necessity. That was not a fear he had now, and that, more than anything, illuminated the gravity of his situation in a way nothing else could have.

Bending his knees, he gripped the back of her thighs and lifted her, opening her legs to hover her cunt over his raging cock. She reached between them and took him in hand, positioning him at the slitted entrance to her plush pussy. She rubbed the plum-sized head against her, coating them both in the slickness of their combined arousal. The feel of her satiny skin against the tender tip of his dick was so good his breath hissed out between his clenched teeth.

He lowered her slowly, a low pained growl rumbling in his chest at the feel of her opening to the pressure of his rigidly stiff penis. It was like sliding into a wet fist, the heat and pressure of her delicious cunt a shattering pleasure around his naked cock.

She inclined her head toward him, her hair spilling all around them. Her lips were parted on panting breaths, a soft whine in her throat as he slowly fed more of his brutally thick erection into her. She was breathtakingly beautiful always, but impossibly more so when she was taking his cock. Her hedonistic pleasure in his possession was as necessary as the feel of her squeezing him in greedy pulses.

Her hips began to move in tiny circles, screwing him deeper into her, massaging his ferociously stiff length.

He held her aloft, his legs trembling against his self-restraint. "Ireland… you're going to make me come before I've given you all of my cock."

"Hurry!" she demanded, fighting his grip. "You're going too slow."

He nipped her full lower lip, then soothed the sting with his tongue. "Let me savor you, *cher*. You're always in a rush."

She caught his face in her hands, her eyes wild. "Start fucking, Ronan. *Now!*"

The ferocity of her lust was incendiary fuel for his desire. Snarling, he pinned her to the wall with a powering drive of his hips, burying his cock in her to the root. She screamed her pleasure, the sound reverberating in the small space and spurring him past any hope of control. He fucked her hard and furiously, driving deep and dragging back out again, her pussy gripping his dick so tightly he had to work back inside her with heavy thrusts.

She fucked him back with strength and passion, clinging to his shoulders as she tightened and released her powerful thighs, lifting and lowering in rhythm with his surges.

"*Dieu*, I can't live without this," he moaned, already so close to coming. His hips pounded against hers, his whole body electrified by the sizzling ecstasy radiating from the place where they were joined. His cock was ruthless in its hunger for the feel of her, plunging and withdrawing until he was fucking her in near-mindless euphoria.

"I'm going to come," she gasped, her body tightening and trembling. He adjusted the angle of her hips to stroke her pussy high and hard, driving the pleasure into her, knowing how phenomenal it felt to be deep inside her when she came. She sobbed and tensed, then fell into orgasm with a keening cry, her decadent cunt pulling on his cock in tremulous ripples.

His heavy sac drew up tight, his impending climax barreling through him like a freight train. He held it back by will alone, his back teeth grinding as he extended her release as long as possible, giving her pussy the entire length of his impossibly hard erection to clench down on.

Only when she went limp in his arms did he let go, feeling the orgasm surge from the base of his penis and up to spew hot and thick from the broad tip. Throwing his head back, he roared, spilling endlessly. His hips pinning hers to the wall, holding himself at the deepest point as he filled her to overflowing. The climax was relentless, his cock jerking with every hot pulse of semen until his vision dimmed, his jaw ached, and his legs grew weak.

With a grunt of dismay, Ronan felt his muscles give out, and they slid together to the floor. On his knees, he kept a desperate grip on her hips, unwilling to slip from deep inside her cum-filled pussy. Right here, now, she couldn't be more his.

And he couldn't be more hers. Did she know that? As he cuddled her close, their bodies wet with sweat and cum, he marveled that their connection could be both filthy and sweet, tender and merciless. She'd proven so adroitly that she could be everything to him.

Her lips moved over his face, tracing his jaw, the bridge of his nose, the arch of his brows. "We really have to stop meeting like this."

There was a teasing note in her husky voice, but her words sparked panic and frustration, nevertheless. It was intolerable that she could even jest about not having this when he couldn't seem to go even a few hours without it.

Somehow, he gathered the strength to move from kneeling to standing, relying on her strength to keep them joined.

With one arm slung beneath the firm cheeks of her ass and one hand gripping the waistband of his jeans so they didn't slide down, he managed to get them inside. Reaching over his shoulder, she shut the door behind them.

The moonlight was brighter in the condo, affording him the light to see her fully. It seemed impossible for a woman like Ireland Vidal to let him have her like this. He wasn't worthy of her, which he proved by being with her now.

"Do you ever think about what we'd have if Vidal Records weren't a factor?" he asked, longing for everything instead of the bits and pieces he was getting. How wonderful it would've been to go home together from Valentin's, to make love without urgency and to wake her with more unhurried lovemaking before their lazy picnic in the park.

Regret darkened her lovely eyes. "All the time."

Nodding, he offered her his mouth, and she took it with a soul-searing kiss. Even as his blood quickened again, Ronan knew this wasn't sustainable. Something had to give.

She was right about his culpability. He'd had the experience to recognize that she was different and that his reaction to her was unique and powerful. If he'd walked away from her that first night at Jazzie's, maybe they wouldn't be here now. That she hadn't walked away, either, did not absolve him. He'd known who she was and what he was doing to her family.

He had to be the one to make the break, whatever it cost him.

"He came over again." Ireland covered her face with her hand, embarrassed to admit her helpless fascination with the man who'd pitted himself against her family.

"Girl." Alina's voice held more than a note of surprise. And censure.

Dropping her hand, Ireland looked at her best friend on her phone screen. Sitting at her desk in the Vidal offices, she was torn between the lingering elation of a morning spent cuddled up with a gorgeously naked and blissfully sated Ronan Boudreaux and the reality of the situation at work. "I'm a terrible person."

Alina sighed. "No, you're not. You've just finally found the man who can get to you. Unfortunately, your picker is still broken."

"Right? I've got to get over him."

"Or at least out from under him." Alina grinned.

Ireland laughed. "He couldn't be terrible in bed, could he? That would be too easy. No, he's got to be a sexy beast who gets off on getting me off. I've had more orgasms this week than all the rest of my life combined. I had no idea a man could love going down on a woman as much as Ronan does, although he swears it's my effect on him that makes him enjoy it so much."

Alina shook her head. "Lucky bitch."

"Not for long." She winced. "Gideon gets back from his trip tomorrow. Depending on whether Christopher laid out what's happening in a voicemail or just asked for a callback, Gideon could know about the situation with Ronan at any moment."

And the thought of the two men she loved so deeply facing off—

No. She did not just think that. She was tired, that's all. It was a mental slip.

"Well..." Alina winced, too. "On the plus side, Gideon will be busy with the masquerade. Might buy you another weekend of hot monkey sex before the inevitable showdown between those two smoking hot specimens of male perfection."

"God." Ireland's eyes squeezed shut. "I can't keep fucking Ronan. It's got to stop."

"Oh, it will as soon as Gideon gets involved. He'll run the McCaffreys out of town before they know what hit them."

"I'm not sure that's true." Ireland chewed on her lower lip. "Ronan would've anticipated my brother and planned for him. I've thrown Ronan off his game a bit, he admits that. But I've seen him with my father and Christopher, and he's capable of being just as frightening as Gideon can be."

"No offense—you know I love your dad and Christopher—but going toe to toe with them is nothing like facing off with Gideon Cross."

"That's true, but I think they're more evenly matched than you realize."

"You think?"

"Ronan clawed his way to where he is now, from abject poverty to a position of wealth and power. And while he's

Gideon's age, his forty years of living have been much harder to survive than my brother's. I can't see him backing down without a brutal fight."

And the possibility of a nasty, protracted battle between the man she was addicted to and the brother she adored made her stomach twist into knots of anxiety.

Her head lifted at a knock on her partially closed door. "Hang on, Alina. Yes?" she called out.

The door's opening widened, and Angus McLeod poked his head in. "Is it a bad time, lass? Your assistant isn't in yet."

She straightened. A glance at the clock told her he'd arrived just before nine. She'd told him she was available at his convenience. "No, not at all. Come in." She looked at Alina. "I'll call you back."

"I'll be waiting with bated breath, whatever the hell that means."

Ending the call, Ireland gestured for Angus to take a seat. He entered, dressed in jeans and a plaid dress shirt worn as Ronan also preferred—with an open collar and rolled-up sleeves. He had a leather messenger bag slung over his shoulder, and he pulled it into his lap as he settled his heavily muscled, impossingly tall frame into one of her visitors' chairs.

He rubbed at the grizzled stubble on his jaw. "Things have changed drastically around here, I see."

"Yes, we played musical chairs—or offices, as the case may be—but everyone still has a seat."

"Because of Ronan Boudreaux?"

Just hearing Ronan's name in Angus's Scots burr made her back tense, an instinctive need to shield and defend him rising. And wasn't that as insane as everything else between her and Ronan? She felt the same protective drive for both her father and the man who threatened him. "In part. He's a shareholder."

"I'm sorry to hear that," he said grimly. "Boudreaux makes his fortune by taking over troubled businesses and selling their assets for profit."

"Yes, I know." She almost didn't say more, but everyone would soon know how vulnerable Vidal Records was. "He's got us on the chopping block now. I don't know if I can fend him off, but I'm trying. We haven't given up hope yet."

His lips compressed into a tight line, then he continued. "I've lived many lives. In one of them, I hunted people who didn't want to be found. You pick up a few things in that line of work, and I'll tell you there is something very wrong with Boudreaux."

It took Ireland a second to recognize that she was shaking her head because she was actively suppressing the urge to deny what he was saying. Her trust in Ronan was firmly anchored in a way that brooked no doubt. She had an ear for lies, a sixth sense so to speak, and it had yet to warn her when it came to him.

So she was relieved when all she said was, "What do you mean?"

Angus began his report. "He was born Ronan Liam McCaffrey to Emma Olivia McCaffrey. No father was named on the birth certificate. A standard background check revealed little of note beyond a name change in adulthood when he added the Boudreaux, which he uses sporadically. When I dug deeper, I found an expunged juvenile record. When he was fifteen, he was convicted of manslaughter in the death of a police officer."

She blinked rapidly, her brain misfiring. "Are we talking about the same man?"

Digging into his bag, Angus withdrew a mugshot and slid it across the desktop to her. She pulled it closer with trembling fingers, staring at a young man who was unmistakably Ronan. His face was gaunt, his beautiful gray eyes dark and haunted, the sockets sunken and bruised. His tawny hair looked like it'd been hacked short with a dull pocketknife.

Time is a luxury I've enjoyed too little of, he'd told her.

She released her breath in a rush, her hand splaying across the image to protect it. That Angus had gotten his hands on the expunged record wasn't so much surprising as impressive. It reminded her of just how far-reaching her brother's power was.

"That's him?" Angus queried.

"Yes."

His curt nod told her he'd had no doubts. "Boudreaux warranted a closer look, so I flew down to Louisiana."

"You did?" Why was she surprised? Of course, he would be thorough; Gideon would expect nothing less.

"I was once told that to hear gossip in the South, you need to be sippin' sweet tea and sitting close enough to whisper to." His attempt to shift his burr to a drawl failed spectacularly. "So, I drove to the parish where the Boudreauxes are based to find that not a single person would speak a negative word about any member of the family. His childhood and criminal history do not exist there, and if you mention either to someone, they won't look you in the eye, and they stink of fear."

Ireland sat back in her chair, rocking a little to expend the chaotic energy brewing inside her. There was a growing sense of disconnection, the feeling that she and Angus were discussing two very different people.

"If you make general inquiries, the residents boast about him and his father, Lucas Courtland Boudreaux, the youngest son of the family matriarch, Harper Fleur Landry Boudreaux."

"So, he knows who his father is, despite him not being named on the birth certificate?"

"My guess is he figured it out later in life and rectified it with the name change." He flipped through a folder in his bag, searching. "I can't adequately express how strangely people in the area reacted when discussing the Boudreauxes. They're eager and delighted to share all the good works the family does for the community, and there's a collective infatuation with them. But there's also the sense that the family protects its image aggressively. A waitress in a neighboring parish told me that the earliest businesses targeted by Ronan were rivals of the family."

Withdrawing another photo, he pushed it across to her.

The entire room twisted and juddered back into place. She lifted the photo to study it closer. The resemblance between Ronan and Lucas was so uncanny that it took her a moment to identify the differences.

The man photographed appeared to be ten to fifteen years younger when his picture was taken than Ronan was now. He had a broad, cocky, million-dollar smile that was so incongruous with his circumstances, as if he didn't fear the consequences ahead of him. He had tawny hair similar to his son's, although it was a darker shade. Well-dressed in the style of the time, he looked like a man with everything going for him—aside from the booking number placard in his hands.

"Lucas was arrested, too?" she asked, incredulous.

"And convicted. Of first-degree rape. He's been incarcerated in Angola prison for over forty years. His case is being championed by the Innocence Project, which is seeking to have the DNA evidence retested and eyewitnesses reexamined." He gave her a cynical look. "From the reactions of people I talked to, I'd have some concerns about coercion and intimidation being a factor in any recanted testimony."

"*Forty* years?" The sentence fit the crime in her opinion but seemed unusually high. Then again, her criminal legal knowledge came from Hollywood productions.

"In Louisiana, the mandatory sentence is either death or life without parole."

"Jesus. More states should take their cues from Louisiana." She put the two mugshots side by side, staring at the boy who looked as if he hadn't eaten well in far too long, if ever, and his father, who looked like the world was served to him on a silver platter.

"Being claimed by the Boudreauxes is what allowed Ronan to enter polite society. He's engaged to Scarlett Olivia Claiborne, the only daughter of a family more prominent than the Boudreauxes." Angus reached into his bag again and withdrew yet another photo. "There's general elation about the match."

Ireland felt the blood drain from her face, and her stomach soured with acidic heat. She looked helplessly down at the photo Angus placed in front of her, unable even to touch it like she had the others. The woman pictured was a lovely blonde with long cascading curls, big cornflower blue eyes, and a wide smile. She was so perfect she was almost doll-like.

Angus provided an additional photograph, one of Ronan and Scarlett together in front of a step and repeat backdrop for a charity event. Scarlett wore a wide-brimmed sun hat and white lace dress, while Ronan was dressed in a linen suit of soft tan. His smile held all his charm and charisma, while Scarlett's was confident and engaging. Her gloved hand on his proffered arm was unmistakably proprietary. With Ronan's hair worn shorter, much like his father's, he didn't look like the man in whose arms she'd lain just hours ago. He looked like the angelic twin of the devilish seducer with whom she'd spent the past several days revealing her most personal vulnerabilities and aspirations.

Her vision blurred with hot, stinging tears. The searing intimacy they'd shared took on a sinister and painful connotation. She waited for the cleansing rage to rise so she could weaponize it and confront Ronan head-on. But what she felt was a smothering agony that made it hard to expand her lungs.

Pushing the pile of photos back to Angus, Ireland tried breathing through the urge to vomit into the trashcan beside her desk. It was a joke that she could find the biggest loser in any room to hook up with, but she had felt a bone-deep certainty about Ronan that she'd depended on. To be so wrong about a feeling that felt so…*right*? What else had she misjudged or underestimated? How badly was she fucking everything up?

She stood on shaky legs, wanting to leave the room, the building, the city…

The ringing of her desk phone startled her enough to make her jump. Angus didn't even blink. She fumbled the receiver, dropping it on the desktop where it clattered noisily, aggravating her fraying composure.

"Yes?" she answered, appalled at her voice's hoarseness. She felt Angus's examining gaze and knew she was revealing too much of her inner turmoil. She didn't know how to pretend feeling okay when she wasn't.

"Hey, boss," Matt greeted her. "You don't have a meeting scheduled, but your door's closed, so I'm checking to see if you've got a minute for Brett Kline. He's saying there's a problem with the studio he booked downstairs. Neither of the two Mr. Vidals are in the office yet."

Brett was saying something in the background. She looked at Angus. "I have to handle an issue with one of our artists. Could you give me a few minutes?"

"No need. I'll leave you to it."

She spoke into the receiver. "I'll come out and get Brett in a minute, Matt."

"Sure thing."

Angus stood and withdrew a folder from his bag as she hung

up. Sliding the photos into it, he left the folder on her desktop. “Your copy of my report. I have to warn you…” He waited until he had her full attention. “The Boudreauxes will know that someone’s been asking around. I positioned myself as a true crime podcaster researching Lucas’s case, but if they’re as protective of their reputation as I believe, they won’t just take my word for it. Whatever plans he has for this company may accelerate.”

Opening her top drawer, Ireland swiped the folder into it. “Ronan says he targeted Vidal Records because of a vendetta against my dad, who denies knowing anything about Ronan at all, although he admits to knowing a man who looks like him, which has to be Lucas, right?”

Angus’s interest sharpened; she could tell even without any outward sign. “Not necessarily. The Boudreauxes are a large brood. If two of the men look alike, there will likely be more among them with similar appearances. I’ll see what I can find.”

“Thank you for this, Angus.”

“Of course. I’ll be in touch.”

Rounding her desk, she walked with him to the door and opened it, summoning the inner strength to focus on the immediate problems facing her. Confronting Ronan would have to wait until she was sure she wouldn’t break down in tears in front of him. She would not humiliate herself that way or give him the satisfaction of seeing how he’d wounded her.

The first inkling of fury began to warm the block of ice in her gut.

Angus headed toward the elevators, and Ireland managed a smile for Brett, whose dimple flashed when he grinned back. The lead singer of Six-Ninths hadn’t changed his rocker-chic style in years. He still wore his hair short and bleached at the tips. Lean and tall, his arms were covered in sleeves of black and gray tattoos of various people, places, sayings, and things, and his green eyes gave her an appreciative once-over.

"Hey, Irie," he greeted her, using the nickname he'd given her that only the band used. "Got a question for you since you're the boss now, I'm told."

She extended an arm toward her office in invitation, then followed him in. "Let's hope I have an answer for you."

"Your dad wanted us in the studio right away to record 'First Kiss Goodbye,' our new single." He faced her once he reached her desk, choosing not to sit. "Did you hear the rough sample we sent?"

"I sure did," she lied with what she hoped was an enthusiastic smile, remaining on the visitors' side of her desk with him. "It's fantastic, Brett. I'm thrilled for all of us."

He nodded energetically, clearly excited. "Right? We *know* we've got it with this one. Anyway, he'd sent us some pics of your new studios, and we're ready to roll, but I guess you're not…?"

Her smile didn't falter. Although Six-Ninths had been around long enough to know how things worked, it wasn't unusual for artists to question the support they were receiving—or not—from their label, especially when they were particularly proud of what they were working on. "That's not true at all. We've been working hard to get everything ready for a big drop. Christopher will review the promotional plans with you this afternoon, and you'll be pleased with them."

"I meant the new studios aren't ready," he clarified. "Sorry. I'm jetlagged and under-caffeinated. So, we're trying to figure out where we're supposed to go."

She opened her mouth to say more, but a sinking feeling silenced her. "Let me see what you're talking about."

"There's nothing to see—that's my point. The control and

machine rooms are prepped for installation, but there's no equipment yet. And I gotta tell you, Irie, I'm concerned that you don't know that."

Ireland was striding toward the elevators before he finished talking, then she took the stairs to get to the second floor faster. She burst through the door to the main hallway and found the rest of Six-Ninths talking with Chantal. It was impossible for Ireland to smile at anyone, with tears of frustration and heartache clogging her throat.

"We were here until around three," Chantal was telling Darrin Rumsfeld, the Six-Ninths' drummer. "Everything was here then."

Ireland exited the machine room, now just an empty space with wires scattered all over the floor and a temperature that felt below freezing without the servers generating heat. She couldn't say a word to anyone, afraid if she opened her mouth, only a piercing scream would erupt. She took the stairs back up to the executive floor. When she exited the stairwell, she saw Jules sitting at the conference table and marched over to him.

Thrusting the glass door open, she glared. "Where's your brother?"

His lips curved into a malicious smile that was more of a sneer. "*Bon matin* to you, too, Lizzie."

"Fuck you. Where's Ronan?"

Laughing, he rocked back in his chair and checked his watch. "I'd say he's about an hour away from landing in Lafayette. Never saw anyone pack that fast, but when my brother's done, he moves on to what's next and doesn't look back."

The news was a blow so severe she felt it like a punch. That she didn't double over was inexplicable. "Why are you still here?"

"I like to throw the last handful of dirt on the coffin."

Setting her hands on the table, she leaned toward him and took sharp satisfaction when he rolled his chair back a few inches. "Your family has made itself my mission in life. You might be too stupid to be scared about that now, and I'm fine with that because that'll just make me more terrifying later."

He scoffed as she shoved away from the table, nursing her rage as fuel.

She flashed him a smile that was all teeth. "Tell your brother to give my regards to Scarlett... at least until I get around to giving them to her personally."

Jules leaped to his feet. "You keep her out of this!"

Flipping him the bird over her shoulder, she stormed back out through the glass door just as her father exited the elevator.

Ronan angled the stick to guide the helicopter around again, allowing himself to take in another view of the lush paradise below. The mighty Mississippi River glittered sinuously through a verdant landscape dotted with ancient live oaks and blanketed in short, swaying grasses. A resplendent mansion sat like a sentinel on the shore, surrounded by acres of riotously colorful gardens and manicured walkways. The air was fragranced with the perfume of hundreds of blooming flowers, the soft breeze diffusing some of the sultry humidity.

Bellefleur. The pride of the parish and state.

Built in the Greek Revival style, the square manse was two and a half stories tall and enveloped by a colonnade of twenty massive columns. An enormous gallery wrapped completely around, affording every room access to the outside. The home had been built by another family in 1852, and as a plantation, it once grew tobacco. It fell into Boudreaux hands in 1868, and now no one was sure where the family had been rooted before that.

As Ronan descended to the helipad on the rear lawn, he thought of what it would be like to bring Ireland here. Would she hear the music of this place as he did? The steady, inexorable surge of the river to the sea. The buzzing of bees as they collected pollen. Would she dance with him in a midnight garden to the sounds of the cicadas, crickets, and katydids?

He felt a twinge of regret that a Vidal would never be welcome here; she would have to change her name.

As he settled his Hill HX50 on the ground, he saw the bright yellow Lotus Emira parked in the circular drive. And once he completed the after-landing checklist and exited the aircraft, he saw the Lotus's driver watching him from the rear gallery. It would be hard to miss Scarlett Claiborne at any time—she made sure of that—but the fact that she was naked guaranteed he noticed her.

With one hand on the ornamental iron railing, she blew him a kiss. She'd tossed her long blond hair over her shoulders so nothing would impede his view of her generous tits, trim waist, and full hips. She had even ensured that her pussy was visible between the ornate spindles. Her petite, curvy body was the envy and desire of many but couldn't be more different from that of the woman who enflamed him beyond all rational thought.

Scarlett didn't call out to him, which might have attracted the attention of the residents in the adjacent rooms. She only liked to flirt with danger, which is why she was hellbent on marrying him, but she was as protective of her reputation as any member of his family or hers.

Taking the three short steps up to the rear entrance of the mansion, Ronan pulled off his mirrored aviator sunglasses and hooked them onto his open shirt collar. Entering through the screen door, he strolled the long central hallway to his grand-mère's study, passing beneath a heavy crystal chandelier and the mural of a cloudy blue sky that had been painted on the ceiling ages ago.

He'd arrived in time for lunch but wouldn't eat much here despite the rather pitiful breakfast he'd scavenged at Ireland's. They'd have to work on stocking her pantry so he could feed them both properly. He could eat comfortably with her. She quieted the noise in his head that food—or more specifically, the lack of it he'd experienced in childhood—created. Sitting at the immense dining table that seated thirty of his relatives was a boisterous good time, filled with humorous conversation and scathing anecdotes, but all of the chaos made it impossible for him to be mindful of what he was putting into his mouth. So, he'd pick his way through the meal and look forward to eating more robustly later with Ireland.

The study door was open. The substantial mahogany desk at the room's far end was too large for the woman sitting behind it. Her hair was primarily white with thick streaks of dark blond swirled through it. She wore it in an elaborate chignon, revealing a long, graceful neck and massive sapphires dangling from her ears. At eighty-two years old, Harper Boudreaux was still spry, which she credited to her nightly tumbler of two fingers of whiskey.

His grand-mère was the bright spot in an otherwise dark room, the walls covered in a burgundy damask wallpaper and the dark wood floors covered with an Aubusson rug in a similar hue to the walls. Generations of male Boudreauxes had conducted family business here, and when Harper had taken over the task, she'd left the baroquely masculine room as it had always been.

He knocked and waited on the threshold. She glanced up

with a fearsome glower that immediately brightened into a dazzling smile and bright eyes.

"Ronan! I didn't hear you land. Does that mean you drove, or am I going deaf?" She stood effortlessly, her posture still perfect. Dressed in a long, slender navy skirt and white gauze blouse, she looked cool and ready for business.

He lengthened his stride to reach her before she had to walk too far. "I'm a stealthy bastard, grand-mère, you know this."

"Not a bastard," she corrected sternly, extending both hands to him and returning his *les bises*. "Your father would've done right by you had Vidal not gotten in the way. Thankfully, that is all behind us now. Look how long your hair has grown! And you've lost weight. Should I be worried that you've been too busy to look after yourself?"

"The hair was laziness, now it's by design. The weight… well" —he flashed a big smile— "I've been exercising a lot recently."

"We'll get you a trim and fatten you up a little. You've been missed terribly. Scarlett hurried over when I told her you'd be home today. She'll be spending the weekend with us. And so will you," she finished as if the matter was decided.

Harper Boudreaux was tough, and she had to be. Managing the many Boudreaux siblings, cousins, aunts, and uncles was like herding cats. She also managed the estate and the family's finances and investments. She'd only recently begun delegating some of the charity and church work to his generation of Boudreauxes.

"Sounds like a party," he said cheerily. "I regret not being able to stay for it."

Her eyes were a deep, dark blue, and they took on a hardened glint, even as she continued smiling with welcome. Harper didn't like being denied. "You can stay at least one night before you head home."

"Ah, home," he said fondly, thinking of Marcelle and the comfort of being entirely himself. "I'm eager to see it, even if only long enough to switch out the clothes I'm traveling with."

He was one of the few in the Boudreaux family who didn't live at Bellefleur. And as much as he admired the grand old lady who ran the estate, Jules and Claudette weren't welcomed here as family, only as occasional guests for rare public events and festivities. Harper wanted everyone to forget that he hadn't been raised as a Boudreaux, and she'd educated him in the requisite social skills required to pass among the civilized. But he could never live behind the façade long term; it was too taxing.

She tutted at him. "What's so pressing that you have to leave as soon as you arrive?"

"I'm heading back to New York."

"*Non*," she dismissed. "You're needed here."

He gave her a patient, resolute look.

She sighed heavily and gestured for him to sit on one of the two matching settees. "If you're not finished there, why return at all? You can afford to buy new clothes."

"You know why." Tugging up his slacks, he sat gingerly. While Harper often insisted the delicate-looking, centuries-old furniture could bear his weight, he didn't entirely trust that. "I want to tell Lucas personally how and why the plan has changed."

And today was Harper's scheduled video call with her son, so this was Ronan's chance. It was a standing appointment afforded to his grand-mère by good planning *and* breeding—there were benefits to coming from old money, which he'd learned by watching, not doing. Harper had seen to it that he was trained as necessary to prevent embarrassing her or the family, but he would always be the boy from the bayou.

"Don't call your papa by his name," she admonished. "And what's changed? We haven't discussed making any adjustments to the plan."

Ronan shook his head. He was only going to explain the situation once to them both. But he could tell her something that wouldn't matter at all to Lucas. "We lost the warehouse in Queens to Cross Industries. I've already told Owen Claiborne."

And Scarlett's father hadn't taken the news well. Owen hoped to expand the Claiborne import-export business beyond the Gulf to the East Coast. Ronan so rarely failed to succeed that many assumed he was infallible.

Harper's gaze narrowed. "How?"

"The daughter, Ireland, is more formidable than anticipated."

When his grand-mère's eyes narrowed and her lips compressed with displeasure, he realized he might have inadvertently revealed his admiration in his tone. So be it. A bit of forewarning before the call might actually help smooth his way forward.

"Ronan!" Scarlett's breathy voice came from the doorway. "I wasn't sure that was you with your hair so long. Although I do like the savage look on you."

She'd put some clothes on—sandals with elaborate heels and a floral halter dress that might've been demure but for the plunging neckline that revealed her impressive cleavage. Her hair was now up in a ponytail, and large round diamonds sparkled from her ears.

He stood as she entered. "Aren't you a vision," he drawled, careful to avert his mouth when her *la bise* strayed too close. She smelled of roses and honeysuckle, which conversely reminded him of how Ireland's spicy floral scent drove him wild. "That dress was meant to be worn by you."

The sly look she gave him said she caught the double meaning of his compliment.

"Lawd, have I missed you!" she told him as she sat on the settee he'd been occupying. "It's terminally boring when you're not here. I should've gone with you to New York. I could've shopped while you worked and made sure you fit some fun in there, too. You work too hard, Ronan."

Absolutely not trusting the curved leg settee with both of them on it, Ronan went to the bar cart instead. "Can I get you ladies anything?"

"It's too early to drink," Scarlett said—for Harper's benefit. He knew she lied because he'd watched her pour whiskey from a flask into her lemonade at more than one charity event.

"Nothing for me, thank you," his grand-mère replied.

Agreeing with Scarlett, he opened a small bottle of soda water and drank deeply. He did like the woman, always had. When he was roped into being the token Boudreaux at an event, Scarlett's presence made it bearable. They'd tangled in the sheets a few times, and she had been a pleasant diversion. He'd known to fuck her like a lady—not too rough or sweaty, no teeth marks or bruises. Not that he was ever or had ever been as passionate with any woman as he was with Ireland, but he couldn't say he'd ever even lusted after Scarlett. She was willing, and he was able; that was all.

Still, despite his sedate performance in bed, Scarlett was perversely excited by the fear his past evoked in her. What went on in her pretty head, he didn't know, but having a woman get off on being afraid of him was not a turn-on. And now that he'd mated with his tigress, he was ruined for the casual sex he'd indulged in before. If he wasn't burning alive from the inside out, he didn't want it.

"Ronan's planning on leaving again this afternoon," Harper told Scarlett, wily in her quest for support.

"No!" Scarlett protested. "You've just returned, *cher*. I've hardly had time to even look at you."

"I've met someone." He looked each of them in the eye individually.

"What does that mean?" Harper demanded.

"I've become romantically involved," he elaborated, "with a woman I met in New York."

Scarlett's frown smoothed out, and she smiled confidently. "Well, you have been gone for weeks, and you're a healthy male in your prime... I really should've come along with you."

"Scarlett." Harper's voice held a note of reprimand. No one expected her to remain virginal until marriage, but discretion was the mark of a lady.

His mouth curved at Scarlett's lack of jealousy. "I may be gone for a while longer."

Her fingers drumming on the arm of the settee, Harper studied him. "Don't be ridiculous. Just because the Vidal situation has concluded doesn't mean you have time to waste. There's more to be done here."

"And plenty of Boudreauxes to do it," he countered without heat. "My mind can't be changed, so I urge you not to waste time trying."

Her breath whistled. "How serious is this dalliance of yours?"

He shrugged. "It's early days yet."

"If you're trying to make me jealous," Scarlett drawled, recrossing her legs seductively, "it won't work. You can't live away from here, and a woman making her living in New York isn't moving to our sleepy parish. Let him sow his wild oats, as they say, Ms. Harper. He got a late start after all."

Ronan hadn't expected Scarlett to take his side, but he appreciated it, which he told her with a wink. She preened and returned the gesture.

"That may be," Harper conceded, "but you're forty years old, Ronan. Not only was your father a grown man when I was your age, with three older siblings, but you were one of several grandchildren."

"Almost forty." He grinned. "And if you're counting on me to contribute to your extensive brood of great-grandchildren, don't."

A soft chiming sound drifted through the air. Harper and Scarlett both stood immediately at the familiar reminder alarm. "We'll see you at lunch, Scarlett."

"Yes, Ms. Harper. I'll save you a seat by me, Ronan."

He inclined his head. "Thank you."

"*De rien.*" Scarlett shut the door behind her when she left.

His grand-mère used a remote to power on the big monitor on the wall, then she logged into the video program that charged them in ten-minute increments to speak with Lucas Boudreaux.

When Lucas appeared, Ronan heard Harper's sharp inhalation. He knew his face, so like his father's, made Lucas's four decades of hard labor even more apparent. There was a hardened look to the man, a flatness in his gray eyes that revealed the cost of living in a cage, fighting for dominance and survival among lethal criminals with nothing to lose but a lifetime of captivity.

Ronan had felt and seen a similar change happening in himself before he'd crossed paths with his father in the state's penal system. If he hadn't come under Lucas's protection while institutionalized, he might not be alive today. He might also be even more of an animal than his childhood had made him.

"*Comment ça va?*" Wearing a chambray shirt over a white T-shirt, Lucas greeted them with a wide smile. "How are my two favorite people? I take it there's grand news since Ronan is home."

Harper sat with perfect posture, hands linked in her lap. "Ronan tells me the plans have changed."

"Oh?" Lucas brushed back his grizzled hair, which was more blond than his mother's but with a similar pattern.

Ronan's arms crossed. "Chris Vidal, Sr. has lost control of his business. He has no stake in it whatsoever now."

His father flashed a smile so bright he could see a glimpse of the man Lucas had once been. "You did it. I knew you could, but a man learns not to get his hopes up after a while, you know?"

"I know." And he did. All too well.

"Why is it relevant that he has no stake in a company that no longer exists?" Harper asked shrewdly.

Giving her a brief, appreciative grin, Ronan explained, "Because I'm not going to kill it just yet. Chris Vidal was the problem, and now he's not. It could become profitable again under the right hand."

Lucas looked from him to Harper with raised brows.

Harper's cool gaze was intimidating. "You don't run businesses, Ronan, you ruin them."

"That's true. But I've been thinking perhaps it's time I built one up instead. And why not music? One of my great loves." He could tell the argument wasn't landing and switched tactics. "Plus, dismantling the business will be over too quickly. Much more painful, I think, for Vidal to watch me running it instead."

Nodding, Lucas grinned, but this time, it was full of malice.

"I like the way you think, baw. Always have. You know how to make things hurt. That's a valuable skill."

"It's the girl, isn't it?" Harper scowled. "The daughter. She's why you're doing this."

"The daughter?" Lucas frowned, and then his expression cleared. "You're fucking his daughter?" Throwing his head back, he laughed raucously. "*Mon dieu*, that's rich! It must be killing him."

"Stop laughing!" Harper ordered curtly, her expression inflexible. "You said you're romantically involved with her, Ronan. That it might be serious."

Ronan felt a warning tingling down his spine and heeded it as always. He began to choose his words more carefully. "A gentleman discusses his liaisons with respect—you taught me that, grand-mère."

"You can make an exception for the Vidal woman."

He laughed with feigned nonchalance. "She and I wage war by day and truce by night. It may be less exciting without the war," he lied. "If so, I think the business might suit Jules and help settle him, although his distaste for New York surpasses mine."

"Jules Robicheaux is not my concern," she said icily.

"*Mais non*, he's mine," he countered, smoothly hiding his irritation. "We must also consider Gideon Cross. Taking the business over rather than under should help defuse a protracted battle we can't afford. *Forbes* recently published an article on how costly the competition between Cross Industries and LanCorp has been for both companies. It's worth a read."

A knock came to the study door.

"*Vas t'en!*" Harper yelled curtly.

The door opened anyway, and Scarlett peeked her pretty face

around the door. "*Désolée*. Ronan, Jules called. He's trying to reach you. It's an emergency, or I wouldn't have bothered you."

Realizing he left his phone in the chopper, Ronan shot his father and grand-mère an apologetic glance. "*Pardon*."

"Can't it wait?" Harper asked.

"Clearly not," he answered, heading toward the door.

"We're in the middle of a discussion!" she called after him.

"I've caught you both up." He paused while still in view of the webcam. "How are things going with the attorneys?"

Lucas shrugged. "Slow as molasses, but they tell me things are progressing. Our lawyers are staying on top of the Project's lawyers. But like I said, you learn not to get your hopes up."

"It's good to see you, Dad," he said. "I pray it's not long before I get to do so in person instead."

"*Merci*, son. Watch your back with the Vidals. None of them can be trusted."

Nodding, he exited the room and found Scarlett in the hallway. He closed the door softly, and she launched herself at him, pressing her lips to his before he knew what she intended. Once, twice. Swift pecks. Just as quickly, she pulled away with a mischievous smile.

"Give a kiss to Jules and Claudette for me, *cher*. I'd give you one, but you're *involved*."

"Stay out of trouble," he told her over his shoulder, discreetly wiping his mouth.

"Never."

He smiled ruefully as he opened the pilot side door and removed his phone from its hands-free station. The number of missed calls sobered him, and he dialed back.

"Pour l'amour de dieu!" Jules shouted without preamble. "You can't just fall off the face of the earth and leave us with this mess!"

"Calm down. What mess?"

"She had the fire department evacuate our entire floor! They stood in their gear and watched Claudy and me pack up everything."

Frowning, he circled the exterior of the helicopter, inspecting it. "You're not making sense. There was a fire at Vidal Records?"

"Non, gros bête! We've been evicted from the hotel! And she was waiting in the lobby to tell us we're not welcome in any Cross Industries property. We're trying to book a flight home or find a rental instead because we don't know which hotels are Cross's and I won't be humiliated further!"

"I assume you're talking about Ireland."

"Who else, couillion? We're driving around in a taxi with nowhere to go!"

He climbed into the pilot seat, snapped his phone back into the holder, and secured his seatbelt. "What did you do to get kicked out?" he asked patiently.

"Why am *I* at fault?" Jules yelled.

Ronan heard Claudette admonish their brother to lower his voice. "Because Ireland wasn't on the warpath when I left her this morning."

"*Oui*, well, whatever sedative your dick dispensed wore off!"

"Jules—" he began harshly.

"*Beau-frère*," Claudette greeted him, sounding as serene as always, "Jules is neglecting to tell you that he had the recording studios emptied overnight."

Ronan froze with his fingers on a switch, his heart skipping a beat before it began pounding. "He did *what?!*"

"We agreed!" Jules shouted. "We discussed it, and you agreed!"

"I said I would fucking handle it!"

"Also," Claudette continued, "Ireland knows about Scarlett."

The sudden tension in his back was painful. “What the hell does that mean?!”

“Nothing good,” she guessed.

Cursing, he hung up and speed-dialed Ireland, racing through the run-up to takeoff. The call didn’t even ring; it just went to voicemail. Jules called back, and he skipped the incoming call, trying Ireland again before he accepted that he’d probably been blocked. “*Maudit!*”

He called the Vidal offices.

“Ireland Vidal’s office,” Matt answered. “How may I help you?”

“Matt, it’s Ronan McCaffrey. Can I speak to Ireland, please?”

“Sorry, second boss,” he chirped. “No can do. She did leave a message for you, though. Fuck off, eat shit, and die—that’s the message. I didn’t say it; she did.”

His jaw clenched. “Tell her I’ll be there in four hours, and she can give me the message personally.”

“You got a death wish?” Matt asked, still with that same bright cheerfulness. “I’ll pass your message on. Have a nice day.”

Furious and worried at once, Ronan pulled his headset on and communicated with the tower while waiting for the engine to spool up. Once it had, he engaged the clutch, and the rotor began to turn, quickly picking up speed.

The spirits were laughing at him; he just knew it. Every time he thought he was making some headway, he was back to being the asshole.

Fine.

Damn it.

Harper Boudreaux heard the helicopter this time. The rotor's whine increased until the aircraft lifted off, and the sound gradually moved away. She looked at her son on the screen before her, her thoughts sorting and churning.

"This is a problem," she said.

"Why? I find it amusing."

"This girl is different. I can see it in his eyes, hear it in his voice. She's influencing him."

"You don't find it romantic?" Lucas teased, but the humor didn't reach his eyes.

"I won't have her ruining everything. Ronan needs to conclude his business there and come home. There's work to be done here. Scarlett is here. I can't have him lingering in New York, especially not over a Vidal."

"Carefully, *Mere*, before someone listening takes the harmless words of a loving grandmother the wrong way." His voice was light, his smile wide, but the warning was in his eyes.

Harper giggled as if they'd shared a joke, but her festering anger was truly making itself felt today.

Scarlett was what Ronan needed. The girl was clever, well-bred, and knew how to smooth the way for him in social settings. And she wasn't demanding. A baby or two, and Scarlett would let him roam. He could have it all, everything he deserved. And Harper knew he was fond of Scarlett and that they'd already been intimate on more than one occasion. For Ronan to indulge more than once meant there was at least a small spark between them. That was more than enough.

And Scarlett knew she had to work together with Harper to keep Ronan in line and was more than willing to do so.

Losing Lucas had wounded Harper as nothing else ever had or could. The damage to the family's reputation was intolerable, even with most of the parish agreeing that her son could not have done what he was falsely accused of. And because Lucas wasn't where he should've been, Ronan had been lost to them for years. He would never be the man he could've been had she raised him from infancy. Two lost generations because of Vidal.

Harper would not allow the man's daughter to finish the job of removing Ronan from both her grasp and his family's influence.

It was Vidal's turn to feel her loss and suffering. She would see to it and bring her boy home.

fifteen

RONAN DIDN'T NEED ANY FURTHER REASON TO SAVE Vidal Records beyond Ireland herself, but sitting in the conference room after hours, without the piped music and enthusiastic, colorfully clothed employees, made him realize what would be lost if he continued with his initial, long-gestated plan.

The creative musical energy that thrived here held a certain magic. He'd seen firsthand that it was hard, often thankless work, and he understood why Ireland was conflicted about it. Making and enjoying music was next to spiritual, but for a record label, the finished product was a commodity to be sold and had a sliding scale of value. It was far too easy to fall in love with a song, which made it that much harder to decide it wouldn't appeal to enough listeners to be financially feasible to distribute.

Still, he was growing increasingly more excited by the thought of building something rather than tearing it down and doing so alongside Ireland, who fought so fiercely for the people and things that mattered to her. If, one day, she fought for him and whatever this thing was between them with equal ferocity...

Well, he wouldn't be worthy of it, but he was working on that.

He picked up the phone and dialed the number he'd searched for in the company records. He had decided to come to the offices to make the call because he wasn't sure she'd answer without Vidal Records showing on her Caller ID and because he had nowhere else to go now that he'd lost his hotel room. He laughed ruefully. There were vipers in his family, but he didn't worry about Ireland's ability to handle them like she was so deftly handling him.

"My god, girl," Alina answered, sounding thoroughly exasperated. "You promised to leave work and go punch things at the studio!"

The unexpected revelation straightened Ronan's slumped shoulders. "Alina, it's Ronan. Please don't hang up."

There was a wary pause on the other end. "How did you get this number?" she asked finally.

He opened the saved bookmarks in his browser. "You're a contractor with Vidal. Your contact info is in the system."

"Isn't it illegal to use my information for personal reasons?"

"No. It is an invasion of your privacy, though, and I'm sorry for it, but desperate men do desperate things." Like he was doing right now by calling Alina Rurik while simultaneously wracking his brain for the article he'd saved about the Krav Maga gym Ireland trained at. He swore silently. He had to find it to find her.

"If you're hoping to sweet talk your way into another round of crazed jungle sex with her, you're delusional."

"I'm never not hoping for that with her," he said, scrolling down the list of his bookmarks, searching. "But right now, I just want to explain what happened and how I'm addressing it."

She snorted. "How, exactly, do you address cheating on your fiancée?"

He went very still. For fuck's sake, could this day get *any* worse? He winced. Of course it could—depending on whatever else Ireland thought she knew. “I’m not engaged. Have never been engaged. Who told her otherwise? Jules?”

“Why would she or I believe any-fucking-thing you say?”

“Because I can prove it.” And if he had to bring Scarlett to New York to do so, he would.

Alina sighed heavily. “It doesn’t matter. You’re not the right guy for her, and for so many reasons, there’s not enough paper in the world to write them all down. That you can tear Vidal Records into pieces, knowing what that’s doing to her—”

“It was a mistake,” he interrupted. “A miscommunication. I’m fixing it.”

“So, she finally realizes you’re too toxic even for her, and you miraculously find a solution that you couldn’t find earlier in the week?”

When she put it like that… “I’m in this fight for my family, Alina. That made it harder for me to realize that I’m prepared to fight for Ireland, too.”

“You know what? I don’t care. Listen, I’m not your ally and never will be. Ireland has dated some exceptional assholes but you… You, Ronan, are in a class by yourself. If you ever contact me again, I’m calling the cops.”

The line went silent.

“*Merde*,” he breathed, setting the phone down and removing his glasses. Closing his eyes, he pinched the bridge of his nose.

If that was a taste of what Ireland had in store for him, he didn’t know if there was any chance at all for him to make things right. And hadn’t that been the struggle all along? Everything had gone wrong long before they’d met, and he’d been trying to paddle upstream, over raging rapids, ever since. Damned if he wasn’t exhausted by it all, and he knew she was, too.

But even as he sat there, telling himself to fly home as Jules and Claudette had done earlier, he *craved* her and couldn't turn it off. More, he didn't want to.

Opening his eyes, he straightened. The name of the Krav Maga gym returned to him in a flash. He pushed back from the table. If Ireland was done with him, so be it. But she would hear the truth before he walked away.

Parker Smith's Krav Maga gym in Brooklyn was housed in a brick-faced warehouse in a revitalized industrial area. Flanked on one side by a trampoline park and a nutritional supplement company on the other, it boasted two massive delivery bay doors that could be opened for airflow. When Ronan entered, he saw rows of aluminum bleachers against one wall and dozens of students sparring on mats throughout the vast space.

Smith himself was easy to identify, mainly because Ronan had just seen his photo. He was also the only figure moving from mat to mat, giving instruction and praise as needed. Rangy and sleekly muscular with skin that reminded Ronan of café au lait, Smith was far stronger than his lithe body looked, and he was a highly skilled instructor as well, which he demonstrated by escaping the grasp of someone behind him. It was a move Ronan recognized because it was the one Ireland had used on him when she left his hotel room.

Even with her long hair restrained in a tight bun on top of her head, Ireland was impossible to miss. She was so tall, her legs miles long, her body graceful yet powerful. She was sparring with a man more than double her size and holding her own, which made it easier for Ronan to observe her in action.

He knew she could handle herself, but she was still vulnerable—and infinitely precious to him. She could continue being the fierce, impetuous, reckless, and fearless woman she was with him if things worked out the way he hoped. Her family kept her insulated to protect her, but he wouldn't have to cage her to keep her safe. Danger would never get through him to her—ever.

It didn't take Smith long to spot him and walk over. The man examined him from head to toe with keen dark eyes and extended his hand with a welcoming smile. "Parker Smith. Welcome in."

Smith's handshake was powerful enough to feel the bite of his wedding ring. Ronan returned the gesture with a nod. "Ronan McCaffrey."

"What brings you in tonight, Ronan?"

"This day has been kicking my ass." He watched Ireland grab her opponent from behind so the guy could practice breaking the hold. "Figured I might as well make it literal."

Smith laughed. "I haven't had that one before."

Tearing his gaze away from Ireland, Ronan glanced at Smith, catching the grandmaster giving his physique a thorough, examining study as a potential client. "I need to get on a mat with Ireland Vidal."

"Is that so?" Smith's gaze narrowed on him. "I still haven't decided whether you'll get on a mat. Period. Do you have any experience?"

"No."

"How much do you think you know about Krav Maga?"

"Not a damned thing."

"Then you'll start with me," he declared with a decisive nod of his shaved head.

"I'm here to spar with Ireland," Ronan reiterated smoothly, if intractably.

Rounding on him, Smith's posture was loose and relaxed, but he was bristling. "I'll make two things clear to you, man. One:

my studio is not a place to hookup. Two: that woman could kill you in under a minute without you laying a single finger on her."

Ronan huffed a humorless laugh. "Now that I *do* know."

"*What the fuck are you doing here?*"

He smiled inwardly at the sound of Ireland's voice but knew better than to do so outwardly. Turning, he faced her. "Hello, *cher*. We have some things to discuss."

Dieu, but she was absolutely stunning. Taking the opportunity to drink her in, Ronan almost wished she had flaws, even just one. Anything that might offer him some hope of surviving her. But no, she was perfect. In too many ways to count.

Her face was flushed, and there was a fine sheen of sweat on her exposed skin. That he wasn't responsible for her glow was a shame. Still, she smelled deliciously of hardworking woman and her perfume. He could find her in darkness by those two scents, the one combination on earth capable of overriding his highly evolved self-preservation instincts.

She shot him an incredulous look. "Was blocking your number not a clue that I don't want to talk to you?"

He remembered standing in the lobby of Vidal Records and taking a last look into her eyes before she found out who he was. He'd known that would be the last time she would ever look at him with untarnished trust and affection.

The way she looked at him now was beyond brutal after what he'd once had with her.

Smith came into Ronan's view and got in his face. "Are you a fucking problem? You come *here*, of all places, to harass one of my students? You got a death wish?"

"You're the second person to ask me that today," he drawled. "It must be true. And yes, *cher*, I got the message, but I have some things to say, and you'll hear them. If you need to hit me while I talk, so be it. I did give you carte blanche to use my body for your pleasure."

Her beautiful eyes narrowed dangerously, then they sparked with a maliciously eager light. Ronan felt a surge of triumph. He'd watched her confront that idiot in Jazzie's and saw the soul-crushing indifference on her face when she'd looked at the guy. Now, he saw hurt and disappointment, which wounded him but also revealed that she still felt *something,* which was far better than nothing.

"I don't mind breaking this guy in," she said to Smith without looking away from Ronan. "In fact, I'd really enjoy it."

Smith looked between them grimly. "My studio isn't a therapist's office. If you two have issues, take them somewhere else."

"At least half the people in here right now are here to blow off steam," Ireland countered. "Three minutes max, Parker, and he'll be out of here."

Ronan's brows lifted. She was *really* pissed if she needed three minutes to whale on him.

"It's not a fair fight," Smith pointed out.

Ronan laughed inwardly because he knew Smith wasn't worried about Ireland. Yes, his greater size and strength made him a threat to her, but a couple dozen people in the room would step in if he crossed a line.

Ireland's smile was vicious. "Oh, I'm sure Ronan learned how to defend himself with a face and body like he has."

It struck him abruptly that she knew about his record somehow. She let him know with the challenge in her eyes and the bitterness that compressed her lushly seductive mouth. His shock turned to horror, followed swiftly by grim resignation.

At that moment, he didn't know whether he would've told her at some point. Part of him thought it was better if she never knew. Another part wanted her to accept him despite his past, for her to know every dark and ugly secret he had and want him anyway.

"And maybe I won't land every hit." She flashed another razor-sharp smile. "Or maybe I will."

He growled low in his throat. "I don't doubt it."

Smith snapped his fingers and waved his hand, clearing the combatants off the nearest mat. "Make it quick," he told her.

Ronan focused only on her, mentally preparing for battle: a swift one on the mat and a far more difficult one after. When this was over, he had to keep Ireland close enough to figure out if what they had was fleeting or something he'd fight the world for.

She padded barefoot onto the mat. He went to the nearest bleacher bench and sat to remove his shoes and socks. Before heading over, he'd changed into gym shorts and a T-shirt. She wore a black sports bra and matching leggings, the skintight clothing revealing all the slight curves of her flawlessly sexy body.

Standing, he joined her. She widened the spread of her legs, settled her weight, and held her arms up with bent elbows. He found her defensive position of power outrageously arousing, especially considering his current circumstances.

She beckoned him with a flex of her hand and a wicked gleam in her eyes. Resigned, he shook out his body, trying to limber up.

Lunging without warning, she caught him in the shoulder with a palm strike, sending him stumbling back a few steps.

Ronan got back into place, his jaw tightening grimly. He focused more closely as they began to circle each other. Curious students started to draw closer to watch. Ireland feinted, then lashed out with her foot. His leg gave out under the blow, and he fell to one knee. A man in the room shouted, "Go, Ireland!"

She laughed, clearly enjoying herself, which was the only reason he clambered to his feet.

"You just going to stand there and bleed?" she asked.

"I'm not—" His head snapped back, and pain exploded in his mouth. "*Sacre bleu!*"

"What'd he say?" someone called out.

Tasting blood, Ronan rubbed his jaw and considered how to end this. He lowered a little, looking for an opening, remembering how he'd charged out of her elevator like a raging bull the night before and pinned her to the wall with his cock. She wasn't going to be so accommodating now. He saw an opening and tackled her, shifting to take the hit to the floor, then rolling her under him. Lowering his head, he went to give her a quick kiss before she knew it was coming…

He was flat on his back and winded, to the sound of more whistles and cheers. He couldn't quite grasp how she'd shifted and kicked him off. All he knew for sure was that his pectorals throbbed from the imprint of her heels.

"She's giving a masterclass," Parker called out so the entire warehouse could hear.

Ireland stood over where he lay sprawled. "Bet you wish you'd stayed home with your fiancée."

Someone gave a long, slow whistle while others went *oooooh.*

"I'm *not* engaged," he bit out.

"Does Scarlett know that?" she asked sweetly.

"Scarlett," a woman repeated.

"Yes," he answered vehemently. "She knows that. Everyone knows that."

"Everyone who doesn't live in your parish?" Her gaze was hot. "Because everyone there says you're engaged."

"*Pour l'amour de dieu!* I'm. Not. Engaged!" How did she know so damned much?

Cross, he thought dourly. Her brother had the money and power to expose expunged criminal history. And Ronan was going to face the brunt of that power at some point...

He rolled onto all fours. Next thing, he was sprawled on his face by a kick in the ass.

The roar of laughter was deafening.

Cursing the saints, Ronan gave up on playing nice and sprang to his feet, pivoting quickly to avoid another swipe of her leg. Bouncing a bit on the balls of his feet, he raised his hands and ducked another palm thrust. His lip was pulsing with pain, his mouth awash in the metallic taste of blood.

"I'll put you on a video call with her," he told her, deflecting another jab. *Maudit*, she was fast. He ducked her incoming fist. "You can ask her yourself!"

There were more *ooooohs,* and he started to feel like they were on a reality TV show.

Jaw set with determination, Ireland eyed him grimly. They circled, their footsteps the only sound in the now quiet room.

"And I'm sorry about the studios," he said, feinting when she got too close to force her to retreat. "They'll be up and running by the morning."

And he'd bled cash to get it done. The company that had taken the equipment off their hands had charged three times what they'd paid to return it all.

"What do you want me to say?" she snapped. "Thank you?"

He leaped to avoid another leg swipe. "Jules acted without my knowledge."

Darting forward, she caught him in the shoulder with her palm. "You don't seem to know what you're doing with this takeover," she taunted. "Why not just give up and go home?"

"Why not save Vidal instead? *Oof!*" He doubled over, gasping, still feeling the sole of her foot in his gut.

She stopped moving, her breathing rapid. "What?"

Ronan straightened and grabbed her, pulling her in for a hard, open-mouthed kiss and holding her to it with a hand cupping her head. The pain in his lip was like fire, but her flavor soothed him and quenched his thirst. There was a weighted silence around them, but when she didn't resist him, it broke with raucous applause.

When she gripped his hips, he lifted his head and held her luminous gaze. "I said, let's save it. Together."

"Okay, that's enough!" Smith yelled, herding the crowd away from them. "Show's over! Time to do what you came here to do, people! Let's go!"

Ireland pulled away from him. She licked his blood off her lip, and that turned him on so fiercely it was only the physical pain he felt that kept him from getting hard.

Shaking her head, she said faintly, "I don't understand."

"Give me a chance to explain." He fought the urge to take her hand and keep her from leaving. "All of it. I'll lay out my entire life for you."

Smith walked over. "You two good now?"

She hesitated. "I don't know."

"Well, get the hell out of here if you're not here to work. You're distracting."

Ireland stepped outside Parker's studio with Ronan beside her, and it felt surreal. For one, seeing him outside of work in a routine part of her life felt intimate. And two, she *had* believed he'd finished what he came here to do and gone home. She'd lived with that thought for hours that felt like days because the emotional pain was so merciless.

What was he doing to her? How was he doing it?

She felt the intensity of his focus on her as they paused together on the sidewalk under a streetlamp. His energy was so fierce.

“Can we get a drink?” he asked. “Or coffee? Dinner, maybe?”

He was so heart-stoppingly handsome, standing before her so earnest and penitent. The longing was like a vortex, pulling her inexorably down.

Shaking her head, she said, “When I’m with you, I feel like I know you. I would swear to it. But then I learn things about you that don’t align with who I think you are, and it’s such a mindfuck.”

The entrance door opened, and another student walked out. He looked at both of them and asked, “Everything all right?”

“We’re good, Dak,” she told him with a reassuring smile. “Thanks for checking.”

“See you later.” He headed down the street.

Ronan stood there unmoving, watchful and waiting. “You do know me, Ireland. I’ve never been more honest with anyone. It’s… instinctual with you. It has been from the first.”

“You killed a cop, Ronan,” she whispered, trembling even though it wasn’t cold. It felt damn near psychotic to *know* something but to *feel* something else.

His face changed, his features sharpening, his mouth compressing briefly. “I killed the man who murdered my mother. He was also Jules’ and Claudette’s father. Him being a cop had nothing to do with any of it aside from extending my sentence.”

Her lips parted, her breathing shallow.

“I don’t regret it,” he said hotly. “I’d do it again, and I’m only sorry I didn’t do it sooner. Maybe my mother would still be alive today.”

“Oh… My god…” She listed over to the bench outside the

studio's entrance and sat, eventually realizing that she'd been locked with tension all day, fighting herself and grieving what she'd lost. Not so much because Ronan had left, but because she'd thought she never truly knew him.

He sat beside her and stared down at the ground. "I was at Marcelle's one afternoon. She was putting together a meal for our family. It was the one day of the week when my mother was home. I was fifteen at the time. Jules was six. Claudy was five. Irish twins, they call it, when two siblings are born within the same year."

The picture of him at that age was fresh in her mind. The hollowed cheeks and eyes. The signs of gross neglect. She wouldn't ever forget it. It was now an indelible part of him in her memories. "Please don't say more. I had no right to dig for information you didn't want me to know."

"I don't mind telling you," he said gravely. "I would have eventually."

"So, we'll wait until then." She reached over and laid her palm on Ronan's knee. He immediately covered her hand with his, the warmth of his skin making her aware of how cold her fingers were.

The door opened, and three people walked out: two guys and a woman she knew. Ireland jerked her chin in greeting and managed a wan smile.

Taking her hand in both of his, he chafed it to warm her. He caught her gaze and held it, nodding toward the entrance. "Half a dozen cops were working out in there. You detailed my sins for all to hear, but not this one. You didn't tell Alina about it, either, did you?"

Ireland looked away. She hadn't allowed herself to examine why she'd kept his past to herself. "Your history is not for me to share."

"Bullshit. You thought I'd destroyed your business and went home to a secret fiancée, but you kept this terrible thing you knew about me to yourself. You didn't believe it could be what it sounds like, did you? And you were protecting me, still, as you've been doing the whole time."

She opened her mouth to say something but didn't know what. She closed it again.

His smile flashed briefly in the shadows, there and then gone. "Except for when I manage to *really* piss you off. Then you cost me millions and evict me into the street."

Leaning into her, he pressed a kiss to her temple. "Let's go somewhere. Anywhere."

She didn't answer right away. Then, with a long slow exhale, Ireland slouched into the bench. "We've got to end this, Ronan."

He stiffened beside her. "Let me finish explaining."

"That's not why." She squeezed his hand. "I appreciate that you're willing to save Vidal. I can't tell you how much, but I will."

"It's not necessary."

"It is. And once I get my head on straight, I'll write you a letter and thank you. But if you really, truly think about it, there's no way to make this work long-term, and we're wading in too deep for something that can't last."

"Ireland..." He lifted her hand to his mouth and kissed her knuckles. "Let's just take it one day at a time."

She shifted toward him. "You're just going to come into the offices every day and work side by side with my father, the man you came here to destroy? Just like that?"

His throat worked on a swallow, but he was otherwise motionless. "No. He can't be involved. In any way. I'll take his office and figure out the rest with your help and maybe even Christopher's."

Straightening, she spoke with resolve. “Are you going to bring Marcelle up here?” she pressed. “And Marie Laveau? What about Jules and Claudette? You all shared a hotel suite. You work together. You’re very close, and I think I understand why now. Do *they* want to base themselves here? Or are you thinking you’ll commute a few days a week?”

“I don’t have it all figured out yet.” He raked a hand through his hair. “You could travel, too. You love New Orleans.”

“Who doesn’t? It’s unique in all the world.” *Like you are.* “But you're suggesting we split our lives between two places and two families. If I go down there with you, I’ll strain your relationship with your family. And let’s not get into how *my* family will react. My brother is coming home tomorrow,” she warned gently. “Christopher will drag Gideon into this first thing.”

People began to file out of the studio in a semi-steady stream.

She stood and felt the stiffness that had begun to settle into her muscles. She’d missed too many days in the studio dealing with work and Ronan—she’d feel it in the morning. She could add those physical aches and pains to the emotional ones she was feeling and be a complete package of misery and suffering.

Ronan stood with her and followed as she walked away from the studio.

“I don’t think we have to look that far ahead, Ireland. We start and end the day together and deal with whatever happens in between as it comes.”

“That sounds like winging it instead of an actionable plan.”

“We’re smart, we’ll figure it out.” His tone was light, but the subtle tension in his body belied his teasing.

“I want you,” Ireland said matter-of-factly, pulling out her phone to order a rideshare pickup. “I haven’t ever wanted anything as badly.”

"Why do I hear a *but* in there?" he asked gruffly, his hands shoved into the pockets of his shorts.

She still couldn't believe he'd come back to New York, that he'd tracked her down to tell her he was fixing the mess he'd made. But it was too late. It had always been too late.

"But I don't want to live a life split in two, Ronan," she finished.

Catching her by the elbow, he stopped her. "You know you can't pick and choose who you feel this way about. Do you think you'll find this again? You're young, *cher*, but you're not naive."

He was angry. Ireland could see it, hear it. And she was angry, too. But at the circumstances, not him. She cupped his face in her hand, then lifted onto her toes to kiss the side of his mouth. His torn lip looked painful, and she regretted hitting him. She hadn't been herself since she met him, in good and bad ways. And she knew he was acting out of character, too.

Jules thinks I've lost my mind, he'd told her.

Ronan caught her by the hips, kissing her back, heedless of his injury.

It felt so wonderful to be with him, near him, kissing him. It was so hard to push away, and he resisted her efforts to do so.

"Stop," she muttered against his desperate kisses. "Stop. *Stop!*"

Wrenching away, Ireland put distance between them, her lips tingling from contact with his. Misery spread like a chilling fog through her chest, making it hard to catch her breath. "I can't do this, Ronan. It's too high a price to pay to belong to you."

His hands were white-knuckled at his sides, but he didn't pursue her. "You don't think I'm worth it."

"You are," she said, digging deep for the strength to keep backing away. "But I can't afford you. And once you really think about it, you'll see the same is true for you, too."

WAITING FOR THE SECOND POT OF COFFEE TO FINISH brewing, Eva watched Chase, Raúl, her father, Angus, and Gideon survey the floorplan and evacuation routes of the Bellingham Hotel and its ballroom while standing around her penthouse dining table.

This was usually one of the more exciting days of the year for her, but she couldn't work up even the slightest bit of anticipation. She'd consider bowing out if it were any other event, but the masquerade was highly publicized. Guests worked for months with designers to curate their fashions to highlight elaborate masks that fit the year's theme, and the photographs from the red carpet were widely circulated for a week or more after the event. While she and Gideon no longer walked the red carpet of *any* event after her mother's murder, declining to attend the masquerade altogether wasn't an option because she wouldn't give whoever was sending them gruesome rhymes the satisfaction of seeing her hide.

Pulling the now-full carafe out of the coffeemaker, Eva carried it to the table and refilled the mugs that needed refreshing. It was half past eight in the morning, but Gideon had been focused on security for the masquerade since they'd found the crossbow bolt.

They'd left the beach early, returning to the city Thursday evening. It was no longer considered safe for them to be at the Outer Banks house, so they hadn't spent another night. While the team gathered information and evidence, Gideon had broken the communications embargo they'd always maintained at the beach house—yet another choice that had been taken from them —to work on beefing up security at the masquerade, which was already substantial and would now be exceptionally so. Many of their guests would attend with their own security personnel, which was usually a logistical nightmare but appreciated this year.

Gideon caught her by the waist when she came close, pressing a brief kiss to her temple even as his eyes remained trained on the specific areas around the ballroom and its mezzanine that Chase was pointing out to him. Her husband was always aware of her and physically affectionate, but he'd been paying *too* close attention to her, and she knew he was concerned. He often asked her how she was feeling, and the truth was that she didn't know.

For her husband, there was life before the crossbow bolt and life after, with a clearly delineated line between the two, but nothing was different for her. Their situation was precisely the same, and its effect on their lives—for her—was also unchanged.

She sighed and returned to the kitchen. It was a mistake to have brought up her desire for a child when she had. Her timing could not have been worse. Gideon was altered by her confession; she could feel it. There was an edgy impatience to how he was tackling the issue of their safety as if the urgency of her biological clock was something he now felt. The others could feel the difference, too. She saw the furtive glances they sent Gideon's way, and their elevated somberness was an oppressive weight in the air.

Gideon loved her too much. Knowing she wanted something only he could give her was driving him hard, and he would push himself harder for her than for himself. While he still spoke with his usual measured command, seemingly as calm and collected as ever, his energy felt almost…frantic.

Putting the carafe back on the warming plate, she gripped the edge of the countertop and bowed her head. It would be a long day followed by an even longer evening. Then they'd have the weekend to face how they were trapped in their penthouse, unable to travel as they'd planned because a stalker was close enough to know where they'd be even when they acted spontaneously.

"*Eva.*"

Her father's voice had her straightening in a rush, gathering her self-control as best she could. She and Gideon couldn't both be off their game simultaneously. One had to support the other, so she would shore him up and give him whatever strength she could.

"Yes?" She faced her dad with her shoulders back and chin lifted. "Bet you're not happy about missing the excitement at the beach."

"Excitement is not the word I'd use," he said gruffly. His silvery gaze—which he'd passed down to her—was dark and turbulent. "Can we agree that you won't make scheduling decisions for me moving forward? If I want to be somewhere, I should damn well be there."

She released her pent-up breath in a quick, tremulous rush. "We always felt so safe there. And anonymous. Plus, sometimes we get frisky on the deck."

"I know when to take a break."

He came to her. He was so tall and broad-shouldered that he blocked her view of the dining table and the other men behind him until he was all she saw. Deep grooves bracketed his mouth, and lines of strain accompanied the concern in his eyes.

"I'm sorry," she murmured, hating that he was under so much stress, too.

"Hey."

It was crazy how much her father could convey with a single word.

Command, always—he could hush a crowded room in an instant. Today, there was admonition, too, letting her know he didn't appreciate her bottling up her emotions. The note of sympathy, though, arrowed right into her heart. Her throat tightened, and her eyes stung with the threat of tears she couldn't afford to shed. Not while the men she loved were walking on eggshells around her.

He opened his arms and beckoned her closer with both hands. Eva resisted at first, aware of her tenuous grip on her composure. Later, she couldn't recall how she ended up enveloped in the strength and support of his familiar, beloved embrace. She just burrowed in and held on with everything she had.

He rested his cheek against the crown of her head. "There's my girl."

Gideon glanced into the kitchen and saw Victor hugging Eva tightly. It comforted him to see her being taken care of by her dad. He had so much to do that he appreciated the assist. And he understood why Victor needed to hold her close—Eva was the center of the world for both of them.

“We had everything covered already,” Raúl reiterated. “Every person working the event passed background checks and is a longtime employee of Cross Industries or the foundation. No one who’s been employed for less than two years will be staffing the event. We’re just focusing on redundancy at this point.”

Nodding, Gideon pulled out a chair and sat, his body sore from unrelenting tension.

Chase straightened and stretched. “I’ll run by the Bellingham again and reacquaint myself with the ballroom. I’ll also meet with hotel security and triple-check that enough staff are scheduled to cover every ingress point. I still say the mezzanine is a concern, though, and we should close it off.”

Sighing, Gideon nodded, but he knew their guests would be disappointed. The mezzanine’s velvet booths were popular places for private conversation and were one of the reasons they held the masquerade in the Bellingham’s glass-domed ballroom. Unlike the Met Gala in the spring, the foundation allowed guests to take selfies and photographs. “Can we close it off at the top of the staircase rather than below? It’s a popular picture spot.”

Raúl’s considered it. “The problem is it’s a vantage point, so we don’t want people loitering on the stairs. Can you put a photographer there to handle the picture taking so it moves quickly? Maybe more than one?”

“Yes,” Gideon conceded. “I can run with that.”

If they roped off the dual curving staircase at the top and bottom, they could form lines on either side at the base. With the help of assistants, four photographers could position the attendees on each sweeping curve’s high and low ends, and keep things moving

“We’ll have to decorate the mezzanine,” he thought out loud, “to minimize the visual of empty space up there. I’ll ask the events team at the hotel to do what they can.”

"Nothing wide," Angus cautioned. "Nothing anyone can hide behind. Slender trees would be better. Maybe use some of those tiny lights to dress 'em up."

Gideon shot him a surprised but approving look. Fairy lights weren't something he'd expected the Scot to be aware of. Then again, not much escaped Angus' keen eye. "Good idea."

Chase looked at Angus. "Want to tag along?"

The Scot shook his head. "I've an unrelated matter to discuss with Gideon."

"All right. I'll be in touch then." Chase moved quickly through the living room and left.

Raúl grabbed a seat at the other end of the table and pulled his laptop out to work. Eva and her father sat at the kitchen island, talking over coffee. Gideon sat back in his chair, feeling the warning signs of an imminent headache.

"You and Eva could use a nap," Angus noted. "Make sure you both get one. You should be as alert as possible tonight."

"Christopher is calling at nine to tell me what the hell is happening at Vidal," Gideon said wearily. "I should've known something was wrong and asked more questions when Ireland came to me the other night—I just didn't want to step on her toes. I'd planned to find out how the company was doing but had other things on my mind."

"You've got a lot on your plate, lad. I hate to add more to it."

Gideon gave him a level look. "But you have something."

Angus nodded. "Did you have a chance to review the dossier I sent you on Boudreaux?"

"Not yet. But the situation with Vidal will get my full attention this weekend."

Reaching into his bag, Angus withdrew a folder and opened it on the table. He pushed the photos inside up and out of the way. Gideon recognized a mugshot when he saw one, and there were multiple of the same guy at different ages of his life.

Now intensely curious, he leaned forward and spread the photos to see more than partial images. "This is the guy who maneuvered Chris out of the company? He's got a rap sheet? For what?"

Angus found the paper he was looking for and handed it over.

Gideon read through it, his brows lifting. He flipped it over, then shuffled through the other papers. "What did he get arrested for the second time?"

"Different man. The father."

He lifted both photos to study them side by side. "Fascinating."

"Your sister says Chris is the reason Boudreaux has targeted Vidal Records. That it's a personal vendetta of some sort. I'm looking into it since she didn't know more, but you need to understand this isn't just business. Something brought him all this way with a commitment to losing substantial money."

"Hey!" Eva called out behind him. "Whose pictures are you looking at?"

"They're mugshots, angel."

"Really?"

Her voice was more animated than he'd heard in days, which drew his attention to her. She hopped off the barstool and headed his way, stopping at his side with her hand on his shoulder.

"Oh, my god," she breathed, taking the photo of the older man from him. "I thought he looked familiar. This is the guy Ireland's seeing."

Gideon's back stiffened abruptly. "What do you mean?"

"No, wait." She frowned. "This is an old picture. I didn't see the date. Or the clothes, for that matter. Crazy resemblance, though. It's fucking weird."

Shifting in his seat to better look up at her, he said more firmly, "Go back to what you said about Ireland dating someone."

Eva dropped the photo on the table and slid the teenager's mugshot closer. "You should hear her talk about him. Actually, you probably shouldn't. You wouldn't like it."

"When did she first tell you about him?" Angus asked, pulling out a more recent photo and handing it to her.

"*That's* him. His hair's a lot longer now, though. Longer than yours." She ran a hand over Gideon's head. "She told me about him last weekend."

"Repeat what she said." Gideon caught his wife's hand and tugged her onto his lap. "Then tell me why you didn't say anything to me about it."

"They met in a bar and went to dinner with his friends. I kept it to myself because you *might* be a tad overprotective, ace." She set the picture down.

"I trust my instincts. They led me to you."

She kissed him. A soft press of her lush lips to his that he'd needed. "I saw them together when we took Lucky to the park. I got a bad feeling from him, to be honest. There's just something...off. But then, I might be overprotective, too."

"That's why we walked so long," he said reflectively. "You were looking for them."

Raúl stood and came over, looking at the photographs.

Draping her arms around his neck, Eva gave him a crooked half-smile. "Can't get anything past you, baby. Yes, I wanted to see them together because she was so excited about him. She's never talked about anyone else she's dated in quite the same way.

I almost asked Angus to look into him, but it seems you got to it first."

"Ireland asked me to," the Scot told her.

"I've seen this dude," Raúl murmured, pulling out his phone and swiping at the screen. "This morning."

Shouts and catcalls erupted from the speaker as he set the phone down on the tabletop. They all leaned over to watch the video he cued up for them.

"That's Ireland," Eva murmured. "Ooooh, good hit."

Gideon's initial curiosity was now laser-focused interest as he watched his sister put Ronan McCaffrey Boudreaux through his paces at Parker Smith's studio. The person who filmed the short video was positioned behind his sister, so Ireland's face was seen only occasionally in profile. But he knew how she moved her body, just as Eva did.

When Boudreaux caught his sister in an aggressive, possessive kiss that she not only didn't reject but participated in, Gideon felt an alarming chill settle over him.

"My wife sent me that this morning," Raúl explained. "It was posted last night. Apparently, it's romantic to watch a woman kick a man's ass and then get kissed senseless."

"Holy shit, it's got over a quarter million views already!" Eva exclaimed, drawing Gideon's attention to the rapidly increasing likes count.

Gently urging his wife up from his lap, Gideon stood. His earlier soul-deep fatigue was now replaced by restless energy. He started walking toward the front door.

"Are you going over there?" Eva asked, running up beside him.

He couldn't decide whether he wanted Boudreaux to be at his sister's. He wanted a face-to-face but also knew what it meant if the man was there this early in the day.

"Send me a link to that video," he barked over his shoulder at Raúl. "And find out where he's staying." *It had better not be with Ireland...*

He'd initially planned to advise Christopher on what could be done to secure control of Vidal—and provide capital, if necessary. The situation was now drastically different.

Boudreaux should've limited his scope to just the company. But he'd involved Ireland.

So now the man would be dealing with him.

Ireland jolted when her leg vibrated yet again, her phone ringing silently in the thigh holster she wore beneath her formal gown. She'd turned the ringer off but couldn't turn the phone itself off because she was emceeing the bachelor auction. She needed to know and be prepared if something changed at the last minute.

Reaching into the thigh-high slit of her blue ombre dress, she pulled her phone out, saw Gideon's face on the screen, and sighed. She sent the call to voicemail and texted instead, as she'd been doing all day.

I'm about to walk on stage

She slid the phone back into place. The thigh holster was meant to be worn athletically, like when running in shorts without pockets, but she'd discovered it worked great for formal events, too. And with a bracelet that hid a lip gloss wand, she could go hands-free at events and not bother with coordinating tiny purses with her dress.

"I can't believe you've gone all day without answering him." Alina fidgeted while looking stunning in a strapless diaphanous peach dress with petal-like embellishments that fluttered every time she moved. Her rose gold mask had peach-colored feathers and ribbons on one side. "It's giving me anxiety."

"Hello? My brother and I are in the same damn ballroom together now! It's not that I don't want to talk to him, just that I'd rather do it in person."

So, she'd been answering his calls with texts. Which she could tell was pissing Gideon off by his tone—at least what tone she could gather from letters strung together into words. Her brother never resorted to using exclamation points to convey his mood, which somehow made his short commands to pick up and answer his calls even more worrying. She hadn't listened to his voicemails because she was edgy enough already.

Ireland smoothed the front of her silk dress with trembling hands. It was strange how strung out she felt, as if her body was overcaffeinated—or slipping into a state of withdrawal. She realized that this was the longest stretch of time she'd gone without seeing Ronan since they'd met.

How long would it take to feel normal again? To not feel like something vital was missing?

"Why aren't you nervous?" Alina asked. "I just have to escort the guys on and off, and my palms are sweaty, and I have heart palpitations."

"When have I ever been nervous onstage? I could run this auction in my sleep now." It was actually a lot of fun and her favorite part of the Crossroads Foundation's annual masquerade ball. "And you look blissfully calm when you glide across the stage."

Peeking through a gap in the stage curtain, she surveyed the Bellingham Hotel's massive ballroom. The guests were a who's who of Manhattan society, along with political figures, celebrities, and other billionaires like her brother.

It was great having the event as a distraction, but she dreaded the weekend ahead. She needed to stay too busy to think about Ronan and where he might be, what he might be doing, and who he might be doing it with. She'd made the right decision for herself but had no idea what the impact would be for Vidal.

Was he still willing to let her try to save the company? Was he still planning on helping her do it? If so, perhaps they could design a schedule where she'd be out of the office on the days he commuted, at least until she got over her attraction to him and could be around him without becoming desperate to *always* be with him.

Or maybe he'd only considered saving Vidal if they were sleeping together, and that offer was no longer on the table. She sighed. Not that it mattered now that Gideon knew. She hoped to convince her brother to let her do what she could without intervention, but she doubted either of her brothers believed she could turn Vidal around with just guts and determination. At least her dad had given her a shot.

She could really use one of Ronan's hugs right now, not to mention his affirmations that she was fierce, fabulous, dangerous, and powerful. Was she still a tigress when she wasn't his?

"You're thinking about him," Alina noted, studying her. "Ronan, I mean. I can tell because you get this lost, sad look on your face."

Giving her best friend a skeptical look, Ireland pointed out the obvious. "I'm wearing a mask."

"They don't cover up *that* much, and you know it. Plus, I know you." She reached over and squeezed Ireland's hand. "I'm sorry this is hard for you."

"Yeah, well..." She was sorry, too. For all of it.

The stage manager approached them briskly, pulling down

the mic on her headset to say, “We’re ready in five. Are you good to start?”

“Hell yeah.” Ireland rubbed her hands together. “Let’s raise some money!”

Ronan entered the packed ballroom and surveyed the room for Ireland. Gideon Cross and his wife were the first people he spotted because they remained stationary while guests circled and approached them as if they were royalty with an audience of sycophants. And also because he knew what the Crosses looked like even while masked. He couldn’t say the same for the rest of the attendees.

He still couldn’t quite believe he was there, that Ireland hadn’t removed his name from the guest list. Her phone still blocked his number, and she hadn’t come into the Vidal offices at all. He’d waited for her there all day, wanting her to see that the recording studios were up and running as he’d promised they would be, with Six-Ninths and two young female singers busy inside them all day. They’d all still been hard at work when he’d finally remembered Ireland’s invitation after listening to her voicemails again because he missed the sound of her voice.

Laughing silently to himself, he thought again how humbling it was to be kicked to the curb by a woman who occupied his every waking thought. He *had* known that she could cut him off at any moment like she did every man she became involved with. And that she would do so quickly.

I’ve never been with anyone long enough for it to become serious, she’d told him. *I tend to check out of relationships fairly quickly.*

It was some sort of self-defense mechanism, and he would

get to the root of it. He'd committed to that decision when he acknowledged the slim chance that maybe she'd ended whatever they had, not because of the reasons she'd given him but because that was what she always did.

He searched for her, his gaze sweeping over the massive room repeatedly. Cross should've disappeared in such a crowd of loud colors and outrageous masks. While many of the male guests in the room wore colorful suits in various textured fabrics, Cross wore a standard tuxedo and rather plain mask of pure black with simple embellishments.

His wife was also markedly less flamboyant in her attire than the other women present. Eva Cross's gown of gray silk draped a petite, voluptuous figure similar to Scarlett's. Her mask was a feminine version of her husband's but in silver. She was, however, dripping with millions of dollars in precious gems at her throat, ears, wrists, and fingers. They were sometimes referred to as the Richard Burton and Elizabeth Taylor of today, with Cross often making headlines for gifting his wife with exceptionally rare jewelry.

A now-familiar sensation gripped Ronan, and he knew Ireland was close. He searched more intensely for her tall, slim figure, unsure of whether her hair would be worn up or down. The music faded into silence, and an announcer's voice projected from the speakers.

"And now, welcome back our emcee, Ireland Vidal!"

The room erupted in applause. Facing the stage, he watched her enter from the wings with her outrageously sexy feline stride, which was both aggressive and erotic at once. She looked like the goddess she was, her willowy body hugged in an aqua gown that became steadily darker in hue from her hips to the floor as if she'd just stepped out of water. Her mask covered only one eye and was decorated with a profusion of peacock feathers that flared from her shoulder to the top of her head. Her long hair was unrestrained and swayed behind her as she reached center stage. She held a microphone in one hand and a slip of paper in the other.

Ronan had never wanted anything or anyone more. It took supreme effort not to cross the room and climb the stage to claim her, every instinct screaming at him that she belonged to him in some way he didn't yet comprehend.

"I have what you've all been waiting for," she began, her smile lighting up the room as she waved the paper in her hand.

And then she found him, her gaze unerring and intense. Her smile held firm, but her body went still. They simply looked at one another for a long moment, electric awareness coursing between them.

"Our final bachelor has arrived!" she exclaimed with a fiendish smile, and the room's energy changed. "He may not be punctual, but he's worth the wait. Ladies and gentlemen, Ronan McCaffrey!"

Pour l'amour de dieu!

Eva felt Gideon's arm tense beneath her fingers as Ireland announced Ronan McCaffrey to the room. She tilted her face up to his, about to remind him to keep a lid on his simmering temper when Richard Stanton walked up to them.

Her mother's widower smiled at them both. "I'm going to call it a night, you two. I was waiting to hear how much was raised, but I'm fading fast."

"Always good to see you," Gideon said, loud enough to be heard over the crowd's sudden boisterous excitement at his sister's announcement of an additional bachelor to the auction.

She could hear the fury in his voice and noted how his gaze was fixed beyond Richard to someone in the crowd. She was too short to see anything, and her agitation increased.

Her stepfather exchanged a brief backslapping hug with Gideon, then he moved to her and gripped her by the shoulders. He took a long look before pressing a brief, dry kiss to her cheek. He was dapper in his tuxedo, fit and trim as ever. However, time had begun to curve his back, and sadly, slow him down. The way he walked was noticeably stiff.

It hurt Eva's heart, even as she hoped to be as healthy when she was his age.

Gideon gently removed her hand from his arm. "Excuse me."

To her horror, her husband left her side with an angry stride. She looked helplessly at Richard, unable to leave him.

His lips parted as he moved to say something, then closed on a forlorn smile as he changed his mind.

Eva knew he still grieved her mother deeply and that their close resemblance was why he'd avoided seeing her for almost a year after Lauren—the woman he knew as Monica—had passed. She was glad they'd been able to move past that and reach a point where they lunched together at least twice a month and enjoyed the holidays together.

"Thank you so much for coming, Richard," she told him warmly, even as she dreaded the possibility of a confrontation between her husband and Ireland's man.

"Wouldn't miss it for anything, Eva love. Like your mother, you know how to throw a party."

"Are we still on for lunch Wednesday?"

"Yes. I wouldn't miss that, either."

They hugged, and he left her, but the guests had once again moved closer to the stage. There were round tables that sat twelve, and everyone had a seat, but most chose to walk around or loiter by the bars. And when the auction was in progress, many chose to stand on the dance floor in front of the stage. Since that was where she was, Eva found herself hemmed in. There were many disadvantages to being short, and pushing her way through a shoulder-to-shoulder crowd was one of them.

"Hey, baby girl."

Eva turned in relief at the sound of Cary's voice. "Hey. Can you see where Gideon is?"

"I passed him on the way over. Let me tell you, the Red Seas parted for the look of mayhem on his face. Who pissed him off?" Cary looked as debonair as a classic Hollywood leading man in his Brioni tux.

"Ireland and that guy." She pointed at Ronan as he crossed the stage. He cut a dashing figure dressed in a white dinner jacket over his black tuxedo slacks. His mask had elaborate curved horns like a ram or forest god, and when he drew abreast of Ireland in her towering stilettos, they were nearly eye to eye.

Cary whistled. "Saved the best for last, I see."

The guests seemed to agree, especially when Ireland reached up and removed Ronan's mask, revealing his stunningly handsome face. A tangible stir was felt. That Ronan only had eyes for Ireland was evident to all, and her returning stare was so heated with yearning that Eva winced thinking about Gideon seeing it.

"The sexual tension between those two is thicker than his hard-on," Cary noted.

"Not that you can tell from here," Eva countered drily.

"I refuse to fantasize a small cock on a man that gorgeous."

She shook her head and dug her phone out of her clutch to text Gideon, half-listening as Ireland relayed Ronan's attributes to the crowd. She knew her husband was thinking of only one thing: the man was a convicted murderer who had designs on his sister.

Disaster seemed inevitable.

Ronan McCaffrey Boudreaux brought in the largest auction bid of all time: twenty-five thousand dollars. The winning bidder was a hotel heiress, and Ireland would've been outrageously, irrationally jealous if she'd had time to think about it. But she didn't have time to worry about anything beyond the next five minutes when she spotted her brother moving toward the stage with Chase, Raúl, and two hotel security guards.

"Come with me," she said urgently, grabbing Ronan's hand and pulling him to the wings.

He didn't resist; instead, seemed completely happy to follow her and totally oblivious to the threats closing in around him. A confrontation with her brother was inevitable, but after avoiding Gideon's calls all day, she knew he was already unhappy with her. Surely, there was a way to have him in a neutral mood, at the very least, before he met Ronan for the first time.

Frantic, she debated where to go. The security at the event was so tight she could hardly move without bumping into someone in either the hotel's security uniform or someone in a black suit wearing an earpiece. She pushed through a door into an unfamiliar service hallway.

"Left or right?" she asked him curtly, indecisive in her panic.

"Right," he answered smoothly as if nothing at all was wrong with anything.

Her heels clicked frantically as she rushed with no destination in mind. She flashed a smile when she spotted a hotel security guard standing in front of a service elevator. "Mind if we use that?" she asked sweetly.

"It's to the mezzanine," he replied, "which is closed." Then his gaze narrowed briefly, then widened with recognition. “Sorry, Ms. Vidal. Go ahead.”

“Thanks.” She and Ronan stepped into the elevator. It had only one button to ascend the one floor and she pushed it repeatedly as if that would make the doors shut faster.

The service elevator was slower than the guest elevator, leaving her trapped in a small space with Ronan’s mouthwatering scent and even more mouthwatering body. She backed into the rear corner, but he followed, his gaze hot on her face.

“I can’t believe you just sold me, *cher*,” he drawled, his fingers brushing over her cheek in a tingling caress.

“You shouldn’t have come here. My brother is hunting you down now.”

“How else could I talk to you before the weekend?”

She groaned. “You’re not supposed to talk to me at all!”

He gave her a patient look as the doors opened. Pushing him out of the way, she exited the elevator and hurried to the railing, looking down at the guests below and searching for her brother and his goons.

Ronan joined her at the railing but leaned back against it, facing her. “You made some valid points last night,” he began smoothly. “But I have a proposal for you.”

She glanced at him, then looked away. “Hurry up. I’ve got to get you out of here.”

His mouth curved in a knowing, indulgent smile. “Still protective, I see. A good sign for me. Listen, you said you don’t want to live two lives, but you’ve only experienced one. You have to come home with me and try out the other one before you reject it out of hand.”

“That’s insane,” she said tersely.

“Is it, though? Basing decisions on supposition instead of facts is bad business.”

She looked at him again.

His one raised brow challenged her. "What do you have to lose?" he cajoled. "You'll have a lovely time, at the very least."

Shaking her head, she looked down again and found Gideon surveying the crowd from the stage. "I'm going back down there to distract my brother. When you see me with him, you're going downstairs and leaving. Got it? You. Are. Leaving. Before he finds you."

Ireland started back toward the elevator, and he caught her arm, releasing her quickly and lifting both hands in a gesture of surrender. "I'll go," he promised. "But I'll wait for you at the Teterboro airport until midnight. If you show up, we'll enjoy the weekend and decide about the future on Sunday. If you don't show up, you won't see me again. We'll work around each other."

She looked at him for a long minute, wanting everything he offered almost as badly as she was afraid to want it. The urge to kiss him, press against him, was physically painful.

Turning away, Ireland left him behind to find Gideon.

Ronan watched the guests from the mezzanine, noting how Cross, with two men in nondescript black suits and two hotel security guards, was surveying the crowd.

For him, apparently. He was almost flattered.

Cross would be a *trevail*, though. He wasn't at all happy about that, considering what trouble the man's sister was giving him.

Exhaling heavily, he damned himself for offering Ireland the choice he had. She'd been so harried and rushed, though. He'd acted on instinct, as he always did with her, sensing—hopefully correctly—that adding urgency via a midnight deadline would work in his favor.

He spotted her down below, the aqua hue of her dress eye-catching even among so many brightly attired guests. She was hunting for her brother, and he did the same, realizing that he'd lost sight of Cross while looking for his sister. He did find the woman who'd paid twenty-five thousand dollars for a two-hour lunch with him and sighed. Ireland certainly had inventive and devious ways to punish him. And here he stood, eager for more. What *had* she done to him?

Feeling his phone buzz in his jacket pocket, Ronan pulled it out and saw another missed call from his grand-mère and a text from his brother.

> I have never been more worried about you. I feel an intervention is necessary.

Closing his eyes briefly, he considered how best to soothe his family's concerns. How would his siblings react when he brought Ireland home with him? Because he refused even to consider that his tigress wouldn't accompany him. And he would not be taking her to Bellefleur, that was certain. Harper could be the loveliest and most welcome hostess, but she could also be quite vicious. All while couching her sentiments in Southern charm, of course.

He looked at his phone and realized he hadn't given himself much time, either. The clock was ticking for him, too. It wouldn't do for him not to be there at midnight when she arrived.

Ireland *would* come.

Wouldn't she?

Sliding his phone back into his pocket, Ronan turned toward the elevator.

And found himself facing Gideon Cross.

Ireland couldn't believe she couldn't find Gideon. Everyone in the room was there for him and wanted an audience, however brief. How could he just disappear?

She looked up at the mezzanine, but no one was there. The service elevator was hidden in an alcove and not visible from below, so Ronan was either on his way down or had already made his way out.

"There you are," Alina said, coming up beside her. "Where'd you go? What happened to Ronan? You were both gone when I came out to escort him off."

She looked at her best friend and could almost hear a ticking clock. It was stupid. She needed to forget Ronan had shown up at all. The man's audacity was astounding. He had a death wish or something. Thank god, Gideon didn't know about Ronan's criminal history.

Ice settled like a brick in her gut. Unless Angus had shared his report with her brother. Would he do that? Damn it. Why hadn't she clarified that she was counting on his discretion?

"Hey," Alina said, snapping her fingers in front of Ireland's face. "Are you okay? You don't look so good."

Ireland grabbed Alina's hands in her own. "Ronan asked me to go home with him for the weekend. To meet him at the airport at midnight."

Her best friend's eyes widened. "Seriously? And you're thinking about going?"

"If I don't, he says I'll never see him again."

"Isn't that what you wanted?" She squeezed Ireland's cold fingers.

"I did. Now, I don't know." And why not? She'd broken things off. Earlier in the evening, she'd told herself that she was at least one day into getting over him. One day at a time, she'd eventually return to normal.

And then he'd appeared, looking like a pagan god in his horned mask, still looking every inch the Southern gentleman in his white dinner jacket. A lion in sheep's clothing. And she'd wanted him so keenly she'd trembling with it.

"He says I can't say I don't want to try when I haven't really tried," she told Alina.

"Honey, you don't even know if you can trust him when he keeps such big secrets."

"But I do trust him," she confessed. "When he tells me things, I believe him. I just… I feel like…"

She shrugged lamely but began to quiver with excitement. Alina gave her a gentle, loving smile and then hugged her tightly.

"Go," she urged. "You'll have to hurry."

Fully committed now, Ireland hurried through the hotel, ordering a rideshare pickup on the way. She kept her head down to avoid making eye contact with anyone who might try to stop her for conversation. Taking one last look at the make, model, and license plate info of the car picking her up, she slipped her phone back into the sleeve on her thigh.

She rushed through the automatic doors, leaving the almost too-cool air conditioning for the warmth and humidity outside. The weather would be even muggier in New Orleans, and she perversely looked forward to it because being pressed against Ronan's body when they were both slick with sweat was an outrageous turn-on for her. She couldn't explain it.

The rideshare pickup area was packed. Several cars were lined up in numbered stalls while a row of waiting vehicles hugged the walkway. She saw the model car she was expecting and quickened her pace to see if it was her assigned vehicle and driver. When the back door to a black Chevy Suburban opened in front of her, she shifted to go around it.

Ireland realized too late that someone was closer behind her than was comfortable. By the time she got out of her head enough to acknowledge the warning tingle racing down her spine, a hand clamped on her forearm. Shifting her weight, she spun and prepared to strike…

…and was smothered in black velvet from behind. Unable to see or breathe, her momentum was used to shove her into the backseat of the SUV. She screamed but was muffled by the voluminous material that pinned her arms to her sides. The sound of terror cut off abruptly as her breath was knocked from her by brutal impact with the rear seat. A big male body smelling of stale cigarettes crowded in behind her. Someone opened the front passenger door and climbed in.

Both doors slammed shut. The Suburban's tires squealed in protest at the sudden hard acceleration. Then, the SUV lurched forward and sped away.

Ronan and Ireland's story continues in

Illusive

A CROSSROADS NOVEL

Character Illustration featuring Ireland & Ronan by Penny Mae Harris

Sylvia Day is the #1 *New York Times*, No. 1 *Sunday Times* & internationally bestselling author of over twenty award-winning novels, including ten *New York Times* and thirteen *USA Today* bestsellers. She is a number one bestselling author in twenty-nine countries, with translations in forty-one languages and over twenty million copies of her books in print.

sylviaday.com

facebook.com/AuthorSylviaDay
instagram.com/sylvia_day
tiktok.com/@authorsylviaday
pinterest.com/sylviaday
threads.net/@sylvia_day
bookbub.com/authors/sylvia-day
goodreads.com/sylviaday
youtube.com/@SylviaDay
x.com/SylDay